Dream

Aisling Trilogy
Book 2

Carole Cummings

ROCKY RIDGE BOOKS

Dream, Aisling Trilogy Book 2
Copyright © Carole Cummings 2020
Cover art © TL Bland
Interior layout and design by P.D. Singer

Cover content is for illustrative purposes only and any person depicted on the cover is a model.

Maps created using a template courtesy of freefantasymaps.org

Print ISBN: 978-1-62622-091-1

First Edition published 2011 by Prizm Books

Second Edition published 2017 DSP Publications

Third Edition published 2020

Rocky Ridge Books
Box 6922
Broomfield, CO 80021

For Julia

CYNEWÍSAN
(THE COMMON FAITH)

THE GUILD

RÍOCHT
(THE DOMINION)

CILDTROG

OLD BRIDGE

LIND

THE RIDINGS

CHESTER

GREEN BASIN

PUTNAM

KENLEY

DUDLEY

GLOSSARY

Æledfýres

(āel-et-fēr-es) God of fire. Brother of the Father. One of what are known as the old gods. Also referred to as dearg-dur or daeva.

Ælíf

(āel-if) Given name of the Mother; literally translated as "eternal."

Aire

(ə-rā) Literally translated as "danger."

Aisling

(ă-ēsh-ling) Literally translated as "dream." In Ríocht's culture the Aisling is also referred to as the Chosen, a holy figure who is called on once a year to ask the Father for His favor and blessings, and then convey those blessings onto the people.

Brethren

A band of priests cast out of the Guild and reformed as a more fanatical sect dedicated to the Father.

Brionglóid

(briŋ-lóid) Given name of the Father; literally translated as "dream."

Célnes

(sāl-nəs) Goddess of the wind. Sister of the Mother. One of what are known as the old gods, or the gods of the Four Corners.

Chester

A midsized city south of Lind.

Chosen

See Aisling.

Cildtrog

A holy place in Lind; literally translated as "cradle."

Cliabhán

(klē-ə-bän) Cradle.

Coimirceoir

(kim-òl-ēk-āórr) Literally translated as "guardian."

Commonwealth

See Cynewísan.

Cynewísan

(kin-ə-wiss-än) Also referred to as the Commonwealth. A conglomeration of united provinces with a democratic government overseen by their elected Elders. Bordered to the north and east by Ríocht.

Daeva

Vampire.

Dearg-dur

Incubus; soul-eater.

Deartháireacha

(dē-ath-air-rēch-ə) Brothers.

Díepe

(dē-əp-ā) Goddess of water. Sister of the Mother. One of what are known as the old gods, or the gods of the Four Corners.

Dudley

A small village south of Putnam.

Ealdordéman

(al-dòr-de-mòn) Chief judge.

Eorðbúgigend

(ē-ərthpā-gēg-ānd) God of the earth. Brother of the Father. One of what are known as the old gods, or the gods of the Four Corners.

Father

The patron deity of Ríocht. God of music, harmony of the seasons, beauty, the stars, and dreams.

Fæðme

(fa-äm-ə) Womb.

First Tongue

The language of the old gods and the first clans.

Flównysse

(flō-win-üss-e) A major river that runs a southeasterly course from the mountains on Lind's northern border.

Foreládtéowes

(fär-eläd-tā-äw-es) Chief; leader.

Gníomhaire

(gə-nēv-əm-h'er) Literally translated as "agent."

Guild

The governing body of Ríocht.

Lind

A province of Cynewísan known for its Old Ones, a governing assembly of magic users and healers. Its denizens are devoted to the Mother and are highly secretive, keeping themselves as isolated from the rest of the Commonwealth as is possible. It sits in the northeast corner of Cynewísan. Ríocht sits at its northern and eastern borders.

Mother

The patron deity of Cynewísan. Goddess of cultivating, reaping, comfort, nurturing, protection, and war.

North Tongue

Native language of Ríocht.

Old Bridge

A tiny hamlet in northern Cynewísan, northwest of Putnam.

Putnam

A major city in the mideastern region of Cynewísan (also referred to the Commonwealth).

Ríocht

(rē-äkht) Also referred to as the Dominion. A highly religious and patriarchal country governed by priests sworn to the Father, their patron deity. Bordered to the west and south by Cynewísan.

Wæpenbora

(wap-en-bär-ó) Weapon-bearer; warrior-knight.

Wæterþéotan

(wat-er-thā-ät-an) Conduit; floodgate.

Weardas

(we-órd-ós) Watchmen; guards; ones who stand post.

The Story So Far....

Putnam's First Constable, Dallin Brayden, is called upon to question a man brought in as a witness to murder. From the moment Dallin encounters the man who claims to be Wilfred Calder, things begin to skew off-kilter—from the not-quite-recognition Dallin feels when he first lays eyes on Wil to the fact that one man beat another to death, apparently as a result of an argument over Wil himself. Before Dallin can get answers, Wil skips town. It seems Wil is actually the Aisling, the Chosen of his country—Ríocht—sporadically at war with Dallin's country, Cynewísan (also known as the Commonwealth), for as long as anyone can remember. And the return of Wil to Ríocht is the only thing that will keep the war horns from blowing this time. Dallin is commanded by the chief of Putnam's constabulary to track Wil down and bring him back.

Dallin sets off on Wil's trail, and notices there are others on it as well, others who have burned an entire village and murdered its denizens in their pursuit. Dallin finally catches up with Wil in Dudley just as Wil's pursuers do. A violent confrontation ensues, and once Dallin takes care of those who are after Wil, Wil once again tries to run from Dallin. Dallin jails him with the cooperation of Dudley's sheriff.

Under Dallin's interrogation, Wil tells a tale of decades-long captivity and addiction, and a man, Síofra, who kidnapped an infant Wil and had been keeping him prisoner in order to control his magic until the Brethren—Wil's other pursuers, and self-appointed agents of the Father, Ríocht's patron deity—stormed Ríocht's citadel and took Wil away. It wasn't a rescue, Wil says, just another kidnapping, and his captivity no less horrifying than it had been with Síofra. Wil is the Aisling, he tells Dallin, one who can enter the dreams of others, and manipulate them into doing his bidding. Wil also says Dallin is the Guardian, a being of magic meant to guard against the Aisling and his power.

Dallin doesn't believe in magic, but he's seen plenty of evidence that Wil is in danger, and that returning him to Ríocht and Síofra would be no less perilous—both to Wil and Cynewísan. Despite his orders to capture and return Ríocht's Chosen, Dallin decides he needs to protect Wil, if he can get Wil to trust him. Before he can even try, the Brethren attack the jail. Dallin and Dudley's militia manage to fight them off, after which Dallin and Wil flee into the wilderness.

They decide to head to Lind, the northern country where Dallin was born, the place out of which Dallin's mother smuggled him when he was a boy and Lind was attacked, apparently by forces sent by Síofra and looking for Dallin. Dallin barely remembers it, but he thinks it's the place there might be answers, and they have nowhere else to turn.

On their way, they stop at an inn for the night, during which Dallin dreams things that seem to confirm what Wil has told him. The Mother comes to him in the dream and tells Dallin he is indeed the Guardian, and he's meant to protect the Aisling, not protect against him. She calls on Dallin to guard her precious Gift.

Dallin wakes, still disbelieving, but then he makes a joke that Wil should prove it all to him by making it rain. Wil does.

CHAPTER 1

"Hey. Hey, Wil, c'mon, wake up."

Wil swatted blindly, realizing too late in his sleep stupor that he'd done it with his right hand. A low hiss skidded through his teeth, and he curled the now throbbing hand—*thank you, Brayden*—to his chest. He dragged open hazy eyes. Shut one. Squinted.

"Are you all right?" Brayden's tone was all urgent disquiet. When Wil only blinked in muzzy irritation, Brayden's face pinched up with worry, and he took Wil by the shoulders to roughly sit him up. "C'mon now, say something, do *one thing* I ask, all right? I'm drowning here."

Annoyed, Wil shrugged out of the grip. "Get off, will you? 'M *sleeping*."

And why was he annoyed and not afraid? Where had his reflexes gone, damn it?

A balled-up something came at Wil's nose—*another handkerchief? What the hell?*—pressing a little too roughly. Wil tried swatting that away too, but Brayden shook his head.

"Just calm down. You're bleeding."

I

And if that wasn't the dumbest contradiction Wil had ever heard.

"What...? Why am I—?"

"What were you dreaming?" Brayden gently but intractably tipped Wil's head back, pressing fingers at either side of the bridge of Wil's nose.

Wil fumbled at the handkerchief and squinted fuzzily at the ceiling. "Coffee." He frowned. "I was dreaming about coffee, and... rain, I think, but I don't—" Suspicion crowded out the sleep haze and murky confusion. "Why d'you care?"

Wil pushed Brayden's hand away and snatched the handkerchief. Brayden let him, leaping back as though Wil had just spit hot coals at him. He just stood there, looking down at Wil with a mix of disbelief and too-cogent dismay, shaking his head slowly back and forth.

Wil couldn't decide between bewilderment, apprehension, or pique. "*What?*"

Brayden didn't say anything, just stared, still shaking his head like he was trying to deny Wil's very existence, before he turned slowly, stunned gaze going inexorably to the little window above the cupboard. Staring, as though the steady drops of rain had mesmerized—

The rain.

It all slipped into place, snapped into a broader shape, like those puzzle pieces Brayden was always on about. Every bit of blood in Wil's body dropped to his gut, leaving him cold and sickeningly numb. "Oh *shit.*"

Brayden's hand was tangled in his hair now, as if he'd gone to brush it back and forgotten what he was doing halfway through. "Yeah" was all he said.

His voice was thin and shakier than Wil had ever heard it before. Wil's own dawning dread was somehow temporized by the fact that Brayden looked almost as shocked and repelled as Wil felt.

"You were there." Wil's voice was just as tremulous as Brayden's had been. "How did you—?"

"I've no idea." Brayden turned to look at Wil—dark, intelligent eyes gone wide and near vacant now. He frowned. "No. No, I... I mean, yes. Yes, I do. I *think* I do." He looked at Wil, still knocked for six, but earnest now. "Millard was right. She loves you."

And that was just about enough of that. Wil threw back the tangle of bedding and lurched up, only half noticing the dull spikes of pain that shot through his hips, his thighs, even his arse as he did so. Damn it, he'd had a feeling he was going to pay for a day in the saddle. He ignored it, skirted clumsily around Brayden, and made a dive for his pack on the floor. Wil backed himself out of Brayden's immediate reach, hugging the pack to his chest as though it was going to offer even the smallest protection when Brayden decided to... to... well, to do whatever he meant to do.

Except Brayden didn't look as if he meant to do anything but stare at Wil in troubled bemusement. He merely turned his head and followed Wil with his gaze.

"You're still bleeding," Brayden said quietly. "Looks like it's slowed some, but check your ear too."

Wil swiped at his ear, then his nose, then backed up another few steps and into the wall when Brayden leaned over, retrieved the stained handkerchief from the bed, and held it out. Brayden did it all without taking a single step, the breadth of his reach going from the bed to the wall where Wil cringed without having to so much as stretch. No wonder he wasn't chasing Wil around the room—he could probably reach every corner of it without moving more than two steps.

"Take it." Brayden held the wad of bloody linen out between

his fingers. "I'm not going to hurt you. I'm not going to grab for you. Just take it before you bleed to death."

Slowly, cautiously, Wil reached out, eyes never leaving Brayden's. A shudder he couldn't help swept along his backbone when his bloody fingertips brushed Brayden's knuckles.

"What do you mean to do?" It was small and too timid, mumbled through the ball of blood and linen.

Brayden looked as though he hadn't thought of anything beyond the damned handkerchief. He rubbed at his face, the scratch of callused fingertips against the bristly growth on his chin louder than it should have been, but it was like Wil's senses had trebled. He could hear raindrops searing and sizzling in the flue of the chimney, could hear ash tremble loose from the dying coals in the fireplace and sough down through the grate, could feel the infinitesimal drop in temperature with each one. He would swear he could hear Brayden's heart beating, almost as loud in his ears as his own.

"Do?" Brayden laughed, a low, arched snort without a trace of mirth. "I've been called. No." He frowned, jaw clenched, and cast his gaze out the window. "No. I've been dragged into a calling I didn't even believe ten minutes ago." He shifted his glance to Wil, mouth twisting with bitter irony. "And it's *really* not what you think it is. Whatever sinister things they told you, they were lies. Besides being a foul little shit who drugs and preys on little boys, Síofra's a bloody filthy liar. He lied because he wanted you to be afraid of me. It's why he sent those men to Lind, and... I don't know, but *She* certainly—" He cut himself off, head tilting. "How could you have believed...?" A baffled pause. "How can you look at Her and not see the way She loves you? How could you ever think She means you harm?"

Wil shook his head slowly, inching his way along the wall toward the door, eyes locked to Brayden's. Curiously, Brayden only watched him do it, a peculiar raw interest in his gaze, like he was seeing Wil for the first time and didn't know what to make of him.

"You've seen Her?" Wil couldn't help asking, voice low and hoarse, vibrating with both reluctant wonder and profound betrayal.

Brayden didn't answer the question, merely flicked a look over Wil and said, "You might want to put on some trousers before you bolt. And your boots."

Wil stared. "You'd... I can...?"

Again Brayden didn't answer, only slouched over to the bed, sat heavily, then propped an elbow to his knee and dropped his head into his hand. He rubbed at his brow.

"I don't know what to do," he muttered to the floor. "I'm meant to protect you. She *ordered* me to—She bloody *chastised* me for not doing my job—" A cynical laugh barked out of him, and he looked at Wil. "Except She didn't tell me how I'm supposed to convince you I'm not going to kill you, and I can't prove a negative. The only way I can prove it is to keep not killing you, but you'll go on expecting it, I'll go on terrifying you without meaning to, and when you look at me like that, like I'm the worst monster conjured from your darkest nightmares, it makes me want to take your head off, so how am I supposed to...?" He threw his hands out. "Do I let you go, let you walk right into whatever's out there waiting for you? Do I keep you a prisoner for your own good? *You* tell *me*." Wil saw nothing in his eyes but honest confusion and earnest asking. "What d'you want me to do? What do *you* want?"

It resonated right through Wil's chest, rife with remembered surprise and cautious hope, and he echoed back the answer he'd given the last time the question was put to him. "I want to not be afraid anymore."

Brayden winced, as if hearing the words was another confirma-

5

tion of something he didn't want to believe. Wary, Wil lowered the handkerchief, fairly certain now the bleeding had stopped, and peered curiously at Brayden. It scared Wil a little to see Brayden like this. From the moment Wil had laid eyes on him, Brayden had oozed confidence and good sense, wily intelligence, and the capability to bend any circumstance to what he chose. To go from that to this... disoriented perplexity... it was almost as unnerving as knowing that what had set it off was too real to be denied.

"All right." Brayden sucked in a long, bracing breath. "I want you to not be afraid anymore too, but I don't know how to... I didn't mean to... to...." He waved his great hand about. "I didn't mean to 'follow' you, and I don't even really think I did—I think *She* did—and even if I did, I'll be buggered if I know how, and I've no idea—"

"She was there?"

"She *brought* me. I wouldn't've been there had it not been—"

"You're *always* there." It just... blurted out of Wil, heated and furious, before he realized what he'd said and shut his mouth. He hugged his pack a little closer to his chest.

Brayden blinked over at him, eyebrows twisted tight. "What the hell does *that* mean?"

Wil's teeth clenched, and he shook his head, angry and mortified when tears seared the backs of his eyes.

"You're always *there*." It was maddening, *enraging*, that not only did Brayden really not know, but that Wil couldn't stop himself from enlightening him. "You've always *been* there, Watching me. You just didn't know it, because... because...."

Wil was posturing as if he knew what he was talking about, and strangely, Brayden was listening to him. Inexplicably it drove up Wil's anger until it spilled out his mouth like messy splatters of poison.

"Because you're a great lummox of a man who thinks if he just reasons hard enough and believes hard enough, everything will be as he thinks it should be. You didn't *want* to see, you didn't want to *know*. And now you're going to sit there and tell me that all this time, She's been watching, She's been *seeing*, and you could but you wouldn't, and there I was—" Wil bared his teeth in a snarl. "You want me to believe Síofra lied, made me afraid of you because *he* was afraid of you, and all right, it makes sense, but it doesn't *fix anything*! Where *was* She for all this time? Where were *you*?"

He hadn't any idea that *any* of that was coming. It was as if he was listening from the outside as every word shot from his mouth in little darts of betrayal. His mind was caroming back and forth, remembering everything he'd been told, everything he'd believed, and the possible relief of contemplating it all for lies was almost a bigger betrayal than having been lied to in the first place. It would almost be less wrenching to think that this man—this *Guardian*— was everything Wil had ever thought he was, that he'd just been playing with Wil all this time, letting him suffer through small snatches at hope so it would be all the more painful when he finally took it away.

Believing that She *knew*, that She'd sent Brayden—Her bloody damned *Guardian*—that Brayden had been there at Wil's back all this time and done *nothing*....

He didn't know what to do with himself. There was a chasm at his feet, and he was standing on sand.

"I'm sorry." Brayden's voice was soft, almost small. "I didn't know."

Wil... *slipped.*

"*Why didn't you know?* You were *there*, you were Watching, and He just... sleeps, always *sleeps*, and mumbles things at me I don't understand, tells me She loves me, and then just... just *goes away* when I ask Him for... to make it *stop*. I thought it was...."

Tears were burning Wil's eyes and cheeks, but he didn't care anymore. His throat was rough and sore, but he couldn't stop screaming.

"I thought I was being *punished*, and I couldn't... couldn't make the thing I was being punished for *stop*, and I hated Him because He made me, and I hated Her because She didn't care, and all the while—" A rough snarl nearly closed Wil's throat. "You say She loves me like it's supposed to make everything all right. I don't *want* to know She loves me. I want to think She's dead, or She hates me and laughs when I scream, and now you're *sorry!*"

He threw the pack, hurling it as hard as he could at Brayden's head. Brayden only dipped a little to the side, dark gaze following the pack's trajectory as it bounced on the bed and down to the floor. He looked back at Wil, the regret in his eyes lancing another wrenching spike into Wil's heart.

"What am I supposed to do with 'sorry' *now?*" Wil said, a whisper this time, broken and hollow.

Brayden was silent for a long time, just *looking* at Wil, before he shook his head and pushed out a heavy sigh. "I expect you could tell me to shove it up my arse. But I would ask you to consider that perhaps I might have known, had my home not been attacked before anyone could tell me."

...Oh.

Wil closed his eyes. The softness of the words, the quiet intent behind them it hit Wil right behind the breastbone, sharp and raw.

"I—"

"You didn't know—you were a child. It wasn't your fault. I understand that." Brayden's voice was still quiet, very calm, but there was a slow swell of wrath welling beneath it. "Just give me the same benefit, all right? We've enough blame and blindness between us already, I think."

All Wil's own wrath seemed to have left him. He was disoriented without it. "How do you know...?" His voice was softer than he liked, but he couldn't seem to get enough air. "How do you know you're... you're *not—*?"

"Those marks the Brethren wear." Brayden's teeth were tight, his jaw clenched. "Those tattoos—d'you know what those are?" He didn't wait for Wil to answer. "They're clan marks, the tokens of the Old Ones, Lind's shamans. Only they don't just tattoo them on—they etch them right into their skin. They're runes that spell out *Wæpenbora* in the First Tongue. Do you know what that means?" Again he didn't wait for an answer. "It means paladin, weapon bearer, warrior protector, Mother's soldier. And the funny thing is, written language in Lind is forbidden, except for the shamans. My *father* wore the mark of the *Weardas*—they're only a little different—and *I didn't know* what they meant until ten minutes ago. I didn't bloody *remember*. I'd seen them for the first ten years of my life, and yet I didn't recognize them. I saw them on those men the first night at the inn in Dudley, and I *knew* I'd seen them before, but...."

Brayden's hands closed into fists, that low level of rage still vibrating through him.

"All that meaning and history in a word they likely can't even read, and those men *stole* it all, took it like it belonged to them, and then tried to take away everything it means."

Wil thought about it. Carefully. It still wasn't enough—it was too ambiguous and not nearly enough to stake his life on.

"But how do you *know*?"

Brayden sighed. He looked exhausted already, and it couldn't be past sunup yet.

"Think about it for once, and try to do it without any of Síofra's noise cocking up the logic. You said you saw my mother— she smiled at you, touched your cheek. Does that seem like something the mother of someone meant to kill you would do? I *don't* know, because no one told me, and right, I could still convince myself She was a dream or delusion if I tried really hard—but I *know* now, I can't *stop* knowing, and I can't offer you any better assurance than that.

"I can offer you the relative safety of my protection. You're not helpless, you've survived on your own, but things have changed, and this is... this is fucking *huge*."

Brayden rubbed at his brow, agitated but trying not to show it.

"I can help you, but not if you keep trying to run from me, not if you still insist on believing I'm going to murder you. I can't make you trust me, and I can't keep seeing that, that... *look* in your eyes."

He didn't say that he could force his help if he wanted to. Wil didn't know if it was because Brayden was serious about asking what Wil wanted, or simply because he didn't *have* to say it—it was fairly obvious.

A sharp rap at the door startled them both. Even though it nearly loosed a shriek from Wil's throat, he was almost glad for the interruption. He kept pinging from hope to guilt to suspicion to wrathful outrage, and every word Brayden spoke pushed Wil closer to some kind of edge.

"Open up in there!" someone barked from the other side of the door. More pounding rattled the hinges, this time heavy and impatient. "Open up, I say!"

Wil half expected Brayden to throw himself between Wil and the door. But Brayden merely drew his gun from the holster strapped to his thigh, slipped his hand beneath the bedding, and nodded at Wil.

Wil raised his eyebrows but opened the door cautiously to a red-faced innkeep, hand raised in a fist as though caught midknock and mouth open on more thwarted demands. There was a thick, nasty-looking cudgel hanging by his hip. The innkeep paused when he saw Wil, then leaned in with a wary look.

"There've been complaints from the other guests." The innkeep shot his glance over Wil's shoulder, eyes narrowed in suspicion, presumably at Brayden. "Said there was shouting up here like murder was being done." He looked back at Wil, gaze lingering pointedly—on the yellowing bruises, on the bandaged hand, on Wil's no doubt bloodstained nose and lip, and doubtless his chin as well—his overall disheveled state. The innkeep leaned in and lowered his voice. "Everything all right, lad?"

Wil dropped his gaze, then angled it slowly over his shoulder. Brayden was watching—no warnings in his eyes, no threats, just a cool interest in what Wil would do. Wil was pretty interested himself. If Wil shot the innkeep a desperate glance, whispered to him—*help, I'm afraid, he's kidnapped me*, anything—the innkeep would be an instant ally. Wil could run, and no one would try to stop him but Brayden—maybe not even Brayden. And if Brayden did try, he'd be so occupied with explaining the situation and trying not to get himself arrested that Wil would be long gone before Brayden managed to sort the tangle.

And yet.

Wil somehow found himself nodding. "Thank you, every-thing's fine. I'm afraid I was dreaming and woke with a nosebleed, and I rather...." A warm flush flooded Wil's cheeks, and he swiped at his face, embarrassed, in case there were any residual tears lurk-ing. "I rather went to pieces for a little while, until I finally realized I was awake, and...."

The innkeep still looked chary, eyeing Brayden dubiously over Wil's shoulder. He apparently wasn't going to go away unless he was convinced someone wasn't going to get murdered in one of his rooms, and right now he seemed fairly convinced that Brayden was the one who'd done the damage to Wil.

If the situation weren't so surreal, Wil might've doubled over with preposterous little cackles. *Hahaha, look at this, me coming to the defense of big, scary Constable Brayden, oh the irony....*

Wil cleared his throat and looked down with an uneasy shrug. "I had a.... I was accosted several days ago by brigands—" He waved vaguely at his face with the bandaged hand. "—and I'm afraid some of the effects... linger. I'm very sorry to have disturbed the peace of your establishment."

The innkeep's tense stance softened immediately. He even looked a little abashed. "It's quite all right, there, Mister...?"

"Wil." He gestured over his shoulder. "And this is my companion, Constable Brayden from Putnam." He shot another glance back in time to see Brayden lift a bemused eyebrow.

The innkeep bobbed a nod. "Jarvis." He stuck out his hand to Wil, then smiled apologetically and withdrew it when Wil ruefully waved the wad of bandages that was currently passing as his hand. "Are you well, then, Wil?" It was earnest and solicitous. "I can send for a healer, if you need—"

"No, no, that won't be necessary," Wil assured him quickly. "I've already embarrassed myself enough. I'd just as soon forget any of it happened, if you don't mind."

"As you wish." Jarvis hovered at the door, still frowning concern.

Perhaps Wil had chosen the wrong course of action. Perhaps he should have just barked at the man and got them thrown out. It likely would've been quicker.

"My Elli brews a brilliant headache remedy," Jarvis said with a decisive nod. "I'll have some sent up, shall I? And I don't expect you'll want to come down to breakfast soon, what with...." He cleared his throat. "A tray, yes? Eggs and bread and whatnot. Elli will handle it. I'll send her along."

"Coffee?" Brayden piped in.

Jarvis spared him a wry smile. "Indeed."

Absurdly touched, Wil thanked Jarvis warmly, then slowly shut the door on his smiling face. With the *click* of the latch, all the tension seemed to run out of Wil. He leaned his forehead to the jamb, closed his eyes, and sighed.

"Um." Brayden said from behind. "Companion?"

A droopy little half snort whiffed out of Wil. "Ah, Cynewísan," he muttered to the door. "Where the women wear trousers, the men love men, and the sheep are bored." He turned and leaned his back to the door. "I'd never have got away with that in Ríocht—they'd already have us out on the gibbets." A shrug. "It was either 'companion' or... something else I couldn't think of in the moment."

"It's fine." Brayden waved his hand. "It'll just confirm what he already suspected last night, I expect, and it did rather take care of... other suspicions." He tilted his head, eyeing Wil thoughtfully. "You could've got away."

Wil looked down, chewing his lip. "According to you, I don't need to get away—I'm not a prisoner."

Brayden sighed, slipped the gun out from beneath the bedding, and reholstered it. "Can I ask you something?" His eyes were on his fingers as he resecured the weapon.

"You can ask."

Brayden didn't acknowledge the ambiguity, just nodded. "Last night—well, this morning, I guess—the coffee, the rain...." He stopped fiddling, set his jaw, and looked at Wil straight. "Did I hurt you?"

Wil frowned. "Hurt me?"

"You said it hurt when Síofra... did the things he did."

"Oh." Wil hadn't thought about it until now, what with the blur of... everything that had happened since Brayden had shaken him awake. And now that Wil *was* thinking about it, he wasn't sure if it was a relief or a new worry. "No. You didn't hurt me." Brayden looked so relieved, Wil found himself feeling an odd sort of sympathy. "Then again, you didn't... or rather *I* didn't—" Frustrated that he couldn't seem to find the right words, Wil scowled at the floor. "There was no push." He said it quietly, almost to himself, thinking. "You wanted something, and I chose to give it to you. And it didn't hurt." It was as simple as he could make it, as close to sense as he could come.

"Huh." Brayden deliberated over that for a moment. "Has it ever happened that way before?"

Wil shook his head.

"Then why the bloody nose?"

Wil's mouth twisted sourly. "You keep asking me these things like I know. No one told *me* either, y'know."

Brayden opened his mouth, closed it, then rubbed at his stubbly chin. "You chose to give me something. Why would you do that?"

Wil could feel that embarrassing flush rising to his cheeks again, and he gritted his teeth, annoyed. It wasn't as though the dreams always made sense. In fact, sense was rather a rare thing, in his experience. It had just seemed like something he wanted to do at the time. The truth was he'd felt bad about the things he'd said last night, the way he'd accused Brayden, and coffee had seemed such a small thing. Now it took on significance all out of proportion.

"It hasn't rained in this part of the country for a long time," Wil mumbled fractiously. "If I'd known... if I'd thought of it myself—"

"Right," Brayden was quick to agree. "Rain. That makes sense."

Apparently they both decided to forget about the coffee entirely. Wil was a touch comforted that at least Brayden was as uncomfortable about it all as Wil was. It was small consolation, but consolation it was.

Brayden shifted, still looking uncomfortable and trying really hard not to. "Listen, I've not even had a piss yet." He stood. "I'm going down the hall to take advantage of plumbing while we have it. Then you can have your turn."

Wil had to keep from blinking in surprise that Brayden was going to leave him in the room by himself. It was... strange, this new tentative trust. And Wil didn't even know yet if it was real or merited. He tried not to show his confusion, just shrugged and made himself busy with retrieving his pack from the floor and rummaging in it for nothing in particular.

Brayden watched him for a moment, then walked to the door. Stopped. He looked at Wil over his shoulder.

Wil didn't look up. "I'll be here when you get back."

Brayden only nodded and quit the room.

"You still want to travel today?" Wil angled his gaze to the window with a frown. It was still pouring, and what with his new enlightenment on saddle soreness, he realized he'd been assuming—or hoping—up until now that they'd linger here at the inn until the rain let up.

It was cozy once the fire was rebuilt and stoked, and Wil had got used to sharing the small space. It only got easier after he let go of the tension and made a concerted effort to view things in the new, nonlethal light in which Brayden insisted upon standing. Brayden sat across from Wil on the bed with the tray between them, each of them shoveling down the generous breakfast Mistress Elli had provided. Brayden wasn't lunging at Wil, wasn't trying to stab him with a spoon—not that he'd need to, what with the arsenal strapped all over him—and he wasn't trying to knock Wil unconscious so he could practice his newly learned skills at following. In fact, Brayden seemed even more uncomfortable with the whole idea than Wil was, and Wil wouldn't have ever believed that possible. Although he might change his mind when it came time to sleep again.

Wil shuddered, took a bite of sausage, and chewed it slowly.

Brayden plopped a great glob of runny scrambled eggs onto his toasted bread and chomped it down, chased it with a slurp of coffee, and shrugged. "Provided it stays nice and heavy like this, it'll wash away our tracks. With any luck, anyone coming after us will spend days on the road north before they realize their mistake, while we're safely detouring west and on over to...." He looked down into his coffee. "Um." He shifted a bit, then plucked up a sausage link, examining it with a little too much focus. "We need to discuss our plan again."

Wil raised an eyebrow, curious. He didn't particularly like the idea of drudging through the rain, but he hadn't intended to argue about it. It made too much sense, and Brayden did know what he was doing. Wil never would have thought of rain as a benefit to travel, but he did like the idea of using it to throw off any followers.

"I don't think we should go to Putnam." Brayden looked up at Wil, somber. "I think we should go to Lind."

Wil's breakfast took a slow, rolling tour around his stomach. He shook his head automatically, mouth open on a ready protest.

Brayden held up his hand. "Whatever else is there, they've got answers. They know things we don't, things we need to know so we can figure out what the hell we're supposed to do. In case it's escaped you, besides all of this—" He waved his hand about. "—this Aisling stuff, you've made quite a nasty political mess. If we make a move before we know what we're doing, we could cause a war—a *real* war, like The Fifty Years War, not these little border skirmishes of the last ten years."

"I didn't choose the mess, y'know."

"Well, it's made, so it hardly matters."

"Then why d'you have to *say* it?" Wil caught Brayden's frown, the sardonic tilt to his gaze, and flushed some, but clenched his teeth with a stubborn shake of his head. "I haven't missed the obvious. I'm not slow. But the way you say it...." He spread his hands, caught between anger and bewilderment. "I never asked for this. I only wanted a *life*. I never intended to hurt anyone or cause any political messes. I only *ever* wanted... I only want to be let to *live*. And not drugged 'til I can't even take a piss by myself, or chained to a—" He stood abruptly, agitated, and paced back and forth beside the bed. "I've never even seen a river, except in someone else's dream—I learned to think inside the minds of madmen and dreamers. How fair is *any* of that? And you say these things like I'm supposed to bloody *care* about political messes!"

Wil stopped, took a long, deep breath, and stared levelly at Brayden. "I'm not being ungrateful—I'm *not*—and I understand the enormity of what you're doing, what you risk in doing it. I didn't mean... I never... I'm not belittling it or making light, and I wish I could be as brave. I just...." Wil shrugged heavily and looked down. "I don't want to go anywhere near Lind *or* Putnam, and it's very hard for me to give a damn about a political mess when I know too well what walking back into that trap means. You don't understand. You can't *know*—"

"No, I can't," Brayden agreed. "But I saw Old Bridge last night, and I at least understand the risk you take if we don't keep several steps ahead of the Brethren." He shot a look at the scars on Wil's wrist, then flicked it quickly away, back up to Wil's eyes. "If I'd known, I never would have...." Brayden shook his head, true remorse on his concerned face. "The shackles," he said. "I'm sorry."

Damn it, how could he make Wil go from dread to insight to umbrage in the space of ten words?

"*Pity?*"

"Not pity." Brayden ignored Wil's angry tone, keeping his own mien calm. "Understanding—something I need desperately and you provide sparing little of. If you'd just told me all of this from the beginning...." He set his jaw, clearly annoyed. "What did you think was going to happen? What did you think I would do?" He held a hand up when Wil opened his mouth. "*Besides* killing you, I mean, because if you say that one more bleeding time, I swear—" He growled with a roll of his eyes. "Well, I don't know what I'll do. Killing you now would only prove your point, and I've a contrary nature."

Amazingly, Wil had to smile at the uneasy frustration. It only lasted a moment before he shrugged and looked away.

"I thought Síofra was telling the truth." Wil looked up, solemn now. "You must understand—it wasn't always... that way. He was kind to me at first. He was the closest thing to a parent...." His mouth twisted. "I had no reason to doubt him. I thought he was protecting me, and it wasn't until after I started to rebel against the leaf that it turned... ugly. And even then, I thought it was me, my fault. I was bad, I couldn't behave."

Wil shook his head. "I tried to do more than find you when I went searching about in Lind." His voice had dipped down, lower than he would've preferred, but at least even. "I couldn't read the Old Ones, just like I couldn't read you, and your mother was the only person in the entire village—in the entire *world*—who knew what you were. Lind doesn't just breed giants—they breed Watchers and have done for thousands of years, and no one knows what Lind is about but your shamans, *no one*. Why would they keep it so secret, if there wasn't something terribly sinister beneath it all? How d'you know you're not going to walk me right into a new trap, if I agree to go there with you?"

Brayden was pensive now, listening and brooding down into the dregs of his coffee. After several silent moments, his eyebrows drew together and he shook his head.

"The problem," he began slowly, "is that I don't know *anything*. I'm basing our safety on dreams and conjecture and memories more than half a lifetime old. But the Old Ones *do* know, and I can't believe people who carve 'Mother's Soldier' into their faces exist solely to stamp out the Mother's most loved Gift."

"Just like the Brethren shouldn't exist to usurp and redefine the Father's gift?"

"...All right." Brayden rubbed at his brow. "You're right to be cautious. I know in my gut I'm right, but with religious freaks, who can ever tell?" He slipped his cup onto the peeling surface of the shabby cupboard. "Compromise. We'll head to Lind and find someplace safe for you to stay while I go into the valley and see if I can find something that will help us. I'll gather what information I can, and we'll discuss the next move. Will that do?"

Wil stared at the floor unhappily. Unfortunately it made sense. But Síofra had made sense for a time too. The Brethren had even seemed to make sense for a brief moment of hope. Wil had never liked the idea of going back to Putnam, but even that made sense in a desperate sort of way.

Anyway, Brayden was going out of his way to treat Wil as a partner, an equal voice. Wil thought perhaps that might translate into more freedom on the road, more chance of getting away clean if he found he had to. And if Brayden really was going to find Wil someplace to lie up, safe, by himself... there'd be all kinds of opportunity then.

In the meantime, Brayden was the best chance Wil had of

shaking the Brethren *and* the Guild. And if nothing else came of all this, Wil was certainly eating better than he ever had before Brayden styled himself Wil's protector.

"All right." It was halfhearted and slightly sulky, but Wil couldn't help it. "I imagine Lind is better than Ríocht, at least."

Brayden smirked. "Good, because that was going to be my next suggestion."

Wil stared for a long moment. Then he tilted his head. "Constable Brayden," he said slowly, "did you just make a joke?"

"Um. No?" Brayden flushed. Wil hadn't known he *could*. "I mean—that is, I suppose it wasn't—"

"No, no." A sardonic smile twitched at the corners of Wil's mouth. "You've a sense of humor. Not a very good one, but... well, who knew?"

With directions from Jarvis—quite vocal in his opinion that they should not be venturing out in the rain *what with the young man unwell*—they found a shop on the northern outskirts of the village where Brayden kitted them both with rain gear, waxed cloaks and wide-brimmed hats. Wil caught a look at the heft of the purse Brayden untied from his belt to pay for it, noting with envy the solid glint of gold inside. Wil hadn't thought about it before, but considering the horses, and the inn, and the baths, and all the meals—and now the new gear—and considering all that gold left over in the purse... well, Brayden must be quite wealthy.

They trudged for several miles along the road, the hardpack slipping and depressing under the horses' hoofs. Wil rode with his head turned back for a while, watching with satisfaction as the prints filled with water, then mud, then turned to indistinguishable divots that would no doubt continue to erode as rain pounded the road. He smiled to himself and tipped his head down, oddly amused when a small deluge spilled from the brim.

Wil would never have thought of the hats either, but they did a fine job of keeping the water from dripping over his face and into his eyes. With the hood of the cloak turned up over his head and the hat atop it, no rain spattered down his nape, and with the coat underneath it all, he was probably as comfortable as anyone could be while traveling on horseback through torrential rain. Despite the whole saddle-sore thing.

The horses remained agreeable, even though their coats steamed and they blew plumes of heavy mist into the cold, wet air from their nostrils. Neither one of them turned ornery, though, and Wil made it a point to pat his on her muscled neck every now and then and mentally promised her one of his precious apples when they stopped. All right, and one for Brayden's horse too.

They rode all through the miserable day, skirting down the first random lane they came to off the road and following that until it wound into another and another still. They finally set themselves west through heavy forest. Wil assumed it was midday because Brayden handed him a handful each of hardtack and jerky, apparently meant to be lunch. Wil didn't know what he'd been expecting, but he admitted a touch of disappointment at the fare, if only to himself. It made him wonder what to expect at suppertime. Would they stop at all? And what about sleep? Just how hard did Brayden intend to push? Wil hadn't even thought to ask how many days' ride Lind would be.

The rain was too loud for conversation, so Wil held his questions. Anyway, it was just as well—it seemed as though every conversation they'd ever had started out with penetrating questions from Brayden that Wil didn't want to answer. Silence was just fine.

The pace was slower once they left the road, the horses carefully picking along roots and slippery deadfall. Brayden led today, watching every angle constantly, gaze swiveling in regular wide sweeps about the perimeter, even craning his neck frequently and stretching his gaze up into the trees. Wil did the same but found his own eyes catching on the subtle change of colors from one tree to the next, the way the rain weighted the pine boughs and made them tremble, the slight bit of iridescence in the wet sworls of his horse's mane.

They kept going even after it got so dark Wil couldn't see anymore. The rain hadn't let up, though it wasn't as bad beneath the trees as it had been out in the open. Still, it was going to make a miserable night for sleeping—if Brayden even let them stop for the night. Though perhaps a sleepless night wouldn't be an altogether bad thing. Wil had deliberately not allowed his mind to wander to this morning's events, deliberately not thought about a lot of things, in fact, but if nothing else, the horses were going to need to be rested and fed, and Wil figured Brayden *had* to let them stop eventually.

Wil's stomach was growling by the time Brayden finally called a halt, and his eyelids were drooping. And his thighs were *killing* him. *And* his arse bones hurt. He hadn't even known he *had* arse bones.

He dismounted slowly, clinging to the saddlebow until the ground stopped feeling like it was trying to sway out from under him. His injured hand had been throbbing for hours and miles, probably from the wet and cold, and he kept it securely tucked to his chest beneath cloak and coat.

"This is the densest we'll find in the dark." Brayden seemed to be muttering it to himself as he led his horse over and pushed the reins into Wil's hand. The crossbow had traveled strapped to Brayden's broad back; now he wrangled it out from beneath his cloak and braced it against the nearest tree. The rifle had spent the journey propped across his saddlebow beneath the protection of the cloak. It almost joined the crossbow, but Brayden stopped, shot a sideways glance at Wil, and slung the strap over his shoulder instead, as though that was what he'd meant to do all along.

Wil might've snorted, but he was too busy realizing how deeply the cold had set in to his bones.

Brayden dragged his pack from the saddlebag, freeing the hatchet and shovel from their little loops on the sides. "There's enough around here for a small shelter, at least. We'll need a fire, though, or these cloaks will be no more than useless weight. I hate to do it. I might as well leave a sign that says 'We came this way!' but I haven't much choice."

A fire. It was a nice thought, but unless Brayden was a secret shaman, a fire was likely just wishful thinking. Still, it might be fun to watch him try. Shelter might be a more reasonable expectation, but Wil wasn't even going to guess how.

"What about the horses?"

Brayden paused. "What about them?"

"Well, they need shelter too, right?"

"Not... really?" Brayden sounded bemused. "Horses don't need shelter, not like we do."

"That's stupid." Wil set his hand to his mare's neck, feeling protective. "Of course they do. That's why there are *stables.*"

"Says the man who'd never ridden a horse as of last week—"

"Hey, I *worked* in a stable, in case you for—"

"—*and* who isn't going to be the one building said shelter."

That made Wil pause, but he only shrugged. "I could help. And, I mean, if you're already building a shelter, why not make it big enough for them too? I don't mind sharing."

"Just—" Brayden whipped off his hat with a sigh, tipped it until all the water ran off it, then set it back on his head. "Never mind. I'll see what I can do." It didn't sound very enthusiastic, but

Brayden was all concern a second later when he leaned in and squinted through the darkness at Wil. "How are you after the long ride, anyway? Doing all right?"

Wil's first impulse was to snark that no, he wasn't doing all right, he'd likely never get his knees back together again, and his arse bones had gone from aching to *really* aching, and by the way, he was *starving*, what the fuck, did Brayden have a spare stomach or something?

He ended up nodding, voicing a polite "Fine," then made himself busy with digging out the feedbags and filling them with a few handfuls of oats while Brayden chopped at pine boughs and cursed every time one of them dumped a bucketload of water on his head. Wil thought about telling Brayden it might be easier without the rifle swinging around on its strap behind him, and he needn't worry—Wil had no intention of nicking it and shooting Brayden in the back—but the colorful outbursts were, after all, the most entertainment Wil had had all day.

So Wil kept quiet, smiling into the darkness as he stood with the horses and listened to their slow munching, the sharp sounds of snapping branches, and the occasional irritated mutter in the otherwise silence of the thick forest. It had probably been a good hour or so when the abrupt, brilliant spark of a match near dazzled Wil's eyes; the brighter flare of flames catching and spreading into a small but real campfire near dazzled his reason.

"How did you do that?" Wil demanded, undecided if he was pleased or resentful.

Brayden looked over in Wil's general direction, blinking and squinting around the light. He frowned. "How did I do what?"

Augh. Not only was Brayden able to start fires in the rain, he had no idea why it would amaze someone who hadn't guessed the possibility. Wil stared at Brayden, still undecided if he should be backing away and signing charms or throwing himself at Brayden with a grateful embrace. Brayden had shed his hat somewhere and thrown back the hood of his cloak. The firelight scudded over his face with careful fingers, drawing gold and light touches of claret from hair curling damp and unruly. The effect kept glissading back and forth between primitive forest god and boyish artlessness.

Wil shook himself and shifted his stance. "The fire," he said. "How did you start a fire with wet wood?"

"Oh." Brayden turned back to the smoky fire, feeding it what looked like hacked-up chips and small split branches. "It's easy with pine." He worked steadily, stoking and fanning as he continually added fuel. "You can do it with any kind of wood if you split the bigger branches to get to the dry wood inside and chip away the wet bark. But with pine, there's the sap or resin inside that helps it catch a lot quicker and burn hotter, so the wet outside will dry and burn too." He shrugged, poking at the base of the flames. "We'll have to keep a steady eye on it, else it'll likely sputter, but I need the light to make the shelter, and we might as well have a hot supper while we're at it."

Huh. Wil thought of all the times he'd shivered in the rain, crouching in some damp little hole if he could find one, or trying to ignore the raindrops on his eyelids if he couldn't. "That's...." He swallowed his self-consciousness with an effort. "Will you show me?"

Brayden didn't even raise his eyebrows. "Of course, but right now there are other priorities, all right? Between fuel for the fire and the shelter, I'll need to cut quite a lot more." He flicked a glance toward the horses and muttered, "Apparently *a lot* more," though it didn't sound *too* morose. With a sigh, he jerked his chin at Wil. "D'you know how to hobble?"

Wil rolled his eyes. "I *did* work in a stable, y'know."

"So you keep reminding me."

"Well, I did!"

"For two weeks," Brayden said, not *quite* under his breath. Then, louder, "That doesn't answer my question."

"*Yes*, I know how to hobble horses." Wil had already taken some lengths of rope from his horse's saddlebag and was looping them to size. He didn't say he didn't *like* to do it, that he thought it was a little bit mean, because he'd probably just get that same *what the fuck?* look he'd gotten about the shelter.

"Well, could you take care of them and then come over here? I could use a hand."

The mares were still munching tiredly and unlikely to wander off, but Wil clumsily braided the knots—stupid soggy bandages—mostly by feel in the dim light of the small fire, and then looped the hobbles around the fore fetlocks of both horses. Neither one of them even twitched, but Wil quietly apologized anyway and made his mental promise of the apples a verbal one before he went to help Brayden.

Brayden had already started without him, moving beyond the small circle of wavering light. All Wil had to do was follow the grunted curses in the dark.

"Good." Brayden took Wil by the shoulders, stood a little too close behind him, and guided his left hand up over his head. Wil was already gripping a thick, crosshatched bundle of prickly branches before he thought to shrug Brayden off, and by then Brayden was already rattling off instructions. "All right, feel how these are connected by this one joint? I need you to hold that tight, and don't let them loose while I lift the other end and get it secured in those branches over there."

What with his eyes having to adjust to the dark all over again, Wil couldn't see two feet in front of his face, so he decided to take Brayden's word that there were indeed branches "over there."

"It's going to be heavy for a few minutes, so be ready." Brayden let go of Wil's hand and was gone.

It did indeed get very heavy, and Wil had a hard time of it, what with the bark digging into his hand and the circulation in his arm slowing to a near halt by the time Brayden was satisfied and told Wil he could let go. Relieved, Wil dropped his arm to his side, backing up a few paces and right into a shallow trench filled with water.

"Watch out for that." Brayden smirked as he passed by. "Your ladies won't appreciate you fouling their trough." And then he just moved on to the next section of branches.

So *that* was what the shovel had been for.

Scowling, Wil dragged his now muddy and waterlogged boot from the muck. His toes squelched.

"That wasn't funny."

"It was, a little."

Wil notched the scowl up into a glare.

They repeated the process three more times, the last corner of the shelter so close to the small fire that Wil had to wrap his arm around the tree Brayden was working on to keep from tottering into the flames.

It wasn't until some feeling leached back into Wil's arm that he took a good look at what Brayden had done. It was terribly impressive. Wil had been expecting something like a lean-to, but Brayden had more or less built a roof made of pine boughs laced and woven together using the branches of the surrounding trees as supports. Higher on one side than the other "so the water will run off and we won't end up buried beneath a small forest," Brayden told him.

"Wooooow." Wil stared up and turned in a circle. "This is very fine." He grinned. "You definitely have your uses, Constable Brayden."

Brayden only stared for a moment, then cleared his throat and looked away. "I do try." He rubbed at the back of his neck and then gestured at the horses. "I know you know how to curry. Why don't you take care of them, and I'll take care of supper."

Still smiling despite his squishy boot, Wil nodded agreeably and went to do as bid.

"It's best if you do it away from you." Brayden was watching carefully as Wil trimmed wet bark away from pine branches. "Do it toward you and slip...." Brayden opened a hand and shrugged.

Wil nodded and adjusted his hold, the heft and grip of Brayden's wicked dagger a surprisingly comfortable fit in Wil's palm. It had been awkward going, getting used to doing it with his left hand, but once Wil caught the rhythm, his speed picked up considerably.

Brayden was working on the bigger limbs with the hatchet. He sat on the ground atop one of the saddles, propping the branches from shoulder to ground between his legs and hacking off chunks in a steady spray. His boots were already half-buried in bark and curled shims. He was angled away from the fire, gaze shifting constantly to different points in the forest and doglegging around the curtain of the cloaks with every other sweep.

Wil sat on his bit of carpet with his back leaning against his own saddle, legs stretched out and feet crossed at the ankle. His boots sat next to the fire, drying, his stockings hanging over their sides. The detritus from his own work steadily piled in his lap, and every once in a while he stopped to brush it away and wiggled his toes in the warmth of the flames.

Supper had been an interesting stew made from lumps of jerky and selections from the sacks of dried vegetables in Brayden's pack. It was amazing what a little salt could do for the flavor of what would have otherwise been rather bland fare. Combined with the hardtack, two diced potatoes from Wil's pack, and one each of the somewhat bruised apples afterward, Wil's stomach had stopped complaining, and with the activity and the warmth from the fire, the chill in his bones was starting to recede.

They'd hung their cloaks from the branches closest to the fire, hopefully to dry a bit before morning and providing a flimsy boundary between themselves and the horses—which, if it wasn't exactly a marker of civilization, was at least a reflection of it. With the excuse of making sure the horses were set for the night and checking the hobbles, Wil had earlier ducked around the makeshift curtain to make good on his promise of treats from his rapidly depleting store of apples. It was all right—both mares nickered happily at him and seemed to enjoy them a lot more than he did. Anyway, he wasn't likely to starve without them. And if Brayden had been watching from the other side of the drying cloaks and snorting at Wil's altruism, he at least had the perspicacity to pretend he hadn't been.

"So, I've been thinking." Brayden tossed one trimmed branch toward the pile near the fire and picked up another.

"Oh, good."

Brayden shot Wil a sideways glance but didn't acknowledge the sarcastic bent to Wil's retort. "It's a character flaw." The corner of Brayden's mouth turned up when Wil chuckled. "Seriously, though, there are so many things in all this business that don't connect, so many loose threads flapping about in a windstorm. My job is to find answers, and it's a habit I don't intend to shake. And since you're the only one here...."

Surprisingly, Wil's supper still sat pleasantly in his stomach and didn't roil about in agitation. He hewed away several sprigs from his branch, slicing away their small stumps. "I don't know what answers I can give you. But I suppose it's your right to ask."

"I appreciate that." Brayden went silent again until he'd finished with the limb he was working on and chucked it over to join the others. He flipped the hatchet's blade into the soft ground between his feet and turned to Wil. "Why didn't you ever kill Síofra?"

The name, coming so abruptly like that, hit Wil in a way that made him startle. The knife skidded along the branch, and he tightened his fingers around it, pausing for a moment to make himself start breathing again. Consciously pretending none of it had just happened, Wil made his hands not shake and resumed shaving away bark. He didn't answer.

"I've seen you kill," Brayden went on determinedly. "It takes a certain cold-bloodedness to do what you did, and what happened with that man in the cell...." He shook his head with a frown. "You're full of rage—I can see it every time his name or the Brethren come up—and you're not incapable, so why haven't you just taken him out?"

Wil was quiet for several long moments, staring at his hands but not really seeing, whittling the branch away to a weak, flexible spike. "You didn't see me kill. You saw me abuse a corpse." He shot Brayden a hard look, then looked back down at his hands. "If you'd seen me kill, you likely would have seen terror first and then surprise that the man had let me get close enough to knee him in the stones to get him down." He dropped the branch, leaned to the side, and stabbed at the ground with the knife, leaving it hilt-up between them. "The rage came after." He looked up at Brayden, seeing nothing in his eyes but interest. Wil turned his gaze to the fire. "You would name me a murderer, then?"

"No. I think you're a killer. Some would see no distinction, but those are the ones who've never had to choose between someone else's life and their own."

Wil was slightly taken aback to hear his own estimation of Brayden turned back on him like that. "I never killed Síofra because I couldn't." He flicked a glance over at Brayden, shrugged, and turned away again. "There was no question of doing it when he followed me into dreams—I couldn't do anything but what he told me to do. And by the time I was grown enough... well." A bitter snort. "Leaf and violence are rather mutually exclusive."

Brayden pondered that for a moment in silence. After a short stretch of it, he ventured, "All right, but what about... well, can't you follow *him*?" He leaned forward. "You describe what you do as tending the threads. Can't you sort of...." His hands waved about, and he shook his head. "I don't know, can't you find his thread and... rip it out?"

Wil gritted his teeth. "If it were that easy, you really think I wouldn't've done it already?"

"Well, that's rather the question, innit?"

It was so... reasonable. Why did the man have to be so damned *reasonable*?

"I don't *know* why I can't." Wil sat up abruptly, swatting shavings from his trousers to keep from looking at Brayden. "I don't know why I can't find him, or why he can't find me. He did it once, right? You'd think he'd've caught up to me within days, but somehow he can't. And I can't hunt him down, or the damned Brethren, either—believe me, I've tried—and yes, I would've taken them *all* out if I could've done, and what's more, I don't *care* if that makes me a murderer."

He took a long breath, trying to calm the anger that was ramming through his veins, but it didn't work. "Put me aside for a moment. Pretend I'm not a person and it doesn't matter what happens to me. Look at what Síofra's already done. Look at what the Brethren want to do. Is it murder to take men like that from out the world? Is it murder to do it before they can kill who knows how many others—and not for any kind of higher purpose, but because they think it's their *right*?"

Brayden rubbed a hand over his mouth. "No. But I'll admit I'm a little surprised to know you've thought of it in those terms." He shook his head when Wil's mouth dropped open. "I don't mean it in a bad way, I only mean that... well, I understand why the politics of all this mean little to you—it's right that they should. And it would be just as right if you didn't give a rat's arse about what those men could do with that power if they managed to get hold of you." He shrugged. "You've every right to not give a fuck about the rest of the world. I'm just somewhat...." He paused, searching for the right word. "I'm impressed that you do."

Wil was caught between indignation at being judged so, and an embarrassing grudging pleasure at being assessed as something other than a... well, as something other than a mutinous little badger. He looked down, cheeks heating.

"Don't be too impressed," he muttered to his knees. "If I had to choose between another, even someone I liked, and letting one of them get me, I'd choose me, and it wouldn't necessarily have anything to do with worrying about anyone else's fate. Given that choice, there is no one I wouldn't throw in front of a bullet." He looked at Brayden straight. "I can't go back. I *can't*. There are worse things than death—I know, I've lived them—and I can't...." His jaw clenched tight. "I *won't*. And if I have to throw *myself* in front of a bullet, or cut my own throat to prevent it, I'll do it, and I don't care what that makes me."

Brayden stared at him, eyes slitted and brow contorted in a thoughtful frown. "We've spent an awful lot of time on your need or lack thereof to fear me." He tilted his head. "Do I need to fear you?"

Again there was cool interest and sincere curiosity but no condemnation. The question was straightforward and genuine. Wil almost barked a sharp laugh at the idea of this man, of all people, fearing him—Brayden was almost an entire person wider, after all. In the end, Wil decided to return the favor of bluntness in kind.

He wrested Brayden's knife from its seat in the ground and held it out hilt-first. "I don't intend to murder you in your sleep." He shot a pointed glance at the rifle propped against a tree, Brayden between it and Wil. And he hadn't missed the way Brayden had practically slept atop his weapons last night. "I don't intend to steal one of your guns and shoot you in the back. I choose to trust you because I believe perhaps Síofra did lie and you're not what I've always thought you. I believe you want to help, and I think any danger from you will be unintentional. But I won't trust you blindly. If it comes to a choice between you or me...." He waggled the knife. "I'll still choose me."

Brayden didn't so much as blink. "Fair enough." He nodded at the knife. "Keep it."

Wil frowned, caught off guard, and let his hand fall open, the knife balanced across his palm. "It's a nice knife."

"It is. My foster father gave it to me when I was inducted into the army. It's served me well."

"You were in the army?" Wil didn't know why he was so surprised. Brayden was exactly the type. Honor, duty, rectitude—all those things necessary to men who fancied themselves guardians of anything and liked to play with guns. It was amazing, upon reflection, that it had taken Brayden so long to admit what he was, regardless of what he was meant to guard.

Wil's frown deepened, the knife a growing weight in his hand. "Were you an officer?"

33

Brayden did have an air about him of one who'd been giving orders all his life and was used to having them followed.

Brayden only waved at the knife. "It's a good blade."

Wil didn't miss the deliberate change of subject, but he didn't pursue it just now. "Then why would you give it to me?"

Brayden didn't answer—just leaned toward the fire, poked at the coals with a long stick. He stood, propped the rifle on his shoulder, and turned his back to the fire and Wil. "Get some sleep. If the weather lets up tomorrow, I'll teach you to shoot, so you—" He turned with a frown, waving at the sky. "D'you, um... d'you make it stop too?"

Wil blinked. "I haven't before. Should I?"

Brayden thought about it for a moment, then shook his head. "I can't think why. Anyway, if the weather lets up, I'll teach you to shoot so you can take a watch. In the meantime, at least one of us should get some rest." He adjusted the rifle's strap and walked away.

Wil raised his eyebrows and looked at the knife in his outstretched hand, then let his arm drop. He refused to let himself ponder it, at least not tonight. Instead he turned the knife over in his hands, watching the firelight glance and shiver over its etched surface, its sharp edge. He smiled, then slipped the dagger beneath the saddle.

The clearing was silent, the air still heavy and rimy with yesterday's rain. They'd struck out south when they broke camp this morning, the forest petering out along the way, from dense and thick to sparser growth that grudgingly let through moody, erratic sunlight. Fewer evergreens here—more oaks and elms—and the leaves and deadfall on the forest floor slipped and slid in the muck beneath their feet and the horses' hoofs. Dead vines wound thick and treacherous, so the speed they should have gained through clearer paths was canceled out by another day of cautious stepping. Still, they'd covered a lot more ground than Wil had ever done walking.

Now, though, Wil stood unmoving. Concentrating, his back straight, head slightly bent to the left, one eye closed as he took careful aim at the target. He vibrated just a little, anticipation leaking through the cool metal against his skin and resonating eagerly beneath his touch. A long, calm breath, finger twitching on the trigger, and... *pull*—

Wil blinked. Frowned.

"No, you're forgetting the safety again."

"I'm *not* forgetting it." Wil took the gun's butt plate from his shoulder, pointed the barrel at the ground as Brayden had instructed—six *thousand* times—and tilted it to point at the little catch behind the trigger. "Every time I go to shoot, my finger slides the safety back on."

"Mm, well, that's because it's designed for right-handed people, I expect. You'll just have to get used to it."

Wil scowled and began the process once more. There was a lot to remember, and he hadn't even got a shot off yet. Stupid-picky-bossy Constable Brayden had made him learn the various parts of the gun first, and what they did, quizzing him relentlessly as they'd ridden through the day. Once they'd finally stopped for the night— earlier than yesterday so they'd still have some light left—Wil was instructed and quizzed on how to load and pump it. And all of that before he was even allowed to touch the poxy thing, except to point at various parts and name them.

Even though the rain had let up before dawn and the day was alternately bright and gray and not as cold, Wil found himself in a somewhat sour mood, and Brayden's patience was noticeably thinner than usual. The combination was either going to result in one of them with the shotgun up his arse, or Wil in eventual giddy hysterics on the ground.

And, well, maybe Wil should be more accommodating. Brayden hadn't slept at all, and Wil had—quite well, in fact, as soon as he'd convinced himself Brayden wasn't going to try the trick from the night before again. Still, there had been blissful relief this morning when Wil woke to the smell of coffee and the knowledge he'd been as alone inside his head as he could be. Brayden's dark shape had been behind him as always, at his back, Watching, but that was all, and strangely, it hadn't been unnerving.

"All right, start over," Brayden said sternly. "Cock it first and slide the—"

"Slide the safety on, right. I can't apply the safety without first cocking it, then I brace the butt plate to my shoulder like so—"

"Not too firmly—"

"*Not too firmly* because there will be a kick—"

"Recoil."

Wil dipped the barrel back down and sent a sideways glare at Brayden. "What bloody *difference* does it make?"

"The difference," Brayden said slowly, "is that it's called a *recoil* and not a *kick*."

Wil held back a growl and turned his attention back to the gun and the target. "Not exactly the strong, silent type, are you, then?" It came out from between clenched teeth. "*Fine*, there will be a *recoil*, and if my grip is too firm I'll end up with a broken shoulder." Wil rolled his eyes, forcibly relaxing his jaw before he ground his teeth away, and sighted down the long barrel and across the clearing, aiming for the bundle of sticks Brayden had strung from a branch as a target. "If you'd just let me use one of the handguns, I wouldn't be having this—"

"I keep telling you, they're not as accurate and they don't—"

"They don't have the same range, yes, so you've said, but I bet they're a lot easier to use one-handed."

"You'd think, but not really."

"Easy for you to say. You don't have to pump this thing with a broken hand."

"Your hand isn't broken. A couple of fingers and a few bones are."

Like the fact that it was "a *few*" bones and not *all* of them was supposed to make some kind of difference.

"And your wrist is only sprained, don't whinge, and we've already taken care of pumping. You did just fine when you did it the other—why am I even—? You know...." Brayden took a long breath. "Do I look like I don't know what I'm doing?"

That was the truly irritating part—it would be so much easier to maintain annoyance if Brayden *did* look like he didn't know what he was doing. As it was, it was too obvious he knew exactly what he was doing, and if Wil ever wanted to defend himself from a range longer than whacking distance, all he could do was listen and try to learn.

Wil sighed, checked the safety by feel—he'd slid it over again when he'd slipped his finger over the trigger, damn it—and put it back into firing position.

"All right, I'm sighted, the safety is off, and my grip is as relaxed as I can make it. Can I shoot now?"

Brayden took a step to the side. "As you will."

The reply was so unexpected, Wil had to stop himself from releasing his firing stance in exasperation before he realized he'd been given a *Go ahead* rather than a *No, no, stop, you're doing it wrong, start again.* He had to blink a few times and flex his fingers. Despite himself he checked the safety another three times before determinedly curling his finger around the trigger and slowing his breathing to a low, even in-and-out. The bundle of sticks hung maybe fifty feet away, and he concentrated on the brown of the wood, the tan of the string holding them together, the over-and-under loop of the knot....

It wasn't a bundle of sticks—it was Síofra's smug, smiling face.

And then it was all so... *easy.*

Brayden had been right—there was a healthy recoil to the thing. Had Wil been gripping it tight as he'd done the first few times, his arm would likely right now be several yards behind him. His ears rang dully, the sharp, acrid bite of gunpowder in his nose, and oily smoke in a thin cloud around his head. He blinked, turned first to Brayden, then followed Brayden's surprised gaze to the target.

The sticks were still held together in what used to be the center of the bundle, but now they spiraled crazily on the end of the string, the trajectory lopsided and erratic because Wil's shot had sheared them in half. One end of ragged splinters twirled against the string at a sharp angle, the other end dipping and weaving in a wild orbit of unscathed kindling.

Wil stared, then turned to Brayden, who peered back with a surprised look that might have been somewhat insulting if Wil wasn't so stunned himself.

"I hit it." It was rather stupid and redundant, but... well, he'd *hit* it. He'd actually *hit* it.

"You did." Brayden's faint lurking smile of approval did things to Wil's pride he refused to admit. "All right, what next?"

Wil had to think about it. He'd never expected to get this far. The instructions about what came after still lived in a haze of *It'll never happen, so why bother.*

"Pump the forend," he heard himself say. "Expel the spent shell and reengage the safety."

"Good. Do it."

Wil did, gripping the forend barrel-up in his left hand as Brayden had shown him and giving the rifle a sharp jerk down, then up. Ordinarily, Brayden had been careful to note, one would keep the gun braced to one's shoulder and maintain the firing stance while completing this task, but Wil had tried and hadn't been able to pump the thing with his damaged right hand, so Brayden had shown him an alternative. This way held the risk of too much time between shots, Brayden had told him, and vulnerability of exposure, but it was better than trying to fumble through clumsily recocking the thing and getting shot while you stood there cursing at it.

"Anyway, this way I could shoot from the saddle and still keep hold of the reins," Wil had enthused—back when he was still more bloodthirsty than tired.

"Right" had been Brayden's laconic reply, "and end up on your arse from the recoil or from the horse getting spooked and throwing you. Not all horses are made for the cavalry, y'know. They have to be trained not to bolt at loud noises, which is why we left them back at the campsite."

He seemed to revel in bursting bubbles.

"How d'you know that?" Wil had asked somewhat truculently, refusing to let go of his bubble just yet. "Do you know *everything*?"

"Because I was *in* the cavalry," Brayden had informed him. "And yes, I *do* know everything, or at least more than you do, so *if* you please—show me how you load that cartridge."

Wil had rolled his eyes, sighed out loud like a five-year-old, then did what Brayden instructed. Now Wil completed the task of pumping and expelling one-handed, swaying back to avoid getting hit by the spent cartridge as it spun out from the bolt. He pointed the rifle's barrel at the ground and slid the safety into position, looking up at Brayden with a grin he couldn't have kept from his face if he'd just shot his own foot off.

"Very good." Brayden nodded. "Now, let's back you up a few dozen paces and see if that was just a lucky shot."

Wil gaped. "A *lucky shot?*" He followed Brayden back to a new position, mouth flapping. "It was bloody *beautiful*. What d'you *mean*, 'lucky shot'?"

Brayden merely shrugged. "It may well be that you're a naturally brilliant shot. It may also be that we have just witnessed conditions that will never be repeated. The only way to tell for sure is to repeat them."

Damn the man—there was that annoying reason again.

It wasn't until his second shot that Wil began to appreciate the undeniable *power* in his hands. He'd thought he'd known what to expect the first time, but it had all happened so fast he didn't really remember any individual, distinct impressions. This time *everything* made an impression: the line of focus from the end of the barrel to the target, and how it fuzzed out everything in its periphery; the feel of cool metal against his cheekbone as he sighted down; how the forend made itself a gentle cushion against the bandages on his right hand; the almost tender resistance of the trigger against his finger as he steadily pulled it back....

The awesome *punch* of the recoil as it vibrated from his hands and up his arms, through his shoulder and chest, and on down his backbone to the ground.

He was still standing there in his firing stance, *feeling* it all, when Brayden's big hand clapped to Wil's shoulder, gripped tight, and shook.

"Un-bloody-*believable!*" Brayden laughed and shook Wil again in his enthusiasm. "I have *never* seen anyone shoot dead-on like that, not the first time. You're brilliant!"

Wil felt pretty brilliant. He lowered the gun, cocked it and ejected the cartridge, then slid the safety into place, breathing in the scent of metal oil and spent gunpowder. He hadn't just taken off the other end of the twigs this time—he'd pulverized them and turned it all into a shower of fluttering splinters and smoking twine. He'd never known destruction could be so beautiful.

A grin curled his mouth, and he looked over at Brayden, seeing his own pleasure reflected back at him. Even the heavy hand gripping his shoulder wasn't very heavy.

"I want to shoot something bigger."

It was growing too dark to see when Brayden finally managed to drag Wil away from their makeshift target range and head back to camp. Wil's arms were sore and a little shaky, and his shoulder was probably going to be bruised, but he was still too high for any of it to worm through the euphoric haze. Brayden had been more than accommodating, finding bigger and bigger things to shoot from farther and farther away until he got tired of setting up targets and just had Wil shoot the trunks of trees. Not quite as satisfying—they didn't fly apart the way sticks and piles of leaves or small stones did—but it did help Wil adjust his aim.

"We're blazing a trail miles wide for anyone to follow," Brayden had muttered. "Let's just hope they miss where we turned off, and they might miss us altogether."

Wil absolutely *could not* bring himself to care.

They'd determined that his accuracy began to flag pretty badly after about two hundred paces, but he almost never missed at closer range. Wil had been somewhat surprised that he never got tired of shooting, of watching targets go to pieces at the end of his focus, but each time was a new thrill. He kept expecting his enthusiasm to wane—and Brayden was likely hoping for it—but it never did, not even when Brayden pointed out somberly that watching a man's head explode through your sights was not quite as thrilling.

Wil considered that seriously, then privately concluded it probably depended on exactly whose head it was.

"So, did you learn to shoot in the army?" he asked Brayden as they walked back to camp, the rifle a comfortable weight against his back as it hung from its strap around his shoulder.

"No, my foster father taught me."

"The one who gave you the knife?"

A lift of sandy eyebrows. "I only had the one."

"Did you like him?"

"I like both my foster parents just fine. They still live in Putnam, and I have dinner with them almost every week."

Huh. Interesting. Brayden really did have an actual life. "But you don't live with them?"

"No. Not for a very long time."

"Well, why not?"

"Because when children become adults, they move out on their own. It's just the way it's done."

Wil took this in with interest. "So you don't hate them, then?"

"Of course not. Why would I hate them?" Brayden sounded genuinely mystified by the question.

"Well, you said your foster father gave you that knife, and you just sort of... handed it over to someone you barely know. I thought, if you liked him, you would've wanted to keep it."

"You do have a different way of looking at things."

Wil tried to find condemnation in the tone but couldn't.

Brayden waved a hand. "I gave you the knife because... well, did you look at the inscription?"

Wil considered the casual assumption in the question, thought about dodging it, but... well, dodging was seeming less and less necessary anymore.

"I can't read." The challenge in the tone was more overt than Wil had meant.

Brayden, as he seemed to do with everything, rose to the dare in his own way. "No? You've not taught yourself that too?" It was a sardonic drawl, and he didn't allow Wil time for a retort. "I'll show it to you once we've a fire going. It'll explain better than I can."

They walked in silence for a moment before Wil frowned and asked, "You were an officer in the army, weren't you?"

"I was. Captain."

"For how long?"

"I did two four-year tours."

"Volunteer or conscripted?"

"Volunteer."

Wil hadn't really needed to ask that question—Brayden was definitely the volunteer sort. And Wil would bet he'd volunteered and served out of honor and duty, not the three square meals and respectable pay many others did it for, or even the opportunity to shoot at people with impunity. Wil didn't think Brayden shot at anyone with impunity, even if the censure was only from himself.

"I saw a regiment of the cavalry once." Wil smiled at the memory. "They looked very sharp in their red and gold. I quite envied their boots, and they all had brilliant mounts. They even made those stupid helms look good."

"Hey!" Brayden looked like he was trying to be offended, but he couldn't keep the smile from out his voice. "They might not be the sexiest things in the world, but they serve the very useful purpose of resisting all manner of sharp implements aimed at one's head."

"I just *said* they made them look good." Wil slid his gaze over to Brayden with a sly bit of a smirk. "I'll bet the pretty girls got all swoony over you, kitted out in your officer's surcoat and all, didn't they?" Brayden didn't answer, just rolled his eyes and watched his boots. Wil grinned. "Ha, I knew it—the pretty boys, then."

Brayden shook his head with a low chuckle. "*Now* who's the chatty one?"

"Hey, I answer all *your* questions. And you ask a bloody *lot* of questions."

"Maybe." Brayden sighed. "But you make me walk through fire first."

"Keeps the bugs away."

Brayden chuffed out a small laugh and ran a hand through his hair. "You've a very odd sense of humor."

"I'm a very odd person."

Brayden was quiet for a moment. "You're not, you know." His voice was low and frank but still quite amiable.

Wil frowned. "Not what?"

"You're not odd." Brayden stopped and looked at Wil steadily through the thick-falling darkness. "You could be a maniac who runs about attacking children. You could be a drooling imbecile. You could be a depraved cutthroat who lurks in dark alleys and murders for a billet or two. You could be an infinite number of foul things—you could have lain down and died and let Old Bridge be your grave.

"Instead you're a man who is more than capable of killing but only does it when he has to, and you don't let anyone else's mores tell you when 'have to' is. You take hold of every single thing in your grasp and value it, things I've taken for granted my whole life and never had the first clue were precious. You learn things faster than anyone I've ever seen, and yet you keep thinking you have to defend your intelligence.

"You've invented your own way of being, and perhaps it might be 'odd' to one who has no idea of the life you've led, but to one who does...." Brayden paused, searching, then shrugged. "To one who does, it's... it's.... I haven't got a word. It's *astounding*." He took a step closer, dark eyes strangely alive and perceptive in the murk. "You're not odd. You're just who you are, and I think you've done bloody well, for all you've been through."

Wil stared, eyes narrowed against the dark. What was... what was with the... the.... Well, Wil wasn't sure exactly what it was, but he figured it was at least close to flattery.

"You know," Wil said slowly, "I meant it when I said I didn't intend to murder you in your sleep."

Brayden snorted. Then he laughed. "And that's something else. You trust absolutely no one and wouldn't believe a kind word from the Mother Herself." His laughter dried up, and he cleared his throat. "Sorry, bad example. But you know, you should be... I don't know, you should've been another Síofra. You should've imprinted on him like a kitten imprints on a goat if it's the first thing it sees. But you didn't—you fought him every way you could, and you don't even know how impressive that is."

That was the second time Brayden had said that. *Impressed.* Rising discomfort was very nearly making Wil squirm. What the hell?

"I thought I was a vicious little shit."

"You are." Brayden turned and started walking again. "But you say it like it's a bad thing. C'mon, I hear the horses."

No shelter was necessary tonight, so setting up camp was relatively quick and easy. As it had been last night, Wil took care of the horses—sneaking them each another of his dwindling store of apples and getting those disgusting horse-kisses as thanks—and Brayden took care of supper. Wil kept the rifle with him, unwilling to release his new friend yet until they sat by the small fire to eat, at which point he laid it carefully on the ground in easy reach. Talk, being unnecessary, was fairly scarce until they'd finished eating and cleaning up. Afterward Wil, intrigued by Brayden's earlier hints, slipped the knife from out his boot. It had been a comfortable weight against his calf all day. It was bulkier than the little dirk had been—he was grateful all over again for the thicker stockings—and he had to wear it on the opposite side in consideration of his right hand, but he'd grown used to it almost immediately.

He held it slanted into the chancy glow of the fire, lightly tracing a finger over the string of finely etched symbols engraved in its surface. "So what does it say?"

"That?" Brayden moved in closer. He smiled. "That's just my name. The thing I wanted to show you is on the other side."

Wil turned the knife over, examined the wider swath of glyphs on its opposite side, then turned it again. "That's awfully long for just your short little name."

"Well, it's both my names." Brayden leaned in and pointed at one little group of runes. "Dallin." And then the next. "Brayden."

"Your name is Dallin?" Why had Wil never even considered the fact that Brayden must have a given name? Dallin. It was... nice. Not as harsh-sounding as Wil would've expected, considering Brayden's build. Wil would've guessed Stone or Bear or something equally descriptive. He peered over at Brayden, more interested than he would have thought. "What's it mean?"

"Why d'you want to know?" Brayden's tone was somewhat cagey—not unkind, but just edging on suspicion.

Wil shrugged. "I don't know. I'm just interested. The people of the Commonwealth seem to put a lot of stock in what names mean. I was very glad to learn what Wilfred Calder meant."

"'River of stones.'" Brayden stared into the fire with a frown. "And 'much peace.'"

"Peaceful River." Wil nodded. "It's nice, isn't it? I want to live by one someday. I want to stare into the water all day long and then watch the stars dance over it all night. I want to listen to the music the current sings and nothing else until I get tired and hungry and can't listen anymore."

Brayden was looking at him now, gaze penetrating. "That's a very good wish. And perhaps you'll get it. There's a river runs through Cildtrog, you know. That's the valley below Lind."

Wil hadn't known, though with the amount of time he'd spent spying there, he wondered why. Perhaps it was the very one Wilfred Calder had been named for. He wasn't sure how he felt about that.

"Dallin," Brayden said, "means 'pride's people.' It also means 'from the valley.' Brayden means 'brave.'" He shrugged, pensive. "My father told me that as long as I never forgot my name, I'd always know my way home."

"Well, I expect forgetting your own name isn't much of a danger."

Wil meant it lightly, but it made Brayden's frown deepen.

"You'd think. But She seemed to think I have done."

Wil couldn't help the way his stomach dropped a little. He also couldn't help the curiosity. "What did...?" He chewed his lip. "What did She tell you?"

Brayden turned his gaze slowly from the fire to fix it on Wil. "She said I'd forgotten my name." And then he shook his head, troubled gaze flicking over Wil's shoulder and taking an absent sweep around the camp. "I am Dallin Brayden from the valley of Cildtrog, Lind's Cradle," he told the darkness. "I am the twelfth Brayden, possibly the last of my line, son of Ailen and Aldercy. I know my name, I *haven't* forgotten, I know my way home, and I've no idea—" He frowned. "What?"

Wil's stomach had taken another bit of a dip about halfway through.

He will dragoon you to the Cliabhán, *make of you a sacrifice....*

He shook his head. A harsh little snort burbled in his throat, and he clenched his teeth. Why was he so surprised?

"They call where we're going a cradle?"

"Cildtrog. It means 'cradle' in the First Tongue. Lind sits in the hills above it. Why? What's wrong?"

That weary snort pushed again, and Wil let it come. He rubbed at his face. "One of the prophecies." He was bone-weary all of a sudden. "Maybe it was another lie." He peered up at Brayden, the light of the fire sparking in his dark eyes, bringing back that forest-god effect and making Wil shiver just a little. "I *hope* it was a lie. Because if it wasn't, we're both in the process of making the biggest mistake of our lives." He looked away. "I'm used to betrayal. You're not, and I don't think you could stand it."

Not many things could take this man down, Wil thought, a bit of pity mixed with the chagrin. The bigger a person's heart, he'd come to believe, the deeper the blade of treachery plunged. Brayden, for all his gruff arrogance and bossy "I know better than you do" ways, had a heart that would one day do him in.

Brayden stared at him—just *stared* at him—then leaned in, closed his hand over Wil's, and took the knife from him gently. He turned it over. Firelight hit the long dagger, scattershot over Brayden's fingers as he tilted it, tipping in so close his shoulder was touching Wil's. He slipped his wide finger along the blade, tiny scores in the smooth metal sliding beneath his fingertip in rhythm to his words:

"The Mother's Blessing upon this blade

May you use it never in anger

May it protect you and cleanse your Path of foes

May it remind you always that you are the Mother's Beloved Son"

Wil scowled and leaned away. A low ache was starting to

bloom behind his eyes, and he rubbed at it, annoyed, though he couldn't quite tell why.

"I know you're angry," Brayden said quietly. "I know you feel betrayed, and I won't argue that you shouldn't. I can't begin to guess at the mind of the Divine, and even if I could, I won't pretend there is any reason good enough or important enough to justify what's happened to you."

He held the knife out again to Wil, hilt-first, as Wil had done last night.

"But I saw Her face, I saw Her eyes. She loves you, and She made sure She dragged me from a lifetime of ignorance and borderline belief to do what She, for whatever reason, can't, and I don't intend to displease Her by getting you captured or killed. If you can't believe in Her, believe in *me*. You wanted to know why She didn't help you—I *am* that help. I'm sorry I took so long to get here." Brayden waggled the knife between his fingers, its blade catching shards of fleeting brilliance from the fire that spiked into Wil's eyes and made them burn. "I gave this to you because right now I think you need it more than I do. Maybe you can't read it, but that doesn't mean you can't understand it."

Wil stared at the blade, at the words that had been senseless little scratches on metal five minutes ago but had already seared themselves into his heart with the tangled, ruthless burn of chaotic conflagration. Firelight glanced and shivered over its honed blue-white edge. Wil blinked desperately, refusing to let traitorous tears sabotage his last and best bulwark of safety, refusing to let the jagged lump in his throat choke him.

He stood calmly and slipped the strap of the rifle over his shoulder. "I believe I've the watch tonight," he told Brayden quietly and stepped away.

"Wil."

Soft but urgent. Wil paused but didn't look back.

"Do I look like I don't know what I'm doing?" Brayden asked him gently.

Wil dipped his head, eyes shut tight, both unwilling and unable to say any of the raw, livid things lumping in his throat. So he merely turned and walked away.

It wasn't until he was already pacing his second slow sweep around the perimeter that he realized the damned knife was in his hand.

CHAPTER 2

Dallin didn't jolt this time, didn't wake panting and shaking. He merely opened his eyes, sighed up at the stars, and groaned.

"Fucking *hell*."

Of all the things around which this mess could have centered, it just *had* to be dreams, didn't it? Just his luck. The groan turned into a light growl.

He shook his head, listening to Wil's soft footfalls in the damp undergrowth, walking his watch.

It was funny—two days ago Dallin wouldn't have even considered allowing Wil to leave his sight, let alone stand guard while Dallin slept. Now he wasn't even surprised that Wil hadn't taken the opportunity to skive off. Relieved, yes, but not really surprised. It wasn't trust, at least not the sort of trust with which Dallin was familiar. It was... something else. Mutual need, perhaps. After all, there were no illusions that Wil would stick with him if Dallin proved to be other than an asset in keeping them both alive. Wil wasn't here for Dallin's dazzling personality.

The horses gave a few sleepy nickers, hoofs shifting quietly.

Dallin smirked when he heard Wil stop to speak a few soft words to them, then gruff a grumbling curse when one of them blew on him. Wil's affection for them was grudging but real and growing. And Dallin hadn't missed the fact that most of Wil's precious apples were serving as treats for them every night. For someone who'd looked like he was willing to fight to the death to take the damned apples along with him in the first place, and who professed to disliking horses in general in the second, the nightly surreptitious gift-giving was awfully damned funny. And now Wil had more or less forbidden Dallin from hobbling them, wanting to know how Dallin would feel if someone tied *his* feet together, and insisted on long pickets instead. Since they were out of thicker forest and there was no danger of one of them wrapping herself around a tree, Dallin hadn't argued.

He grinned and scratched the bristly growth on his chin.

"Why don't you shave that off?" Wil's voice was soft and low in the dark, a mild note of amusement.

Dallin stretched with a long groan. "What, it doesn't make me look rugged and fierce?"

"It makes you look like you've got fleas, because you can't stop scratching at it."

Probably true. Dallin hadn't grown a beard since he was in his teens and trying to prove he could, and he'd remembered days ago why he'd shaved it off immediately thereafter.

"I thought perhaps it might be useful once we got out of those places where we wanted to be recognized."

"A disguise?" Wil snorted. "P'raps if you shaved off a foot each of breadth and height. Otherwise you stand out more than I do, beard or no."

"Well...." Dallin scratched again—he couldn't help it. "True, I suppose, but it at least makes me feel like I'm doing something to disguise myself. How's that?" He turned back again. "You don't shave at all, do you?"

He'd been wondering about that for days. Every time he thought to ask about it, there was always something more pressing going on.

Wil didn't answer, only struck his gaze out into the darkness and gave it a wide sweep. "What're you doing up? It's hours yet 'til sunrise."

Dallin sighed. Back to the nonanswers again.

He rubbed at a crick in his neck. "Dreams."

"Hm." Wil walked slowly over to stand in front of him, rifle held across his torso like he'd been born to the stance. Dallin could just make out the lift of a dark eyebrow in the glow of the dying embers, the hint of a smirk. "Looking for some sympathy, Constable?"

"From you?" Dallin looked away. "I wouldn't presume."

He couldn't imagine the sorts of dreams Wil had to live through every night and then forget every morning just to maintain his unique sanity. Let alone what had gone on before. Expecting sympathy from him wouldn't just be thoughtless; it would be obscene.

Although Dallin was going to have to tell Wil about his own dreams soon, explain what he'd seen and put forth his theory. If Dallin had really been watching the last moments of someone else's life, and not merely hallucinating and letting his mind run wild, Wil should know he hadn't been abandoned all these years as he obviously thought—in fact, he had a right to know. Except how did one tell someone his own enraged denial and belief that he'd been betrayed was in fact what had perpetuated that betrayal? How did Dallin explain that the lack of trust and hope, which had been beaten out of Wil, seemed to be exactly what had prevented help from finding him?

Dallin decided, for now, that he didn't. At least not in the middle of the night when that man was standing over him with a loaded gun.

...Or when he was almost comfortable in Dallin's presence for a change and making stupid jokes at his expense. Almost smiling.

"All's quiet, then?"

Wil merely nodded. "Look what I found." He crouched down, settling the rifle across his knees and tilting his hand into the dim, wavering light.

Dallin squinted, then reached out and plucked a textured, triangular stone from Wil's palm. "Arrowhead?"

"Chert." Wil's mouth had a slight curl upward at one corner. "From when the clans were still wandering folk." He wasn't smiling yet, but his voice was, and his face in the soft gold of the failing fire was full of interest and discovery. "See those marks there on either side?"

Dallin nodded.

"Pressure flaking, which means it's *old* old, ancient old—like the-first-people-who-used-stone-tools old."

Dallin lifted his eyebrows. All thoughts of allowing violent dreams and gloomy conjecture to spoil the pleasant moment were decisively throttled and pushed away.

He held the little projectile back out between his fingers. "How do you know all that?"

Wil shrugged and took the relic back, frowning. "Dunno. Sometimes I just know things. Most of it's pretty useless, generally, but...." The tip of his finger ran lightly over the edge. "People aren't the only ones who dream. The stones and soil have longer memories and sleep more deeply."

Dallin opened his mouth... closed it. Decided he had nothing intelligent to say and so kept his lips buttoned tight. There were only so many fantastic anecdotes he could take in at a time, and he'd reached his limit days ago. And he didn't even want to *think* about what it might be like to not only have the charge of tending the dreams of all the people in the world, but also the world itself—rock and stone, leaf and soil. Once again, watching Wil quietly communing with something Dallin himself would likely have passed over as just another stone amidst the debris of nature, Dallin adjusted his definitions of sanity and... wisdom, perhaps?

Of all the lessons Wil had taught himself, Dallin mused, peering soberly at Wil's surprisingly gentle expression in the flickering light, that was probably the most valuable—snapping up every single thing in his reach without shame or hesitation.

Dallin grinned. "You're like a crow picking at shiny bits."

Wil flicked a doubtful look at him.

"In a very *good* way," Dallin assured him. "*I* never would've seen it. How did you find it? In the dark, no less."

Wil thought about it for a moment before he leaned in and dropped his voice to a grave whisper. "The voices in my head told me where to look."

Dallin snapped a startled look up. *Voices?* As if everything else wasn't bad enough, now there were bloody *voices?* How much more—?

Except bloody Wil was bloody *laughing.* "Fucking hell, your *face!*"

Dallin could've punched him right in the mouth. "Oh, *funny.*" Except it sort of was, and ridiculously relieved, Dallin couldn't keep the grudging half grin off his face. "That sense of humor of yours is either going to do me in or get you throttled. I'm knee-deep in the surreal, and you're cracking wise." He shook his head, trying not to laugh. "Seriously, how'd you find it?"

Wil shrugged, flipped the stone in his palm, and pocketed it. "Dunno. Just did." He stood. "Brother Millard called me a crow too." A peculiar little smile was working at the corners of his mouth. He looked back at Dallin, curious. "What's a chimera?"

Dallin winced. It had been nearly cheerful between them for a moment there. "Well...." He considered dodging the question— sometimes lies really were kinder than truths—but decided prevaricating would be disrespectful at best, tentative trust-breaking at worst. "It's a dream." He made his voice even, straightforward. "Usually an unattainable dream."

"Huh." Wil thought about it for a moment. "Sometimes I wonder...." He trailed off, frowning off into the darkness. "Have you noticed that Aisling means 'dream' and not 'dreamer'?" His voice was soft, somewhat flat, the humor of a moment ago gone completely. He looked back at Dallin. "Isn't that strange?"

"A little. But translations get bollixed all the time." Dallin stood, groaning as the bones in his spine cracked and realigned themselves. He turned to Wil. "Everyone thinks about that now and again. You're as real as I am. Don't borrow trouble."

Wil cocked his head. "And what makes you so sure *you're* real?"

It wasn't one of his odd little jokes, and he wasn't being difficult—the question was genuine. And far too big for Dallin to address before coffee.

"Sometimes you make my brain hurt," he told Wil tiredly. He stepped away from the bedroll, waved a hand toward it, then went to wake the fire. "I won't be getting back to sleep. You might as well have it for a few hours."

"Oh." Wil shook his head. "I didn't mean to disturb—"

"You didn't. I told you—dreams. I'd just as soon not chance any more tonight. They're not terribly pleasant." Dallin threw some kindling on the smoldering bones of the fire and jerked his chin at the bedroll. "Honestly. One of us should be alert in the morning."

Wil peered at him thoughtfully for a moment, considering, then nodded, looked down at the rifle, and reluctantly held it out. "You, um... want this back?"

Dallin held back the snort, but not the twitch of a smirk. "I wouldn't dream of coming between the two of you." He shifted some bits of timber onto the coals and went to hunt through his pack for the coffee.

If he kept giving his weapons away, *he* might end up being the one who needed protection.

Dawn found Dallin poring over his map—a wide roll of leather, browning and curling at the edges—when Wil snorted awake and blinked over at him with a wide, lazy yawn. "This," he slurred contentedly, "is a very comfortable bedroll."

Dallin didn't look up, but he smiled as he took a slurp of his coffee. "Well, you'll have to drag yourself out of it soon. I want to get started as soon as we can." He tilted a curious look at Wil. "D'you know that your fingers are always moving when you sleep?"

Wil paused in midstretch to frown up at the sky for a moment. He grimaced. "Yeah, so? You snore." He lifted his hands, squinting at them, fingers of the left hand flexing and wavering in front of his nose. "Why the rush? Something wrong?"

"No, no." Dallin turned his gaze to the map. "It's time we started being proper fugitives and trying to hide our trail a bit better. Besides a change of course, that'll mean no more target practice or evening fires. Sorry."

Wil sat up and rolled his shoulders, tipping his head from side to side, the bones in his neck cracking so loud it made Dallin wince. "I'm already a brilliant shot." Wil smirked. "I don't need to practice." He grinned as he stood and stepped several feet away and behind a tree. "So which way are we heading, then?"

"If I haven't got us completely lost"—Dallin traced a finger over the worn lines of the map—"Chester is only a week's ride northeast from here, and not much in between, so we can avoid being seen if we're careful. We can stop there, sell the horses, and replenish our supplies—we need more ammunition, and our water's getting low, so no more unnecessary washing either, I'm afraid. After that we strike northwest and follow the Flównysse all the way to Lind. If the weather holds and we don't run into any trouble or delays, we should come upon Cildtrog's Bounds in... say, ten days, maybe twelve."

He looked up with a lift of eyebrows. Wil was just emerging from around the tree, buttoning his trousers and frowning at the ground.

"Sell the horses?"

Trying to pretend his tone was just curious and not slightly mournful.

Dallin's problem, he decided, was that he didn't spend enough time around people who weren't looking at him from behind bars. If he did, he might stop to consider more how his words affected others. He winced, sincere apology in the shrug he angled at Wil. He'd been thinking only hours ago that Wil was starting to get attached to the horses. Dallin shouldn't have just blurted it like that. Still, it had to be done.

"We wanted to be followed when we started out. And the horses gave us a good head start through the rougher country, but our pursuers will likely be riding harder than we've done. I won't be at all surprised if they can track us through here and all the way to Chester, but once we leave there, we can't risk it. It's a lot easier to follow hoofprints than footprints—especially if they're trying to track us from horseback. Unless they've dogs, we should be able to stay invisible even if they're within a few miles of us." Dallin held out a hand, palm up. "Sorry. It's for the best."

"They're yours. You bought 'em." Wil shrugged with a bit of a scowl. "Don't care, really. Just a little surprised, is all."

Dallin wasn't the least bit fooled, but he let it go. Let go of everything, in fact, that didn't have something to do with the next thirty minutes. He stood, rolled up the map, and headed over toward the packs.

"Porridge for breakfast. Might as well take advantage of our last fire. Start getting your kit together. Breakfast will be ready in about a half hour, and then we'll strike camp."

Wil only offered a sullen "Mm," glowering a bit as he slouched away.

He didn't speak to Dallin for nearly the whole day, giving noncommittal grunts now and again at casual comments and one-word answers to actual questions. It didn't feel like anger. Withdrawal, perhaps. He'd even stopped the habitual patting of his horse's neck, concentrating instead on the sky, the trees, the landscape, but not with that continual interest Dallin had seen the first day's ride north. If Dallin had been feeling unkind, he might have even called it sulking.

Dallin gave him the day. There had been surrenders to sentiment too many times already on this journey—if it weren't for sentiment, Dallin would be on his way back to Putnam with a prisoner in shackles and not on the run with the Dominion's Chosen—and the matter of the horses was just more of the same. The matter of the horses, in fact, was damned important, and Dallin wouldn't even think of selling them if it weren't. Just because the maudlin broodiness was making him twitchy didn't mean he was wrong, damn it.

He held out until it was time to start scouting for a suitable campsite. The silence had been sort of nice, but he'd got used to the occasional ingenuous questions and smartarse commentary, and the absence of it just kept reminding him that he was taking away something from a man who had next to nothing. It didn't matter that Dallin had bought the horses and he could do with them as he pleased; it didn't matter that they'd been nothing to him on this trip but tools to get them from Point A to Point B—he hadn't even bothered to check their papers to see if they'd had names when he bought them—and another two mouths to feed. What mattered was that he'd more or less handed something to Wil, forced it on him, in fact, and now he was taking it back. And causing the retreat of what he'd been amazed to realize was an intriguing personality right back inside a shell of guarded remove.

So Dallin decided nearly ten hours was quite enough. "So, Wil, tell me," he said as they rounded the feet of a range of lofty hills strung like mossy ribs sprouting from a fallen giant's back-bone, "where've you been?" Wil slanted Dallin a suspicious side-ways glance. "I mean," Dallin clarified, "what places have you been to since you've been... um...." How to put this tactfully? "... since you've been out on your own?"

"Lots of places."

"So I assumed. You've been wandering about for, from what you've said, three years or more, and I don't imagine you've been holed up in a cave all this time." Dallin kept his tone light and conversational. "It's almost a straight line southeast from Old Bridge to Putnam. Did you just sort of"—he waved a hand about —"pick a direction and keep going?"

"I didn't...." Wil's eyebrows twisted. "Straight...?"

Wil stared, surprise sliding into that maddening apprehensive antipathy Dallin hadn't missed in the least. What the hell was wrong with him *now*, damn it?

"No." It was grudging, and Wil's posture was closing in on itself again. "I started out...." An uncomfortable shrug and an annoyed huff. "Do you really need to know?"

Dallin blinked at the obvious resentment. The exchange had been fairly innocuous, even by what Dallin was coming to know as Wil's perpetually suspicious standards.

"Is there a reason you don't want to tell me?"

"You mean other than the fact that it's none of your damned business?"

Dallin's own suspicions piqued, despite the good intentions he'd had just a moment ago. His eyes narrowed. "Did you cut a swath of crime from the border on down?"

Wil rolled his eyes. "Maybe I just don't want to talk about it for some of the same reasons you don't want to talk about your time in the army."

That one made Dallin sit back in his saddle. "What the hell does that—?"

"You did things you can't talk about because they'd seem wrong to anyone who wasn't there, right? You've tried once or twice, but the looks on the faces of others made you understand that people would just as soon you kept it all where they couldn't see it. You did things you're maybe not proud of, things you try not to look at now because they make you wonder what kind of person could be capable of them, and then you remember *oh, right, that was me*, and then you understand those looks on the faces of others. But you can't feel the same way they do because you know it was necessary, no matter how low it makes you feel to have done them." Wil pulled rein and turned to glare as Dallin did the same. "I'm not astounding, and there's no reason for you to be impressed —I did what I had to do, and I won't apologize for surviving."

Dallin stared for a long time, meeting the throttled fury in the green eyes with calm consideration. This had nothing whatever to do with any speculations about Dallin's own proposed encounters. This was entirely abject bitterness accumulated before Dallin's existence had even come within Wil's purview of experience. Just how long, Dallin wondered dubiously, did it take for someone whose entire life had consisted of pain and thwarted rage to stop being enraged? Was it possible? Could someone who'd been taught over and over again that every word hid some sort of betrayal ever learn to trust? Should they?

More to the point, did Dallin have the patience to deal with it while he figured it out?

He propped a hand on the saddlebow and leaned into it. "I'm getting a little tired," he said slowly, "of feeling compelled to defend myself over things I haven't done. I wasn't trying to interrogate you. I was trying to get your mind off the horses. I was trying to get to know you—as a person and not as the Guild's tool or the Brethren's prey, since those histories are the only ones you've thus far seen fit to give me. Very grudgingly, I might add, and not without fighting me bitterly tooth and nail first. Quite literally."

Wil opened his mouth, but Dallin held up a hand.

"But since you've brought it up, I wouldn't be half as impressed with you if you *did* apologize for surviving." Dallin paused to let that one sink in. "I don't say things I don't mean, and it's very rare indeed that I misjudge someone badly enough that my considered assessment of them comes back to bite me on the arse. In fact, it's never happened, so if I'm impressed with you, it means you've done things to impress me. Live with it.

"Now, I have been nothing but straight with you and *thought* we'd progressed to a point where you felt more comfortable being straight with me. If we haven't, you should tell me now so I'll know not to bother you again with the respect of asking you questions straight out, instead of hammering answers out of you like I could be doing."

Wil was trying to glare but couldn't seem to find the anger necessary. He looked down at his hands, fingers working over the worn leather of the reins.

"Do you not want to tell me because it's private?" Dallin made his tone less harsh than a moment ago. "Or do you just not know?"

He watched closely as Wil struggled to decide what he wanted to say, too obviously choosing and discarding words before finally electing to speak.

"It would appear that I... that I more or less walked a straight line down the country from Old Bridge to Putnam, with several zigs and zags along the way." Wil shrugged, turning away to scan the hills. "I didn't know it until you said it, and I didn't do it on purpose. It just happened that way."

Dallin waited for more, but Wil just kept casting his glance around the terrain, shifting now and then in the saddle and looking everywhere but at Dallin. Something was there, more than discomfiture, something that bothered Wil—either about the journey itself or things that had happened along it—but whatever it was, he'd rather eat fire than tell Dallin about it.

Dallin held back a sigh. "C'mon, we're losing light. Why don't we give the horses a run while we've clear—?"

"I went where my feet took me." Wil's voice was low, with a peculiar note of challenge beneath it. "Most of the time, I had no idea where I was heading, nor did I usually know the name of the town or village I was in. And neither did I care. Putnam was the only place I ever went to intentionally." He slid his gaze sideways, that same rebellion Dallin had seen for the first time in the cellars of the constabulary settling in his eyes, the clench of his jaw. "Does that seem strange to you?"

Whatever he was getting at, or expecting Dallin to grasp from the cryptic information, it wasn't clicking. *Does that seem strange to you?* Yes. Yes, it did. Almost every damned thing the man said when he was in this sort of mood was strange, and for someone who took what others said annoyingly literally, he could be *the* most obscure pain in the arse when he wanted to be. With more effort than should probably have been necessary, Dallin kept his breathing normal and his mien bland. It had been bloody *small talk*, for pity's sake.

"The horses need a run." Dallin nudged his heels into the chestnut's barrel. "Come on, it's getting dark."

Camp was quiet and routine. Dallin snatched at restless sleep, as it seemed restful sleep was a thing of the past, then took second watch again. They camped atop a butte looking down over a valley that, according to the map and if Dallin had his bearings right, was known as Green Basin. Dallin rolled his eyes—whatever the Ancients might have had going for them, creativity in the naming of their environs wasn't one of them.

He'd chosen the spot mostly because it afforded him an almost complete view of the surrounding landscape, but for a small stretch to the north where a swath of conifers still occluded the line of sight. Since anyone following would likely be coming from the south or east, Dallin didn't spare it much worry. Their perch gave him a clear view of the thin distant ribbon of road that would eventually lead into Chester. Vague blurry figures resolved into the shapes of stray riders in ones and twos, interspersed with the occasional lone wagon tramping at travelers' paces, from what Dallin could make out.

Once the sun fell and night closed around them, he spent several hours scanning the surrounding area—looking for the telltale spark of a campfire, listening for the neigh of a horse, the shout of a man, the report of a gun. He saw and heard nothing but the quiet sounds of the sleeping countryside. Satisfied for the moment, Dallin dubiously climbed into his bedroll, leaving instructions with Wil to wake him in three hours. It was unnecessary, of course —Dallin woke well before, just barely managing to keep the swearing behind his teeth.

Damn it, he hated dreams. Especially recurring ones that made *no sense at all* and were starting to make him feel like his own memories were betraying him, because the dream about his time in the army had nothing to do with reality even a little bit. The other, the one Dallin was coming to think of as the Watcher Dream, had come again after, just as vivid and violent as it had been the night before. And, as it had been the night before, it left him just as angry and shaken.

So after he'd grumbled awake, relieved Wil from watch, and made sure he was safely asleep, Dallin dug out the book Manning had loaned him back in Putnam and waited for a faint tint of dawn so he could make out the words. He hadn't read much past the Aisling legend, but he remembered a mention of the old gods and their fates in there somewhere, and since they seemed to be the point of the damned dreams, he likely wasn't going to be able to set them aside until he figured out why. Even if the dreams were just nonsensical rubbish—which dreams generally were and precisely why Dallin hadn't missed his—perhaps forcing some reason into their crevices would at least take away some of their power. And let him get some bloody *sleep*.

The book didn't have much more than a few passing references. Apparently the old gods were still about but spellbound and trapped inside evergreens somewhere. Which was likely some kind of metaphor for something a lot less poetic, and really not helpful.

Luckily—not only for Dallin's mood, but he suspected for his sanity—Wil was more pleasant when he woke. Wil seemed, in fact, to have made up his mind to forget his pique from yesterday. He was back to his semi-amiable self, though perhaps somewhat subdued. Dallin occupied himself with drawing Wil out further to get both their minds off darker matters, finally succeeding when Dallin happened to mention the Kymberly and Sunny Ramsford in passing.

Wil perked right up. "You know the Ramsfords?"

Dallin had been flailing a little up 'til then, so he latched on to the common thread. "I do, and very well," he answered as he repacked his kit. "For years, in fact. I stood second at their wedding."

"*Get* on."

"Ramsford had some very nice things to say about you, y'know."

"About me?" Wil blinked with a bemused lift of black eyebrows.

Dallin slanted a look up from his crouch near the saddles. "He's the one asked for me on the case. Told my chief he was worried about you and wanted me to see no harm came to you."

Wil's mouth worked. Dallin waited for the sarcastic retorts about what had come of that first night, wondering if he should bring up Wil's own dodging and running in his own defense if he found himself accused. Again. Instead Wil whiffed a small, startled laugh.

"That was very kind of him."

Dallin nodded. "It was. But not surprising. He's a very kind man."

"Mm," Wil agreed readily enough. "And Mistress Sunny too." Dallin nearly laughed out loud when Wil's expression went nearly dreamy. "And she's the most amazing cook. Have you ever had her venison sausage?"

"Ha. It's my recipe. She *stole* it."

Wil's mouth dropped open. *"Really?* You know how to make that?"

Ah-*ha*. Apparently all one had to do to win Wil's regard was feed him.

Dallin flipped his pack closed and cinched the fastenings. "No," he replied with a smirk. "But you should see your face."

The sour look Dallin received in return was priceless.

They spent another day plodding through admittedly beautiful countryside dotted here and there with the rare lone cottage or farmstead, wending slowly back to the road and the almost comfortable rapport they'd achieved in the days previous, making today much more pleasant than yesterday had been. Wil's smirky smile came back, and so did the questions and the sardonic comments on Dallin's answers. Dallin was not the least bit embarrassed or chagrined to admit to himself that he'd missed them.

They made better time than Dallin had anticipated, reaching Chester late in the morning of the fifth day. They'd been passing travelers both coming and going much more frequently this morning, startling the knickers off an old man and his wife traveling by ox cart as they'd led their horses out of a thicket and onto the road right behind them. Dallin had waved a friendly greeting, conscious of his no doubt startling appearance and fully prepared for the couple to either cower and ignore them or pull a weapon on them. They did neither. After the initial distressed alarm, they both slanted annoyed glances over their shoulders, tipped grudging waves, and ambled on.

"Rugged and fierce, eh?" Wil drawled.

Dallin shot him an acerbic smirk as he mounted up. "It's you and your waifish charm. It's counteracting my carefully cultivated air of danger." More likely the fact that they were only a few days out of Lind and people his size weren't as uncommon here as they were farther south, but he saw no need to let Wil in on the logic. "Given another thirty seconds, she'd've been cooing all over you, trying to feed you up on her 'famous pork pies' or some other such specialty."

"*Waifish*" was all Wil snorted as he swung up into the saddle and fell in after Dallin, but the "fuck off" beneath it was heavily implied.

They both made it a point to smile brightly and tip their heads politely as they passed the couple again.

The sun was bright but the day cold, a harsh wind cutting right through their coats and whining in their ears. Chester stretched over the wide, flat summit of a broad knoll, sloping slow and gradual up from the belly of the open valley of Green Basin.

Dallin stopped them just as they started up the incline that led to the gates, dug his hat out of the saddlebags, and handed Wil's to him. Dallin himself likely wouldn't stand out here as much as he did in Putnam, but Wil's dark hair would. "Keep it pulled down, if you can," Dallin told him. "Try not to let anyone get a look at your eyes."

Wil merely nodded, pulled the hat low over his brow, and slanted Dallin a grim, edgy tic of a smile. "Head down, eyes to the ground." He blew a breath between his teeth and set his shoulders.

The gates of the small city were open. The days of battles and skirmishes in this part of the country were over ten years past, and life—as was its wont—picked up as though the strife had never been. A fortress once, the walls were thick stone, cut from the cliffs Dallin knew dressed the steplike formations where the Flównysse carved its way through the countryside. Still strong and kept, but Dallin couldn't help but curl his lip at the fact that the watchtowers were all unmanned. With unrest at the border simmering once again, strongholds like this one were all the more important, and he didn't like that his countrymen had got so lax lately—not when it had only been a little more than a decade since he himself had been defending that border. Guards stood posts at the entrance, but they seemed mostly for show. Dallin didn't see them stop a single soul, either going in or coming out.

"Looks like market day." Wil mumbled it as they dismounted and he craned his neck to have a look 'round the guard. He was already hunching in on himself, the cheek he'd employed on the road earlier all but a memory as his face closed up and his eyes hardened, narrowing warily.

It made Dallin understand fully just how much Wil had opened up on their journey. Even the discomfort of a few days ago didn't compare to this near complete reversal. There was no evidence whatsoever that Wil had ever smiled at all, let alone laughed just this morning and groused good-naturedly about how the dried apples they'd had for breakfast on the road stuck in his teeth. Now he was the slit-eyed creature made of strung nerves who'd pulped an enemy's head; he was the hard-faced man who'd tried to throw himself through iron bars to get at a prisoner. His eyes darted warily, constantly assessing risk and dismissing every-thing else. The earnest young man who'd shown Dallin a prized find in the woods, holding out his hand and offering ingenuous discovery, was gone entirely, tucked away in the amount of time it took him to slide from his saddle.

"Just stick close." Dallin leaned in so he could speak quietly as they led the horses to the gates, dismayed though not really surprised when Wil's instinctive flinching reasserted itself. "We're fine. No one's followed us so far, and there should be no reason anyone would guess we'd come here. We're as safe as we can be."

Wil only shrugged noncommittally, and his gaze never stopped shifting, weighing, calculating. For all that he might as well have been on holiday when they'd been trekking in the wilderness, now Dallin thought Wil might spot trouble even before he did.

"You'll have to check your weapons here."

The gate guard was gruff, bellying up to Wil with a superior look Dallin recognized all too well. He'd seen it often enough on the faces of Elmar and Payton back in Putnam. Men of minimal rank and command, lording it over those who didn't know better because they were the only ones who could be bullied.

Terrific. Just brilliant.

"There's a no-arms edict in Chester on market day. You check 'em here and pick 'em back up on yer way out." The guard reached out toward Wil. "Unshoulder that cannon there, boy, din't ye hear—"

It was only by virtue of reflexes that Dallin managed to get between the guard and Wil as Wil's shoulder dropped, strap sliding down to his crooked elbow, the rifle coming around and across his torso in one smooth sweep. Dallin caught it before Wil could swing it up to firing stance and angled himself in before the guard could lay a hand to Wil's arm and get it bitten off for his trouble.

"He's with me." Dallin made his tone calm and commanding, surreptitiously keeping hold of Wil's arm down low and slightly behind him, feeling the tension and vibrating stress running beneath his fingers. Dallin was a little surprised Wil didn't wrench out of his grip and shoot them both, but Wil stayed still and silent, though Dallin would swear he could hear a low growl rumbling. Dallin's horse stretched her neck, dipping her great nose over and burying it in the crook of Wil's shoulder. Dallin had to choke back a snort as Wil twitched and cursed at her under his breath.

"I assume dispensation is granted to visiting officers?" Dallin said pointedly to the guard.

"And who're *you*?"

Dallin dug out his badge and papers, keeping his hand clamped to Wil's arm. He'd rather not have to show identification —he'd hoped they could slide in and out of Chester without leaving much of a trace, and here they were, stopped at the gates, every passerby goggling and whispering as they sidled along—but there was absolutely no way Dallin was going to allow himself to be disarmed, and he judged flashing his badge to be the lesser risk.

"From Putnam?" The guard squinted suspiciously at the raised lettering around the sword and leaf pattern that was Putnam's seal. "Ye en't from Lind?"

The question shouldn't have surprised Dallin, but it did. "Used to be."

The guard tilted a skeptical stare at first Dallin, then Wil. "What's yer business in Chester?"

"Our business is not yours." Dallin pushed all his years of command into his tone. "But we would be happy to discuss it with your superior, if you feel it necessary. Of course, then we might find it equally necessary to explain how, at least in Putnam, we don't growl at visiting colleagues and attempt to manhandle them at the gates."

In truth, Putnam had no gates, and all visiting officers were required to check in at the constabulary and explain their business upon arrival within the city's limits, but this man didn't need to know that.

The guard glared but backed down a touch. He eyed Wil up and down, gaze going half-lidded with a knowing little smirk, but he addressed his next question to Dallin. "Yer little, uh... *lad* got a badge?"

Dallin's jaw clenched. He'd used the wrong approach—he'd been looking for instant respect when he'd pushed authority into his demand, but what he'd got was instant jealousy and hatred. And since Dallin was too big to bully and had a badge that outranked the guard's, the man chose Wil as his default. The inflection of the word *lad* made the insult to Wil all too clear, and the sudden deliberate interest blooming in the flat stupid eyes made it clearer. Dallin didn't know if he was indignant on Wil's behalf or his own.

"As I *said*," Dallin made his tone low and dangerous, "he's with me."

"Who he's *with* makes no nevermind."

The guard was still eyeing Wil in a way that was beginning to make Dallin's skin crawl. Wil saw it too, tensing even more.

"It's what he's *got* that matters." The guard waggled his eyebrows. "Don't know what sorts of arrangements they have out Putnam way, but here you'll have to—"

"You finish that sentence," Dallin said between his teeth, "and it'll be the last your tongue sees of your filthy mouth. For the Mother's sake, man, you're *on duty*!"

The guard's lip twitched, but the hateful smile remained. "If he en't got a badge, he can't carry a gun."

He slid another slow glance over Wil, very clearly and purposefully lewd, then slanted it up to Dallin, challenging. Bluffing. Baiting. Ugh, he looked just like Elmar with his square, stupid face and smug air. Poking and provoking just because he could.

"Either he hands it over," the guard went on with his pompous little smirk, "or he's with *me*, and you can pick *him* up on yer way out."

Dallin made himself breathe evenly, made himself think it

through. Knowing it was all a bluff wasn't helping. He didn't like being provoked. The thought of giving in to this grandiose boor was repugnant, but the only two alternatives were to turn around and leave or demand to see the man's superior. And Dallin didn't want to do either. He supposed there was always the alternative of beating the shit out of the foul troll. Or letting Wil shoot him. But either of those would likely call attention to them they really didn't want.

Dallin ground his teeth as he turned to Wil. "You'll have to give it up."

Wil tilted his head, peering at Dallin from the corner of his eye as he gave the horse a light swat and shrugged her away. "I know. I just didn't want him touching me. And I... he's...." Wil clenched his jaw with a huff. "I don't want his grubby paws touching *it*, either."

Dallin thought about that too. Carefully. Then he smirked.

"As you wish." He held out his hand. "Give it to me, then."

Wil gave Dallin a curious frown, then slid the strap from his elbow, checked the safety on the rifle, and with one last glare for the guard, handed it over to Dallin. Dallin slipped the gun's strap over his own shoulder, and turned back to the guard.

"There. No badge, no gun. We'll be going now. Unless you'd care to go fetch your superior for that little chat?"

The guard gawped, but Dallin nearly let a malicious little grin curl at his mouth when he heard Wil give a very quiet but very satisfied *"Ha"* behind him. The glare the guard gave them was sincere, but the flourishing gesture as he handed back the badge and papers and finally let them pass was grudging and thwarted. Dallin could feel the guard's dead-eyed glower between his shoulder blades well after they cleared the gate and entered the city center. Still seething, Dallin searched for and found a provisional livery with a post to tether the horses, waited impatiently for a call chit, then flipped a gilder to the lad who tendered it with the promise of more if their saddlebags and Dallin's crossbow were unmolested when he came back to claim them. Tucking the receipt into his breast pocket, Dallin pulled Wil over and around a leather worker's stall.

"Sorry about the gate. Took me a bit off guard. And we need to get something very clear." Dallin held the rifle up. "You can't just go about shooting people when they piss you off."

Wil dragged his arm from Dallin's grip and looked down with a bit of a sulk. "I wouldn't've shot him."

It would be very unwise of Dallin to snort right now. "You can't point it at him either, or wave it about, or even make threatening gestures or look at him cross-eyed. I know he's a great knob, but he's got a badge and isn't afraid to use it. You fuck with someone like that and he'll have you in irons just because he can, and I'll have a bugger of a time getting you back. Now, I'm hanging on to this—" Dallin held up the gun again. "—just until we leave Chester. You can have it back again once we're outside the gates, all right? But they've apparently got an actual law against weapons on market day, which makes sense when you think about, and if you get nabbed with it, we'll end up getting more acquainted with the local law than we want to be. And keep the damned knife in your boot. We're lucky they didn't search you at the gate." Dallin slipped the rifle's strap over his shoulder. "Now. I smell roasting meat coming from somewhere—would a hot lunch lift your spirits any?"

Wil looked down, still sullen and scuffing his boot in the dirt like a five-year-old. "Some." The scowl lost some of its fierceness. "A hot lunch and a beer would do better."

And there it was—feed Wil and he'd forgive you just about anything.

Dallin rolled his eyes. "Come on, then."

They were at a gunsmith's stall—Wil ogling the small array of handguns, running careful fingers over each burled grip while Dallin haggled with the owner over the cost of shells—when Wil quietly and casually sauntered up behind Dallin, grabbed his sleeve, and dragged him down. He leaned in.

"Shouldn't've pissed off that guard." It was a low murmur next to Dallin's ear. Wil shot a surreptitious glance at the stall owner and then leaned around Dallin. Dallin thought at first Wil was perusing the knives set out on a black velvet cloth on the table to the side, but Wil's eyes darted a quick sweep to all points beneath the brim of his hat before he picked up a knife and held it up as though he was showing it to Dallin. "There's two of them over by the fountain." Wil turned the knife around in his hand and caught the light with it. "Your friend from the gate and three others are standing across the street, pretending to but not actually buying pasties from a very angry-looking cart owner."

Shit. Shitshit*shit*. Seriously. Could Dallin have *possibly* bungled their supposedly unnoticed entry into Chester more badly? He clenched his teeth, barely resisting the near overwhelming urge to follow Wil's glance.

Instead, Dallin nodded at the knife. "You like that one?" He made it louder than he needed to, but the gunsmith was eyeing them with a touch of suspicion now. Dallin leaned down to Wil, even slipped a serene smile to his face—just a silly, smitten man having a private moment with his companion, perhaps deciding whether or not to treat him to a new blade. "Good eye," he said calmly. "Well done, you." He turned back to the stall's owner. "We'll take that and this." He pointed to the knife in Wil's hand and gathered the ammunition over which he'd been arguing just a moment ago.

Wil grinned, leaning against Dallin and giving the owner a smile that was somehow shy and sly all at once. "Is there perhaps a back way out of here?" He nudged Dallin, sliding his glance down to where Dallin's purse hung from his belt. "A nice, quiet... oh, alley, maybe, where a man could say proper thanks?"

The gunsmith pursed his lips and rolled his eyes, but when Dallin drew four gilders more than necessary from his purse, laying it all out on the counter next the purchases, the gunsmith sighed with a grimace. "Through the curtain past the longbows." It was offered grudgingly, though he swept up the coins in his nimble fingers without hesitation.

"Have you got a sack for all this?" Dallin waited for the man to turn before he leaned down again to Wil to murmur, "You first. Calm and slow, as you've been doing, then wait for me."

Wil didn't even nod, just patted at the small of Dallin's back—almost intimate, like he'd been doing it all his life—and wandered to the rear of the stall to eye up the array of bows. The curtain was drawn but for a slight opening to the side; Wil made to walk past it, did a bit of a double-take, as though something behind it had caught his eye, and angled through.

Dallin had to stop himself from grinning and applauding the performance.

"Don't see too many Linders fraternizing." The gunsmith lifted an eyebrow as he loaded the sack with the ammunition Dallin had just paid too much for. "They're usually in and out o' here without much more than a 'Mother may I' to anyone else." His eyes narrowed—not with suspicion but with interest. "You one o' them exiles?"

Someone driven from the village, ostracized and shunned for any number of things, the most common Dallin remembered being too much collusion with outsiders. Service in the Commonwealth's military was the only exception. The Old Ones didn't abide the thinning and dilution of their flock.

"Yes." Dallin held the man's eye. It felt like a stone in his mouth—he'd never really thought to wonder what his reception in Lind might be, or what they might think of a man who'd run away as a boy and returned as an outlander—but it was the easiest answer and the fastest way to end the conversation and get out of there. The stares of the men behind him were beginning to tingle at the back of Dallin's neck.

The gunsmith merely shrugged as he handed over the sack. "I hope he was worth it."

Dallin withstood the attitude for another moment while he got specifics on the when and where of the livestock auctions, then thanked the gunsmith politely and sauntered as casually as he could manage toward the back of the stall. With a performance that probably wasn't half as convincing as Wil's had been, Dallin slipped through the curtain and out through a small anteroom to the door, ducking down as he made his way through it.

The alley was indeed quiet, no traffic but a young woman pushing a barrow full of vegetables over the broken cobbles. Dallin gave her a nod as she passed, gaze reaching and scanning what appeared to be an otherwise empty stretch of alley. Damn it, if those men had spooked Wil and he'd taken off—

"Down this way" came from behind him, accompanied by a light tug at his elbow.

Dallin only twitched a little as he turned to find Wil at his side.

"Where did you come from?" That space had been decidedly unoccupied two seconds ago. And where the hell were Dallin's reflexes? He couldn't remember the last time someone had success-fully got behind him without him knowing it.

"I can turn myself invisible." Wil said it with a wry wink,

smirking when Dallin's mouth twisted. "I was right there." Wil pointed to a tiny shadowed alcove to the side of the gunsmith's stall and gave Dallin's sleeve another tug. "This whole place is cross-hatched with alleys and little side streets—we could probably get lost if we're not careful, but it'll likely throw those men off for a while."

Dallin just shook his head. "You've been doing pretty well so far." He waved down the alley. "Lead on."

A surprised little half smile flitted over Wil's face, but he only nodded before he turned and led Dallin into a labyrinthine criss-cross of overgrown bricked paths and dirt alleyways that were intersected now and again by neater cobbles and stone walks. The sun slanted lower over the tops of the buildings they passed, roofed variously with thatch, tin, and slate. They were losing time—another two hours 'til the auctions—but losing the guard and his little posse was a bit more important right now.

They fetched up some time later when the random path they were following dead-ended at the rear of a great stone building, stately and dignified, with portcullises that looked like they'd never been closed in their long years and grown over with ivy and the crumpled autumn remnants of wild roses. The characteristics were universal and unmistakable. Dallin grinned.

"A library. Perfect. I've been wishing for Manning and his know-it-all lectures, but this will do very well indeed."

Wil's mouth twisted. "You want to go in there?" He eyed the building, its crouched stone bulk and stained glass windows. "What am I supposed to do in a library?"

"Hm, well, yes, but it might turn out to be important. Or at least somewhat informative. I hope." Dallin shrugged. "It shouldn't take too awfully long, and those men wouldn't venture in there unless they were serving free beer."

Wil scowled up at the wide stone walls for a moment before he sighed, groused *"Anyway,"* and pulled his shoulders up to his ears.

Dallin hadn't noticed until just this second when he'd watched Wil hunch in again that, though the alert wariness had remained all through their diversion through the alleys, the expectant sullenness had disappeared. It was subtle, not a huge difference, but it *was* a difference, a marked distinction between how Wil behaved around Dallin as opposed to everyone else. And now that Dallin was thinking about it—about all the different faces Wil had donned just since they'd arrived at Chester's gates—he realized the resentful look of a man constantly on tenterhooks, just waiting for the next offensive, had only really re-emerged after Wil had been disarmed. He'd been cagey but determined when the guard had moved toward him, but became drawn-in and angrily sharp the moment the rifle left his hands. He'd gone from a man with the confidence of carbine and cartridge at his back to a back-alley grifter like a fish that had grown legs and lungs but still knew how to swim with the sharks. Dallin had more or less handed over the reins to him at the gunsmith's stall, and Wil had taken them up as though he'd been born to this particular saddle. For all Dallin had seen in his years as a constable, he'd never know the underside of a city as well as one who'd spent time in it. Wil was much better at being a sneak than Dallin was.

"What?" Wil's tone was sharp and defensive.

Dallin realized he'd been staring and not moving. He shook his head and breathed a small laugh. "Sorry. It's just that you've impressed me again."

One dark eyebrow rose. "Because I said I'd go to the library with you?"

"Because you got us out of a touchy situation without a shot being fired or a punch being thrown."

Wil rolled his eyes. "You're very easily impressed. Are we going in or not?"

Dallin only waved toward the path that led to the front of the building. Wil scowled and slouched around to the front steps. Smiling slightly, Dallin followed, waiting politely for a clutch of women to pass him before stepping out into the still-busy street as Wil shuffled up the steps ahead of him. They were well away from the main thoroughfare of the market, deeper into the city itself, but plenty of traffic still bustled alongside several stray carts that hadn't been fortunate enough to win a prime location on the square, and Dallin thought about maybe taking a momentary detour to see if offering something more to the god of Wil's stomach might make—

Dallin stopped dead with his foot on the bottom step of the library, body gone tense and rigid. An abrupt, inexplicable shudder was fizzing up Dallin's spine, and instinct sent his gaze in a cursory sweep over the sparser crowd.

It didn't take long to spot him.

Wide and tall, hair the same color as Dallin's but graying, though longer and with beaded braids holding it back at the temples. His dress was similar to those of the general public fanning around him and affording him a wide berth, but plainer, colors bland and tending toward browns and beiges. His face was clean-shaven and deeply tanned. Dallin couldn't really see from here, but his mind's eye etched a string of scars over the right cheekbone at the same instant he realized the man's eyes were pinned over Dallin's shoulder. Wil.

Dallin jerked his head and took a step up the stone stairs—meaning to block the man's line of sight, perhaps, or just get between him and Wil—but Wil seemed to feel something too. His shoulders twitched, and his head ticced to the side before he spun around with a bemused frown. His eye caught Dallin's, questioning. Dallin blinked and shook his head, turning his glance back out into the street.

No bulky figure stood staring; no blond head towered above the crowd.

The ghost of the Watcher from his dream, perhaps? Dedication and devotion to his calling reaching even beyond his foreign, anonymous grave? Or merely the lack of sleep and recent immersion in the bizarre finally catching up with him?

"Something wrong?" Wil asked from behind him.

"...Maybe."

Dallin turned. Wil's expression was clouded, anxious, his good hand gripping the library door's handle in a white-knuckled fist. His gaze kept snapping from Dallin and then out into the street, searching, and back again to Dallin. Dallin wondered if Wil had seen too, or if Dallin's own disquiet was leaking out onto Wil. In fact, Dallin wondered if he'd even seen anything himself, now that the initial rush of apprehension was beginning to subside.

He gave his head a quick shake and pulled a sedate expression to his face. "Thought I saw something, but if it was there, it's gone now." He jerked his chin. "C'mon, we're already running later than we wanted."

Wil stared up at him for a moment, skimmed his glance back out into the street, then only twitched a small nod, pulled the door open, and went inside. Dallin gave the street one last sweep before he followed.

The scents of a library, like its overall appearance—regardless of architecture—were universal and therefore soothingly familiar. Dust and parchment were more palliative to Dallin's senses than a stiff drink would've been. He stood by the door for a moment, just breathing in the scent of beeswax and ink, letting his eyes adjust to the dim light filtering in through the high windows paned in painted leaded glass. It wasn't as big as Putnam's, nor was it as comfortably shabby. The shelves didn't overflow with a mishmash of titles of which only Manning knew the order, but were lined neatly, each volume tucked in its own slot. No squat little stove piled with teapots and saucepans heating the librarian's lunch ticked in the corner, but a central hearth burned with a sensibly sized fire that put off just enough heat for comfort.

Dallin knew just by the neatness of the setting not to expect someone like Manning to greet them, but Chester's librarian still startled him. A spare little woman, gray and just going slightly wizened, who looked as if she was perpetually chewing on the sour-bitter rinds of a lemon. She regarded them suspiciously, mouth pursed as her critical glance roved over their obvious travel wear and Dallin's weapons, pinching impossibly tight when her bright gaze rested on Dallin's head. Dallin started, took off his hat, and nudged Wil to do the same.

"Good afternoon," he began politely. "I was wonder—"

"Ye can't take books 'less you live in Chester." Amazing how the woman managed to bark it so quietly.

Dallin blinked, then shot a quick glare over when Wil snorted. Dallin shook his head. "I wasn't—"

"If ye want a book, ye'll have to show papers and leave five billets deposit."

Dallin frowned this time and pinched at the bridge of his nose. His first impulse was to puff up and cut the woman down to an even smaller size with verbal chastisement and high-handed posturing. His second impulse was to do exactly the opposite of his first impulse. His first impulse, after all, had worked decidedly against them at the gates.

He pasted on a pleasant smile and dipped his head. "We won't be taking any books with us and promise to be more than careful with any you might permit us to look at." He didn't think he'd achieved a look of innocence since he was five years old, but he tried for one anyway. "We're looking for something in particular, something about the gods of the Four Corners. Have you got anything that might help?"

She thought about it, eyes brushing a telltale glance to the center of the far wall before fixing again on Dallin. "You can read?"

It was strange, being assumed a Linder after all this time. Dallin had never met anyone from Lind in the years since he'd left it. He was the only one he knew of who had traveled as far south as Putnam. There, those who knew him just knew him as Dallin, and those who didn't knew him as Constable Brayden. Even in the army, he'd only seen one other who'd appeared to be from Lind, and he'd been just another of the dead over whom Dallin's horse had to pick its way after the last retreat sounded. There, Dallin had first been *that big Brayden lad*, then *yessir, Lieutenant sir*, and finally just *Cap'n*. In Putnam it had taken him years to fit in, and he'd belonged as much as someone like him could. The army and the constabulary were different, valuing skill over heritage. No one had looked at him as though he belonged in Lind since he actually had. It was disconcerting.

"I can read," Dallin answered evenly, watching as the librarian's gaze changed infinitesimally, "exile" now dropping like a little weight behind its reflected judgment.

Interesting.

Dallin had never been on the receiving end of bigotry before. New acquaintances in Putnam usually viewed his origins as a point of interest and then took him for who he was, whether they liked him or not. Not only did this woman apparently disapprove of those from Lind, but she approved of those exiled from it even less. And by the way her lip curled and she avoided looking at Wil altogether, she disapproved of anyone who looked like they might be from Ríocht too, though that wasn't terribly unique. Refugees from Ríocht were few, but they existed nonetheless, and now that Wil didn't have the dubious disguise of his hat to hide his hair color, his heritage was all too plain.

The woman sighed, shook her head, then stepped purposefully around them and toward the spot where her glance had shifted before. She pulled down two books. Dallin felt not even a twinge of guilt when he noted with satisfaction that Manning, for all his disorganized disarray, would never have allowed books in such a state onto his shelves—the bindings were cracking, their weave fraying along the edges of the spines, and no one had bothered to gild the pages to prevent yellowing.

"Let me see your hands."

Show me those hands, now, little man.

Dallin managed to hold back a scowl as he put his hands out.

The librarian had herself a good, long look, her mouth twisting tartly at Dallin's relatively clean hands, apparently unable to find an excuse not to let him touch the books. She blew a great, long-suffering sigh as she shoved them at Dallin, pointing over to a lacquered table in the midst of eight uncomfortable-looking, stiff-backed chairs. Prim and abrupt, she wheeled on her very proper heel and clipped over to her very proper desk, slipped on her very proper spectacles, and sat very properly in her chair.

Dallin rolled his eyes, gave Wil a sour grimace when he noted the covert snorts had never stopped, then plodded over to the table and dropped into one of the small chairs. Wil followed, hiding a grin in his collar.

"Are you all right?" Wil asked through a smirk he didn't even try to hide.

Dallin didn't miss the inflection, the way his own apparently too-oft-voiced question was turned back on him. His mouth twisted. "Very funny."

"It really bothers you, doesn't it?"

"Of course it bothers me." Dallin just barely kept himself from snapping it. "It's ignorant and hidebound, and I find both offensive in the extreme."

"Is that why you got so angry with that guard?"

"I expect I got angry with the guard for the same reason you did."

"I was angry because he was going to take the gun. I *really* like that gun."

Dallin gave him a skeptical grimace. "And what he said didn't bother you at all?"

"Ha." Wil dipped his head a bit and glanced over his shoulder when the librarian loudly cleared her throat. He couldn't seem to lose the smirk. "Did you do all of that because you thought my virtue was insulted?"

Dallin hadn't thought of it in those specific terms, hadn't really thought much about it at all, just reacted. "Well, I just thought... I thought—"

"You thought I'd go to pieces because some skeezy gob thought I was your catamite?" Wil rolled his eyes. "Fuck's sake, Constable, d'you think I've never heard its like before? I know what I look like. Or should I be blushing and covering my ears? I keep forgetting I'm supposed to be impressive. Shall I make as the driven snow so as not to disappoint you?"

"*Disappoint....*" Dallin gaped. "It has nothing to do with.... *I'm* not the one...." He peered over at the pinched-up librarian and lowered his voice. "Is that the way people always talk to you?"

"It's how *you* talked to me back in Putnam."

"That isn't fair." Dallin was flailing, and they both knew it. "I was working from the accounts of others, and you wouldn't tell me what really happened. You wouldn't tell me *anything.*"

Wil seemed absurdly entertained by Dallin's discomfort, but

he only waved it away. "You're right. It was forever ago, and we were different people then."

Dallin frowned over that. It did seem like forever ago, and Wil certainly seemed like a different person, but Dallin felt pretty much the same as ever. Except perhaps more tired.

Wil tapped at the books. He was still smiling, but his gaze was more interested than snarky now. "So what d'you want to know about the old gods? And how come?"

A deliberate change of subject, but Dallin was more than willing to go along with it. "I want to know everything I can find out." He flipped open the first book, trying to put the strange, unsettled embarrassment aside, and started scanning through the pages.

Eorðbúgigend—god of the earth. That was simple enough.

Wil waited for a quiet moment, but when Dallin didn't go on, Wil slid his elbows to the table, folded his arms, and laid his chin atop them. "How come?"

Dallin sighed. "Because I keep dreaming about them." He paused. "Well, not dreaming about *them*, exactly—more like dreaming about people asking me about them and me not knowing the answers."

"Having all the answers is very important to you, isn't it?" Wil stretched his arm out on the table and traced little invisible symbols into its slick surface.

Dallin turned back to the book. "It's my job."

"You want to tell me your dream?" Wil's voice was quieter than it had been, fingers still tracing, his gaze following his own movements but distant. All the humor of a moment ago was gone, but he didn't seem anxious or distressed.

"Why would you want to hear about my dreams?" Dallin flipped some more pages. This Eorðbúgigend fellow was a little boring, apparently spending all his time delving and avoiding everyone, including his fellow deities. "Don't you get enough of all that on your own?" Ah, now this Díepe seemed a bit more promising—the goddess of water, coaxing the hapless into her depths and having her way with them, then spitting them back out, sometimes alive, if they pleased her well enough.

"I can probably tell you what it means, at least."

Dallin snapped his glance up. Wil was still tracing his little patterns, almost stretched out across the table. To another he might look relaxed, even bored—to Dallin he looked pensive.

"I thought you didn't know how... well, how... *things* worked."

Wil shrugged. "Well, no one actually told me, but it's... I've been doing it a long time, y'know." He laid his head on the crook of his elbow and peered at Dallin, that little smirk back again. "And I'm not slow."

Dallin smiled back, drawn. It was quite an offer, considering. And extraordinarily heartening that Wil would even make it. Dallin thought about it for only a mere span of seconds.

"People—people in my dreams, I mean—they keep asking me to sing them the songs of the old gods, and when I can't...." He hesitated. "Well, bad things happen."

"That's not much to go on. Is that all you remember?"

"...No."

Dallin sat back, carding through the various dreams and their possible effects on Wil, and chose the one he thought least likely to disturb either of them. If Wil could indeed discern something in them that squeaked some sense out of it all, Dallin would have to confess the other, the one he knew would be somewhat upsetting. He'd have to do that eventually anyway, but he was loath to do it here with that bitter-boned librarian looking on.

"I'm in the army. Colonel Mancy is there, the one who more or less arranged my promotion, and at first he's telling my commander how he thinks I won't be satisfied until I hack my way into the Dominion and through the Guild's ramparts. He really did say that, I heard it, so it's likely just a memory or something."

Despite the reassurance, Wil tensed just a little. Dallin paused, worried he might take it as yet another sign that Dallin was a danger—he used to live inside the Guild's walls, after all— but Wil merely sat up, rested his chin in his hand, and peered at Dallin steadily.

"Go on."

Dallin blew out a sigh. "Well, then he asks me the words to the songs of the old gods, and when I tell him I don't know them, he turns into Manning—my old tutor—and he keeps shoving books at me, but they're written in a language I don't understand, and he tells me I have to decode them. Except when I tell him I don't have the key to the code, he tells me my father's going to die. I tell him my father's already dead, but then he turns into one of the children from Kenley, only it's just a burnt-up skeleton and it tells me I've forgotten my name." He paused, thinking, trying to eke out details from the murk. "The skeleton has clan marks on its cheek," he added after a moment. "And it's pointing at me like I'm the one who killed it." He grimaced. Now that he'd said it, given it ordinary words as its frame, it sounded a bit silly.

Wil was staring at him, eyes narrowed. He didn't seem to think it was silly. He was pondering it seriously. His fingers went back to their invisible scribbling, gaze following.

"The songs are the key," he said slowly. "The code is whatever you find inside them. Something that will mean something to you, help you figure out where to look for the pieces of your puzzle and understand who you are."

Dallin rubbed at his brow. "I *know* who I am. Let's don't go back to this again—please, I'm begging you."

"I'm not." Wil gave him a slight roll of his eyes. "I'm not saying anything like that. For pity's sake, I sleep while you're walking watch with a loaded gun five paces away from me. Doesn't that tell you anything?"

It told Dallin plenty. He only wondered if the reverse told Wil as much.

"You're a Linder who was taken from Lind when he was a boy." Dallin was somewhat taken aback by the soft authority in Wil's tone. "You are what you've made of yourself, but there are parts of you that you can't possibly know—you didn't even know there *was* such thing as a Guardian. How much more d'you think there is to you that you don't know?"

Dallin had to concede the point. "My father died before he could teach me the songs of my name."

"There you are." Wil opened a hand. "P'raps the songs of the old gods will help you understand your own."

"Which would be very helpful if I could find the bloody songs." Dallin flipped open the second book and began to scan the pages. "These only seem to be tales of the gods themselves, and there's not much of even that. A few paragraphs for each one mixed with a bunch of other mythology that has nothing to do with anything."

Wil looked down into his lap with a brooding frown. "You're a very interesting, very confusing man." He peered up from beneath his lashes, measuring. "You're forever asking questions, seeking answers, but you sometimes miss the most obvious questions, and sometimes the answers are right in front of you and you can't see them." A small smile lifted one corner of his mouth. "You only take one foot at a time from out your quickmud."

"That's...." Dallin frowned. "That's an odd thing to say." He closed the book, hands resting loosely atop it. "You think I'm missing something obvious, then."

He didn't phrase it as a question; it was all too apparent that Wil was attempting to wend his way around to something and perhaps didn't know how to just come out with it. In Dallin's observations thus far, Wil hardly ever "just came out" with *anything* unless he was fairly pissed off at the time, so patience now would probably be advisable. If they were talking about a crime scene or witness statement, Dallin likely would take sincere offense at the contention that he was stumbling blind. Since they were in point of fact talking about dreams and were therefore in Wil's element, so to speak, the allegation wasn't too far off the mark.

"You say the answers are right in front of me." Dallin turned his hands over, palm up on the table. "Will you tell me?"

Wil's smile spread just a touch wider, but it twitched ever so slightly, dipping wry. "Ah, see, there's the obvious question." He looked down at his lap again, fiddling with the slight fray of the linen wrappings around his hand. "I can do better than tell you." He glanced up to gauge reaction. "I can teach you."

Dallin had already been itching to get back on the road as soon as possible. Between their greeting at the gates and the figure that might or might not have been his imagination across the street from the library, the urge to take care of the rest of their business and be gone had worked at his nerves like an itch he couldn't reach between his shoulder blades. Now he was on fire with it. He'd almost wanted to insist Wil teach him those songs right then and there, but he didn't like the idea of doing it while that pinch-mouthed biddy was looking on.

"All right," he said to Wil as they stepped back out onto the library's steps, eyes sweeping habitually but pausing to linger on the spot where he'd seen—*thought* he'd seen—the man earlier. Nothing there to see now. He wasn't sure if he was relieved or disappointed. "We've got to get back toward the square for the auction. Once that's done, we can head back out." A quick look at the position of the sun told him they still had plenty of time. They hadn't been nearly as long in the library as he'd thought they might. He started down the steps. "We should have smooth walking, at least today and tomorrow morning. Things'll get a little more—"

He stopped, and shot his arm out to keep Wil from loping down the steps behind him. "Hold on a moment." Unease was abruptly buzzing all over him, as if a ghost were chiseling right into his backbone, and he had to work hard to suppress the shudders.

Wil halted without protest but peered a question up at Dallin. Something in Dallin's eyes must have been a bit too obvious— Wil's expression changed instantly, gaze shooting from one end of the street to the other. The hardness was back, and his shoulders were just beginning their defensive inward stoop. Dallin couldn't have kept whatever was on his face that had triggered the change off it had he tried. He'd never felt anything like it. Urgent foreboding, a feeling of something impending, something unpleasant. It was crawling all over him.

"What?" Wil nearly whispered it.

Dallin shook his head, his own gaze never resting, scanning the people milling about on the street and looking for anything suspicious, anything at all—a lingering look or even a deliberate not-look, a telltale bulge of a weapon, a hulking shape that looked too much like him....

Still nothing, or at least nothing he could see.

"Nothing, I guess." Dallin's voice was quiet, his tone probably not at all convincing. "I thought...." He shook his head, eyes still moving, troubled. "I don't know—*something*." He turned to Wil. "Don't you feel it?"

It *felt* as though Wil should feel it—it felt as though anyone within a hundred paces should feel it, like it had physical shapes and Dallin just couldn't see them.

"C'mon." Wil tugged anxiously at Dallin's elbow and tried to drag him down the steps. "Let's *go*." Between his teeth this time, and quietly uneasy. Whatever was thrumming through Dallin was now leaking out onto Wil. Wil tugged again. This time Dallin let himself be moved.

His hand went automatically to the revolver strapped to his thigh, flipping the fastenings and resting his fingers lightly on the butt. He reached for Wil's arm and latched on.

"Put your hat back on." Dallin angled them down the steps as Wil complied, and they turned back into the little side lane from which they'd come. "Back to the alleys." Dallin didn't know why he kept his voice so low, but he did, eyes trying to look everywhere at once, words from dreams haunting—*the Watcher is watched*—yammering through his head like a sinister mantra, except he couldn't bloody *see* anything. No one lurked, no one stalked—everywhere he looked, he only saw ordinary people going about their ordinary business on an ordinary market day.

When they reached a crisscross pattern of lanes leading off in six different directions, Dallin pulled Wil over toward a stand of bushes ringing a dooryard behind an ageing heap of stone that likely used to be the very impressive home of some prosperous citizen but was now run down and depressing in its dilapidated gloom. Dallin had to stop a moment and get himself together. There was no good reason for the absurd anxiety, and all he was doing was ramping up Wil's already unpredictable state of being. Except Dallin couldn't find that cool reserve, the remove that normally walked him through tense situations.

The Watcher is watched.

And yet there was nothing—no one—there. Anywhere.

"Is it gone?" Wil eyed Dallin with trepidation and as close to dread as Dallin had seen since they'd shown Dudley their backs.

It wasn't gone; it was getting worse, and the afternoon sun was whining in Dallin's head with an insectile buzz that was drilling into his teeth, making his peripheral vision too bright and too sharp. They were being watched, and it wasn't just in his head; it was real. He could feel it all the way to his bones.

Dallin didn't answer, instead throwing his glance over the spider web of alleyways, then choosing a random direction and tugging Wil's arm again. "This way."

Amazingly, Wil didn't argue, didn't even try to get loose from Dallin's grip, following Dallin without objection or comment. They headed down a dirt lane, winding between squat, decrepit brick structures, the purpose of which Dallin didn't pause to ponder. The atmosphere was growing seedier, the air taking on a rank smell of piss and dirt as they went farther. The buildings crowded together, blocking most of the light.

They passed doorways and niches carefully, Dallin edging around each one first, holding Wil back until Dallin determined they were safe enough to pass by. One or two seemed to serve as living quarters, ragged men lurking in their corners and growling balefully at the sight of Wil, then in turn cowering at the sight of Dallin and even more so at the sight of his weapons. Wil and Dallin passed unmolested until they came upon an alcove outside what appeared to be a less reputable hostel, alleyway strewn with rubbish and the contents of pisspots emptied into the gutters and not washed away.

A haggard woman lurched up from her crouch in the hovel's recess, staggering at Dallin with intent, hands outstretched like she was greeting an old friend. She was thin as wire, dried up and wispy as a husk, eyes sunken and vague above a delicate, near toothless grin. Her muscles twitched with uncontrollable tics, her breathing labored and rheumy. There was a sour smell about her, over and above the pervasive stench of the alley, the clothes hanging off her thin frame rank with ages-old dirt and rot. She was dying, wasting into nothing—Dallin could smell it on her—and the soft, dreamy look all but beat the drum for it. She was this close to death from one thing or another—lung-sick, maybe, or blight, who could tell?—and that beatific look of serene peace in her eyes told Dallin she truly didn't care.

A leaf user.

"Exile!" she cried. "Ye've come! Bless. *Bless*."

She reached for Dallin, fingernails thick and yellowed beneath the layers of grime on her shaking hand. Dallin stepped back to avoid the touch, knocking into Wil, who stood staring with horrified fascination inside grim surprise.

"I've watched, I have." The woman's soft giggle was all the more unnerving for its girlishness. She held her filthy hand out palm up and waggled her taloned fingers. "Redeem your word and I shall redeem mine."

Dallin almost brushed past her—Wil shouldn't be seeing this, and the stiff posture, the inability to drag his revolted gaze away, told Dallin that Wil knew exactly what he was looking at—but something about what she'd said, or maybe just the way she'd said it, made Dallin stop. He stared down at her dirty hand, its meaning universal and very clear.

"Remind me of my word, Miss." Dallin reached to his belt for his purse—slowly, so her abstracted gaze could follow. "You're not the only one watching, after all."

"Ah!" She giggled again and shook her finger. "And I thought I was yer one and only."

Mother's mercy, the woman was trying to be coy. She was bloody *flirting*.

Dallin dragged a smile onto his face, making it as easy and

pleasant as he could. A light shudder ran through Wil, shimmying into Dallin's hand through his grip on Wil's arm, and Dallin squeezed in reassurance.

"Oh, but you are certainly my favorite." Dallin winked and broadened his smile when she giggled some more. He shook the purse. "And what was our agreement?"

"Five gilders." Her gaze was sly, and her smile was going slightly sideways.

Lying, of course. Whatever she'd agreed to do for this "Exile," and whatever price she'd agreed to do it for, it was likely more along the lines of a few billets. Nonetheless, Dallin made quite a business of taking the proper coins from his purse before he turned around and handed the rest to Wil.

"Hold on to that. And get on the other side of me, in case you have to grab for the rifle. Just don't rip my arm off doing it, if there's trouble."

The woman *probably* wasn't dangerous—Wil had been right; leaf and violence were rather mutually exclusive—but she was showing signs of withdrawal, and addicts deprived of their addictions were predictable only in their unpredictability.

Dallin turned back to the woman and held up the coins. He kept silent, merely lifting his eyebrows, expectant.

Her playful smile turned joyous as she stared up at the money, and she clapped her hands like a little girl. Eyes fixed to the gold, she sauntered closer, leaning in conspiratorially. "The one you seek comes to you." Her sour breath puffed too close to Dallin's face, but he kept his mien graciously encouraging. "Wait and Watch." She pulled back and covered her ruined mouth with her hand. The effect was nauseatingly coquettish.

The words made Dallin's eyes narrow slightly, and he didn't know what they were doing to Wil—he daren't look back yet to find out.

It couldn't be what Dallin thought it was. He must be hearing things through his own skewed expectations. All the secrecy that seemed to surround this whole business, men killing for it, and this filthy slum leaf freak *knew*?

"This one I seek," he said, smoothly cordial. "What does he look like?"

The smile fell, but only a little. "Ah, walks in shadows he does, poor lad." Amazingly, she managed to pout through the smile that was more and more making Dallin want to smack it off her skull-like face. "He's the feel of the culled, but I know him when we sleep." Her head fell back, and her arms crossed over her small, flat breasts. "Touches my brow with his tattered fingers, plucks at my thread, and sings me to dancing." An ungainly bit of a sway, to and fro, and her eyes fell shut. "I know it's him by how he marks me." A spindly hand came up, fingers sweeping at her brow. "Blood to blood." It was a hum, tuneless and ragged.

Dallin actually looked closer to make sure there wasn't in fact a bloody fingerprint on the woman's forehead. He turned to Wil— somewhere between disbelief and confused revelation.

Wil's gaze was pinned to the woman, sickened and horrified but held by macabre fascination. He turned slowly to Dallin, shook his head, mouth working but nothing coming out of it. His eyes were doing that thing they did, going murky and bright at the same time, color twisting inside them.

Dallin's stomach dropped, and he reached out to lay a hand on Wil's shoulder. "Hey. You're all right, there's nothing—"

"—the big one first!" came from almost right behind him. He spun too late, instinctively shoving Wil back before his vision was blocked by something wide and very hard smashing into the side of his head. Damn it, he'd let himself get distracted, forgot the first rule of both offense and defense and let someone get behind him, hit him blind.

Dazed, Dallin staggered. He blinked to keep blackness from taking his vision or his perceptions. There was a scream, and several shouts wound through the dull ringing in Dallin's ears. Everything happened at once.

A tug at the rifle's strap. Wil. Dallin dropped his shoulder and let Wil have the gun. At the same time, Dallin drew the handgun from its holster, all before he'd even completed the turn to face his attackers and put his back to the wall. He shot his glance down to each end of the narrow lane before settling it back on the men in front of them.

There were five of them, the guard from the gate standing foremost, his pig eyes glittering with petty vengeance. Bloody hell, Dallin must have *really* pissed him off.

A sticky rivulet of blood ran down Dallin's temple. A broken length of timber lay at the gate guard's feet. If Dallin was lucky enough to get out of this without much more damage, he was at least going to have a bugger of a headache once the adrenaline wore off.

The woman was on the ground, on her knees, crawling about and collecting the gilders that had scattered from Dallin's hand. She peered up at Dallin as she scrabbled up the last gilder, and gave him a happy grin. Dallin resisted the urge to roll his eyes.

Wil stood to Dallin's right, rifle cocked and ready and aimed into the center of the small cluster of men who faced them. Three of them had swords drawn. The other two flashed standard military pistols.

"Back off, and we'll be on our way." Wil's voice was calm. Dallin was absurdly proud of him.

Thirty seconds ago, Wil had been all set to panic. Now, with the rifle once again in his hands, he was cool and more deadly than any of these men could imagine with their small minds.

Two of them snorted. One of them mimed a kiss. They all had

the same look to them—small, mean men who got their few meager pleasures out of making others their prey. This wasn't personal; they were just looking for their twisted version of fun, and Dallin had crossed the gate guard's path on the wrong day. He hated to think what sorts of prison guards they'd make.

"This is my fault," he murmured to Wil. "Sorry. I don't know why, but my instincts have turned to shit."

Wil adjusted his grip, tilting his head and sighting down, the barrel now pointed directly at the gate guard's chest. "After we get out of it, I get to keep the gun."

Dallin didn't dare twitch a smirk, but he wanted to. That rifle looked more at home in Wil's hands than it had ever felt in his, and he wouldn't dream of taking it back now. He reached down, resting his free hand over the new revolver, letting his fingers twitch when he saw one of the men follow the movement with a beady gaze.

"Don't shoot unless you have to." Dallin kept it low and calm. "You counted six before, and there are only five now. Watch for another." He took a deep breath. "Here goes."

Bold, Dallin pushed away from the wall, holding his gun up and out in his left hand. He kept his right hand over the other as he took two slow steps forward.

"I don't know what this man has told you"—Dallin nodded toward the gate guard—"but I am a visiting constable from the province of Putnam, and therefore probably a lot more trouble than you bargained for when you agreed to this little... party." He watched their eyes. Three of them showed obvious surprise, then doubt. "Walk away now, and it goes no further. We'll be gone before day's end."

They stared, all of them still and silent. Dallin watched the eyes of every one of them but mostly kept an eye on the one from the gate. If this went bad, it would be on his signal. It was just how these things went. One stupid leader and a handful of followers who were too used to obeying orders and pretending at loyalty to talk sense into him.

The warning came by way of a flare in the gate guard's eyes. He rushed, sword swinging. With a deep-chested cry, he lunged at Dallin. It was somewhat clumsy, but he was formally trained, so Dallin didn't underestimate him. Dallin turned sideways, flung his arm out, and thoroughly clotheslined him. It sent the guard to his back in the dirt with a breathless snarl. He didn't stop swinging. His blade flashed in the dribs and drabs of sunlight that filtered through the buildings. Dallin had to spin again and dance out of the way to avoid getting his shins sliced up.

Wil was still holding three of them off with the aim of the rifle and a look that would have made Dallin stop and think twice. Another was helping the gate guard up from the ground, staring at Dallin and dragging at the guard's elbow.

Dallin was just wondering again where the sixth had gone when a sharp pain sliced into his lower back, searing and incandescent with bright white agony.

Dallin jerked with a throttled cry. He drove his elbow back first, then followed it with a blind, spinning right hook, the butt of the gun against his palm lending more power to the blow. He didn't even have time to be satisfied with the painful grinding of his knuckles as they mashed into the assailant's jaw, the gratifying *crunch* of tooth and bone vibrating up his arm.

A shot boomed, the heavy *whoof* of air exploding from a broken chest almost muffled beneath the roar. Dallin heard every mechanism in the rifle click and churn as it was pumped and cocked again. Another shot whizzed past Dallin's shoulder. He only noticed vaguely when a warm spray of blood spattered him. He was otherwise occupied with watching the top of a man's head split off from the bottom... otherwise occupied with trying to breathe through pain that was almost sublime in its agony.

"Good shot." Dallin realized it came from him, only it huffed out fuzzy and slurred. His vision pulsed between light and dark in time to the pain radiating up his back, engulfing the whole left side of his body. He reached back, fingers blundering into the hilt of a knife jutting from low in his back. Exquisite, blinding pain vibrated from his touch, sent hot bile to the back of his throat, and sparkled at the edges of his perception. "Shit." He swayed. "This is... this is bad." Not fatal—most important things were higher and on the other side—but bad.

Two more shots rang out. Dallin blinked. His right arm shouldn't feel like it weighed twenty stone, but just raising his gun, pointing it into the blurred mass of moving bodies, made his vision go dark.

"Brayden!"

Dallin blinked again. He shook his head but couldn't clear it. A vague shape that resolved itself into Wil was coming toward him —face fierce and determined, lit from within and as close to actual feral beauty as Dallin had ever seen. He was like some kind of avenging spirit. He was saying something, shouting, but Dallin couldn't hear it. Dallin peered up, wondering why Wil was suddenly so much taller than him. *Oh.* He'd gone down to his knees, oddly disturbed that he couldn't remember when.

"*Hey!*" Fear and real concern slicked through Wil's shout. "C'mon, we have to go." He took hold of Dallin's shoulder. "We have to *go!*"

"Don't shake me," Dallin mumbled, or hoped he did. Shaking would be bad. Shaking would bloody *hurt.* "Can't go." Dallin shook his head, but everything was still too bright around the edges, muddled. "Just... give me a minute."

He just needed to catch his breath, that was all—catch his

breath and clear the tangle of pain that was clouding every thought, turning him slow and stupid, sucking him down into that quickmud everyone kept chastising him about.

"What's wrong?" Wil gripped tighter. "Are you shot? Did they get you? I don't see anything—is it your head?"

Muzzy, slow, Dallin blinked up into Wil's face. Then up into the face of the man looming behind him. Noted the beaded braids in the gold-gray hair... the rough, notched scar.

Just how corrupt did an Old One have to be, Dallin wondered dazedly, before the others sliced your Marks from off your face?

"The Watcher is watched." Dallin wheezed out something between a sigh and a thin moan.

Failed. *Failed*, damn it, and he hadn't even started yet.

Vertigo closed him in a hard fist. He dragged his eyes back to Wil's, reached out, gun dropping from his hand as it latched on to Wil's sleeve.

"*Run.*"

CHAPTER 3

Wil just barely kept himself from growling anxious impatience. They must have hit Brayden with that chunk of wood a lot harder than Wil had thought. Wil was going to have a bugger of a time getting Brayden to his feet, let alone out of the alley, before the gunfire started attracting a crowd.

The men had all scattered, except for the two Wil had shot, and Wil had no doubt the others would be back within minutes with reinforcements. The scraggy woman was cowering in the doorway of what Wil assumed was the hostel's kitchen, clutching her gold to her thin chest and singing to herself, that eerie smile still pulling at her mouth. Before, her sudden appearance and the realization of what she was had thrown him almost completely. Now he dismissed her.

He yanked his arm out of Brayden's grip, leaning in until Brayden's gaze fixed and focused on Wil's face. "We have to *go*." Wil only just kept from snarling it. "Get up. We don't have time for this."

But Brayden just grabbed hold of Wil again, this time

clenching a fist to the collar of Wil's coat. "Go." A breathless grunt, urgent and fierce. *"Run!"*

"I'm *trying* to, damn it, would you—"

Wil stopped short. He hadn't noticed the look in Brayden's eyes until just this moment, hadn't seen the stress, the pain, the urgent command. The way he dragged his oddly hazy gaze away from Wil and pointed it over Wil's shoulder, the clench of his jaw and the flare of determined anger. Hadn't noticed that Brayden had dropped both his guns to the dirt.

Brayden was *never* without his guns.

There was a prickle at the back of Wil's neck, a bulky shadow falling over Brayden's face and stretching out behind him. Wil turned slowly, pulling his reluctant glance up even while his stomach began a queasy descent to the ground.

He knew right away why Brayden had told him to run, knew right away this was some very serious shit and more than enough reason for retreat. There was no confusion when Wil saw the ragged scar roping over the man's cheek, no naïve guessing at what might have caused it. Instead there was a sick sort of awe, a sinking curl of dread that leached into marrow and turned his limbs to water.

How wicked do you have to be, some small, lost-little-boy part of his mind wanted to know, *before they take your Marks away? What offense could be so desperately base?*

Brayden growled again, shoving at Wil, and nearly sent him sprawling to his arse in the dirt. Wil kept his balance, staggering up and then backing to the side and slightly behind Brayden. The rifle's stock was resting against Wil's hip, his finger reflexively sliding over the safety to make sure it was disengaged. He brought the gun up to rest in the cradle of his shoulder when the man raised a big hand.

"Is this how your Guardian guards you?" The man's voice was

gruff and graveled, harsh, and the smile in his eyes made some-thing inside Wil go loose and cold.

Brayden was trying to get up, to stand between Wil and the man. He planted one booted foot solid to the dirt, then had to pause to lean over his knee and catch his breath. It took a moment for the hilt of the knife jutting from Brayden's lower back, the growing stain of blood on his coat, to jumble into sense in Wil's head.

Oh. So that's what he's doing down there.

Wil clenched his jaw, a low tremor wanting to take control of him, but he wouldn't let it. Fuckfuckfuck, what the hell was he supposed to do now?

"For the Mother's sake," Brayden wheezed through his teeth, turning a quick snarl on Wil over his shoulder, "will you just *go?*"

He turned quickly back to the man who stood calmly in front of him, trying again to get to his feet, but it looked like his left leg didn't want to cooperate.

"Exile," Brayden growled.

"Watcher." The man dipped his head, mouth turning up at one corner in a smirk that sent a shiver down Wil's spine. The hard blue eyes dismissed Brayden and turned to Wil. The man turned his hands palms up. "You see I am not armed. I am no threat to you."

Run. He told you to go, he said *it, absolution, you owe him noth-ing, so just go!*

"What do you want?" Wil was relieved his voice was steady and not as reedy as he'd feared.

"Ah, we all want so badly." The woman giggled and smoothed her torn, ragged skirts about her ankles. "Give them what they think they want to keep them from taking what they don't know you have." Her birdlike hands fluttered in the air in front of her face, and she laughed again.

A small shock went through Wil. He frowned at the filthy woman, a grimy little oracle leaking portents like pus from a wound. How many times had he told himself that same thing? How many times had he used it as an excuse for deeds he didn't want to remember?

"We never give 'em anything that matters." She mumbled it to her fingers, then flashed her ruined grin at the man Brayden had called Exile. "Keep it so well, it hides even from our own." She giggled.

The man ignored it all entirely and let his smile spread a little wider. "Does he take you to the Cradle, lad?"

Wil jolted—he couldn't help it.

"Ah, but you're no lad, are you, then?" The man nodded sagely, tilted his head. "Did you think they'd just let you walk right in?" His voice had dipped down, conspiratory and filled with mock concern. "Did it never occur to you that there were others who seek?"

He took a step forward, but Brayden let loose a rumbling growl and drew his short sword from its sheath. It shook as he held it up, not much of a threat, but the man stopped, eyes narrowed.

There was something wrong about him, something... off. He gave off threat like it breathed from his pores—he *knew* what they were, both of them—and yet there was circumspection in his mien, as though he was looking for more.

And why was Wil not running? What the fuck was wrong with him?

The woman staggered to her feet and threw herself at the big man, taking him in a bony embrace. "*Exile.*" She buried her face in the sleeve of his coat. "Ye've waited so very long to take Her children in hand." She looked up at him, pleading. "Will She take my hand, then?"

The man's smile turned shrewd. He slipped his arm around

the woman but kept peering down at Wil, cunning. "D'you want what she has, then? I see the look in your eye. I see the need." He tightened his grip around the woman. She laid her head to his chest, and he let her. "Look at her, lad. She doesn't hurt. She's not afraid. How long has it been since you felt so still?"

Wil shook his head and backed an involuntary step, caught off guard by how quickly and deeply the want overwhelmed him.

He wanted to shoot the dirty little woman so he wouldn't have to look at her anymore. Wouldn't have to wonder how close the resemblance might have been. Wouldn't have to remember the serene drift and tranquility that went hand in hand with the pain. Wouldn't have to know he still wanted it so badly he'd consider killing for it and then killing himself if he managed to get it.

"Wil," Brayden wheezed, "if you don't move right now, I swear I'll shoot you myself."

A small flick of the man's hand, and Brayden flinched. He was too obviously trying to hold back a gasp, but it burst from his chest in a labored hiss. He almost toppled to the side. His sword flew from his hand as he clutched at the ground. It landed next to the gun he'd dropped, less than a few inches from his splayed fingers, but he didn't snatch it up—Wil wasn't even sure he'd seen it. Brayden's head was bowed, chest expanding and contracting too quickly, trying to breathe through the pain.

It did something inside Wil, something cold and strangely possessive, a yammering little interior *mineminemine* snapping through him as he watched this strange pretender's little gesture, watched Brayden react to it like the man had just reached out and twisted the knife. Watched Brayden try to hold back a cry of pain and *still* attempt to keep himself between this man and Wil.

It was absurd, it made no sense whatsoever, it was a thought worthy of the six-year-old Locke had named him. But damn it, the

Guardian was *his*—his gift, Millard had said so—and Wil was bloody tired of people taking what was his and making free with it.

"I'm going," he told Brayden, low and even, "but you're coming with me."

He needed his good hand for the gun, so he stooped down and slipped his right shoulder under Brayden's left. As carefully as he could, Wil wrangled Brayden's thick arm over his shoulder. It was very telling that Brayden couldn't seem to shrug him off.

Instead, Brayden wrapped his arm around Wil's neck and dragged him in. "Don't be an idiot—I'll catch up if I can, but this is not apples and potatoes. You've nothing to prove. Look at him—don't you know what he is? They took his *Marks*."

And yet had left him alive, knowing what he apparently knew, setting him loose in a world they hadn't trusted for thousands of years, to do with the knowledge what he would.

It didn't make sense. A clan that didn't even tell its own people what it was about, allowing their secret to slip through their borders in the form of a disgraced Old One?

Wil looked the man over thoroughly, noting the calm, calculated challenge, the lack of malice in the measuring stare. The way he kept peering at Brayden with a badly hidden look of muted urgency. The too-obvious lack of any sort of assault on Wil himself, his mind or his person, despite the small show of power against Brayden.

The scars that were too young and pink against his tanned, leathery cheek.

Wil shifted his glance down to his own wrist, then back up at the man. Wil gently disengaged from Brayden and stood. "No, they didn't take his Marks. He did it himself. Or maybe had another do it for him." He tilted his head. "He can't hurt me. He hasn't got the power."

"How nice for you, because he's been mucking with *my* head since we got here."

It made sense. Unless something had gone very wrong with Brayden's reflexes, no one could have ordinarily got behind him, let alone stuck a knife in him. He'd been acting odd for hours, twitchy and unlike his usual confident self. And now that he thought about it, Wil himself had managed to sneak up behind Brayden earlier, and he hadn't even been trying. Combined with the way one small gesture from the man had seemed to rip right through Brayden, Wil thought it wouldn't do at all to assume anything or underestimate this man. There was a sinister air about him, but in the same way a hurricane was sinister, a flood—a force of nature, the sole purpose of which was to move from Point A to Point B, and if you couldn't survive the onslaught... well, it wasn't personal.

"He hasn't done anything you can't fight or do back ten times harder." Wil scowled when the man's smile curled sardonic. "He's a test."

"In case the obvious has escaped you yet again," Brayden ground out, "magic is slightly beyond my skills."

Wil almost pitied him. Brayden probably would have lived his whole life very happily believing what he'd just said.

The far-off shrill of a whistle broke in Wil's ears, a renewed sense of urgency drumming a choppy *rat-a-tat* on his nerves. People from the hostel and the building next to it were peering down at them through dirty windows—Wil could feel their stares like buzzing insects over his nape.

They needed to go—should already be gone—but a risk was one thing, blind stupidity entirely another.

Wary, keeping a close eye on the man, Wil crouched behind Brayden and reached for the hilt of the knife jutting from Brayden's back—

"Ah-ah. Don't do that." The man's tone was mild, but there was alarm threaded through there somewhere. It was enough to make Wil pause. "It's the only thing keeping him from bleeding out. Best to let a healer take care of that." When Wil only set his jaw, the man shrugged. "Unless that's what you want. But somehow I don't think it is."

Wil gave him a scowl and turned to Brayden. "Is that true?"

"Close enough, I guess." Brayden winced and pulled in a sharp breath. "Though it's not seeming such a bad alternative just now."

"Don't be such a big baby. It's just a scratch." It came out far too jagged and worried for the levity—or even wishful thinking— Wil was going for.

"Aren't you supposed to be running?"

"Aren't you supposed to be trying not to die?"

Wil stood and regarded the man with narrowed eyes. "Did you know this would happen?" He jerked his chin sharply in Brayden's direction, indicating the fight, the wound... everything.

The man shrugged. "I was not as careful in my seeking as I might have been."

"Then you can fix your mistake." It was terse and angry. "I assume you're as skilled at healing as you are at... other things. Shaman." Wil nodded toward Brayden. "Help him up." He caught Brayden's expression of anger and dismay. "Do I look like I don't know what I'm doing?"

Brayden was sucking air in through his teeth now, sweating, face twisted in a perplexed grimace of pain. "Yeah." He gave a slight jerky nod. "Yeah, you sorta do."

Wil almost twitched a smile. "Shut up. Trust me."

The man pushed the woman away from him gently, murmuring something to her that turned her vacant smile nearly beatific. She glided back to her little alcove, crouched down in its corner, and daintily adjusted her skirts. Happy as a child, she waved at Wil.

Wil raised his eyebrows a bit but didn't wave back, just kept an eye on the man, who knelt, guided Brayden's arm over his shoulders, and levered them both up from the dirt. Once Brayden was up and the swaying had subsided, Wil darted out to retrieve Brayden's guns and sword. The guns Wil jammed into his own coat pockets, but the sword he slid carefully back into its sheath on Brayden's hip.

"Where?"

"The Temple." The man adjusted his grip on Brayden. "I'll lead, you cover."

Wil raised the gun again, gripping the forend, and gave it a rough jerk to cock it. He slipped it back beneath his arm. The shot he'd fired from the hip had hit its mark pretty well the last time, so he stuck with it. And that one-handed cocking thing was very much coming in handy. He let his face set harsh.

"Don't fuck with me."

The man's expression was annoyingly skeptical. "You would kill me now?" He seemed more curious than surprised.

Brayden whiffled a hoarse little snort and creased a pained smile at Wil. "Well, he's only just met you."

Wil only smirked and shot his glance to one dead body, then the other. He let the situation speak for him. He turned his gaze hard upon the man. "What is your name?"

"Calder," the man told him. "Barret Calder."

Brayden shot Wil a keen, startled glance.

Wil only sighed, wondering why he wasn't the least bit surprised.

"The Temple, then. Hurry."

They didn't venture out into the street but hobbled along some of the same alleys and pathways Wil had traveled with Brayden mere moments ago, taking twists and turns that wound toward the more prosperous residences, to the business district, and on through the slums again. Several times they had to duck behind stray bushes or into a shadowed alcove to avoid a passerby, but by and large the way was fairly clear, the majority of the city's residents attending to their market business. Wil tried to keep track of their path, tried to remember where they'd zigged then zagged, but it only took a few minutes before he was completely lost and dependent upon the strange man who'd turned out to be surprisingly gentle as he dragged Brayden through the underbelly of Chester.

Wil watched their backs, turning frequently and scanning behind them. He even went so far as to scrutinize the ground itself, scuffing out with the heel of his boot the occasional drops of blood that leaked slowly from Brayden's wound. All the twists and turns in the world wouldn't help them if they left a trail as clear as that behind them.

As he'd watched Brayden do on many occasions, Wil scudded his glance to all points—even up to the roofs of the buildings they passed—examining every shape and shadow for threat. Shouts and whistles still reached them, but they were far off, still concentrating the search on where they'd been rather than where they might be now.

Brayden had gone notably silent—absorbed, Wil guessed, with keeping his feet moving and breathing through what was likely some terrifically acute pain. He lurched more clumsily than he'd done before, losing more blood the longer they wended about. Wil noted with dismay the spreading blotch darkening the back of Brayden's coat around the knife's hilt, and it was only likely to get worse once they got where they were going. Wil was still doubtful about not pulling that dagger out—it seemed so counterintuitive—but he wasn't sure enough of himself to go against it.

It took perhaps ten minutes. It felt like forever.

The Temple was smaller than the one Wil had seen in Putnam, though its architecture was otherwise identical in its plain, unadorned stateliness. The man—Calder, Wil made himself acknowledge—led them past several doors around back, helping Brayden carefully down a small stone stairway hidden beneath a tangle of dead vine and bracken and winding down below the level of the alley to a damp, moldy landing in a recess so dark and deep it was almost like stepping into night. A thick, squat wooden door slouched at the bottom, small enough that Wil wondered how they were going to manage to squeeze Brayden through it. Wil kept alert, sweaty fingers twitching nervously around the trigger of the gun. If betrayal was imminent, it would come quickly and from the other side of that door.

The cloying scent of incense was the first thing to hit Wil when the door creaked open. The suspicious look of the narrow man on the other side of it was the second. Wil almost smiled—now *this* was what he'd imagined a shaman should look like.

The lean form was backlit by a low torch sconced in the damp stone wall behind him. His hair was brown and longish but combed back from his severe face and tied at the nape with a small length of plain leather. A very basic brown robe was worn open and slung over simple woven tunic and trousers. The only things remarkable about the man were the warmth that bloomed beneath the hard suspicion when he recognized his guest, and then the genuine concern he aimed directly and immediately at Brayden.

"Oh, save me, what've ye brought me this time?" he chided by way of welcome. He swung the door open wide and gestured them anxiously through.

"Brother Shaw," Calder greeted the shaman, "I've brought you trouble as I've never done before." He angled Brayden through the door first, then gestured over his shoulder for Wil to follow. "It would do us all well if no one learned of our presence. You'd best get your kit."

Shaw didn't argue or hesitate, merely headed toward a darkened doorway arched in stone. Along the way he plucked a torch from its sconce on the wall, carrying it before him and gesturing them all after. Calder nodded and made to conduct Brayden through, but Brayden jerked to as close to alertness as he'd been since they left the alley and pressed his hand to the wall to stop them.

"Wil." Concern and confusion both. Brayden tried to turn his head, but the pain must have been lacing throughout his whole body, because his movements were stiff and clumsy.

Wil stepped around to save him the trouble. "Right here." He tried a heartening smirk. "Are you all right?"

Brayden was drawn and pale, thick, clammy sweat greasing his fringe to his brow, dark eyes peering at Wil like chary little animals from the deeping of a stygian cave, but he tried to smile back. "My fault. I'm sorry. This isn't what—"

"It's my turn on watch." Wil pushed confidence and as much command as he could muster into his tone. "Trust me."

"Watch the Watcher." Brayden puffed a weak chuckle, gaze going fuzzy and trying not to. He nodded and swallowed thickly. "I think I'm going to be sick."

"Don't do that," Calder told him, serious beneath the small encouraging smile. "It'll likely hurt like a bugger."

Brayden nodded again, blinking blearily at Wil. He let go of the wall, dropping his hand to Wil's, still wrapped around the rifle. "Keep it close. Choose you. Understand?" He peered at Wil through layers of pain, trying to clear the murk that was blurring the intensity in his eyes. "*Wil.* Understand? Choose—"

"I understand." Wil pried Brayden's great hand from around his own and shot his glance over Brayden's shoulder to meet Calder's sober gaze. Warning. He pulled up one more smile for Brayden. "The hearts of mountains, yeah? Show me that contrary nature. Impress me."

It was almost belatedly that Wil thought of Millard, of how he'd known simply by shaking Brayden's hand.

He snatched at Calder's elbow. "You can't let that man touch him." He slid a look over at Shaw, busy with preparations for surgery, then back to Calder. "He'll know, he'll *see*."

Calder merely shook his head and gave Wil's hand a light pat. "Lad," he said quietly, "Shaw is the rare man who won't see when blindness is necessary and won't ask questions you shouldn't answer. Trust him as you do me."

Wil gave him a flat look. "Are you trying to be funny?"

Calder didn't even waste time or effort on reassurances Wil wouldn't believe anyway, only smirked and went to join Shaw.

Shaw was quick and precise, bullying Calder into getting Brayden laid out facedown on a cot that was much too small for him. Wil tried to stop Shaw from cutting Brayden's coat—and his shirt and vest and trousers, but mostly the coat—from him, but Shaw patiently explained that as much of the surrounding fabric as possible must be removed so he could get a good look at the position and angle of the wound before removing the blade. Wil gave Brayden an apologetic shrug and let Shaw proceed. Brayden was nearly past protest but managed to growl his dissent when he heard Shaw mention mæting, and Wil didn't back down from that objection. They used valerian and arnica instead. A lot of it.

Wil was chided by Shaw several times—gently at first and then rather insistently—for keeping the rifle poised across his torso and himself propped against the damp stone wall, but Wil refused to be moved on either point. He suffered himself to be chivvied into a far corner only because Shaw wouldn't stop sighing at him every time he tripped over him, and because he still had a good view and semitactical angle, but that was the only concession he made. These men might be Brayden's best chance, but that didn't mean Wil had to trust them utterly.

For the most part, he watched quietly, listening to the dulcet chatter between the two men as they worked and alert for anything suspicious. But he didn't really know what they were talking about in the first place, and in the second place, the many sharp little implements Shaw was using were plenty suspicious, but they were obviously healing tools. Wil only continued to follow the actions and words carefully, assuming he'd know somehow if something began to go wrong.

After much serious discussion between Calder and Shaw, the blood was sluiced from Brayden's bared back, leaving only the knife and the small bits of fabric caught by its blade. Shaw unfolded a thin green blanket and covered Brayden's legs, then cleansed the area around the knife with water and two oils, pausing now and again when Brayden loosed a small gasp or moan. It had the feel of unnecessary ritual to Wil, but it didn't seem to be causing an inordinate amount of pain, and he didn't know enough about it to object, so he kept silent. He watched with interest as Calder removed a small carved token from a pouch on his belt, kissed it, then placed it between his palms. His eyes fell closed, hands pressed together in front of his chest, head slightly bowed. Shaw only stood over Brayden and waited, patiently eyeing Calder, with quick glances down to Brayden's face now and again.

Even in the warm glow of two torches and five oil lamps,

Brayden was still ashen, his skin going waxy, hair plastered to his face in sticky swirls of gold darkening to ochre with sweat. He appeared deeply asleep, but Wil noted the frequent twitch of a frown twisting his eyebrows, the clenching and unclenching of his fist where it lay on the cot near his hip.

Calder leaned over the narrow bed, the little charm still between his hands as he hovered them over the knife, rubbing the token between his palms in rhythm to the low chant that flowed from his softly moving lips. A healing song in the First Tongue, likely persuading the Mother to look upon Her child and send Her blessings upon the path toward healing. At least Wil assumed. Hoped.

The song wound into the silence, working itself to a low crescendo. Shaw seemed to have been waiting for it. He splayed the fingers of one hand to either side of the blade, took hold of the hilt with the other, and slowly drew it out. Brayden didn't cry out, but his fist clenched tight, knuckles white, and his jaw clamped, the muscles of his broad back contracting and bunching beneath pallid skin as he clawed in a harsh, shallow breath and held it.

Shaw worked quickly, staunching the slow ooze of blood with herb-soaked cloths, douching the wound with an infusion of oil and water. Brayden's face remained pinched and drawn with pain, scrunching into a stony grimace, his pallor going nearly white when Shaw's long fingers dipped down into the wound. Shaw's eyes closed as he bowed his head, concentrating.

Calder began his song again, different this time—more soothing than insistent, the tone more beseeching than demanding. It seemed hours went by while Shaw's long fingers worked, Calder's chanting wending into time itself, stretching it and then pressing it narrow, until the hymn finally wound down, and Calder withdrew. He was sweating and breathing hard as he tipped a weary nod to Shaw. Shaw only grimaced, jerked a quick negation, and sank his fingers into Brayden's wound yet again.

Wil watched it for as long as he could. "That's hurting him. Aren't you through yet?"

"It's deep." Shaw's eyes were shut tight, head tilting slightly to the side. "I need to see if it's hit anything important."

Wil was under the impression that pretty much everything in there was fairly important. "Well, give him something more for the pain."

The silent clenching and twitching was more unnerving than screaming would've been. Wil was beginning to feel an absurd phantom pain in his own lower back every time Shaw's fingers moved. The whole business was setting Wil's teeth on edge.

Shaw only shook his head. "I've given him enough for two men. I daren't—"

"He's the size of *three* men. Look at his face, he can feel everything you're—"

"More might kill him," Calder put in evenly. "Shall we take the chance?"

He stared at Wil, challenging; Wil stared back, fuming. If he knew a little more about all this healing business....

Wil backed down, slouched against the wall, and shut his mouth.

A small eternity later, Shaw slumped back, finally withdrawing his fingers then reaching for a clean cloth to mop up the blood. "Nothing vital." He said it more to Calder than to Wil, but he politely shuttled his glance between them a few times.

Calder loosed a small sigh, shoulders drooping.

Wil decided "nothing vital" wasn't precise enough. "So he'll be all right?"

"The blade missed all of the organs." Shaw sorted through his kit again before he came up with a suture needle. "Very fortunate.

But it was long and the wound very deep. He's lost a lot of blood, but he's very fit and should rebuild from that quickly. If we can avoid infection...." He shrugged and shot Wil an apologetic glance.

"And how do we avoid infection?"

Shaw sighed, and turned a dour look on Calder. "We hope," Calder answered.

Two shamans—one of them an Old One, the most powerful clan elders in the known world, renowned for their magic and healing skills—and they were going to leave it up to *hope*? Wil scowled. *Not bloody likely.*

"Do the—?" Wil shot a quick glance to Shaw and then back again to Calder. He stepped in close and lowered his voice. "Is the Guardian a shaman?"

Calder puffed a jaded little snort. "Lad," he said slowly, "the Guardian is *the* Shaman."

Wil nodded, satisfied, then went back to his stance against the wall. Kept watching.

He counted fourteen sutures, wincing every time the tiny curved needle dipped and pulled. It would probably leave a worthy scar, at least. Wil hadn't noticed before—he hadn't really looked—but Brayden's lack of additional scars was fairly remarkable, now that Wil thought about it. Brayden had spent eight years in the military, quite in the thick of it, from the little he'd divulged. It was strange that he was relatively unmarked. He was obviously very good at what he did Wil had been rather impressed with the smooth, curling moves in the alley, the dependence not on brute force but finesse and brains—but Wil had to wonder if it was even possible to be *that* good.

Once the suturing was done, it was all rather anticlimactic. Brayden seemed to finally sink into a heavy sleep—painless, at least in the depths of it, Wil hoped—breathing going deep and even, a slight touch of color leaching back into otherwise waxen features. Calder helped with lifting and turning while Shaw changed the sheet then wound a bandage around Brayden's torso before covering him with a thick blanket Calder retrieved from... well, Wil didn't know, but somewhere else. Shaw tried to get Wil to come away, but Calder didn't even bother to argue—he brought Wil a chair and propped it next the cot without a word.

Wil peered at Calder sideways with a frown as he sank slowly into the uncomfortable thing. There hadn't been much of a chance to even think, let alone ask questions, but now that they were here, more or less trapped in this damp basement and placing too much trust in people they didn't know, one question rose to the fore.

"Why?" Wil made a vague gesture toward his own face and let his gaze settle on the scar stretching over Calder's cheek. "It seems a little over the top for the purpose of a mere test."

"And it would be, if that were why I'd done it." Calder leaned into the wall, gaze shifting between Wil and Brayden. "Only one may venture beyond the Bounds wearing the Marks. Only one's path has been blessed." He shrugged. "We do what we must."

"It must've hurt." Wil didn't just mean physical pain. He only knew probably half of what those Marks meant to their wearers. To remove them must have been like losing a limb.

Calder merely shrugged. "We do what we must."

"Did he do it for you?" Wil jerked his chin toward Shaw, still puttering silently, flitting in and out of the close little room with fresh potions and clean water.

Calder tilted a vague little smile. "He is the only one I would trust for such a business."

Wil sighed and sagged down in the chair, feeling the events of the day settle into his bones. He'd been half expecting the pain in his hand to flare and renew itself, what with how much he'd been using it today, but it failed to throb or ache. He was glad. Considering what Brayden had been through, the residual ache of a few broken fingers seemed quite petty. The ache of an empty belly, on the other hand, was another thing entirely. Now that the anxiety was receding, hunger was starting to tap lightly. That made Wil think of the packs in the saddlebags, which in turn made him think of—

"Someone needs to retrieve the horses." Calder was just sinking down into another rickety chair and didn't seem at all impressed by Wil's sudden demand. "We left them at the temporary posts by the gates. Has Shaw got a boy or someone who could go and get them?" Brayden had put the claim chit in his breast pocket—Wil had watched him do it. He hoped no one had pitched the clothes they'd cut up. The money and Brayden's handguns were distributed through Wil's own pockets.

Calder shook his head. "They'll be watching. Can't chance it."

Wil opened his mouth to protest but couldn't come up with anything reasonable with which to negate the statement. Except that he wanted them back, but he didn't think Calder would be moved by that vague sentiment.

"What'll happen to them?"

Calder shrugged, unconcerned. "When no one claims them by the time the gates close tonight, they'll likely go to the common livery for boarding by the city."

"Where is that? We need the packs, at least."

Wil could sneak in easily, he was sure—wait 'til after dark, slip in, retrieve the packs, and slip back out again. He was good at it. He'd often suspected he'd make a good thief, should he ever decide to put his mind to it.

"Let it go for now." Calder closed his eyes and rubbed at the back of his neck. "You've come away with your lives. Let that be enough for tonight."

"No thanks to you." Wil couldn't help the bitter little growl. He glanced at Brayden, lying on his stomach, face scrunched into the flat pillow and feet jutting out over the edge of the flat mattress. Wil got up without thinking, angling to the foot of the small bed, and pulled the blanket down to cover Brayden more evenly. "What were you doing to him?" He tucked the blanket's corners around Brayden's bare feet. "He said you'd been mucking about in his head, and no one could've got behind him otherwise." He straightened to level a mild glare at Calder. "Whatever you were doing, it was cocking up his reflexes."

Calder sighed. "We didn't know where either of you had gone. We didn't know what had become of you." He lifted a cagey look up at Wil. "Nor what you'd become. I had to know."

Wil walked slowly back to his chair, and sat down. "And are you satisfied now?" He kept his voice deliberately soft and even, but a slight bit of challenge leaked into the tone.

"I know what he is." Calder nodded toward Brayden. "Better than he does, I expect, else I wouldn't've been able to touch him, let alone cock anything up." He looked down at his big hands, then angled a shrewd sideways stare at Wil. "What you are is an entirely different matter."

Wil snorted. "Is this where I'm meant to come over all weepy and spill my guts?" He hunched down in his chair, jaw clenched. He twitched his chin toward Brayden. "He knows. If he chooses to trust you with it, then I'll abide by his decision." He slanted his gaze back toward Calder, hard. "Right now it only matters who *I* trust. I trust *him*."

He let the rest hang there, unspoken.

Then frowned as the truth of the statement sank in.

Calder didn't seem to take offense, only sighed again, weary and resigned. "His magic has a green feel to it, new and largely unclaimed." A frown wrinkled his browned forehead. "He fears it, I think."

Wil thought about it for a moment, then shook his head. "He

fears very little. He denies it because his life made it necessary to disbelieve. Give him time."

"It isn't mine to give." Calder paused, faded blue gaze sliding sideways. "And you may not have it." It was quiet, no judgment.

Wil flicked out a hand, palm up, with a shrug. "When you've lived outside of time...." It was his turn to pause, discomfited suddenly that he was speaking so freely. He slouched down and looked away. "It's all relative."

"That tells me very little. And I don't mind telling you that the only reason you're a guest in the Temple and not a prisoner is because I could read *him*"—Calder jerked his chin at Brayden —"which I shouldn't have been able to do." He looked Wil over keenly, lips pursed. "Where've you *been*, lad?"

Genuine concern and distress. Accompanied by a vast question without any simple answers, regardless of the angle from which it was approached.

Wil stared at Brayden in the light of the lamps, at the steadiness of his breathing, at the intermittent flick and twitch of his eyebrows as a spasm of pain worked its lethargic way through the haze of sedatives and exhaustion.

"I think...."

Wil looked down at the rifle propped across his knees, picked at the dirty linen wrapped about his hand. Thought about how he'd walked a straight line for three years, his feet leading him inexorably even when his head tried to direct him otherwise. Thought about Brayden's commander's apparent remarks, how Brayden had fought his way into Ríocht and tried to fight on into the Guild itself. How he obviously had no idea he'd a motivation other than duty to his country.

Wil rubbed at his brow. "Seeking," he muttered to his lap, blinked up at Calder, and then quickly looked away again. He cleared his throat. "Is there anything to eat around here?"

They mustered up some cold vegetable pies for both Wil and Calder, Shaw apologizing for the lack of gravy. Wil ate them dry and with no complaints. The vegetables were tender and the crust divinely flaky, and cold filled his belly just as well as hot did. A cup of deep red wine accompanied the meal, its flavor rich and woody with a touch of smoke beneath it. It was overtly suspicious, terribly rude, and a little bit silly, considering he'd wolfed down the food without a second thought, but Wil waited until Calder had taken a sip of his wine before Wil did the same.

"We've had visitors," Shaw told them when he bustled back down to collect their dishes. "The Guard is going door to door, looking for an exile and his fey companion." He glanced at Wil with an apologetic shrug as he doused several of the lamps. "Remarkably little description on you, though—apparently no one got a good look at you."

Wil shot a look at Brayden's lax face and smiled something tired and cheerless. Well, Brayden's beard had done little good by way of disguise, but the hats seemed to have fulfilled their purpose. Wil propped his elbow on the small cupboard to the side of his chair and rested his head on his palm. *You do have your uses, Constable Brayden. Sorry they weren't terribly useful to you.*

"You're safe enough here," Shaw went on. "The Chester constabulary has no jurisdiction on Temple grounds, and we've the right to grant sanctuary, if it comes to it, though it'll be best if we keep your presence from them entirely." He waved at the doorway. "I've prepared a cot for you in the next room. Clean water for washing. I'm afraid the bathroom is little more than an indoor privy, but it'll do best if you stay down here and out of sight. The priests and initiates can be trusted to keep silent, but the fewer who know you're here, the fewer chances of mistakes or missteps."

Wil agreed wholeheartedly with the logic. He offered sincere thanks as Shaw retired, but he didn't move yet from his uncomfortable seat.

Calder, however, stood slowly, then stared down at Brayden for quite a while before he turned his sharp eyes on Wil. "Pleasant dreams." He kept his gaze even and unflinching as Wil gave him a deliberately unfriendly look, then merely nodded and quit the little room, leaving Wil alone with Brayden for the first time since they'd burst onto the road this morning.

"Is it wrong that I keep wanting to tell him to fuck off?" Wil muttered quietly. Brayden, of course, didn't answer, just twitched his eyebrows a hair and slept on. Good. Sleep was a better healer than any infusion, in Wil's admittedly slim experience, and Brayden had got sparing little of it over the past days, instead watching over Wil in the deeps of night. "My turn on watch." Wil sprawled as much as he could against the stiff back of the chair, toed off his boots, and gingerly propped his feet on the edge of the cot. The waiting cot Shaw had referred to didn't even occur to Wil. He merely got as comfortable as was possible under the circumstances and settled in for a long night.

Surprisingly, he didn't even try not to doze.

"Tell me about the gift," he asks Father. "Tell me how to help him."

Father smiles dreamily, sighs a song. "At last the binding begins." It's dulcet and slow. "Weave it well."

"I don't know what that means." He can't help the anger. He's tired of hints and allusions and nonsense advice that means nothing. "Can't you just say it, damn it, just for once?"

But Father only closes his eyes, a lone tear leaking from one corner. "You accept a cage like you belong in one, beautiful Gift."

Another sigh, this one deep and wrenchingly sad. "And yet the keys to your prison are right within your grasp."

And then He's gone, leaving Wil alone but not alone. Wil turns and looks behind him.

He's not surprised to find Brayden here, Watching as always, but he is rather surprised by Brayden's hereness, his presence, which has always before been more a part of the background and not as finely etched and clear as it is now.

Certainly no threat.

Brayden's dark eyes near blaze at Wil, urgent beneath the unruly fringe of gold. Wil is both startled and discomfited that Brayden looks just as unhealthy here as he did lying on that too-small cot—face sheened with a thin, clammy sweat, pale and wan, wide shoulders somewhat stooped. Brayden doesn't say anything, doesn't intrude, though Wil can tell he wants to, he's almost vibrating with it, but he just keeps Watching, and Wil wonders for the first time ever if it's because Brayden can't say anything, can't intrude, not unless Wil allows it—demands or requests it.

He thinks about it. For quite a long while. He's been avoiding this for days and days—they both have—and if he does this now, opens the door, he doesn't know if he'll be able to close it again. More to the point, he doesn't know if he'll want to, and that scares him quite a bit more. He's grown to like Brayden, trust him more than he should—why else would Wil have hesitated in that alley, insisted upon dragging Brayden with him, instead of taking the opportunity to run?—and he can't really explain it, but Brayden's opinion matters to him. Wil gives a shit what Brayden thinks.

Perhaps because Brayden seems to think so well of Wil, and it makes Wil childishly pleased.

Wil sighs, moving toward Brayden slowly, no longer afraid of Brayden himself nor what he might do to Wil—Brayden won't do anything harmful, Wil knows that now—but a little bit afraid of what Brayden apparently needs to tell him, show him, the urgency and asking in his eyes making Wil shiver and slow his steps. He stops just in front of Brayden, peering closely for a moment, somewhat surprised he's not nearly as much shorter than Brayden as he'd thought. Brayden looms so large in the waking world, and Wil does his best not to—he'd never noticed before that Brayden is only perhaps half a head taller than him.

It matters very little, Wil thinks, but it's interesting.

"You're here." Wil can't help the twitch of a smile in response to Brayden's tired shrug.

"Apparently...." Brayden's voice is hoarse and strained. "Apparently I'm always here."

Wil shrugs too, belated apology for previous declarations made from within tangled bitterness.

Brayden's mouth turns down in a scowl, and he reaches out to take Wil's hand, frowning at the bloodied fingertips. "Why d'you do this to yourself?"

Wil doesn't answer, just watches with interest as Brayden smooths his fingers over ragged flesh, sores closing up and healing beneath his touch, and Brayden doesn't even see it. Wil wonders if it had happened that first time but can't remember. A tiny shock goes through Wil, a twinge of power that runs from Brayden's fingers into his own. There's a slight shiver from Brayden, but he otherwise appears to have no idea.

Wil looks Brayden over thoroughly, registering the new lines spidering at the corners of Brayden's mouth, knows them for pain lines, and Wil's own mouth pinches up in worry.

"D'you feel it even here?"

Brayden sucks in a long breath, looks like he wants to negate it with a shake of his head, but ends up nodding instead. "It's bad. Worse than I thought. I may have mucked this up entirely. I'm sorry."

"You still don't understand, do you?" Wil has to smile in exasperated wonder. "You're as chosen as I am. You've the gifts of a shaman—the gift of the Shaman, I'm told—if you'd only look inward."

"I don't like to look inward. I never find anything there I want to look at."

Wil shrugs. "You might be surprised."

"And what would you find if you looked inward?" Brayden's voice and gaze are both very kind, but implacable. "I'm sorry, it'll be hard, but I think it's why I'm here. I think it's part of my job, and I can't take the chance I'll be gone before you dare it."

Wil scowls, surprised by how fierce it is, surprised by how the words hit him like an undeniable punch in the gut. "You're not going any—"

"Likely not." Wil can tell Brayden doesn't really believe it, not yet, at any rate. "But it's something I should have told you already. You need to know it, and I can't take the chance that you won't understand when you really need to." Brayden holds out his hand, palm up. "Come with me?"

He wants to make it a demand—Wil can see it bubbling behind his eyes—but he's refraining, relying on a trust that wasn't there as little as two days ago but strong enough now that Brayden feels confident in testing it. It doesn't irk Wil as he would have thought; instead, it makes him smile.

"I've nowhere else to be." He stretches out his hand and lays it lightly in Brayden's. "Lead on."

The regret is almost instantaneous. He doesn't know what he was expecting—he didn't think he'd been expecting anything—but the sensation of finding himself behind the eyes of another is intrusive and unnerving and absolutely bloody terrifying. It's only the fact that he can still feel Brayden's great hand around his, holding on, tethering—"It's important, I swear I wouldn't show you, else"—

that Wil doesn't scream and jerk away, but purposefully controls his breathing, answers "Just don't leave me alone in here," and lets himself be guided.

Wandering, searching, years and years of searching and anxiety and worry, and still his charge stays hidden—hides from him. It's deliberate, he can feel it, and he can't fathom it, but there's trouble, deep fear and pain within the knowing, and so he keeps searching, moving from one blank road to another. The Old Ones are no help— they can't find him either, lost his thread the moment they heard the final cry from the last Guardian, filled with betrayal and rage and the deep regret of failure. And now the Aisling has been waiting for nearly two decades, waiting for a new Guardian to grow and learn and train and finally come find him, but failure has marked the search from the first step.

Others have gone before him while he grew and earned his Marks—twice-brave men, for they'd taken on the calling without the blessings that would shield them, stepping into the shoes of the Guardian without the Guardian's protections, without even the barest knowledge of the Guardian or his charge. None of them have returned, all of them blank roads, and their blood cries out to him, but it's only so much noise beneath the cries and screams of the Aisling. He writhes with it—it's under his skin—and he near weeps, because he can hear but he can't see, and he tries to call out, to soothe, to beseech, but there is too much rage. It's like a wall of anger and agony, and he can't break through it. His charge will not hear him, refuses him, refuses the Mother, so he is blind but not deaf, and he keeps searching.

One name stands out amidst the cacophony of bewildered pain, but it's blurred and garbled, indecipherable, as though it's being deliberately skewed, but snarled over and over again through rage and agony and deep, dark, betrayed hopelessness. He answers, or tries to answer, calling out his own name, begging the Aisling—Just let me through, I've come to help you, the Mother hears your call—trying to break through the desperate denial, but it butts up against a wall so thick and strong it only lances back into him, choking him with his own thwarted rage.

He is hunted here in the land of his enemies, and he can't hide among them, for he has the look of the Coimirceoir. He can change his hair, can speak the language, but he can't change his size, and so he ventures among them only when he has to and only fleetingly—there and gone before they have a chance to think about why he doesn't belong. Still, his trail is followed, he can feel it. He doesn't know by whom, but if they know of him, they know of the Aisling, so he allows a slip now and then, leaves a marker.

He's close, he's been close for days now, circling around the city cautiously, hearing the cries waking and dreaming, but he couldn't determine the where until tonight. Tonight he saw. Tonight he understood.

The Turning—the one night a year when the Aisling is brought before the people, blesses them—it revealed him. They know now he Watches, and they know he's close, for he couldn't keep back his shout of dismay when the huddled figure tottered on the parapet, moved with too-obvious intent. Foolish and reckless, he'd made a run for the gates, shown himself, and beyond anything he'd imagined, he'd been recognized. They shouldn't know, they shouldn't understand, and yet he'd seen them understanding as he stood there at the gates trying to figure the best way through them; saw them recognize him even through the henna in his hair and beard and the cloak snugged 'round his hunched shoulders.

So he lets them follow, lets them believe he is unaware that the Watcher is watched. Not too quickly, or they'll know he knows, but he can't wait too long. The Aisling's pain is his own now, and his choices are few.

He allows them to come upon him in the deeps of night, allows *them to accost him. He'll give them a token fight until he sees their numbers, then take out all but one and force from him the final key. But surprise works against him, for they wear his Mark, they have power they shouldn't, and it's harder than it should be to thwart it and regain his advantage. The Mother's blessing shields him, but not enough—there are too many. He takes seven down to three and then one, his own wounds many and mostly superficial, but one leaks blood that seeps near black from just below his ribs, and he thinks perhaps it's mortal.*

He can't die, he can't—it's already been too long, and the Aisling suffers. He can't leave him here to endure through another two decades, waiting and not knowing. He staunches the bleeding as best he can, but he's weak now, tired, and the one man left knows it. The survivor chuckles, blood seeping from between his lips, down his chin, his own wound gory and open, a deep gouge down his chest to his belly.

"The Aisling belongs to us, brave Watcher," he says. "We Watch and shall have what is ours, where you have failed in your blindness. We are the Guardians now."

"He belongs to no one." It's a snarl, somewhere between pain and fury, and he clenches his teeth against both, lifeblood leaking from between his fingers. "He is his own, and he suffers—I can hear his cries, and you dare to call yourself Guardian! What do they do to him in those towers?"

He doesn't really want to know, doesn't really want to put pictures with the sounds that wind through his head. He wants to kill this man, squeeze the last breath from his throat and smile as he does it, so this pretender will know with his dying thought that the true Guardian will heed his call, will shatter whatever cogs of their sick scheme are grinding even now.

"We are called by the Father." The man spits weakly, blood and saliva making wide tracks over pale skin. "Born in the blood of your

predecessor that was fed to the Father so that He may break the bonds your Mother cast upon Him. The Aisling suffers now for his weakness, his very life a blasphemy, for he serves the Guild as he should the Father. Dúil. Elemental. He deserves no name. He rejects the Mother, and Her soldiers will not have him, but the day of the new Watchers approaches."

The man is insane, blue eyes on fire above his stolen mark. He speaks as though the Father were some ghoulish revenant wakened by the blood of fallen Guardians, and the Mother his gaoler.

"You do not speak of the Father," he rebukes the man. "You blaspheme of dearg-dur, of daeva. The Mother and the Father do not suffer either to live. It is law! You twist your own religion and make of the Mother's gift a tool for—"

He sees the flash of the knife too late, tries to cry out as it buries itself in his throat, but his own blood chokes him. He falls back, eyes wide, staring at the stars that wink and sing his thread into the weave of a shroud.

It is complete. He has failed.

"Forgive me."

He speaks it to no one but pushes it through the cracks in the wall the Aisling builds against him. The stars belong to the Father, but he reaches out to them, sings his story into their hearts, so at least they may know what happened here.

"Your Mother is dead, Watcher." The man leans over him, blots out the stars, and the knife flashes again, slashes the Marks from off his cheek. "We die together now."

The man's voice is weaker, and he doesn't know if it's because he is fading or the man is. He doesn't think it matters. He is dying, he has failed, and the Aisling is left once again bereft of his gift, tricked and entangled while his Guardian leaks his life on alien ground, this false guardian's lies in his ears.

"Mother!" his heart calls. "Hear me. I have failed in my task,

and so I call the next." He takes one last look at the stars, listens to them twine his dirge with the new song of another, and closes his eyes.

"Brayden," he gurgles through the blood pooled in his mouth, in his throat, drowning him. "Avenge us all."

And behind his eyes, enwombed in stillness as his lungs give up their struggle, enwrapped in silence as his heart beats its last, the Mother pulls his head to Her breast and weeps quietly into his hair.

Brayden stands next to him as Wil opens his eyes, roosting back into himself like tired feet into comfortable old boots, stretching against his own skin until it settles firm around him. He notices the hand first, still wrapped around his. He thinks he should be jerking back, but his reflexes abandoned him days ago where Brayden is concerned, and the whole business seems rather silly to him now, so he doesn't.

"What's dearg-dur?"

"Incubus," Brayden replies. "Soul-eater."

Wil nods, unsurprised. "You're not the first." Brayden doesn't answer him, only gives his hand a bit of a squeeze, doesn't let go. "I've been...."

He'd been living that not-life for bloody decades, tricked into believing betrayal, into committing his own.

"You're the third?"

Brayden nods slowly. "You weren't forgotten." His voice is low and soothing, like he's trying to gentle a spooked horse.

Wil can't help but put Brayden's face on those others, can't help the weight of responsibility, the guilt, the sorrow. "How do I ever atone for this?"

"You don't," Brayden says forcefully. "Fifty or more years of treachery, Wil. Fifty or more years of being lied to."

It sounds so... easy. Wil would like to believe it, except.... "Oh." He closes his eyes. "No wonder She hates me."

"Hey." Brayden's hand tightens around Wil's, squeezing hard. "If that were the case, would I be here?"

It would almost be easier if he weren't. It would almost be easier if Wil had just died back there in Ríocht, never knowing any of this.

"Wil," Brayden insists, "this isn't yours."

"How can it be anyone else's? He died because I wouldn't hear him."

"You wouldn't hear him because you couldn't. He died because he was just a second or two too slow."

A wet, humorless laugh wends from Wil. "And what of you, then? Do I get to watch it happen through my own eyes next time?"

"Maybe," Brayden answers steadily. "But this is what I've chosen."

Wil shakes his head. "You were dragged into it, you said it yourself. You had no more choice than—"

He stops short when Brayden lifts an eyebrow, a smile curling clever and knowing. "There it is. Don't take on the choices of others. You'll never get yourself from out that cage."

Wil jolts, frowning, and looks down. Thinks about cages and prisons and keys....

"C'mon, then," Brayden says, softly cajoling. "I've brought you a present."

The sound of running water sluices over Wil's senses, supple and comforting. He peers up, a tired smile curling at his mouth, though there are tears on his cheeks—someone else's grief, his own a paltry offering intertwined. He leaves them there, unashamed.

"How did you do this?"

Brayden smiles and shrugs. "It's a dream, innit?" He nods at the river. "The Flównysse. I'm not sure how precise it is. It's been years, but this is how I remember it."

"It's beautiful."

It is. The current flows clear and blue-green, rippling over stones dark and beslimed, smoothed by time streaming over and past, ages of gentle unseen destruction. Starlight sinks into its liquid furrows, placid breakers winking and swelling, then moving on, carrying a bit of night downstream in their crest and curl. He can hear the voices of the stars inside the flux and flow, humming along with the rush in almost perfect synchronicity with the tender breeze that lifts his fringe from his brow, whiffles teasing fingers through his hair, and brushes the lightest of kisses over his cheek. The horror and sorrow of a moment ago are still thrumming beneath it all, coursing along as surely as the river runs, but their edges have stopped slicing into his heart, his conscience. It allows him to look at it all with a mind as clear as the rippling water. He wonders if that's why Brayden chose this place, and thinks yes, quite likely.

He turns his face up to the stars. "They kept the tale safe." He looks back at their faces reflected bright and soft on the water. "Their memories are long, but they never dream. There is so much more I would know from them."

Brayden is silent for a moment, then: "You see why I had to show you."

It isn't a question, but it wants to be. The anxious curl of it is almost a plea for understanding and forgiveness.

"I see." Wil turns to Brayden, finally pulling his hand free, but not for the sake of discomfort. "I'm sorry."

A long sigh winds from Brayden's broad chest. "So'm I."

"I'm right to trust you." Wil almost feels like a little boy looking for approval, but somehow, with Brayden, he can't.

"I hope so." Brayden casts his glance out over the river. He looks sad. "Be careful of Calder. I don't know why, but something...." He pauses, shakes his head—perplexed, maybe, but resolute. "Shaw seems all right. If anything happens, you stay with him, you hear? If I can't—"

"Shaw is not the Guardian." Wil pushes stern command into his tone. "You said you chose this. Well, I choose you. You've dragged me through weeks of trials and persuasions, and you can't cut out on me just when you've managed to convince me you know what you're doing."

Brayden rubs at his brow, frustrated. "But I don't know what I'm doing, that's the point. I've been guessing, stumbling blind, and now look where it's got us—got you. I almost got you killed, and I don't know if I'm going to—"

He pauses and chokes out a shaky sigh. He doesn't have to finish—Wil knows what he was going to say—and Wil has to keep himself from growling derision, rolling his eyes at the stubborn insistence on standing on ground that can be seen.

Wil sets his shoulders, determined. Brayden's talking about dying, as though he's already accepting it, and it pisses Wil off. "Men died because I wouldn't see. If you won't, it may be me next time."

Brayden shakes his head. "I don't know what that means. What am I not seeing?"

"Heal my hand." Wil holds up his right hand. There were no bandages around it only a moment ago, but there are now because he willed it so. He deliberately draws the knife from his boot to slice away dirty linen, pulling it back to reveal fingers that are no longer fat and tight but still somewhat bruised, and from the looks of them, permanently crooked. His wrist is ringed black and green, with smudges of blue and yellow blooming up his forearm.

Brayden takes it all in with a frown. "What are you talking about?"

Wil takes hold of Brayden's hand, turns it palm up, and lays his own atop it. "It's a dream, innit?" he mimics lightly.

"Wil...." Brayden sighs impatiently. "I don't have magic. I can't heal. I'm sorry."

"You can conjure a river, but you can't do me this kindness?"

"It isn't the same thing. This...." Brayden waves his hand around. "It's just a dream."

Wil thinks for a moment. "If you could do anything, would you heal my hand?"

Brayden rolls his eyes. "Of course."

"Then do it. Pretend you can do anything. We'll try flying next." Brayden's scowling, his mouth twisting tight. Wil steps in close, looks up, encouraging. "It doesn't mean anything. It's just a dream, remember? Just try." Brayden is still reluctant, his face pale even here, so Wil knows the pain is leaking through, and he'd like to spare Brayden the reluctant knowing that has to come, but Brayden may well be Wil's only chance. "Take the pain away," Wil demands, insistent now. "Heal me."

Another roll of the eyes, but Brayden doesn't look like he doesn't believe—he looks like he doesn't want to believe, so he hesitates. Wil thinks if he'd instructed Brayden to heal himself, he'd still be cajoling. The fact it's someone else in pain is what moves Brayden, and Wil hides a small smirk in his collar.

He's surprised that it happens so fast; he's downright shocked at the level of intimacy—not only that Brayden initiates it, but that Wil allows it. Wil hadn't even been completely sure he'd been convincing enough, hadn't been sure Brayden would in truth try on his first go, but one moment Brayden's hand holds Wil's loosely in his palm, and the next, long fingers are clamping down, sending stinging bolts of pure energy throbbing through Wil from his fingers and all through his hand and arm, then striating throughout his whole body. He can feel Brayden touching Wil's own soul, truly feel it. And doesn't want it to ever stop. Warm and bursting with reverberant serenity. It does more than heal Wil's hand—it rocks his body and spirit in contented quietude.

It's almost orgasmic in its amity and intimacy.

It's better than leaf. Better than anything. Ever.

Wil takes a long, deep breath, unashamed that he leans into Brayden's chest until he finds his balance, lingering perhaps a few seconds longer than he needs to before he pulls back again.

He'd been a fool to ever think this man duplicitous or wicked. Nothing like this could have come from the heart of malevolence.

Wil turns his hand over, and holds it up in front of Brayden. Wil doesn't say anything, but he doesn't need to—all the bruising is gone, all the swelling, and the bones are as straight as they've ever been. A smile spreads slowly, his fingers flexing, and Wil peers up into Brayden's skeptical face, smirking.

"Remember this" is all he says.

Opens his eyes.

Brayden was already staring at him, that familiar disbelief shining overbright in his bleary, pain-filled gaze. Wil didn't say anything, didn't have to. He shucked the bandaging quickly, impatiently, eager not just for the proof it would grant, but to finally be rid of the dirty, bulky thing. He grinned when he got a look at his knuckles—not swollen, slightly twisted knobs of bone and flesh, but straight and bending only where they were supposed to. He held his hand down where Brayden could see it and wriggled his fingers.

"It doesn't hurt."

Brayden stared for quite some time. before he ventured a shaky reach, as much as he could. Wil slid from the chair and crouched down next the bed. He dipped his head and allowed Brayden to slide rough, cold fingers over Wil's cheekbone, even went so far as to guide Brayden's fingertips to trace the sockets of his eyes, still tender and no doubt as green-black as the fingers had been.

The euphoric peace took Wil again, wound through him. He came back to himself with his forehead pressed to the thick blanket beside Brayden's arm, clumsy, callused fingertips pressing into his scalp, seeking....

Wil dragged himself up, shaking his head, and smiled. "Not those." He didn't know why, exactly, only that it didn't feel right. He took hold of Brayden's hand, tucking it up to rest on the hard, flat pillow.

"Sleep now." Wil adjusted the blanket and drew back. "It's your turn." A slow smirk. "Impress me."

CHAPTER 4

W il was sitting on the cold stone floor, back propped to the wall beside the cot, when Dallin opened his eyes. The ever-present rifle was braced barrel-up to Wil's left, knife at work against a whetstone between upthrust knees. Wil's feet were bare, and he'd shed his coat. By the way his dark hair glistened in the lamplight, he must've had a bath. Dallin squinted, noted the clean clothes, and confirmed his theory. Good. At least someone had been taking care of Wil.

Dallin closed his eyes again.

Mother—strange how the entreaty came to him so naturally— *I'm sorry. I don't think You've chosen very well.*

He would've snorted and rolled his eyes at himself, but it all seemed like too much work. More than half a lifetime spent assuming it all fairy tales and legends to make old men feel better about death, and now....

Now Dallin was neck-deep in things he would have thought devotional dementia only weeks ago. Had committed his word to protecting a man who seemed better able to take care of himself.

What was Dallin even doing here? What was he playing at?

He could have got Wil killed in a grimy little back alley smelling of piss and garbage—and not by Síofra or one of the Brethren, but by petty little men who liked to use their small authority to bully and intimidate.

The low ache of the wound pulsed a dull throb through his awareness, noticeably there but not nearly as acute as he would've thought. The steady *swiff, swiff, swiff* of the blade against the stone whispered a mocking counterpoint.

Is this how your Guardian guards you?

Dallin lying here like a landed fish, and Wil armed and ever at the ready.

Yes, apparently it is. I've spent the last thirty years not learning whatever it is I need to know in order to do whatever job it is that's expected of me, and what I have learned isn't nearly enough. Save me, I'm not ready for this.

Except there was no *not ready*—he was in it, up to his arse, and so was Wil. Dallin had loftily asserted that he was Wil's best chance, had honestly thought he could think and batter their way out of this great stinking mess, and drag Cynewísan out of it with them. He almost laughed—in point of fact, he'd nearly forgotten about Cynewísan.

All right. So he was an arrogant ass.

Now what?

Dallin thought about it. Thought about it hard.

Now, he supposed, he would have to suck it up and use every tool at his disposal to pull both their stones out the fire.

As soon as he figured out what his tools were. And how to use them.

He opened his eyes again and focused on Wil's hands. The right was just a touch paler than the left, but there were no tells otherwise. Wil's fingers moved with nimble poise, stopping every now and then to flick the pad of a thumb over the edge of the blade, checking its bite, then adjusting the grip with quick, agile movements.

Well, there's that, Dallin told himself with some amount of disgust. If he managed to get Wil hurt, Dallin could always heal him again. *Whoops, sorry, didn't mean to let that one lop off your head. Here, let me see if I can fix that for you.*

This time Dallin did roll his eyes.

"Are you going to make a noise?" Wil asked quietly, hands still busy with knife and stone. "Or are you going to just keep lying there pretending you're not awake?"

Dallin sighed, perversely glad when his back and side twinged heavily with the expansion of his chest. "How long?"

Wil paused to blow a small puff of breath over the blade's edge. He held it up to the light and tilted it, examining it closely. "You've been out for almost two days." He skimmed a clever little glance at Dallin out the corner of his eye. "But you knew that."

Dallin had. Some part of him had been aware of everything that had gone on while he slept, as though he'd kept an eye on Wil every moment. And oddly, Wil had let him.

"How are you feeling?" Wil asked.

Dallin thought about it. "Sore. But...." He rotated his shoulders, gave an experimental stretch but truncated it when he felt the sutures pull. "I don't feel like I was almost gutted. I feel like I got a good kick from an ill-tempered horse, but nothing more."

"Hm." Wil spat on the stone and swirled the knife's tip in it.

No further comment, no smug *told you so.* Dallin was... grateful. It was hard enough to accept. And acceptance was fairly important in the application.

Healing. He'd never have believed it.

"You were singing." Dallin's voice was rough and grainy, but he couldn't make himself clear his throat yet.

Wil lowered the knife and looked up, his expression candid. He shrugged. "You asked me to."

"I did, didn't I?"

They'd been by the river again, Wil telling a story about the Father, saying he was translating a song the stars were singing, though Dallin couldn't hear it. So he'd listened to Wil's voice instead, asked him to sing the songs that had been haunting him for too long. Wil had complied easily and with a small smile, sang the tale of how the Father had wooed the Mother with His music and fair looks, His passion and wildness. How She'd captivated Him with Her fierce beauty and elementary honor. How They'd joined Their separate clans and marched on the old gods, their kindred, fought side by side—He with His sword; She with Her bow and quiver—took the powers away from the old gods and banished them, and led Their people out of bondage and fear. Showed them how to use the gifts of the world the gods had once wielded against them—earth, air, fire, and water—and taught them to live out from beneath the yoke of tyranny and oppression. How the people had rejoiced and placed Them on Their thrones—Hers in rock and soil; His in sky and star.

And when Dallin had asked Wil to sing him the songs of the old gods, Wil had done so, spun the histories-cum-legends in a tenor that surprised Dallin in its sweetness and clarity. The story of ugliness and violence had unwound sonorous and dulcet inside the gentle tones, taking something that should have chilled one's bones and singing beauty into it. Dallin had almost wept.

"It's Æledfýres." Dallin watched the oily light stutter over the etchings on the blade that spelled his own name. "The fire god, the one who stole the babies and drank their blood, the one who thieved men's bodies and walked around in them." He let his gaze drift up, catch on Wil's. "Whatever it was with that Watcher—the first one—and wherever the Brethren came from, it started with him."

One dark eyebrow rose. "How can you know that?"

"Dunno. But it fits. Díepe and Célnes were Her sisters, yeah? Goddesses of water and air. That's what the song said. And Eorðbúgigend and Æledfýres were His brothers. Gods of earth and fire." Dallin paused, frowning in thought. "That dream I showed you, that man from the Brethren—he said the first Watcher had been a sacrifice to the Father, that the Father had been reawakened with the man's blood. But it wasn't the Father they'd got hold of. Someone powerful, surely, and dearg-dur...." He peered at Wil. "D'you know of anyone else who fits?"

Wil looked down for a moment, thinking. He shook his head.

"Could it be Síofra?" Dallin asked carefully.

There was no flinch or flare at the name this time, only a slight pinch of Wil's mouth and an almost undetectable shudder. Wil flipped the knife in his hand, and laid it on the floor beside his hip with a muffled chitter of metal to stone.

"I'm not sure how you think I'd know that. Although...." Wil's brow twisted tight. "I've seen them both. If family resemblance means anything, I'd have to say no."

"You see *Him* every night."

It wasn't a question, but Wil nodded anyway. He'd already said as much, groused sullenly, even. Told Dallin how the Father would half wake to spout nonsense at Wil and then go away again. There was anger there, and bitterness, but not nearly as much antipathy as there was for Her, though that seemed more rueful discomfiture now, and Wil had thus far refused to lower his walls enough to let Her in. Not ready yet, and no real blame to Wil, though that wouldn't stop Dallin from continuing to push gently. Whatever they were in for, they would both need Her. And maybe Him too.

"Can you ask Him?"

Wil shrugged this time, surly. "For whatever good it'll do." He peered up at Dallin, measuring. "Can't you?" Dallin's eyebrows rose. Wil waved his hand. "You're the interrogator. You're the investigator. Shouldn't you be asking the questions?"

"Well, I would, but...." Dallin pondered it.

If Wil's inner defenses were what was keeping the Mother from him, if he was blocking Her out, as Dallin was convinced, was it possible that Dallin's own defenses were keeping him from seeing the Father? *He's right there,* Wil had told him, pointing. *He talks to me in His sleep, but He never says anything that makes sense.* But Dallin had only seen more stars reflected on the river.

Maybe it was like the threads, how Dallin had seen them as stars inside clouds, because his mind didn't know how else to interpret them. What little religion he'd been taught since his riving from Lind had been that of planting plays and Turning nights—all of it the Mother, his country's patron—so maybe he didn't see the Father because he didn't know what to look for. Had purposefully forgotten whatever teachings he'd had in his first twelve years.

You have forgotten your name.

For the first time, it made sense, so much that it brought a slight warmth to Dallin's cheeks. *From the valley.* He hadn't forgotten the words, but he'd forgotten what they meant. He'd forgotten what it meant to be a Linder.

He'd forgotten what it meant to *believe.*

Dallin hummed thoughtfully, then nodded. "I think you're right." He smiled when Wil snapped a surprised glance at him. "Next time...." Strange how Dallin just assumed there would be a next time. Strange how Wil let him. "Next time, I'll try." Dallin shifted and stretched his neck. "When is the last time you slept?"

"Too long ago," Shaw blustered as he rammed into the little room, an air of efficient *hurry up* about him, as seemed to be his natural state. Calm and commanding, the air of a military officer rather than a man of religion. Dallin paused at that, but the thought flittered away from him, Shaw's chivvying of Wil too distractingly amusing—especially since it seemed to work so well. "Come then, up with you," Shaw told Wil, before he stopped, his gaze too obviously landing on the bruises that weren't there anymore, and then moving to Wil's hand. Dallin waited for Shaw to say something—a question about the miraculous healing, perhaps, or even an accusation of illegal magicking—and wondered what he'd say in answer. But Shaw pointedly looked away, mouth pursed in disapproval, and jerked his chin at Wil. "You can help me sit this one up, and then off you go." As though he'd seen nothing at all, Shaw turned a pained look on Dallin. "Can't you convince him he shouldn't go about with bare feet?"

Relieved, Dallin only smirked and gave a slight shrug. "If you can figure out how to get him to do anything he doesn't want to do, *please*—give me the secret."

Wil rolled his eyes and stood to help. "Oh, har." His hands were strong but gentle on Dallin's shoulder. "Watch yourself, Constable." He slid down beside the cot, angling Dallin's arm across his shoulders. "I know where you sleep."

When Dallin next came awake, it was Calder who sat beside him, only he hunkered in one of the rickety wooden chairs, not on the floor as Wil tended to do. Calder didn't smile when he saw Dallin was awake, only lifted his eyebrows, reached to the side, and poured water into a mug. It was with something just shy of scorn that Calder eyed the bit of a tremor when Dallin accepted the cup.

There were all kinds of things Dallin could have said, all sorts of defenses—*The raid, she sent me away, no one came looking for me, how was I supposed to know?* He didn't bother. Calder was just as fanatical and rigid in his beliefs as those men from the Brethren were, so any negation would be a waste of breath. And Dallin didn't necessarily give a shit what Calder thought. The only person who had a right to condemn or pardon Dallin was Wil, and he'd proffered his acquittal before Dallin's failures had even been made plain—done it when he'd slipped his shoulder beneath Dallin's and tried to help him off his knees in a dim, stinking alley.

"He told me where he came by the name." Calder's gruff voice was flat.

For reasons he didn't examine, Dallin took a sniff of the water before allowing himself a slow sip, and he didn't try to hide it, either. Warm and tinny, but if there was anything else in it, it had no taste or odor. Suspicious and overcautious, but at the moment, Dallin didn't think there was any such thing. He didn't trust the man.

"Did he?"

They'd never got around to how Wil had come upon those papers. So many other, more urgent matters had crowded out their importance.

"He was a good lad. A good man." Calder's gaze fell to his hands, hung there. "Seeker."

It was said with a bit of awe that Dallin could easily share. A task at least as dangerous as what his own was to be, since the men and women who took it on did so without even knowing the dangers they faced, nor why they faced them, only that the Old Ones asked it, and so they complied.

"I didn't want him to go, but how could I ask him not to? *I?*" Calder shook his head. "It was when I felt him pass that I sent for Shaw to cut my Marks, and when they were gone, I left the Bounds and began to seek." He fixed Dallin with an even stare.

"He said he had entrusted his tale to you. That if you chose to tell me, he would abide it."

Dallin looked away.

"My son died within feet of him," Calder went on, low and with just a slight wobble inside it. "From what he says, he was running away, says he didn't know, didn't see, that Wilfred must've stepped in front of whoever was chasing him. Says he didn't know there'd been violence done until he doubled back to lose his pursuers and found...." Calder didn't choke or sob, but the emotion in his expressionless face was like a spike through Dallin's heart. "Says he didn't know, says it wasn't him, but...." Calder cleared his throat. "But Wilfred found him, y'see, found him when he didn't want to be found, and I've looked straight at death in that man's eyes. You can't tell me he wouldn't—"

"I can tell you exactly that." Dallin kept his tone gentle. "I won't tell you he isn't capable—he's more than that. I will tell you that if he said it wasn't him, then it wasn't him. He doesn't lie."

Slowly, Calder looked up, his stare trenchant but not quite wrathful. "Tell me."

Dallin did. Everything.

Calder sat staring at his hands for quite a while, tanned brow twisted in thought. Or perhaps worry. He stood with a bit of a grunt and stretched his back. Still frowning, he turned to Dallin.

"He's insane, you know."

Dallin scowled. "You've only just met him."

"I could tell you the same thing without *ever* having met him. No one could have lived through that and *not* gone insane."

"Which only makes him unique." Calder's blind surety tweaked Dallin's anger, making him indignant on Wil's behalf.

"You can't judge him by your own standards. I've spent time with him. I've seen his mind work. He may not walk the same lines of sanity others do, but he does amazingly well, and better than some whose sanity would never even be questioned." Dallin's voice was rising, so he paused and took a breath. "Look," he said more calmly, "we're talking about a person who has escaped an unhinged life, dragged off his own path before he'd even had a chance to mark it, and managed to define his own standard of sanity, against every odd imaginable. It may not be the same as yours, but that doesn't make it any less legitimate."

Calder looked at him keenly. "Your defense seems a bit... strident."

"Maybe so. But it's past time someone defended him at all. If it seems strident to you—"

"He's an addict. He still wants it. I *saw* him wanting it."

"And likely will for the rest of his life. But he didn't take it when you *oh so kindly* offered it, did he?"

"And how long d'you think that'll last? If I offered it to him right now—"

"Then you'd best hope I haven't a gun within reach." Dallin shoved that one out through his teeth. His blood was pounding, throbbing hot behind his brow. "Have you ever seen someone coming down from leaf? Ever seen them twist with muscle spasms, stomach cramps, tremors, sweats? Ever watched the agony, heard the screams? Most don't even live through it." Dallin's lip curled up in a snarl he couldn't have helped if he'd tried. "If I respected the man for nothing else, the fact that he didn't stumble out from Old Bridge and right into a leaf den would be enough. The further fact that he's been on his own for three years, living in the sorriest state of poverty *I've* ever seen, and didn't end up dead from an overdose is *more* than enough." He let his eyes narrow, allowing the threat inside them to flare out plainly. "I *ever* catch you making that offer—even talking about it to him—and *his* sanity isn't the one you'll need to worry about."

Calder's jaw was tight, his eyes hard. "Have you any idea what kind of power we're dealing with here? D'you know what could happen if that man's mind broke?" He held his hands out, palm up. "Your responsibility is not only to him."

Dallin's blood went from hot to cold all at once, dropping like lead to his belly. Calder had said it as though he was talking about putting down a dog that had gone rabid, that same righteous look in his eye as those men from the Brethren.

"You," Dallin said slowly, "are not the Guardian. You've no call or right to even *consider* it."

"And you *are* the Guardian?" Calder shook his head with a derisive curl of his lip. "You don't even know what it is."

"And I imagine you're sure you do." Dallin allowed every bit of scorn that was needling his nerves into his tone. "People like you...." He shook his head, hands clenching into fists. He wondered suddenly where his guns were, wondered where Wil was, and hoped he was still clinging to that rifle. "I've seen your sort a little too often. You're no better than any of those men he's been dealing with all his life. And I'll tell you this—the fact that he runs from people like you is the best marker of sanity I've seen in him yet. So bloody sure you *know*, so bloody sure there's only one right answer and you're the one who's got it."

Calder's color was up now, eyes blazing. "Not the only one. Generations of—"

"Generations of pious certainty, right, yes, I know. Generations of secrecy and silence that contributed directly to Síofra's ability to do what he did." Dallin set his jaw. "You and your Old Ones—when you discovered your Aisling was gone, stolen, what did you do? Did you send your seekers to the corners, check with the sheriffs and constabularies? Hire bounty hunters or even an independent canvasser?" He snorted derision. "No, you didn't—you sent men who had no idea what they were even looking for out to their deaths. *Useless* deaths.

"I lived in Putnam for almost *thirty bleeding years*—I wasn't hiding, I didn't change my name—and no one once came along asking why an obvious Linder was so far from Lind. If your search for Wil was as half-arsed, and from what I've seen I'm pretty sure it was, then you people are the last ones who have any right to question a damned thing about him, let alone presume to judge his sanity against your own insane standards."

"*You people.* Is that what we are, then? And what does that make you?"

You have forgotten your name.

Dallin shook his head.

Yeah? Well, maybe that's not such a bad thing.

He thought about Calder's question... decided Wil's words suited best for an answer: "I am what I've made myself. And Wil is what he's made *him*self. We are neither of us your creatures, and you don't get to decide to execute him because you don't like his version of sanity."

"Sometimes our responsibilities are unpleasant. That doesn't make us any less responsible." Calder looked like he wanted to hit something. "If you knew the power—"

"I've got a pretty good idea." It wasn't a lie—Dallin had his suspicions, had seen and felt the edges of that power in its near physical manifestation in that cell in Dudley and again inside his own dreams. "And the fact that he's not used it to burn the world, despite having every reason to despise it and everyone in it, should be enough proof—"

"Because *he* doesn't know his power yet! And if nothing else, I can give Síofra credit for that much—he kept it buried, and likely for exactly that reason!"

Dallin boggled. "Are you really going to stand there and tell me that anything that man did was *right*?" The very idea filled him with crawling disgust. "You know, I must say that I've wondered why the Mother hadn't just gone to one of the Old Ones, told you where I was, told you where Wil was, made everyone's lives a little easier. Now I think I see why She came to me instead."

That stopped Calder dead. "*She...?*" His eyes widened. He might have even paled beneath his leathery tan. "You've seen Her?"

It wasn't just surprise—it was *shock*. And without even really thinking about it, Dallin knew what it meant.

Calder hadn't seen Her, at least not when it came to this. Calder was working even more blind than Dallin was.

Dallin rubbed at his brow, edging *this close* to real abhorrence.

Calder spouted these things as though She'd whispered them into his own ear, and yet he had less of an idea what She really wanted than Dallin did. And Calder likely wouldn't listen if She told him.

He was no bloody better than the rest of them.

"I've my orders from *Her*." Dallin made it perhaps a bit more snide than necessary. "And you'll understand if I choose to take Her word for what She wants rather than yours. And what She wants is for me to take care of Her Gift. Which, I must assume, means I shouldn't allow fanatical zealots who think they know better to put him down because he scares them and they don't know what to do with him." He kept the glare as he sat back. "If you've a problem, I suggest you take it up with Her."

Even though they both knew Calder couldn't.

Calder was silent for several long moments of confused fuming. Dallin waited it out, mildly surprised when Calder finally uncurled hands that had gone fisted and nodded slowly. He bowed his stiff neck and placed a hand over his heart.

"Forgive me, Guardian." It was steady and respectful. "I do not question the Mother's purpose, and I should not have questioned yours." Calder's head dipped lower in sincere-seeming deference. "I am at your service."

Dallin stared. He didn't know what to say yet, so he stayed silent.

"I have assumed and presumed." Calder looked at Dallin straight. "If you cannot pardon me, allow me to offer atonement—allow me to help you prepare for what you must face. It is the best recompense I can offer."

Suspicion still knocked lightly at Dallin's nerves, but it was residual and fading. Calder really seemed to mean what he was saying.

"There is much we need to know."

Calder dipped his head on a measured nod. "There is much I can tell you."

Dallin didn't even feel it necessary to think about it. "After supper." That should give him enough time to catch Wil up on all of... this.

Calder's nod this time was low enough to pass for a bow. "As you wish." He turned with slow dignity... stopped.

Dallin was just as surprised to see Wil leaning against the doorframe as Calder seemed to be. There was no rifle hanging by its strap over Wil's shoulder; he looked strangely small and naked without it. His posture appeared relaxed—arms crossed over his chest, one bare foot propped atop the other, head tilted to the side —but his eyes were alive with sage fire, cagey and distrustful, and burning into Calder. Dallin had seen the look before. He swallowed down the rush of apprehension.

"Wil," Dallin said quietly, but Calder held up his hand.

"Aisling." This time Calder did bow. "Your servant."

Wil merely shot a dark glance at Dallin. It was fascinating to watch the brilliance in Wil's chaotic gaze dulling, calming.

"Don't call me that." Wil straightened, then moved into the room and brushed deliberately past Calder. "We'll see you after supper." Clear dismissal.

Dallin only watched as Calder nodded respectfully then quietly left the room.

The change in Calder was astounding—gone from haughty near-contempt to almost reverence with the mere mention of the Mother. It was convenient, surely, but still unsettling. Calder had accepted it, after all, with no proof, only Dallin's assertion. What might happen if someone else made a claim, just as lacking in evidence, that Wil needed to die? Dallin was telling the truth, certainly, but Calder had no way of knowing that. Would Calder believe another just as easily?

Wil stood by the bed for a moment, grimacing as he brushed a glance over the chair Calder had just vacated. Dallin recalled how Wil hadn't wanted the gate guard to touch him, and wondered if this was more of the same. It was unimportant in the scheme of things, so Dallin dismissed it as Wil peered down at him, considering. With a bit of effort, Dallin shifted his legs, then waved toward the now-open space on the small cot. Wil sank down with no hesitation, but the silence was somewhat uncomfortable.

Dallin attempted to break it with a bit of levity. "Where's your friend?"

Wil tilted a questioning frown, so Dallin smirked and gestured at Wil's shoulder where the rifle undeniably wasn't.

Wil's brow untwisted. "It makes Shaw nervous. He's been kind to me, so I thought...." He shrugged.

Dallin suspected "kind to me" likely translated into "fed me," but refrained from making the comment. And it certainly spoke to Shaw's character that Wil would part with the gun to soothe his unease. Dallin wished he'd had time to get Wil's thoughts on Calder before the last hour or so had happened.

"Where *is* Shaw?"

Wil waved a hand. "He's got patients. A mum and her little one've got... I forget what he called it. Nothing serious, but they're sick, and he didn't want them to see me, so he shooed me off."

"Shooed you off from where?"

That got a twitch of a smile. "He's got his own rooms, with a stove and everything. Calder's staying up there with him." The smile faded. "Shaw smuggled me up when I asked him if he had any books for you—you should see this place, all the back stairs and passageways. It's even more of a maze than the city is. And then he showed me how to make these brilliant little... well, he called them skillet cakes, but they were more like biscuits."

Funny, how Wil remembered what Shaw had called the treats but not the name of whatever sickness the two patients had. Dallin would have chuckled, except for the statement buried within.

Wil had asked for books. For Dallin.

Dallin was absurdly touched. "Sounds like you had an interesting morning."

Wil's gaze scudded over to the door and quickly back again. His expression went sour. "Mm." He shook it off. "And how are you feeling?"

"Amazingly well. Still pretty sore, and oddly shaky, but that's all. Well, thirsty."

"From losing so much blood. The shakiness. That's what Shaw said. You're to drink a lot of water and eat. He should be by with your lunch soon."

It made sense to Dallin. A simpler and more pleasant therapy than it might have been. "Now if I could just get some damned clothes."

Wil's glance flicked over Dallin's bare chest, then quickly to his own lap. He shifted on the undersized mattress. His mouth pinched down tight.

"Calder wouldn't let me go after the packs. And Shaw said if he gave you back your trousers, you'd just be hobbling about before you should do."

It could have been worse, Dallin supposed—at least they'd left him his drawers.

"Well, as much as I'd like to have my clothes back, and every-thing else, I'm afraid I have to agree with Calder. It's too much of a risk for you to go traipsing about the city." Dallin managed to stretch a bit without it actually killing him. "Leave the matter of the packs, all right? We'll figure something else out. You've still got the money, yeah?"

Wil nodded. "And your guns."

"Good man. If we have to, we'll just buy all new supplies. I know it would hurt to lose your things, but...."

Wil waved in a gesture that was trying to be dismissive. "I'll see what I can do about getting you some clothes."

He went silent again, fingers picking restlessly at each other now that there was no bandage to fuss with anymore. His head was bowed, hair hanging down to cover his face.

Dallin sighed. "How much did you hear?"

"Is there anyone, d'you suppose"—Wil dragged a leg up and propped an elbow to his knee—"who *doesn't* want to kill me?"

Well. That answered that question.

Dallin had an almost overwhelming urge to draw Wil in, except he didn't know if that would get him bitten for his trouble. "*I* don't want to kill you."

Wil scrubbed a hand over his face. "Well, yes." He looked over at Dallin with a small, thoughtful smile. "There's always you."

He said it like he really believed it. Dallin was idiotically buoyed.

"Wil." Dallin pushed force into the tone. "This isn't about you, all right? You can't take what he says any more to heart than you'd do with Síofra."

By the slight twitch, Dallin guessed Wil had taken an awful lot of what Síofra said to heart. Dallin cursed the man silently and violently, wondering just how deep the damage really went. He didn't fear its depths the way Calder apparently did, but Dallin worried Wil would never really be free of its echoes.

"He's an extremist," Dallin went on evenly, "with all the bigotry and mania that extremism entails." He laid a hand to Wil's shoulder. "We're going to have to handle him carefully, but it's nothing to do with you."

"Of course it's to do with me. His Aisling isn't perfect, maybe even crazy, so he—"

"*First* of all, you are not *his* anything, and don't let him treat you like it for even a second. Did you see how he bowed to you? That's who you are to him. Take advantage of it." Dallin squeezed Wil's shoulder. "Second of all, 'Aisling' is not who you are. The way I see it, it's a job, and one you're still learning. It doesn't have to be *you* unless you choose it."

Wil peered at him, dubious. "You really believe that?"

"I live it. If I didn't, I'd never have taken those shackles off you that first night in Dudley. Constable Brayden is... well, *was* my title. It's never been my name."

"You mean like...." Wil tilted his head, pensive. "Like... you've been a soldier and a constable, but you've always been Dallin?"

"Yes." Dallin smiled. "Exactly like that."

Wil looked down, thinking. Eventually he shifted infinitesimally, then leaned in just the tiniest bit. "Do *you* think I'm mad?" His voice was steady but very soft.

Dallin resisted the urge to open his mouth immediately on a sharp negation. It was a serious question—the answer would carry weight with Wil. Dallin could see the little bit of hope intertwined with rueful expectation. So Dallin paused and gave the question the careful consideration it merited.

He answered just as carefully. "I think you're different. I think what I might once have seen as madness is more just a way of coping and carrying on that I never would have thought of. The simple fact that you now and then wonder about your sanity tells me you're saner than a lot of people I know—Calder not the least of them. D'you think he *ever* wonders about his sanity, or if he's even right? D'you think Síofra ever did? The Brethren?" Dallin shook his head. "If they're all like Calder, I may want to rethink going to Lind too."

Bugger all. They were running out of places to turn. No wonder Wil had kept moving and as out of sight as possible since he'd been running.

"No." Wil said it with quiet conviction. He looked at Dallin with a surprisingly determined set to his face. "We have to go there. We have to listen to whatever Calder has to tell us, and we have to go to Lind. I need to know."

So did Dallin, when it came to it.

"He was talking about power." Wil peered at Dallin with canny interest. "So were you."

Dallin let his hand fall away from Wil's shoulder. "And this surprises you?"

"I don't know." Wil stood slowly, and distractedly took to pacing in small circles beside the bed. "Calder said Síofra buried it." He stopped and turned back to Dallin, gaze sharp. "How could he do that?"

"How are your fingers not broken anymore?" Dallin shrugged. "*I* don't know. I don't know that I *have* to know—it's happened, it's real. I imagine I should just accept it, learn to use it, and keep moving."

"All right... all right, yes, but...." Wil started pacing again. His head was down now, eyes to the floor, and his voice had gone lower. "If you'd never known, never realized...." He waved a hand around—ironically, the one that had been broken only a few days ago. "Accept it, you said. *Accept* it, like it's that easy, but if you'd never accepted it—" He stopped again, turned his back, his hand coming up to run roughly through his hair. He was breathing hard, agitated.

Dallin frowned. "Does it frighten you?"

A small, cynical laugh whiffed out of Wil. "Frighten me." He shook his head. "It frightens me that it doesn't frighten me." He turned around to peer at Dallin,. "If I'd known... if I'd...." There were tears in Wil's eyes, face screwing up in bewildered grief and anger. "Five *decades*."

Oh.... Dallin closed his eyes. Shit.

"Listen to me." Dallin took hold of Wil's arm, and dragged him in until he met Dallin's eyes. "*Listen* to me. You keep taking on things that aren't yours. You didn't know—he kept you from knowing. I don't know how, and it doesn't matter, but you know now, or you will after tonight. Because I swear, even if Calder tells us nothing we don't already know, we *will* find out what we need to know before this night is through. *Somehow*."

Dallin wasn't just saying it to make Wil feel better. He was damned sick and tired of guessing, of trying to fit half hints into blank spaces far too big for them to stretch into connections. If Calder couldn't tell them everything they needed, Dallin would... well, he didn't know what he'd do—give the dream thing another try, shake the answers out of the Father, if he had to—but enough was enough. That inner push to *hurry*, get themselves gone, was starting to knock in his chest again, chitter over his nape like there were eyes on him, just as it had been that last day in Dudley.

Wil was staring at him—head tilted to the side, brow creased, not in hostility but in concentrated interest. "So you think it's real? You think I can... you think there's more?"

"Wil," Dallin answered tiredly, "I think there's so much more that the effort of holding it back makes you bleed. I think there's so much more that if you're not very careful in how you use it, you could lose yourself."

"And you're not afraid?"

"Of you?" Dallin shook his head. "No. If you ever turn that power on me, it'll likely be because I've done something stupid enough to deserve it." He let go of Wil's arm. "*For* you? Yes, very much." He paused. "But you're not. You said a moment ago you weren't afraid. So what is this about?"

"I think I lied." Wil paced away again, bare feet slow and silent on the stone floor. He stopped halfway across the room, back turned. "Or not *lied*, exactly, but... I'm afraid but I'm not afraid, and that... it *should* scare me, except I want it, and it doesn't scare me, which scares the shit out of me."

"You want what? Power?" Dallin raised his eyebrows. "Are we talking about revenge?"

Wil turned, somewhat ponderous and deliberate, and looked at Dallin straight. "And what if we were?"

Dallin thought about it. Very carefully.

"For almost ten years, my job has been the law. And the law frowns upon revenge." Dallin shook his head. "But there are very clear benefits to, as I think you once put it, removing certain people from out the world. And I can't even pretend that I haven't got a personal interest in all this." He scratched at his chin. "If you're asking would I stop you... probably not. I don't think it's my place or my job to decide right and wrong for you. But I'd like to think you wouldn't need me to."

"What d'you think your job is?"

"To take care of you." Dallin frowned. "No—to make sure you

know how to take care of yourself. Better than you were, I mean. Watcher, Guardian... what was the other?—Intermediary—none of these names mean gaoler or keeper, and that's what I think Calder thinks it ought to be. But we agreed to do this on my terms, and I'm going to hold you to that."

"And your terms being...?"

"Wil—" Dallin sighed and rubbed at his brow. "If you've not figured that out by now, there is nothing I can say that you'll trust."

Wil looked down. "I think...." He hesitated, a slight flush to his cheeks. "I think you're the only one in the world I *do* trust."

Dallin was as close as he'd ever been to poleaxed. Even closer than he'd been after that first dream. Even closer than he'd been when Wil had knelt in the dirt beside him and tried to help him up. It was... nearly boggling in its depth. Wil trusted no one—*no one*. The weight of it should have been choking, but it wasn't. It was oddly bracing.

Dallin nodded slowly. "Thank you." He made himself stop there. Anything more would make it cheap.

Wil just flushed a slightly deeper shade of pink and jerked a small nod. "Shaw should be by with lunch in a little bit." It was mumbled as he turned and walked quickly from the room.

Dallin slumped back, turning his gaze up to the ceiling. He groaned. And wondered why he felt as though he'd just run several leagues. With a boulder on his back.

The dream this time wasn't unnerving. Merely confusing.

Dallin was back in the alley, except it was on fire this time, and he knew Wil was just on the other side of it. Dallin could hear him shouting, but he couldn't tell what Wil was saying. He kept yelling at Wil, telling him to run, get away from the flames, but the gate guard turned into the little burned corpses screeching their songs, drowning out Dallin's voice until Calder stepped through them, waved a hand, and scattered them to ash.

He knows your purpose, Calder told him gravely, *and yet he gives you his trust*. He shook his head, sadness and condemnation both. *He was weaned on betrayal—would you cage him now?* And then he held out his hand, a tiny golden frog perched in the middle of his palm, its bulbous little eyes staring bold and unblinking at Dallin.

I won't betray him, Dallin argued, stung. *I wouldn't*. But he was standing in a boat now, the river rising and roiling, and again he couldn't make himself heard. And then it didn't matter, because someone was shooting at him. Dallin's guns were in his hands, aiming at the ashes of the skeletons, when Shaw shook him awake.

Dallin didn't wake groaning or cursing. There was no point anymore. He merely blinked away the blurriness and dragged himself up to let Shaw poke at the bandages, marvel and remark upon how quickly Dallin was healing, then *tsk* and evade the question when Dallin asked if Shaw might be persuaded to find or buy him some clothes.

"Eat your supper," Shaw chastised lightly and pushed a tray at him.

Dallin sighed, tucking into the bread and the fish crusted in pepper. Wil had said he'd see what he could do about clothes, so Dallin decided to leave him to it. Wil obviously had a better rapport with Shaw than Dallin did.

He took a sip of weak white wine. "Where's Wil?"

Shaw frowned. "I don't know." He peered around the small room as though he thought perhaps Wil was skulking in a corner and had simply been overlooked. "I thought he'd be here. He's not been?"

There was no reason in the world for Dallin's stomach to dip down like it did, no reason for his mind to start racing off in every cynical direction. "No." He tilted his head. "Calder?"

Shaw waved a hand. "Never can tell with that one. Like a ghost, sometimes—comes and goes."

"More coming than going just now," Calder growled from the door, prodding a stone-faced Wil in front of him.

Dallin hadn't realized how very sure he was that something terrible was in the process of happening until he sagged with relief at the sight of them. Strange how Wil skiving off wasn't the first thing that sprang to Dallin's mind anymore.

They had their coats on. Wil's cheeks were red, and his eyes glistened as though he'd been out in the cold. And it was the first time Dallin had seen Wil shod since they'd arrived.

Dallin was almost afraid to ask, but he did anyway. "Where've you been?" And then the packs caught his eye. He winced. "Oh hell." He shot Wil a glare. "What did you *do*?"

"I did as you said." Wil's reply was brusque. He even grinned. "I took advantage."

"I *said* to let the matter of the packs *go*. In fact, I'm pretty sure those were my exact words. What part did you not understand?"

"I took care of it, all right? You're welcome. You've clothes now. Here." Wil pulled Dallin's pack away from Calder, half dragged it over to the cot, and dumped it to the mattress with a strained grunt. "And it wasn't easy." Wil shot a glower toward Calder.

Calder rolled his eyes and turned to Shaw. "Would you excuse us? There are things you'll not want to hear."

Shaw was hiding a small smile behind long fingers. "And things I wish I could." His smile curled wider, eyes twinkling. He jerked his head toward Dallin. "Make sure he eats it all. And he's not drinking enough." He flashed a crooked smile over at Wil, who gave him a bit of a grin in return and tipped his head. With a stifled snort, Shaw quit the room.

Calder wasted no time in turning on Wil. "It was plenty easy after you pulled that trick with—" He sputtered and turned to Dallin. "Did you know he could do that?" He snapped back around to Wil, pointing at Dallin. "Why don't you tell your Guardian how you've been using your magic?"

Dallin looked at Wil with narrowed eyes. *You didn't.* But the smug look Wil gave back told Dallin that yes, indeed, Wil had.

Dallin rolled his eyes. "Oh, for fuck's sake."

"To put it lightly," Calder agreed.

Dallin ignored him and looked at Wil. "Are you all right?" The last time Wil had gotten someone to bend to his will that way, after all, he'd ended up gushing a couple pints of blood from his nose.

"It was just a little push." Wil's tone was just this side shy of defensive. "I just needed the lad to tell me where the packs were and then forget he saw me, that's all."

Dallin's teeth clenched. "*Wil*—"

"A little nosebleed. Teeny tiny, it was nothing. And it wasn't like in Dudley—the boy's fine, I swear, ask Calder. Who, by the way"—the scowl Wil turned on Calder looked deeply offended —"was almost no help *at all*."

Calder's jaw tightened. "If you'd bloody *warned* me—"

"Well, if I'd warned *you*, I would've warned *him*, wouldn't I?"

Dallin was getting a much clearer picture of how events had likely played out than he thought perhaps he wanted.

"You wouldn't've *needed* to warn me if you'd just stayed out behind the stable as I told you." Calder turned to Dallin. "It was safe back there—no reason in the world for him to have followed after—but he wouldn't stay put."

Wil merely continued to scowl, flushing. "I wanted to make sure the horses were being cared for. Like I *said*." He turned to

Dallin too. "Miri's left hock was swelling, and I wanted to make sure they were putting liniment on it. And Sunny gets twitchy if Miri isn't right there, so I had to make sure they were stalled next to each other."

Dallin stared. There were so many things to be addressed in that last exchange, but the first straw he latched onto was—"You named the horses?"

"Well, someone had to."

Dallin's mind went blank. "Which is which?"

"Yours is Sunny."

Calder was rubbing at his eyes as though he was trying to keep his brain from escaping through the sockets. Wil, on the other hand, was quite proud of himself—had handed over that pack like a cat dropping a dead mole on the front step—and now had a defiant set to his chin Dallin recognized all too well. Dallin couldn't find the words he'd need to get through to Wil yet, so he turned on Calder instead.

"What were you *thinking*? I *thought* we were staying out of sight."

"We *were* out of sight. It's well past dark, and we stayed to the backstreets."

"What were you even doing taking him out in the first place? He's got a pocket full of gilders, for pity's sake. There was no need to take a risk. We could have just as easily—"

"It was my doing," Wil cut in boldly. "I told him I was going with or without him, but it would be easier if he came along. Your pack is huge, y'know." He shot another glare at Calder. "And it *would've* been easier, if Grandda here hadn't got all arsey and decided I was some kind of dimwitted bonehead who didn't know how to put one foot in front of the other without his help."

"I think you're confusing 'arsey' with cautious," Calder snapped. "A distinction you might do well to learn."

It was getting clearer and clearer with every word. Dallin could just imagine what the walk back to the temple had been like.

Wil turned on Dallin, then. "D'you think I'm helpless too?" He waved a hand at Calder. "You sound just like *him*."

"Damn it, Wil, *no*." With less effort than he'd expected, Dallin stood, then took the few steps over to stand in front of Wil. "You *know* I don't think that." It was as low and even as he could make it. "But Calder's right—you've got to be more cautious than that. I understand that what you've got in that pack means a lot to you, but do you understand you just risked yourself for what amounts to a couple changes of clothes and a few rotting apples? When are you going to understand you've nothing to prove?"

In truth, Dallin couldn't help a bit of reluctant sympathy. Calder styled himself, after all, as some sort of servant to the Aisling, and there the Aisling had been, declaring he had every intention of doing something—well, Dallin might as well call it what it was—something incredibly *stupid*, and Calder's only choice was to come along. Dallin supposed he should be grateful Calder hadn't tried to tackle Wil and chain him to a wall, though Dallin would have been a lot more grateful if Calder had done the wiser thing and woken Dallin. Who knew if Dallin would've got Wil to leave it, but his chances were a lot higher than Calder's. Obviously.

"Perhaps I've nothing to prove to *you*." Wil's voice was too soft.

Dallin slumped, suddenly feeling somehow small and... mean.

"And we *were* cautious," Wil went on, once again grabbing at confidence through what he insisted upon seeing as a job well done. "No one saw us but that lad, and he won't remember any of it."

They were getting nowhere. In this sort of mood and with Calder looking on, Wil was never going to admit to Dallin—much less to himself—that anything about this evening had been ill-advised.

"Anyway." Wil shrugged. "If we hadn't gone, we wouldn't've known about the notices."

Dallin winced. He didn't really have to ask—he rather guessed —but he did anyway.

"Notices?"

Wil gave him a hopeful look. "The drawings don't look anything like you."

Calder rolled his eyes again. They must have been close enough, Dallin reflected morosely, that at least Wil and Calder had recognized him and identified the placards for what they were —neither one of them, after all, could read.

It was only with a very determined effort that Dallin held back a groan. He decided a tactical retreat was the only intelligent strategy right now.

"It doesn't matter. We need to get ourselves gone. We've been here too long already, and wanted bills are only one more reason." Dallin sat back down on the cot and shifted his glance between Wil and Calder. "We've other, more important, things to take care of right now, and we need to take care of them before we leave here." He let his gaze rest on Calder, steady. "We need to decide where we're going."

As expected, Calder frowned, alarmed. "Surely you mean to go to Lind. I've already sent ahead for—"

"We don't mean to go anywhere until we know what we're walking into." Wil cut his glance to the chair and nodded for Calder to sit. Once Calder did, Wil stepped over to the cot, heaved Dallin's pack to the floor, and sat as well. He turned to Dallin. "You eat. I've a feeling you're going to need your strength."

Dallin's eyebrows went up. Apparently Wil was taking full advantage of this "servant" thing. Dallin couldn't say he disagreed with the logic. Anyway, Wil was the one on the line here, so it seemed only fair. Dallin gave Wil a nod, pulled the tray closer, and poked at the cold fish.

"He thinks I know more than I do." Dallin kept it low, so only Wil would hear. "Let's try to keep it that way, yeah?" He wasn't sure exactly why, but it seemed right.

Wil only gave Dallin's arm a quick subtle pat before turning to Calder. He paused briefly, then set his shoulders, bracing.

"Does it hurt you that I call myself Wil?"

Not at all the question Dallin had been expecting. Nor Calder, it seemed. Calder's brow twisted tight for the briefest of seconds before he schooled his mien calm.

"Not in the way you expect. Nor, in truth, in the way I would've expected." Calder eyed Wil with no apparent guile. "It... disturbs me that it is the only name you know. And I believe Wilfred would have willingly shared it, had he been able." Calder laid a hand over his heart. "He would be pleased, and I would be pleased, if you chose to keep it."

Wil's jaw twitched, and he swallowed, but that was the only outward reaction. "Thank you. It would please me too." His fingers wound together, clamping tight. "Have I a true name?" It was almost unbearably soft.

"The Old Ones have called you Aisling since we joined our cause to yours. The old songs sometimes name you *Coimeádaí*."

"Keeper," Wil translated aside for Dallin.

Dallin frowned but kept silent. Keeper? Of what?

Wil turned back to Calder. "I want to know what your Old Ones are to the Aisling. Why would you think it your right to kill me?"

Dallin blinked. That was certainly direct.

Calder sat back in his chair. "I would never consider it a right. Nor a pleasure. Say rather... responsibility."

"I'll say nothing of the kind. And that doesn't answer my question."

Calder breathed a leaden sigh, then stood to walk a slow circuit around the tiny room before fetching up behind the chair. He gripped the back and leaned into it.

"This"—he waved at Wil and Dallin—"has never happened before. Centuries of Watching, Guarding, and nothing so unspeakable has ever befallen our charge. Since I was ordained, my purpose, my very life, has been you. When the Old Ones heard the cries of young Devon—your first Guardian—you went silent. And so did the Mother and the Father.

"For more than fifty years, every shaman in Lind has medi-tated for hours each day—searching, seeking, praying to the Mother and the Father that They might guide us, show us. Always They have remained silent. We wondered if perhaps we had displeased Them in some way—wondered if our task was taken from us—but still, new Guardians were born. So we trained them to their purpose, sent them out, hoping, and twice we heard the death song and the new call." Calder looked at Dallin. "And then we lost one unordained. We waited and we watched, and we sent our Seekers, but no new Guardian was born to us, no call came, and still the Aisling was lost. We feared... so many things." His gaze went back to Wil. "We never guessed...."

There was a pause, strained silence, before Wil broke it with quiet absolution. "I'm not asking for apology. Only that you help me now." He leaned forward, nearly beseeching. "Tell me what I need to know. Tell me what I *am*!"

Calder's hands tightened on the back of the chair. His head dipped down, beaded braids swaying lightly amidst gray-gold. "You place me in a dilemma." He peered up beneath tangled brows. "It is not my place, and yet...." He frowned at Dallin.

Dallin hadn't noticed until now that his fingers had been busy making crumbs out of a thick slice of bread. The fish had already suffered a similar fate. He looked down at his hands, took a bite of crust he didn't really want, and chewed it slowly.

"If you're saying it's my place...." Dallin scowled down at the ruins of his supper and pushed the plate aside. He thought about this one carefully.

Calder already saw Dallin as weak. The accusation writhed in that pale blue gaze every time Dallin moved a bit too slowly or didn't cover a tremor quick enough. If Calder thought Dallin wasn't up to the job of Guardian, would he start speculating about the advantages of putting Dallin out of the way? Calder was capable, certainly. Men like him were capable of worse things—after all, one of their greatest assets was their ability to defend horrific actions with right-eous purpose. And Dallin had been thinking only a little while ago that he was in over his head, that perhaps Wil might be better served by someone who knew what they were doing.

But did Dallin want to give Calder, or someone else like him, even the slightest excuse to usurp him? This man who'd been arguing only hours ago that it might be best for the world if Wil was got out of the way before he realized what he could do?

What *could* Wil do?—that was the real question. And why did Dallin seem to have a better idea than Wil himself did?

Dallin's eyes narrowed.

He'd seen the power, touched the boundary of it. It had been worlds greater than the paltry thrum that had run through Dallin when he'd held Wil's broken fingers in his palm. And when Dallin had said earlier that Wil had yet to burn the world, Calder had responded as if it were a real possibility—no surprise, only anxiety at the prospect.

No. No, the *real* question was: what would happen to Wil if someone like Calder was there when he found out what he could do?

...if Grandda here hadn't got all arsey and decided I was some kind of dimwitted bonehead....

It wasn't an exaggeration, and it wasn't mere disgruntled grumbling.

Wil was clay to Calder—to all the Old Ones, for all Dallin knew. Calder already treated Wil like a child. A holy child, held in reverence, to be sure, but still a child. Someone to be molded and perhaps even punished if he didn't conform to tradition and legend. And when had Wil ever conformed to *anything*?

More worrying still, the argument with Calder earlier told Dallin just how severe a punishment these people were willing to carry out in the name of that tradition and legend.

"I know what the Mother told me." Dallin said it slowly, phrasing it carefully. "I wish for Wil to hear it in the words of the Old Ones."

He left it there. First lesson in interrogation: give a subject the first leading push, then sit back and wait to see if he hanged himself.

Calder merely nodded. No flare of suspicion Dallin could detect. Calder's faded blue gaze went directly to Wil and stayed there.

"You ask what you are. It would be easier to ask what you are not. Not immortal. Not invulnerable. Our people chose the Mother for our patron for Her strength and wisdom, set the Father lower because His wisdom was imperfect in your making, and yet we came to understand that it was wiser than simple men would guess at first to create a being with so much power and make him vulnerable. We came to understand that the Mother's wisdom in the making of the Guardian merely complemented the Father's. So we have kept always the Aisling safe, as the Mother intended, treasured Her Gift from Her beloved, as She does. We have guided Her gift to the Father—"

"Yes, yes, *yes*," Wil cut in impatiently. "We know the story. We don't need your version of history. You train Guardians to keep the Aisling on his proper leash, which doesn't answer *any* of my questions." He stood, pointing to the floor at Calder's feet. "You stood *right there* this morning and tried to talk my Guardian into killing me. I want to know *why*."

The look between them was almost charged, thick and nearly tactile. Dallin might as well have not even been in the room. Still, he kept his face impassive, hopefully unreadable, and only alternated his glance from one to the other.

Calder shook his head. "You have broken the laws of the Father. That alone is cause for judgment."

Wil's mouth pressed tight, and he slowly sank back down to the cot.

"You mean because he did the things he did for Síofra," Dallin tilted his head. "Except those 'crimes' were the result of *your* failure."

"And so judgment would be put aside." Calder twisted a grimace. "Which leaves us with the question of the danger the Aisling now presents to us." His eyes went to Wil again. "Do you even know what lives inside you? Do you know what's been given to your safekeeping? When I asked you if you thought we'd simply let you walk into Lind unaccosted, it wasn't merely rhetoric. Even if your intention is to prostrate yourself before the Old Ones, take up your task, and devote yourself to your purpose...." He sighed. "It may already be too late. We have never received the Gift so late. The damage may be too great."

Prostrate. Ha. Dallin thought that was likely it right there, the reason Calder's thoughts and intentions had turned so abruptly to execution—you only had to know Wil for a few moments, see the refusal to bend or submit, to know he wouldn't prostrate himself before anything or anyone. Was this the "damage" to which Calder referred? Calder spoke of being a servant, of being at their service, but what sort of service did the Old Ones think they owed the Aisling, really?

Caught and caged—was that it, then? Was Lind little more than a prison for the one they purported to serve and protect? Dallin would like to know what sort of lives of Wil's predecessors had been lived. Had they devoted themselves to their purpose willingly, or were the Old Ones no better than Síofra, snipping a child from his roots, molding him into what they deemed he should be?

"What danger am I to you?" Wil asked softly.

Dallin wished Wil hadn't. Dallin was close to knowing. He wasn't sure how, and logical explanations for the fantastic, or even the mundanely odd, had stopped being important some time ago —*what is* was what was important now.

Perhaps it was the slow absorption of the messages from the dreams finally sinking in. Perhaps it was simply the accumulation of facts and the inevitability of them ultimately starting to fall together into a readable pattern. Dallin neither knew nor cared, but he could almost feel the knowledge knocking at his consciousness, and it was big. He wanted to get it clear in his own head first, so he could break it to Wil in ways that wouldn't hurt, but he couldn't ask Wil to wait anymore—not after Dallin had taken so long to get to him in the first place, and certainly not after failing to see what so many of these capricious messages were trying to tell him in all the time after.

Do you know what's been given to your safekeeping?

Dúil. Elemental.

Coimeádaí. Keeper.

Damn it, that one had been more or less lobbed right at his

face, and Dallin had nearly missed it. Mother's mercy, Wil had made it *rain*.

So, when Calder opened his mouth to answer, Dallin spoke instead.

"You are a danger to all." Dallin waited for a beat until Wil turned to him, frowning. "You are a danger to yourself. *Coimeádaí. Dúil.*" He tapped lightly at Wil's breastbone. "You are the keeper of the strength of the old gods, and it's been suppressed for too long now. It's beating at your mind, your spirit. I know you feel it. I can see you feeling it sometimes." Dallin met Wil's gaze with candid respect. "You've been holding it back, only letting a little out at a time, and that only when you need it to survive. It needs to breathe, and you're not letting it. That's why you bleed. That's why it's so hard to stop pushing once you start. And sooner or later, it's going to break through. Break *you*." He jerked his chin at Calder but didn't take his eyes from Wil. "He thinks you can't control it. He thinks you're weak. He's afraid you'll let it loose on the world, and the Old Ones' failure will be complete."

Wil stared at him, eyes slightly narrowed, irises made of shifting verdigris. "And what do *you* think?"

"I think you are many things. But weak has *never* been one of them." Dallin shot his glance over to Calder, then quickly back to Wil again. "There's more here." He murmured it low and to Wil alone. "I need to think about this, and I need more. Just give me some time."

Dallin turned back to Calder. "Does Lind know what the Guild is about?"

"We did not know what Síofra had done." Calder lifted his chin. "We knew that they sought, but not that they had found, let alone...." His mouth tightened. "They were once our brethren, you see."

Wil stiffened, but for Dallin, more pieces fell into place.

"The Brethren—you know of them."

Calder's eyes went hard. "They are not so secret as they would like."

"Then *speak*," Wil said through his teeth.

Calder dipped a deferential nod. "It was time before time. An alliance. Before times of war for our countries, together the Old Ones and the Guild fostered the Gifts of the Mother and the Father until both were ready to take up their tasks. And once the Aisling and the Guardian left our collective borders, we would simply wait for the next call and begin the cycle anew.

"We have lost count of the years. Long before the first Brayden walked Lind's soil, the Aisling warned the Old Ones, spoke a prophecy, told us our brethren were not brothers in truth, that they would betray us, betray the Aisling. When next the call of the Aisling came not to the Guild, but to the Old Ones instead, the Guild claimed treachery. They cut ties with Lind, cast out their priests, executed some, and plunged our lands into perpetual war. The soldiers of our countries, even the generals and the elders, believe they fight for petty things—border disputes, trade routes, waterways—but always the clandestine demands are the same: *Give us the Aisling.*

"After the purge of the Guild, those who were cast out disappeared for generations until they re-emerged just before the first border war as the Brethren. Since then, we have Watched them as well. Watched as they fell from grace and degenerated into what they are today—no honor, no true calling."

"No intelligence," Dallin muttered.

Calder's mouth drew down, and he peered at Wil soberly. "I suspect young Wilfred found you by following them. Unhappy providence for him, but...." He sighed. "A link in the chain of fate, for it has brought us all here."

Providence. Fate. Dallin didn't believe in any of it, never had.

Circumstance and coincidence, and a young man who'd followed a lead that led him toward what he sought. It was more than it seemed anyone in this whole sorry scenario had possessed the brains to do.

"So, since this break," Dallin said slowly, thinking, "the Brethren have been a sort of... crazier version of the Guild, and you've managed to keep the Aisling from both of them." He paused as Calder nodded. "And it never occurred to *any* of you to put spies on the Guild when Wil went missing?"

"Our spies infest Ríocht, and we do not cringe at acquiring information through blood. The Chosen had been a fraud for centuries. We did not guess the Guild would be bold enough to present the true Aisling as the impostor. We did not guess that if they had the true Aisling, they would not have shown their hand and wiped us from the world with his glance." Again, Calder turned to Wil, hand over his heart. "They hid you before our eyes. There is no apology that would be abject enough."

Wil was just sitting there, staring. Dallin couldn't guess what he was thinking. Wil's face was a blank mask until Dallin leaned in, nudged Wil a bit with his elbow, and lowered his voice to a near whisper. "All right?"

A grim little snort puffed out of Wil, and he closed his eyes. "Can we be done?"

Dallin would rather not—he'd rather get it done all to the once —but apparently it was hitting Wil pretty hard, hard enough to begin a slide into withdrawal, and that would be damned inconvenient right now. Still, Wil was a lot tougher than he looked.

"Can you stand one more?"

Wil shrugged. "I expect that will depend upon the answer."

"Right." Dallin sighed. "Sorry." He turned to Calder. "Why Lind? What's there for him?"

Calder's eyebrows shot up. Dallin thought it had likely never even crossed Calder's mind that, now they were being more or less welcomed, they might decide not to accept.

"Protection." Calder shifted his glance to Wil, softening it just the smallest bit. "Rebirth. An awakening to your Self. Your design." He tempered his rough voice to a tone that was kind and likely as near to gentle as it got. "One cannot be reborn without returning to the Womb."

Wil jolted and breathed a throttled gasp. He was pale, wide-eyed, but his gaze was pointed toward the floor, unseeing. What Calder had said meant very little to Dallin, but it apparently meant an awful lot to Wil.

"All right." Dallin laid his hand to Wil's shoulder. "Sorry. We're done now." He shot a pointed glance to Calder. "Thank you. Give us the night, would you? We'll pick it up again in the morning."

Calder peered at Wil with something close to worry, then at Dallin with a slight touch of suspicion in his faded gaze. He didn't argue, merely nodded at Dallin, then dipped a bow to Wil. "Tomorrow, then" was all he said before he turned and quit the room.

Dallin turned immediately to Wil. "What is it? You've gone nearly white."

"Have I?" Wil leaned over, propping an elbow to his knee and dropping his head into his hand. "Just... I mean, Father... He says these things to me, and they make no sense—and I think about them, all the time, I can't *stop* thinking about them, trying to understand, but I never can. And then *he* just...." Wil's free hand came up to wave toward the door. "He just opens his mouth and it falls out, and suddenly it almost makes sense, I almost know what it means, but... but...." Wil looked at Dallin, clearly and unashamedly distressed. "But there's the Cradle—'caught and caged,' right?—and I don't know if I *want* to understand it."

Dallin could only shake his head. "I'm not sure I know what you're saying."

"I'm saying that I'm beginning to think all of this has been a waste of time. Why did I even *bother*—?" Wil's jaw clenched tight, and he shook his head. "I'm beginning to think that no matter how I interpret any prophecy, no matter where it came from or who spoke it, whether they were lying or telling the truth, they all come down to the same bloody thing, and there's no getting away from it."

Dallin frowned.

The interesting thing about Wil.... All right, there were many interesting things about Wil, but the *most* interesting thing was how he believed in bloody *everything*. For all Wil had lived through, for all the surface cynicism, he talked about things Dallin had always thought of as myth and legend as though there was no question whatsoever. Even having seen and spoken to the Mother Herself hadn't depleted Dallin's healthy doubt and—he'd like to think—his reasoning. Wil had been given every reason in the world, and then some, to distrust magic, and yet here he was, accepting the words of a shaman he'd never met before and erstwhile prophecies spoken by, for all they knew, ancient lunatics.

Wil was—incredibly, implausibly, and against all sense and reason—an idealist. With the widest, most contrary streak of fatalism Dallin had ever witnessed. An idealistic fatalist—what the hell was Dallin supposed to do with *that*?

He scratched at his chin. "I've no idea where this came from." He gave Wil's shoulder a light squeeze. "But in my experience, the truth of a prophecy is in direct proportion to the sanity of the one who believes it. *Anything* can be twisted about to mean something if you try hard enough."

"And what if I gave you a prophecy? Would you believe it?"

Dallin paused. Yes, he probably would, in fact, but now was not the time for such an admission.

"Is this about what that man said in Dudley? 'Caught and caged'? Did something Calder said remind you?" Dallin waited, but Wil didn't answer. "All right, think about it, then. Hasn't that one already come to pass? I did throw you in a cell, after all. But let's don't forget I let you out. So that one's over and done, yeah?"

It made perfect sense to Dallin—so much, in fact, that he was rather proud of himself for thinking of it so quickly.

But Wil's eyes squeezed shut, and he rubbed at his forehead.

"You're to be my end, you know."

It was said so calmly, so matter-of-factly, that Dallin had to repeat it to himself a few times before it would make sense. And then he couldn't help the flare of old rage. He shoved it back, let his hand slip from Wil's shoulder, and made himself respond with unruffled patience.

"We've been through this. I refuse to be what—"

"I've *seen* it! Did you think you scared me close to pissing my pants back in Putnam merely because of your size?" Wil shook his head, mouth turning down into a bitter grimace. "I recognized you. And I don't just mean that you looked like a Watcher should look —I recognized *you*."

Dallin opened his mouth to object, but Wil cut him off.

"You know it's true. You know it, because I saw you recognize me too. And then I saw you bury it. I saw you willfully disbelieve it, and you've been willfully disbelieving it ever since." All the fire went out of Wil. He sagged. "I thought I could use it, use *you*, until you finally let yourself see it—and I reckoned you *would* see it eventually, because... well, because that's how prophecies go. I thought I'd use you to get away from those men, and then I'd get away from you."

Dallin thought about that at some length, didn't bother trying to deny it—not even to himself. He *had* recognized Wil the moment he'd seen him. He hadn't known what to make of it then, so he'd brushed it off, attributed it to salacious tricks, to Wil's eyes, to Dallin's own strange fascination....

Wil looked away, eyes glistening but still somehow dull and tired. "None of it matters now."

Dallin thought about that too, thought about making calm arguments, offering objective logic. But what came out was a low growl between his teeth—"The *fuck* it doesn't!"

Absurdly, Wil chuckled—something dark and dry and utterly devoid of humor. "I'm sorry." He scrubbed both hands roughly over his face, then blinked over at Dallin. "I know how all of this sounds, and I'm only making it worse. But when I say it doesn't matter.... It doesn't matter in the same way anymore." He frowned sharply. "I meant it when I said I trust you. And I know when you give your word, you keep it. So I'll ask for it in this last thing—don't leave me alive inside a cage."

Again, Dallin had to think about the words, analyze them, fit them into shapes in his mind that made sense. It only took a second this time before the anger snapped all through him, swiffing across a network of nerves like the crack of a whip, twanging every last one of them.

What the fuck? Just what the *fuck?*

He stood slowly, then just as slowly paced the width of the small room, pausing to stare at the wall for a moment, trying to breathe evenly. His fist came up, slamming at the stone, before he even realized he was moving. He wheeled about and turned on Wil.

"You son of a *bitch*."

"I've no one else to ask!" Wil cried. "What if it's all some trick? What if the Cradle is the trap Síofra always said it was? According to Calder, a whole bloody *lot* of what Síofra said was true. For that matter, what if we never even get there at all? What if Síofra or the Brethren catch us first? Is that how you'd see me live?"

It hit Dallin like a punch in the gut, leaving him winded. "What the hell *is* this? How did we get from nonsense prophecies to... *here?*—and in the space of thirty bloody seconds!"

"Thirty seconds for *you.*" Wil's tone had turned derisive. "C'mon, Constable, you're the detective, you're the one with your feet locked in your quickmud. Look at me and tell me you're as shocked as all that. D'you think this is a new thought for me? Except before, I had no one I could trust enough to ask, no one who... who *cared.* I've been looking at you over my shoulder all my life, *waiting* for it. I'm not asking you for anything you're not bound to give."

The warble of Wil's voice, the grayness of his face—it should have made Dallin stop, calm himself, think it through, but he was too caught up in his own indignant outrage.

"How many times—" Dallin had to pause for a second, because he was actually *snarling.* "How many times do I have to prove I'm no danger to you? It was lies, *all* of it. Those things Calder said—don't you know what it means? Síofra knew about Lind, he knew about me. He never needed you to find me—he had you do it because he knew it would make you afraid of me. There is no reason—"

"That isn't what—!" Wil bent over his knees and took several long breaths. Slowly, as though the entire world had just been set on his shoulders, he got up, stepped over, and stood in front of Dallin. His gaze was steady.

"I'm not accusing you of murder." Wil's eyes were brilliant and glittering—bleakly despairing but far too composed. "I'm asking you for a mercy." He stooped down, and pulled the knife from his boot. "Here. If there is no other way, you'll put this blade through my heart and twist, or even put your hands 'round my throat if it comes to it, snap my neck—"

"*Stop!*"

Dallin's arm shot out, knocking away Wil's hand. The knife went clattering and skidding across the stone floor. Dallin just watched it for a moment, marking the flash of golden lamplight on honed steel as it fetched up against a corner of the doorframe. It was too far away, the lettering much too small, but Dallin would swear he could read the blessing etched on its blade as though it were written in fire. He looked away, let his head fall back, staring at the ceiling and trying to slow his breathing. He hadn't realized his back was to the wall, hadn't realized he'd retreated as Wil had advanced. There were very few things to which Dallin had ever given ground in fear, but *this*... this was making him recoil and almost cower.

Wil meant it—every word. He was, in all sincerity, asking Dallin to be his suicide—

No. Not asking. Wil just said he'd seen it, knew it would happen anyway. He wasn't asking for something he was sure was already coming—he was absolving Dallin before it came.

It should have been darkly touching. It was, after all, probably the most profound show of trust and regard possible, and from someone who almost never showed either. It was, instead, enraging.

"I should hate you for this." Dallin was seething. "Did you have no thought for me once your corpse dangled at the ends of my hands?"

And what of that? Why, when that particular image rippled in his mind's eye, did Dallin suddenly feel like he might drop to his knees and weep? When had Wil gone from a pain-in-the-arse renegade to someone Dallin would sincerely mourn if he were suddenly not here anymore? Damn it, had Dallin gone and gotten attached to a man who suffered no attachments?

Fucking sentiment. It really was going to be the end of Dallin one day.

Wil was silent for a long time before he finally cleared his throat. "No." And again. "No. I didn't. I'm sorry."

"Well, you ought to be." The anger was subsiding to a low simmer in the shadow of Wil's subdued sadness. Dallin took hold of Wil's arms, shook lightly. "I've seen you give up before. But you only give up until you realize you *can't* give up, and then the badger shows its teeth. Whatever this is...." Dallin's hands tightened unintentionally, and he had to willfully relax his grip. "Wil, I understand what you're saying, I do, but it isn't the time for this. You haven't even lived a real life yet."

"I'm not even sure I want a life anymore." That exhausted defeat Dallin had seen back in Putnam was creeping into Wil's dull gaze, the slump of his shoulders. "I can't stand the.... It *hurts*, I can't.... It's all full of knives, knives everywhere, and they'll never let me live it."

Dallin blinked to keep the sudden flare of emotion from leaking out his eyes. "A month ago you said you had a life wish as deep as the sea."

"A month, a year, a thousand years...." Wil laughed, hollow and humorless. "Well... I may have changed my mind." He swiped tiredly at his eyes. There were tears on his cheeks. "Is it so cowardly?" The misery and pleading in Wil's gaze made Dallin want to look away, but he didn't. "I can't go back, and I can't go on to something that might be just as... I *can't*." He puffed out a small gasp through throttled tears, dazed and hopeless. "Save me, I can't take *more*."

He meant it. Dallin heard it in the threads of Wil's ragged voice, saw it in the tears that still tracked from eyes gone desolate—

saw the despair, the misery, plain and so real it thumped in Dallin's own chest. Damn it, Wil had been so confident when he'd walked in with those packs, so proud. He'd been almost bloody *shining*, and now....

Again that silent, hollow cry of loss moved through Dallin, that image of Wil's lifeless eyes staring at him from above Dallin's own wide hands. Then the betrayed, agonized shrieks of one trapped in endless torment.

The treacherous knowledge of which would be worse.

"You're not going back." Dallin made it a vow, quietly fierce. "And if you want my word so badly, I'll give it—I won't see you caged. I won't let it happen, and if it comes to it...."

He stopped, clenched his teeth, the quiet hope in Wil's eyes almost more than Dallin could stand.

"If it comes to it...?"

Dallin shut his eyes. He pushed Wil back and let go of his arms.

"A bullet is faster. And less painful for us both."

Long silence, thick and nearly choking, then Wil's cold hand reached for Dallin's, squeezed.

"Look at me," Wil said softly, "and say it again."

Mother save or damn him, Dallin did.

He hadn't thought he'd sleep, almost thinks he didn't, but there's the river, and there's Wil standing over it, staring down into its rushing depths. Dallin wonders what he sees down there, wonders if Wil can hear the reflections of the stars as well as the stars themselves, and wonders if their songs are any different.

He remembers thinking Wil beautiful once as he'd stared, shock-still, into Wil's eyes for the first time. Dallin allows himself to think it again now as he watches the breeze lift dark silk from a clear brow, watches peace spread over the face that had looked at him before with misery and asking. Wil should always wear that smile. Dallin wishes he could give it to him, wrap it up in a bow, offer it in the palm of his hand like a promise.

"You can't give smiles," someone had told Dallin once. He thinks it was Corliss. "You can only give reasons for them."

He used to be surprised by how tall Wil is, but he isn't anymore. Now he thinks Wil's not nearly so tall as he ought to be, ought to tower over the world, though Dallin knows the strength and beauty on the inside don't always manifest in the physical. Still, though... Dallin can't really imagine Wil looking any other way. Can't imagine he would want him to.

Dallin rubs at his eyes. He sighs and shakes his head.

Fucking sentiment.

"Weft and warp." A whisper in a low tenor.

It might have startled him, coming from directly behind him like that, but the tone is dulcet and musical, soothing all by itself, like its own song, so Dallin only turns, curious. Several things at once occur to him:

He knows exactly who it is before whom he stands. Knows exactly where Wil got his dark hair and fair skin and that sad, tilted smile. Knows exactly where Wil got those eyes and the burning life inside them.

Huh, Dallin thinks abstractly as his glance takes in the smooth cheek, so that's why he never has to shave. You made him in Your own image.

He is Wil refined, polished. Tall enough to touch the moon, and yet somehow Dallin looks Him in the eye. He is elegant twilight personified, with all the power and majesty of the stars. He is perfect complement to His beloved. Night to Her day. Star to Her sun.

Only somehow, for all His beauty, Dallin thinks the bit of the

Mother in Wil—that earthy humor in his eyes, the occasional winsome artlessness—is more beguiling. Dallin wonders without guilt if that's sacrilegious.

He dips his head. Bowing and kneeling hadn't seemed the way of it with the Mother, and it doesn't seem to be the way of it now either, but respect is the way of it with Dallin, so he settles for the low nod.

"You're dying." Dallin hadn't meant to say that—certainly not by way of greeting—hadn't even really been aware he owned the knowledge until it tripped out his mouth. But now that he's said it, he doesn't really need confirmation. He knows it. He can smell it.

The Father merely sighs, shifts a slight shrug, and waves a pale, long-fingered hand at the sky. "They begin the weave of my shroud. But they do not yet sing my dirge."

Dallin frowns and turns to look at Wil. Wil looks back now, shifting his glance between Dallin and the Father, but he doesn't move from beside the water.

"You should tell him." Dallin turns back. "He thinks you sleep. He thinks you won't help him."

The Father's eyes drift to Wil, turning just as sad as the Mother's had done. "And would you have me tell him that my hope lies in his hands?" He shakes His head. "Too many burdens."

"Yes," Dallin answers boldly, "I would tell him. His strength is nearly bottomless, but he grieves for the wrong reasons. Do you think he wouldn't help you if he knew?"

"On the contrary, I have no doubt that he would." The Father sighs again. "Apples and potatoes. He accepts a cage like he belongs in one."

Dallin blinks to hear his own words come out someone else's mouth—this Someone Else.

The Father's image flickers before Dallin's eyes, winks out for the briefest of seconds, then flashes back into focus again. "Time is short." His voice is a little lower than before, the smooth tenor going slightly weak and tinny. "Hear me, my brave gift. Your heart is true. Do not second-guess it. You have the soul of a Guardian and the mind of a constable—follow them both. No fate is unchanging. No destiny is set."

He flickers again, dwindling to a glint of intense eyes, before wavering back into clarity.

Dallin frowns, thinks about it, brow drawing down and twisting. "It's Your brother, isn't it? He's doing something to You, taking Your strength, and it's killing You. You're not even here."

He's a dream within a dream. What was that Wil had said?

"Have you noticed that Aisling means 'dream' and not 'dreamer'? Isn't that strange?"

And then Dallin's attempt at reassurance thrown back at him with casual cynicism—"And what makes you so sure you're real?"

Dallin stops thinking about it before his mind trips and falls down. He doesn't know what it's costing Him to do this, but it must be a lot—to sap the strength of a god....

The Father smiles—delighted and open—so very much like Wil that Dallin almost smiles back, but it seems wrong somehow, so he doesn't.

"There," He says. "You feared She had not chosen well. You would doubt even the word of your Makers." His smile is approving. "Your own convictions disprove your doubt." He nods toward Wil. "His choice is what matters." He fades, almost transparent, then regains His substance. "He chooses you. I would have you see to it that he continues to choose himself as well. Our fates are joined, but mine is not his to save. You've more than one calling, Shaman."

And then he's gone, winks out without so much as a faint gleam to mark that he'd been there. Dallin blinks and frowns. Not quite as cryptic as Wil's experience, apparently, but still Dallin *wonders why They seem loath to just come right out and say things clearly. If he ever gets hold of one of Them again, he's going to ask.*

He puts it away to ponder later as he turns and walks through tall, frosted grass until he fetches up beside Wil. Wil doesn't look up as Dallin approaches, just tilts his head back, peers up at the stars.

It's strange how natural it's become, Dallin muses. He doesn't groan and gripe when he finds himself here anymore; Wil doesn't flinch and back away from him. Dallin never would have thought it.

He doesn't speak first. He's not sure why, but it seems wrong to him. Intrusive. If Wil wants Dallin's input, he'll surely ask for it—demand it, more likely, Dallin thinks with a small smile—and if he doesn't, well. Dallin will simply Watch. The most basic right a person should have, Dallin believes, is solitude inside one's own head, so he gives Wil the choice to reach for it.

"We are their children." Wil slides a look at Dallin, then jerks his chin at the sky. "We're all made of stardust, you know—forged in the crucible of their hearts. Our world is not the only one. Sometimes I can see the shadows of others inside their songs."

Dallin's mouth twists. He considers that silently for a long while, then decides it's just a little too big for him. Wil, with his open mind and vast belief—things like that are for him to know and see. Dallin will just let Wil know it for both of them.

"He's sick." Dallin's voice is unintentionally hushed, but he doesn't make any effort to amend it. "He's not sleeping, and He's not disregarding you. There's something wrong with Him."

Wil snaps his glance at Dallin, frowning.

"He didn't want me to tell you," Dallin goes on. "He said you've enough burdens, and I agree, but I thought you deserve to know."

Wil is silent. He drags a hand through his hair, pushes it from his eyes, stares down into the water. Dallin catches a faint glimmer at the corner of his eye.

"Thank you," Wil whispers, trying to thwart the tears.

Dallin hadn't realized he was going to do it, but his arm slips around Wil's shoulders, relaxed and natural, as though he does it all the time. Wil doesn't pull back, so Dallin leaves it there.

"Too much has been kept from you." Dallin tightens his grip. "This grief is a clean one, and yours if you choose to hold it. It's not His right to keep it."

Dallin cringes at the boldness, but it's nothing he wouldn't've said to Him directly if given the chance. Even gods can be fallible, Dallin knows that now, and he really doesn't think this one at least would strike him down for knowing it.

"I never...." Wil shakes his head, quickly swiping his sleeve across his eyes. "It keeps... sneaking up on me." He peers up at Dallin, eyes luminous as they always are here, but somber, the burning somewhat muted. "You see me." It comes out low and mildly confounded.

Dallin raises an eyebrow. "Well, of course. You're here, aren't you?"

"That isn't what I mean." Wil looks away again. Slowly, as if he doesn't really know how to do it, his head tilts to rest on Dallin's shoulder. "It doesn't matter. I'm just... glad."

That's all the sense Dallin needs. He smiles, sighs, then turns his gaze out over the river. He hopes it still looks the same, hopes Wil has a chance to stand beside it and watch it like this—peacefully and with gladness in his heart.

They stand for quite a while, just looking, listening, the breeze flicking strands of dark hair up to brush against Dallin's cheek. Wil is warm against him, loose and relaxed, so much so that Dallin is disappointed when Wil stirs, pulls away a bit, and turns. The disappointment turns to puzzlement when Wil reaches up, lightly takes hold of Dallin's shirt, and tugs... turns to astonishment when Wil drags Dallin down, kisses him.

It's warm and soft, but firm, Wil's mouth gently insistent. Dallin hesitates for only a second, molding his mouth to meet it, holding back a small groan with all his will when Wil's hand slips to Dallin's nape, pulls him in. Deep and close to imperative. Dallin hears a low hum from Wil, answers back with a shaky one of his own.

It's a dream, Dallin tells himself dazedly. No harm done, it's just a dream.

And then it's over, Wil drawing back, laying a light brush of lips to the corner of Dallin's mouth as he pulls away. Dallin has to restrain himself from following after.

His chest has gone tight. Breathing is more of a labor than it should be. He stares down at Wil. "Why did you do that?"

Wil just smiles. "I wanted to see what it was like."

Is that all? *Dallin wants to ask, but instead he says,* "And what was it like?"

Wil grins this time. "It was nice." *And then, like the Father before him, Wil's gone, leaving Dallin blinking at empty air.*

Empty air, and a river that isn't real, and stars that sing, and other worlds inside them, and gods, and magic, and....

It's a dream. That's all.

"Nice," *Dallin echoes, laughs, because yeah, yes, it really was. He shakes his head.* "Holy fuck."

He had to really think about it to figure out where he was when he opened his eyes. Dark, the faltering gutter of a lamp wicked too low, the faint damp smell of mold overlaid with antiseptic.

Right. The Temple. Chester.

Not standing by the river. Not kissing Wil.

Kissing Wil.

Dallin scrubbed roughly at his face.

What the hell had he been thinking? Then again, thought hadn't exactly entered into the equation.

A dream. It was just a dream.

Maybe it really was. How was he supposed to tell the difference anymore? Maybe Wil hadn't really been there at all. Maybe the whole thing with the Father had been merely Dallin's buried wish to confirm his own theories, and the whole thing with Wil had been....

Shit, shit, *shit*. What *had* the whole thing with Wil been? What the hell was Dallin doing making Wil an erotic player in Dallin's apparently too-active imagination? Was Dallin a deviant and he'd just never known it before?

It had been too long, that was all it was. Dallin thought back, trying to bring to mind the last time anyone had touched him with intent. Corliss's brother, that night she'd introduced them at her birthday party, and it hadn't lasted long after....

Mother's mercy, had it really been more than a year ago?

Dallin flung an arm over his eyes. Groaned.

Kissing Wil.

"Holy. *Fuck.*"

"You're awake."

It was low and sonorous, gravid.

Dallin jolted up, almost not even noticing the sharp pinch and flaring burn of the still healing wound, and pitched his glance to the doorway.

Backlit by the sconced light in the stone passageway, Wil's lean silhouette slanted against the frame, hair disheveled and loose shirt open. Smudges of low torchlight slipped fingers of gold and carmine through black hair, smoky flame flicking slower than it should over skin pale as the moon, but all Dallin could see was *eyes*. Wil stood there, staring at Dallin for what seemed years, waiting for invitation, maybe, then, when Dallin remained mute, pushed away from the door, prowling silently across the small room. Wil merely looked for a moment, measuring silently, before one leg came up, flung over Dallin's hips, and Wil was kissing him again, pushing him back into the hard pillow.

It wasn't a dream this time. The body against Dallin's was solid and real.

Reaction shot right through him, and he arched just a little, groaned when Wil responded by pressing down, shifting, digging his fingers into Dallin's shoulders.

What the hell are you doing? This isn't a dream, you can't do this.

Long fingers slipped into Dallin's hair, spangling little tingles leaching from them and flushing hot over Dallin's skin.

Yeah? Why the hell not?

Without thought, Dallin's hands came up, slid inside Wil's open shirt, fingers tracing ribs that were well padded with muscle now, sliding around to track the dip that plunged just below the knobs of the spine. Dragged Wil in tighter.

Wil hummed, pulling back slowly, like he didn't really want to, and looked down at Dallin through the darkness, breath light and fast. The fitful light spattered one side of his face, gilded its angles. A small, pleased smile lifted one corner of his mouth.

"Why did you do that?" Dallin bit his tongue too late.

What a stupid question. What did it matter, really? This was a man who reached for what he wanted with no compunction or shame, and what he was reaching for right now was Dallin. Did Dallin really want to argue?

Wil's smile curled wider. "I wanted to see if it was different."

"An experiment?" Dallin almost snorted, but curiosity got the better of him. "And was it?"

Wil's fingertips slid over Dallin's whiskery cheek. "It was nicer without. You don't have it over there, y'know."

Dallin hadn't known that, but he didn't pause to worry about it. "No?"

"No. But this will do."

Without even a moment's deliberation, Dallin decided the beard had outlived its dubious usefulness. He smiled as he tugged Wil back down.

"I'll shave it in the morning," he promised, then pulled Wil in close and kissed him again.

CHAPTER 5

He'd wanted it. He'd wanted it, so he'd taken it. *Life.* A moment of stillness. Forgetfulness. Pleasure, where there was so little. An empty mind—all heat and motion. Oblivion, however temporary. Uncomplicated animal desire.

Except he hadn't expected the animal to... *purr.* A low, rumbling growl somewhere inside him he'd never known existed, and now that he knew, he wanted to shove the thing back into its shadowed den, send it back to its winter sleep. And maybe cut its throat while it slumbered.

He hadn't expected the sweetness. The intimacy. His own failure to back away from either. The refusal to blush at the sounds that had been wrung from him, the eager asking that wound from his throat, raspy and demanding. The willingness to allow those wide hands to guide him into an arrangement of bodies and limbs that wouldn't tear at sutures, and then rock into it all with as close to abandon as he'd ever been.

It wasn't as profound as when his fingers had been healed—it was the intent behind the intimacy that was different. Real emotion. Authentic caring. *Then* he'd backed away. Kept backing away, even as he hung on, bare limbs entwined, watching him sleep, choosing to keep his own eyes open. He didn't want the river, and he didn't want to have to refuse it, so he stayed on this side of dreams.

Dallin.

He tried it silently on his tongue, pressed his lips together.

You've never called me by my name, he'd said... after.

Wil had already been distracted, trying to drag himself from the morass of alien emotions skidding through him, so he'd just let his mouth take the lead: *Would you like me to?*

No one calls me by my first name. Soft musing in the dark, slowly, as if it was a revelation even to himself. *Even the Tanners call me Brayden, or just lad. Not even Manning.* And then he'd turned and pierced Wil with a weighted stare. *Yes. I'd like you to.*

It was like boulders on Wil's back, that stare, but he'd juddered a smile, said it for him—*Dallin*—and grown inexplicably warm and light-headed at the slow curl of a smile he'd got in return, discomfited by the way the name coiled around his tongue and tripped off it so easily.

Sleeping now, perhaps even waiting for him. Wil stared at—

He shut his eyes, teeth clenched.

Dallin. His name is Dallin. You can do him that one courtesy, considering. It's only a name, after all.

Wil stared at Dallin now, wound around Wil's body on the too-small bed, Dallin's grip the only thing keeping Wil from slipping to the floor. Contrarily freeing in its constriction. A slow ache bloomed in Wil's chest, bucking against the hold and burrowing into it at the same time.

Wil sucked in a low breath that shook just a little, despite him. Just looked.

Dallin was... well, he really was quite handsome. Features in perfect proportion—straight nose, strong jaw, kind mouth, dark, intense eyes, wonderfully wide and fit. Anyone who looked at him, regardless of any bias, would have to acknowledge his general attractiveness. The breadth and strength that had been so intimidating once had abruptly turned intoxicating. Sweeter and more generous in the intimate dark than anything Wil had ever experienced—and his experience was hardly limited—and yet the carnal *power* had nearly taken his mind.

Dallin had asked once what Wil slept with men for, and Wil had answered truthfully if not wholly. He'd never slept with anyone for money. Not out of any kind of absurd moral conflict, but because accepting money from the wrong person could mean a quick arrest and immediate induction into a workhouse if one couldn't pay the fine, so Wil had never taken that kind of chance. For survival, though, he'd take any kind of chance, and one night of allowing another to grunt atop him for a while was now and then a fair exchange for not freezing to death.

Anyway, it wasn't as though Wil didn't get his own gratification out of it. Everyone generally got what they wanted, or at least what they thought they wanted. And when someone like Orman showed up...? Well. That was an entirely different sort of survival, but the solution was just as effective, if not more so.

Give them what they think they want to keep them from taking what they don't know you have.

It made Wil shudder, made Dallin shift restlessly in his sleep, so Wil pushed it away.

Perhaps this had been survival of a different sort. Survival of the soul, though that sounded a bit melodramatic. Certainly there had been the physical fascination, but that had barely entered Wil's consciousness before now. He hadn't felt an actual want... *need*, until....

His head was starting to pound. *That isn't a headache; it's your brain trying to claw its way through the stupidity.* He pushed his knuckles into his eyes, pressed hard.

Sorry. I'm a user, didn't you know? I'll use you to make sure I don't get exiled from my own mind, and I'll use you to make myself feel better after having extracted the promise. Just because you happen to honestly care doesn't mean anything, doesn't alter your usefulness. In fact it rather enhances it, doesn't it?

So why did it set every emotion Wil possessed—and some he hadn't known he possessed—into some kind of gyrating spasm?

Because you mean to betray him, and you both know it, and he's going to let you, and you both know that too. And it won't make him stop caring, and that's... it's like....

Like a chain around his neck—constricting, cutting off breath, making it clench in his chest like a mailed fist wringing the juice from a ripe berry, sweetness spilling over cruelty, making the ache of it burn bitter and darkly gentle.

Damn it, all Wil had wanted was to *forget* for a little while.

Slowly, trying not to jostle or disturb, Wil sat up, and peeled himself from out the wide grip. Eased himself from the tangled bedding, tangled limbs, and collected his clothes by the guttering light. Tried not to look down at the sleeping face, tried not to see too much.

Dallin. His name is Dallin.

He had the air of the lonely sort about him. Not in a morose kind of way, or sad-eyed and breathing soulful sighs. The sort who preferred his own company, the sort who chose partners who appealed to his intellect as well as his nethers, someone who didn't seek out a recreational tumble.

The sort who needed a shared evening to Mean Something, who would be prudishly offended if offered an empty tryst... the sort who'd be hurt to realize he'd just had one.

If this evening was any hint, Wil judged somewhat bleakly

that Dallin's last encounter had likely been a while ago—he'd been so bloody *intense*. Dallin would likely be horrified to receive an offer of a tup in exchange for a warm spot to sleep. And then he'd give up his warm spot and hand it to the one who'd offered... and then sleep in the rain, if he had to, just to keep another from selling his soul.

Wil expected his cheeks to flame, but they remained cool.

Because you haven't sold your soul, you bloody stupid idiot— you've gone and given it away. Don't you know you need it?

He plunged into the trousers, and threw on the shirt. Still looking and trying not to, still planted to the spot and trying to walk away.

He should have run. He should have taken off that first day in the rain.

And now it was too late. Now he was caged in a way he'd never even imagined.

"Damn you," Wil whispered unsteadily, trembling with things he didn't understand, didn't want to know about.

Damn you for making me glad your eyes will be the last thing I see. Damn you for making me so bloody sorry for it too. Damn you for making me wish there could be more. Damn you for being so sure there could be.

And damn you, damn you *for showing me what hope is.*

Wil scrubbed at his face, surprised and chagrined that his fingers came away wet.

"Sorry," he whispered, though he wasn't sure exactly what for, then turned and made his blurry way out of the room.

His own little hovel in the makeshift cellar surgery wasn't much of an improvement, though he was alone there, so there was that.

Alone with his thoughts, such as they were. More like a centralized chaos, but still. Wil's and Wil's alone.

The bed was rumpled from when he'd more or less flung himself out of it, and arrowed down the damp stone passageway, aiming for what his brain had been shouting against but his body had been altogether too eager for. And bugger if he hadn't got exactly what he'd thought he'd wanted.

He didn't climb back in. The too-new remembrance of what had been tumbling through what passed for his mind when last he'd left it was just too... something. Raw. Instead Wil just sat in the dark, on the floor, back propped to the cold iron bar that supported the small cot—twin to... the other. Same damn sheets, same damn blanket, same damn hard pillow, except this one didn't smell like—

"Just stop it." He clenched his teeth. "It wasn't anything. You've more important things to worry about."

Dallin.

"Put it away, put it *away*, think about—"

Father.

He drew his knees up, propped his elbows atop them, and rubbed at his temples.

"Why would You tell him and not me? Why would *She*—?" He rubbed harder. "What is it about me?" he whispered, harsh and angry. "All my life, and... and somehow he sees and You don't, and what am I supposed to do with...? Did You just assume I'd go to pieces, go insane like Calder thinks I...? I'd be no use to You then, I expect."

Not that he was much use now.

There was this word people bandied about—love—talked about it sometimes as if it was the beginning and the end, the only reason to be or do, or not be or not do. Wil had seen what he assumed to be love in the eyes of Dallin's mother as she'd dragged her cold fingers across his cheek and made her request. Had seen it in looks exchanged between parents and children, husbands and wives, friends and companions. He'd seen it but hadn't ever held it, understood it, wanted it, because he'd seen its imitation in the eyes of too many, mere lust and greed trying to hide behind it but never quite succeeding.

He was pretty sure there was nothing he loved. He grasped life and freedom because he didn't know how not to, but he'd never really had either, not yet, at least, so he couldn't love them. Anyway, there wasn't much to love about them, at least in his experience. Both were too costly, and the price just kept getting higher.

He loved Father, though. Or at least he assumed the hurt and grief at hearing the things Dallin had told him were some form of love. Perhaps it was merely selfish fear. What was Wil supposed to do, after all, if He suddenly wasn't there anymore? Would Wil wink out too? The world? Was all this running and agonizing and fear for nothing? Was any of it going to matter in the end?

"Stupid question. You know it doesn't matter, at least not to you, and your end is coming a lot quicker than you'd like to believe. And it only gets closer, the faster you run." A growl and a quick jerk of his head. "Why am I even bothering?"

And what of Her? Shouldn't She be doing... *something?* The Father's warrior-goddess, patron to shamans and healers—shouldn't She be using Her own magic? Was that why Father couldn't help Wil?—because She wouldn't help Him?

.... Couldn't?

"She's a bloody goddess." It scraped upward from the anger simmering in Wil's chest and ground out through his teeth. *"Couldn't.* Right."

He scrubbed at his face.

Maybe He hadn't told Wil because there was nothing Wil

could do. Maybe He'd told Dallin because there was something Dallin *could.* Maybe... *maybe....*

"There's always got to be a sacrifice, hasn't there?" The whisper was harsh but not as bleak as Wil would've thought—more cold and detached, resigned. "Is that what I am? Is that why he's here? Some sort of reciprocity for the blood of that first Watcher? Balance out the scale?"

"Devon" came from the door, quiet and steady.

Wil wasn't even startled. He peered up, marked the broad silhouette leaning in the doorway, the failing torch just barely limning features set frank and measuring.

"His name was Devon—your first Guardian." Dallin flipped his hand out, waved it, then crossed his arms over his chest. "It means 'defender.' In case you wanted to know."

Wil hadn't. He let his head drop to his arms, folded across the tops of his knees. "I want to be alone." He winced at the coldness of the dismissal. "I want.... You need your sleep."

"When you're alone," Dallin told him, the barest hint of a smile in his voice, "there's no one about to poke holes in your conspiracy theories. You talk yourself into all manner of dire scenarios, every one of them some evil plan to bring about your end." He paused. Wil could almost feel the piercing gaze cutting through the darkness, flaring into his chest. "So, what was that before?" Dallin's tone was mild this time. "Hedging your bets?"

It made Wil's head snap up and his eyes narrow, strangely indignant despite... everything. "I didn't hear you complaining. Or protesting."

Dallin shrugged. "What man would?"

You would, Wil thought but didn't say. Because he knew, he *knew* Dallin wasn't nearly so unaffected as he was pretending. Trying to make it easy for Wil, maybe, because that was just too... *Dallin.* Trying to make Wil believe that everything he did didn't hurt everyone around him in some way. That when Wil chose himself for the last time, it wouldn't live behind Dallin's eyes for the rest of his life.

Wil's hands fisted.

Why couldn't Dallin have been a selfish bastard like everyone else? Why couldn't he have been a monster?

Why did he have to make Wil give a fuck?

Wil set his jaw. "What do you want?"

"I wanted to know why you were apologizing."

"You were awake." Wil didn't know why he was so surprised— the only time he'd ever seen Dallin sleep deeply enough not to jerk awake at the slightest noise was when he'd been drugged enough to make his teeth swim. "How long have you been standing there?" And why was this great lummox of a man the only one in the world who seemed able to sneak up on Wil? And how much had Wil said aloud?

"Too long." Dallin was staring at the floor, his tone distant. "Not long enough. Something in the middle." His head came up, gaze once again slicing the darkness. "All of this...." He waved a hand between them, then raised it to encompass... well, the universe, for all Wil knew. "It would be so much easier if you'd just be straight with me."

Wil almost laughed. *Straight.* Was there such a thing? Everything had its little hidden passageways and trapdoors—even straight lines had their crooked little flaws, if one looked closely enough.

"Is there something you want?" Wil couldn't help the impatience, overfaced and starting to quiver just a little.

Dallin didn't answer right away. "What do I want?" He shook his head slowly. "You do ask big questions." He shifted against the doorframe, scratching at that stupid beard. "I want you to know that I understand."

Wil puffed a jaded chuckle. Sure he did. Maybe he wouldn't mind explaining it to Wil, then.

"Terrific. Thanks. Good night, Constable."

"It's got to be a difficult thing," Dallin went on quietly, "to ask of someone what you've asked of me, and then come to understand that...." For the first time, he faltered. "You don't think so, but it's better that I... care." His voice was hushed and somewhat uneven.

Wil closed his eyes and dipped his head back down to his knees.

All right. So Dallin did understand. Which made this... really fucking hard. Why did he have to keep making it so *hard?*

"I'll choose me." Wil lifted his gaze, found the low glimmer of Dallin's, and held it. "Right up 'til the end. And I won't care if it's a betrayal. Someone with a gun to your head, or you with a gun to mine—it's all the same. Someone's going to end up with a bullet through the brain, even if I have to pull the trigger myself."

"You say that like you think I didn't already know it." Dallin didn't give Wil time to respond. "I need to know—was... before... was it merely to... seal the deal?"

Seal the deal. Wil would've laughed if he didn't think it would come out a watery sob. A pact made not in blood, but in something Wil hadn't even known he was giving, hadn't even known he'd had. And oh, save him, he hadn't *wanted* to know.

Dallin had been wrong—a lie would be so much easier than being straight. Somehow, Wil couldn't make himself speak it.

"No." He nearly choked on it. "I...." He wanted to bow his head, look away, but he couldn't. "I wanted it. And I knew you'd let me have it, because... because that's what you keep doing, you keep... *caring,* and I don't understand it, but I took it anyway, because that's what *I* keep doing. I didn't mean for it to be... wrong."

"And was it?"

Again, lies wouldn't come. "No. Not for me."

Wil left the *probably for you* unspoken—Dallin was sharp, surely he'd pick up on it.

"Then might I suggest," Dallin said, "that we don't waste whatever time we have?"

Wil shook his head. Damn it, was Dallin really going to make him *say* it?

"I'm using you. I'll keep on using you, as long as you'll let me. And then I'll use you some more. It's what I do."

Inexplicably, Dallin snorted. "I know you believe that. But you also believed once that I'd find great pleasure in killing you." He paused for a moment—not nearly long enough for Wil to process the implications. "You forget that... that I *see* you."

Wil finally allowed himself to look away. He slid his fingers into his hair. "And yet you keep looking." It stung, and he didn't know why.

"Wil." Louder, with a touch of command. "Look at me."

Reluctantly Wil peered up from beneath his fringe.

"You're borrowing trouble. It won't come to it. I won't let it."

If anyone could make that statement truth, Wil reflected bleakly, it would be this man. And yet, no one and nothing could. Wil could argue the point, use some of that reason and logic Dallin was so fond of, but the interesting thing about Dallin was that, for all his quickmud, once he believed in something, the belief became a fundamental part of his being, unshakable.

No... that wasn't right. The belief was there, but buried, held hostage by the sentinels of reason and logic; one merely needed to stymie the sentries to let the belief loose.

And right now, for whatever reason, it seemed Dallin had chosen to believe in Wil.

"I'm going to get you killed," Wil whispered, small and strangled. "I may even end up doing it myself."

And he wanted to hate Dallin for making him give a damn. Except he couldn't.

There's your betrayal, Constable. And it appears I'm not strong enough to gentle the coming blow.

"I don't believe in fate." Dallin's gaze was hard, stubborn. "I don't believe in prophecies. You don't need to believe in anything but yourself. And me. I know what I'm doing now, Wil. I know what this is about."

It made Wil's eyes grow hot. He meant to demand explanations, answers to questions he'd never dared ask, but when he opened his mouth, "All right" was all that came out of it. Resigned. Defeated. Simply and profoundly unable to take another second of misery and all the other tangled emotions twisting in his chest.

Like he'd been waiting for permission, Dallin finally pulled away from the door and took two cautious steps into the room. Stopped. Held out his hand. Waited.

Wil only stared for a long moment, wound tight and vibrating. Some part of him knew exactly what was being offered, and... *wanted* it. Another part was dubious as to how to take it, backing away, *afraid* to take it, sure it wouldn't be there when he reached for it. Sure he wouldn't even recognize it or know what to do with it if he did manage to take hold. Sure it would only make everything hurt more.

But oh... he'd already sipped the sweetness of that pain. A crueler addiction than the leaf, and it had only taken the one taste.

He stood very slowly, almost hoping Dallin would grow impatient, withdraw his outstretched hand with a thwarted scowl, and stalk away. Dallin didn't—he had no end of patience, it seemed— still waiting there when Wil finally gained his feet, staring at the wide hand that had only a little while ago dragged strained cries and hungry whimpers from him... gentled him and held him while he flew apart from the inside out.

Wil took Dallin's hand. And then he stepped in close, took the embrace. Took the comfort inside it.

This was his cage, right here, and he'd gone and walked willingly into it after all. Dallin had said Wil would never get himself out, and Father had said Wil held his own key. Both couldn't be true, and damn it, Wil didn't want to care. He wasn't even sure he knew how.

"The hearts of mountains, remember?" Dallin whispered into Wil's hair. "I'm not done impressing you yet."

Wil juddered out something that was trying very hard to be a sob, but he forced it into a weak laugh instead. "Stop giving me hope. It just isn't funny anymore."

"Hm. Someone once accused me of having no sense of humor." Dallin gave Wil's shoulders a squeeze and pushed him back. "Oh, right, that was you."

The chuckle that rippled out of Wil this time was real, though still a bit watery and rather subdued.

"We're getting out of here." There was more directive in Dallin's tone than before. "I wish I'd thought of all this a few hours ago—we'd already be gone. Now we'll have to wait out the day and leave once it's dark again."

Wil frowned. "Thought of all what?"

"Ah." Dallin dipped a nod and stepped away with a quick scrub at his hair. "About that." He turned back to Wil. "I should apologize. It should have dawned on me before, but...." He waved his hand. "Distractions and blind alleys, and every other diversion meant to throw a hunter off track. I've taken so damned long to come around to it that now I'm.... Well, I've decided to blame it on the tree to the head. Or the lack of sleep, come to it. Getting stabbed didn't help." He peered at Wil with sincere contrition. "Something's coming." If it weren't for the fact that Dallin's voice was so calm, Wil might've given a little start. "I can feel it, and it's close. I mean to be gone before it gets here, but in the meantime, there are some things we should talk about, and I want to do it without Calder hovering." He paused. "Now, or after you've had some sleep?"

Wil rubbed at the back of his neck. "That's kind of a stupid question."

Dallin nodded as though he'd expected exactly that answer and was entirely satisfied that he'd got it. "Right." He made to turn for the door and stopped. "I'm going to put on a shirt. Light some lamps, will you?"

"The thing is...." Dallin's fingers absently traced a crease in the sheet. He hesitated for a moment, thoughtful, before he went on, "The... *shape* of this thing is a lot simpler than I've been thinking. I kept coming at it as though I needed to... well, to use an apt metaphor, needed to find dozens of threads and figure out where they wove into the greater pattern of the mess, then untangle them. Except it's not really a mess."

They'd pushed the little cot against the wall, both of them now using the cold stone for a backrest, the blanket and the more or less useless pillow stuffed behind them as buffers. Wil wondered if the relaxed posture of Dallin's extended form—long legs spilling over the side of the small bed and stretching halfway across the floor—was something new, or if Dallin had looked like this before and Wil just hadn't allowed himself to see it. Rumpled trousers, beltless and so slung a bit low, shirt loose and mostly open; Wil could just see the top of the linen still wrapped around Dallin's muscled torso above the stretched "V" of the opening, a light thatch of curly gold fanning above it. Wil remembered slipping his fingers through that little bit of a ruff, remembered how that wide hand had rested warm on his hip, setting a rhythm that—

That line of thought would do nothing but distract him, so Wil pushed it away. He realized Dallin was staring at him, silent and measuring.

Wil cleared his throat. "Sorry, I'm listening."

"Are you sure you don't want to—"

"No. Now."

Dallin looked down at his hand again, then slowly pulled his gaze back up to meet Wil's. "Some of it will likely be difficult to hear."

Wil shrugged. "Isn't it always?"

This seemed to satisfy Dallin. He nodded, bent one leg up at the knee, and rested his arm loosely atop it.

"It didn't dawn on me until after you'd slipped out earlier. It was sort of strange—I was lying there, and I wasn't sure if I was asleep or not, I thought maybe it had all been a dream, and then I heard you curse me, and then I heard you apologize, all murky-like, and then I wondered if *you* were a dream. Everything just...." Dallin flipped a hand out. "It just tumbled. *Clicked.* All at once. One moment I didn't know, and the next it just started to fall into place—everything. Well, all right, nearly everything. I think." He paused, pensive. "I realized.... Do you remember saying once that you thought it was strange that Aisling means 'dream' and not 'dreamer'?"

Wil nodded slowly, wary now. Something had just curled cold in his gut. "You said I was borrowing trouble." His words were measured, a faint note of accusation he didn't think he really meant beneath them, and it was as though he almost knew why, wanted to know why, but wanted to get up and back away just as badly. "You said translations are always getting bollixed."

"I did." Dallin's mouth went a bit tight. "Except in this case, it's not bollixed translations that are the problem—it's the near complete lack of translations in general. You—the Aisling—it's all been kept so deeply secret that it's like...." He shook his head impatiently. "It doesn't matter, and I don't want to get too far from the point. The point is.... Wil...."

Dallin stopped again, hands going fisted before he realized what he was doing and visibly forced them open. Whatever it was he was trying to get 'round to saying, it must be pretty bad.

The anxiety simmering in Wil's chest was starting to bubble and pop in reaction before he even knew what he was supposed to be reacting *to*.

Wil dipped his head, drew his knees up, and wrapped his arms about them. Drawing himself inward and not even trying not to.

"Please." So much smaller than Wil would've liked. "Just say it."

Dallin sucked in a long breath and laid his big hand on Wil's shoulder. "Earth, air, fire, water. That takes care of the four, but what about their kin, the Father and the Mother? What do they hold sway over?"

What was this, a test? Wil's brow twisted, guarded. All his defenses were suddenly quivering, chewing into his nerves with sharp, panicky little nipping teeth.

"The Mother... healing. Cultivating and reaping. Comfort and nurturing. Protection." Wil flickered a look at Dallin. "War."

Dallin nodded, somberly encouraging. "The Father?"

"Music." Wil's voice was going wobbly, fainter. It was coming, he knew it was coming but *didn't* know it at the same time, and if he let himself, he'd know *what* was coming, and he didn't *want* to know, not ever, but the answers wouldn't stop forcing themselves from out his mouth. "Harmony of the seasons. Beauty. The stars...." His mouth kept working, but his voice abruptly abandoned him.

Dallin leaned in close and wrapped an arm around Wil's shoulders. He dipped his head down and spoke low into Wil's ear.

"Dreams, Wil. He dreamt you into life. Aisling means 'dream' because that's what you are."

Everything went hazy for a moment, gray and muffled. It wasn't a surprise—that was the problem. Wil had known. He'd known forever. He just hadn't *wanted* to know. Because if he knew, that would make him... it would make *everything*....

Pointless. Nothing. All the pain, all the fear... it wasn't even real. Wil wasn't anything but someone else's nightmare.

Without even realizing it, Wil jolted, tried to jerk himself up and away, but Dallin—clever, shrewd Constable Brayden, damn him—had once again been several steps ahead, had got them twined in a position that made it difficult to move, let alone bolt. Dallin's arm locked around Wil's shoulders, curling around and pressing Wil into his chest, Dallin's mouth right next to Wil's ear.

"Listen to me." He whispered it, urgent. "You can't take it literally. It doesn't make you not real. It doesn't make anything empty. It makes you more real than anyone in the whole of the world. You weren't some chance get of random-man-and-random-woman—He wanted *you*, and He set out to make you in the way of His own making. Haven't you ever noticed how much you look like *Him*? He gave to the Mother everything She loved about *Him*. And then He took that dream and made it real." Dallin squeezed tighter. "You're real. It hasn't all been for nothing."

How could he just... *know* like that? How could he speak these impossibly wrenching things and take the knives out of them with only the power of that low, soothing voice?

"Then *why*?" Weak and watery, and Wil hadn't even meant to say anything at all. Every dark thought in his head had just been articulated in that calm basso, strangling him with rationale when all he wanted to do was scream in panic.

Dallin was silent for quite a while, just holding on, before he sighed and ran his hand firmly up and down Wil's arm. "I think the question is rather 'how.' And as soon as it's safe to let you go, I'll tell you what I think the answer is."

Wil squeezed his eyes shut tight and shook his head, only slightly piqued but a lot confused that he didn't really want to be let go at the moment. "Just *say* it."

"You're shaking."

"I'm going to be throwing up in your lap pretty soon if you don't just get on and *say it.*" It wasn't an exaggeration—Wil's stomach was roiling and thumping along in rhythm with his heart, which was in turn trying to drum itself through his rib cage. Surely Dallin could feel it?

"All right." Dallin gave Wil another reassuring squeeze. He sat back, dragging Wil perforce with him, sucked in a long breath, and blew it out slowly. "It's really just a matter of finding Point A and following the path logically. Point A, in this case, is the Father and whatever's wrong with Him. I mean, think about it—who could subdue a god, after all?"

Wil pondered that for a moment, bit back *How the fuck should I know?* and tried to approach it from the side of reason and logic.

"Another god." Wil opened his eyes, narrowed them, and stared at the creased weave of Dallin's shirt in the folds gathered in the crook of his elbow. "Æledfýres. Dearg-dur."

"Right," Dallin agreed. "Wherever he was, is, whatever, someone found him and woke him up, and I'm betting it was Síofra."

Wil dragged himself up to peer at Dallin closely. "What makes you think that?"

"Because the simplest answer is most often the correct one. I think I forgot that for a while. But think about it—thousands of years, these people looked for the Aisling, and then Síofra just stumbles over you? Before you were even born?" Dallin shook his head, a cagey look of cynicism flashing quick-fire over his face. "Even the Old Ones couldn't find you, not unless you wanted them to—they have to be called. And if Síofra had the kind of magic he'd need to do it, he wouldn't've stopped at subduing yours. Someone told him. Most likely the same someone who's... well, I don't know—weakening the Father somehow."

There were several things to be addressed in that. Only one twanged sharp little razor teeth and set them gnawing at Wil's gut.

"Subduing mine?"

"Ah." Dallin rubbed at his mouth. "Right." His other hand was still resting on Wil's shoulder; now it tightened a smidge—a gesture surely meant to be reassuring, but Wil was beginning to recognize it as a nervous habit, a harbinger, which wasn't helping his own anxious state. "This isn't exactly my area of expertise, and I'm still stumbling a little blind here. But what you've got, Wil... it's huge. Don't you know that? Can't you feel it?"

Wil looked away. This was the hardest part to accept, the part that... *hurt*. Offended. Scraped at what little sense he had of right and fair and clawed it raw.

"Hey." Dallin's hand on Wil's shoulder tightened again, then shook lightly. "*Hey.*"

It was the first time in quite a while that Dallin's touch felt heavy. Wil couldn't help it—he shifted a shrug and flinched out of the grip.

"No. I can't feel it."

Wil wanted to feel it. He wanted to touch it, tame it to his hand, direct it wherever he pleased, and... and do what?

Burn the world, as Calder feared? Cure it? A little bit of both? Perhaps aim it at a select few and never have to run again?

"Well," Dallin said slowly, more cautiously than before, "we're going to need to change that. Soon." The mattress dipped heavily to Wil's side as Dallin shifted. "We're going to test it. And then we're going to keep testing it, and you're going to learn to use it, so if we end up coming up against Síofra or anyone else who wants to hurt you or take from you... well. It won't be so easy this time."

Wil paled—he actually felt it. He stared at his hands as they clenched tight in his lap.

Easy.

"What was the word Millard used?" Dallin went on. "Design, right? He said you were blind to yours, that you wouldn't be able to see it until you were ready. So we need to get you ready. Because I'd lay down just about anything that the dreams, the threads—that isn't what you're meant to do."

Before he even knew he was going to do it, Wil sprang from the cot, lurching the few steps across the little room. He came up against the opposite wall all too soon, so he just propped an elbow to it and leaned in. It was abruptly hard to breathe. Through a whining buzz in his head, he heard the cot creak.

"Wil? Are you all—"

"*Don't.*" Wil flung his hand back, warning, acidly satisfied when the creaking stopped abruptly. *Touch me right now and see how fast you lose the hand* rattled at the back of his throat. He choked it off, shook his head, and laid it on his forearm. There were too many things shrieking in his mind, too many questions, too many answers he didn't want, too much anger and fear, and fear of the anger, and all of it clogged in his chest. "There was nothing bloody *easy* about it." Nearly a wheeze, forced past the scalding blockage in his throat.

"I know that. I wasn't—"

"There's nothing bloody *easy* about knowing it now. How d'you know? How d'you know *any* of this? How *can* you.... I don't... *how*—?"

"Because, Wil, it isn't normal to *bleed*. It isn't normal to be in pain all the time. You work your fingers bloody because it's too big for you. It's not your job—it's *His*. When Síofra made you change the patterns, it hurt you because they're not yours to change. You said it yourself." There was a quick pause before Dallin's voice edged sharper. "Who told you it was your task? Was it the Father? Or was it Síofra?"

Wil shook his head. "I don't *know*." Damn it, he was getting awfully bloody sick and tired of repeating that phrase. "No one. Neither. It just...." He pushed away from the wall and turned, slumping back. "It's how it's always been. It's... it *was*... it was the whole *point* of—"

Again Wil bit it back, pushing into the wall as though he was trying to physically recoil from the words themselves. If they were never spoken, perhaps they'd never be true.

"Except it isn't." Dallin said it like the words weren't twisting right into Wil's chest, driving the breath from him. "It never was. Earth, air, fire, water—not dreams, not this... *pushing* thing you do. You shocked the shit out of Calder with that one, y'know. He didn't know you could do it, which means it isn't something any Aisling before you has done. Whatever you started out to be, you've gone beyond it, and I've a feeling you've only just brushed the surface of what you've really got. I think you're—"

"I don't want to talk about this anymore." It was making Wil's head pound and his gut clench. It was making him want to stalk over and clock Dallin just for knowing these things and making Wil know them too.

"We *have* to talk about it. I told you, I don't think there's a whole lot of time. Something's coming—it might even be Síofra. And the way it's crawling up my spine all the time makes me wonder if he was closing in on us when we left Dudley—it feels the same to me, except it's worse—and if he catches up and you're not ready—"

"Ready for *what*? What d'you think it's going to be? What d'you think is going to happen? Have you forgotten what I told you? Do you not understand that it doesn't *matter* what I've got, that whatever it is, he can turn it against me? Use it to make me... damn it, I don't even *know*, I thought... the point, *my* point...." Wil's hands were cramping up, they were fisted so tight. "It's so damned *easy* for you! Made of mountains, for pity's sake, you don't even have to wonder what you're supposed to—I mean, you don't have to.... The reason I even exist—tending the threads, that's what I... and getting away from him fixed my... my *crimes*, or at least started to atone for them, but now I—"

"*Crimes*? Are you out of your bleeding mind?" Dallin stood, stepping quickly over to Wil. He made to reach out but caught himself, clenching his hand into a fist instead and dropping it to his side. "How can you even think you're responsible for that?"

"Because I've only brushed the damned surface, right? It's huge, I've been holding it back, that's what you said, and if I *hadn't* been holding it back—"

"He took it from you, he hurt you while doing it. How can you—"

"And yet you want me to test it, use it, so it won't be so *easy* next time. You can't have it both ways, Dallin. I'm either stronger than him or I'm not. If I'm not, then I'm fucked, and probably you too, if you happen to be standing next to me, and if I am, I should've been able to—"

"Should've been able to *what*?" Dallin's teeth clenched tight. "Understand it in all your six-year-old wisdom? Figure out on your own what it apparently takes a dozen clan elders years to teach and explain? And that's not even considering whatever impact the leaf had."

"He *should've told me!*" Wil cried. "Father.... He should've told me I'd got it all wrong, He should've told me the power was there, and He should've told me how to use it!" His eyes were burning, and he locked his jaw against it. "He should've told me... told me...."

Dallin slumped down, budding anger gone now and replaced instead with a soft sympathy that nonetheless sat heavy on Wil's shoulders. "Told you he was sick?"

"Don't do that. Don't get all nice and compassionate, don't dream up excuses, don't patronize me. If it's there, if it's inside me, if *you* could feel it...." Wil shook his head and looked away, blinking at the blur of threatening tears. "Do me the small courtesy of not excusing everything I do, everything I get wrong, like I'm still that six-year-old without a real thought toward right and wrong. I should've known, and now that I do know, I should be... I don't know what I should be, and there's no excuse for that either. Though I'm sure given enough time you'll manage to think of one. Or fifty."

"Is that what you think I do?" Dallin's voice was low, leaden. He looked... wounded. Trying not to be angry. "You think anything I've *ever* said to you was not exactly what I believed at the time?"

Wil stared down at the great smear of gray that was the cold stone floor. "That's the problem," he answered, hushed and slightly wobbly. "You... believe."

"And your problem is that you won't see what's right in front of you." Dallin's hand twitched again, wanting to reach out, but he restrained himself once more. Wil almost wished he hadn't. "You couldn't see what was inside you while you were at the Guild because Síofra kept it from you. When you finally got away from him, you *wouldn't* see it because that would mean it was there all along. And because you're convinced you deserve to be punished, you won't see now that some things were beyond your control. Wil, look at me."

Dallin waited, but Wil couldn't, simply *could not* drag his gaze up to meet whatever soft look was turned his way.

"Wil...." Dallin's hand came up, fingers gently sliding beneath Wil's chin, tipping his head up. Wil thought about snapping his teeth but couldn't make himself do that either. His eyes caromed into the dark depths of Dallin's, clung there.

"We're talking about the strength of gods here. If whatever's going on is big enough to weaken the Father the way it's doing, do you really think it is or ever has been your 'point' to beat it? When you were *six years old*?" Dallin shook his head, mouth quirked in something that wanted to quiver into a sad smile, but he didn't let it. "Rather an ego you've got there, innit?"

Wil glared, then jerked his chin until Dallin let go. "*Ego*."

"Well, you must think awfully highly of yourself to assume all this was in your control, or should've been."

"And yet you're so bloody sure it could be now."

"...All right, fair enough." Dallin returned to the cot and sank down. "Here's what I think. I think someone—whether it was Síofra or the Brethren or both—tried to get hold of the Father and ended up with that Æledfýres instead. He's sucking the life out of the Father somehow. That's why He's sick, that's why He can't help you, because He needs you to help *Him*, except He doesn't want you to because he's afraid for you.

"I think you're tending the threads because no one else was doing it, and because you're you, you assumed it must be your responsibility. And once Síofra figured out you could do it, that he could follow you when you did do it—that you had the powers of a minor *god*, Wil, think about it—Síofra pushed the rest back—"

Dallin jerked his head back as though struck, eyes gone distant as they peered unseeing at a fissure in the stone to Wil's left.

"No, he didn't push them back." Low and soft, as though Dallin was talking to himself, thinking aloud. "I'll bet good money

Síofra was siphoning them somehow, just like what that other is doing to the Father, so he could take it, have it all at his disposal, and leave you powerless to fight him.

"Except you *did* fight him, every way you could. You must've been tapping those powers somehow all these years, using them to survive when you really shouldn't've done—the leaf should've killed you before ten years was out. Forced withdrawal from it shouldn't've been possible more than... say twice, *maybe*, and certainly not however many times they actually did it. And you definitely don't look your age, let alone like someone addicted to the stuff for fifty years. It must've been like some otherworld tug-o'-war—him trying to drag them out of you and you holding on, not even knowing you *were* holding on.... No wonder it hurt."

Dallin puffed out something dazed and.... Wil couldn't tell. Angry, maybe. *Yeah*, he thought, *definitely really bloody angry*, when Dallin turned those dark eyes on Wil, intense.

"Now tell me I'm wrong."

Wil... couldn't. Stunned and hamstrung by the sudden onslaught of enlightenment, his entire life laid out before him in terms that illuminated and disoriented at the same time.

"I...." He gagged into silence, just shook his head, mute.

"You can't." That low level of throttled rage was simmering just below Dallin's words. "Good. So now that you know it, now that you see...." He stood, stepped over, and planted himself in front of Wil. Dallin didn't stop himself this time but reached out and took hold of Wil's arms. "Tell me you can't do it."

Wil couldn't do that either. He didn't even try.

Because Dallin kept looking at him like Wil really was astounding. Kept looking at him like he thought Wil really could do anything. Prisoner, prey, addict, renegade, killer, user—that was all Wil had ever been, and yet Dallin looked at him and told him he could step into a task meant for a god and bloody made Wil *believe* it.

Didn't he know they were going to be the end of each other? Why wasn't he as terrified as Wil was?

Wil didn't say any of it. Instead he stared into those simmering coals Dallin had for eyes, saw the tender intensity beneath the fury. Vengeance stifled and left to simmer, biding its time 'til it found the ones who'd hurt the one he cared for.

Me, Wil thought stupidly. *The one he cares for—that's me.*

Angry and indignant—for Wil—as it had been at the city's gate.

Righteous Protector; Remorseless Avenger.

Warp and weft.

Wil let himself believe in it, let it enfold him just for a moment, and finally—*finally*—understood why all this so unnerved him.

Something he'd never had, that's what this was, and not something he could tuck away in his pack and clutch to his chest. It could go away or be taken; he could destroy it with his own hands or even a word. He never got to keep anything—it all went away or was stolen, all of it. And he'd never had anything he so badly didn't want to lose.

So what was he supposed to do? Refuse it so it wouldn't hurt when he lost it? Start lamenting now for something he might never have to do?

Or take hold and thieve whatever small pleasures came his way?

He had magic in him. All he had to do was find it and use it. Dallin thought Wil could do it, very plainly *believed* it, and Dallin had never been wrong about anyone, he'd said so.

The power of a minor god—surely that was enough to change fate?

Something rose up in Wil, something he recognized, a rebellion that had more than once kept him alive, kept him from letting his mind snap, kept him from giving in when giving in was the only choice. Defiance. A bone-weary fatigue of looking at the world through eyes wild and wary. A fiery desire to take and hold and expose what was him, lay it out plain and say *This is what I am; acknowledge it, respect it, or leave me be.* A driving *need* to own control over his own destiny—once and for all.

Vicious little shit, he told himself resolutely, *who never bloody quits. It's a good thing—he said so.*

He lifted his chin, locked his gaze onto Dallin's, and took a long, deep breath.

"All right." Wil nodded, resolute. "I want you to shave. And then I want to have sex again. And then I want to sleep. And then...." He set his shoulders. "And then we'll do what *you* want. We'll test."

He'd dreamed alone. Judging by the fact that he wasn't hanging off the side of the small cot, and the lack of warmth swathed to his skin, Wil guessed he'd slept alone too. At least he woke that way.

Dallin's shape had been there, just like always, Watching, but less substantial than that to which Wil had just lately become accustomed. Not sleeping, then.

Wil had looked for Father, had called out, but only got silence in return. Just as well.

Wil stretched and loosed a groan, groping blind for the pillow and dragging it over his head. Burrowed deeper into the sheets. He felt... good. Rested. Content.

It had been slower the second time, more attention spent on exploration and the insistence on feeling every sensation, but no less intense. More of a sharing than a taking. A little more fear inside the pleasure. A tiny smile twitched at the corner of Wil's mouth. A little bit scary was all right. A little bit scary was... rather nice, actually. Reminded him to keep feeling.

"Bloody hell." He smacked himself through the pillow. "Go to bed a man and wake a complete sap. What the fuck?"

The low murmur of voices dug its way through blankets and pillow, teasing at the edge of Wil's hearing. Dallin's voice, and... had to be Calder. Not an argument, which was good—Wil was tired of those. They might need to be careful of Calder, but they needed him nonetheless. They weren't going to get to Lind without him, not without a big, messy incident. Wouldn't that be just Wil's luck?—arriving at the border of a place he'd never wanted to go, only to be shot down for fear of a power he didn't even know how to use.

Irony, thy name is... whatever my name is.

He snorted, then allowed a heavy, satisfied sigh to curl from his chest. He dragged himself up to his elbows, blinking and squinting until the room came into focus. Someone had lit all the lamps in the passageway and the two that framed his doorway. It must be morning. It was hard to tell down here. The only way Wil had kept track that first day was by gauging time by the content of the meals Shaw had brought him. It would be nice to get out of here, breathe clean air, see the sunshine.

"Aren't you up yet?" Dallin's voice, somewhere between teasing and exasperated. What sounded like a muted complaint from Calder, then Dallin again: "He's not a consumptive foundling, y'know. And no one needs *that* much sleep."

Wil rolled his eyes. In fact, he could've done with another several hours, but not because of weariness. It was just nice to have the rare luxury of lounging. Especially considering all the energy he'd expended last night.

He snorted again, still-bleary gaze catching on the little cupboard that had been beside the bed before they'd moved it. The sardonic curl of his mouth turned to a genuine smile. Dallin had left tea. And what looked like several of those ham rolls Shaw had made the other day and over which Wil had nearly gone into an ecstasy of appreciative scrummy noises that might have embarrassed him if anyone but Shaw had heard them.

Wil grinned. Breakfast in bed. Well, sort of. Kind of left there going cold, and he'd have to haul his arse up to reach it all. But still.

"Are you alive down there?"

Dallin's voice again, chiding but with a generous ration of good humor beneath it. Wil could almost see the smile Dallin was likely trying to hide from Calder, couldn't help but answer it with one of his own.

There it was again. Complete and total sap. One good night and Wil came over all wittering idiot. All right, one *really good* night. But still.

Wil flopped down to his back and stretched one more time. "Sort of?"

"Well, get your arse up and moving, yeah? We've got work to do."

A grumbling sigh gusted from out Wil's chest. He sat up and rubbed at his eyes. He peered dubiously at the teapot but more favorably at the food. Probably neither tea nor Dallin's prodding would be enough to move Wil, but those ham rolls were doing the trick.

He snatched up pants and trousers from the floor, slid himself into both, and slouched across to his breakfast. He had one roll stuffed half in his mouth, another in his hand, and one arm through the sleeve of his shirt when Dallin's bulk eclipsed the doorway.

"Sleep well?" The question was casual, Dallin's tone mildly

curious, his face almost boyish now without that stupid beard. His eyes, though....

Wil made himself busy hunting for the other sleeve dangling over his shoulder blade and ducked his head to hide the way his cheeks flared pink. His mouth was full, so he only nodded, shot a look sideways... paused. Very consciously *not smirking*, Wil slowed his movements, stretching more than he needed to, arching his back the slightest bit as he angled his arm into the other sleeve.

Dallin's eyes were narrowing, one corner of his mouth curling up. "You," he said, quiet and a bit hoarse, "are bloody evil."

Wil bit away the half of the roll in his mouth so he could grin. He'd been looked at with lust before. He'd never been looked at like *that*. He might like the chance to get used to it. Which brought to mind this morning's plans. Surprisingly, the thought failed to mute the grin.

"Get rid of Calder?"

"Finally." Dallin rolled his eyes. "And I've asked that he keep Shaw and himself away until we say so. I think it's best we take care of this ourselves, if we can."

Wil had to agree. He didn't think Calder was a bad man, but he didn't trust him entirely either. Betrayal wore many faces, in Wil's experience, and not all of them had evil intent behind them. Sometimes it wore the face of kindness and good intentions.

He took a sip of his tea. "So what's the plan?"

"C'mon down the hall." Dallin waved behind him. "We can get started while I finish cleaning the guns."

Wil nodded. "Be right there." He set the cup atop the cupboard, and finished buttoning his shirt, made a quick visit to the privy, then grabbed up both plate and cup and headed down the passageway.

Dallin was crouched on the floor of his room inspecting an array of semi-assembled weapons taking up half the floor. Wil decided to forgive the fact that Dallin had apparently ransacked Wil's room, looking for the other half of the arsenal Wil had stashed in coat pockets and pack, while Wil had been dead to the world. This sight was worth any imagined invasion. Wil remembered the ritual cleaning and checking back in Dudley and breathed an unconscious little sigh. Dallin had said they were leaving tonight, but this confirmed it. Wil had been feeling itchy to move himself—though apparently not as itchy as Dallin—and this spectacle seemed to set nerves Wil hadn't even known were twitching to rest.

"Can I help?"

"D'you remember how to disassemble and clean the shotgun?"

Wil sat cross-legged on the floor across from Dallin, guns and gun bits splayed between them. He put the plate and cup to the side, and snatched up one of the soft, oily cloths.

"So... how do we go about all... this?"

"Here, these need to stay with you." Dallin handed over the sack of ammunition Wil remembered from the smith's stall when they'd first arrived. "I've kept the knife we bought."

That last was somewhat subdued. Wil let it pass without comment. Any conversation involving knives seemed to rest precariously atop a mountain of explosives, and he wasn't up to treading that carefully just now—not before he'd had at least one cup of tea, anyway. He checked the safety on the rifle, cracked the stock, and emptied the live shells.

"I think what we need to do first"—Dallin squinted one-eyed through the cylinder of the larger of the two handguns—"is to figure out what you'd like to play with." He snapped his wrist, clicking the cylinder into the body of the gun, then laid it aside.

Wil's eyebrows went up. "Play with?"

"We already know you can make it rain. We need to perfect that one, but it's there, you know how to do it, so let's focus on another. Now, if I had my preference—" Dallin cut himself off. "But this is your preference. What would you like to try?"

Wil pulled until the forearm snapped out, then set it aside. He didn't even really have to think about his answer.

"Fire."

Dallin chuckled. "How did I know?"

"Don't be jealous, now." Wil couldn't help the smirk. "If you're very good, we'll drag out what's lurking in you next."

Wil had meant it as a joke, but it made the smile slip from Dallin's face. He cleared his throat.

"All right, fire, then."

Dallin set aside guns and gun bits, stood, and paced over to his pack. He dug out several thick beeswax candles and lit one from the sconce next the door.

Wil had to chuckle. "What *don't* you have in there?"

Dallin merely waved a hand. "Come away from the shells and try to aim... whatever out the door." He gave Wil a speaking look and jerked his chin at the flame. "Let's see what you can do with that."

"...Do?"

"Well, yes. Do." Dallin nodded, encouraging.

Wil rolled his eyes. Dallin was standing there as though he fully expected Wil to just blink his eyes and make the flame change colors or something. And Wil didn't even know where to bloody *start*.

"I don't know *how* to do."

"And you won't unless you give it a try." Dallin sighed concession. "All right, how did you make it rain?"

"Well, *I* don't know." Wil was getting sincerely narked now. "I was asleep, in case you forgot." He paused. "D'you think I have to be asleep for it to work?"

"You weren't asleep in Old Bridge."

Wil looked away. "Well, no, but... I wasn't exactly—"

"Ah-ah." Dallin wagged his finger. "No beating yourself up today. We haven't the time for it. You weren't asleep in Old Bridge, and you certainly weren't asleep in Dudley when you questioned that man. And let's don't forget last night at the stable." The tone was still lightly reproachful about that one. "Think about that and see if they're the same. That is...." His brow screwed up. "See if they... come from the same place, I suppose." He paused, groping for the right words, face brightening when he found them. "Take what you did last night and direct it at the flame."

Wil blinked, all annoyance leaving him with this new proposal. Again, as it had been in that cell in Dudley, it struck him how Dallin was able to take a concept that seemed so overwhelmingly complex and boil it all down to something as simple and fundamental as breathing. Wil blew out a soft little "Huh" and nodded. "All right, then. Let's try."

Dallin looked surprisingly eager as he waved at the candle. "Right here, then."

"Um...." Wil laid aside the pieces of the gun still in his hand and pursed his lips. "D'you think it's wise to be holding it in your hand?"

"Oh." Dallin shot a dubious look at the candle. "Right. Good thinking." Crouching down in the doorway, he tipped the candle and let a small pool of wax gather on the floor, then set the base of the candle in it. Prudently, he stepped back and came to hunker at Wil's side. "All right, that'll do it, then. Go on. Oh, wait."

Dallin got up again, and stepped lightly over to the cupboard beside his bed. Wil hadn't noticed before, but there were three pitchers crowding its top and another four on the floor beside it. The blanket from the bed was in a wet heap right next to it all. Wil raised his eyebrows but didn't comment when Dallin grabbed up a pitcher and the blanket and resumed his position beside him.

"All right, ready now." Dallin nodded at the candle. "Go on, then."

Wil hesitated. Despite the lightness of his mood, the air of potential discovery that had been curling through him since he'd walked into the room, now that it came to it, anxiety was beginning to seep into his nerves.

"*Go on*, he says." Wil could feel the set of his mouth thinning. "If it works, at least I'll come in handy for campfires."

Dallin's hand landed on Wil's shoulder, squeezed. Wil wondered if some part of him had grumbled and griped just so that very thing would happen.

"I'm right here," Dallin offered, steadfast.

Wil sucked in a long, deep breath, trying to shake some of the creeping tension out of himself with a full-body shudder, but it was apparently set to hang on for a while. So was that hand.

He turned to Dallin, a variation of that same childish request he'd made in Dudley on his tongue, but he couldn't hold it back. "Don't go away."

The eyes said it first—fierce, determined and... just *there*. And then the words came to reinforce it. "I'm not going anywhere."

Wil didn't even chastise himself for how heartening it was. He nodded and turned his gaze to the flame.

It only took a moment for the world to drop away, for Wil to let everything but the candle settle into a fuzzed peripheral haze. Slivers of color and light sang from the flame's heart, and Wil reached for them, caught them—

Pushed.

There was no give. There didn't have to be. Everything was already wide open, like it had been waiting for him.

He opened himself wide in return, and let it come.

Not nearly as intrusive as the other. Not nearly as terrifyingly sensual.

It was just as greedy and gluttonous. It wanted just as much.

It was... strange. The same and yet different. There were threads here too—why had Wil never seen that before? why had it never occurred to him to *look?*—but with a different sort of life inside them. Mindless and primal. Frighteningly empty, and yet with so much strength inside the void.

Patterns. He could actually see them, could see how they worked, could see how they twined around themselves to make a whole and then changed in less than an eyeblink, making new shapes to fit into old patterns, winding into an entirely new whole, only to unmake it all in another making.

I think there's so much more that if you're not very careful in how you use it, you could lose yourself.

Wil stretched inside it, reaching out inside forever, and still his grasp was endless.

Oh, Dallin... you don't know how very right you were.

"I can see it." Wil shook his head and breathed a quiet laugh.

"What do you see?"

Wil lifted his hand, tracing the shapes with the tip of his finger, fascinated when they swirled and dipped with his own invisible touch. A chaos of color, right at his fingertips, bending to his will. The flame expanded and churned, reaching impossibly halfway up the doorjamb for a moment until Wil dipped his hand, flattening the flare so it fanned out and spat when it touched the wax.

"I can see how it works." Wil couldn't seem to speak above a reverent whisper. "I can see its heart. I can *touch* it. It's fierce and hungry. It wants to stretch and breathe, eat everything in its path. It loves the burning."

Wil loved the burning. It was as though it were a part of him, an extension of his own body—

No. An extension of his soul. It knew when Wil wanted it to

jump. It knew when he wanted it to kindle down to only a spark at the end of its wick. It wanted to unfold at the end of Wil's hand. It wanted him to flick his fingers and send it leaping out, free it to its hunger.

It wanted *in*. It wanted to eat the emptiness Wil left behind as he swallowed it.

It was amazingly, mind-blowingly beautiful.

"Don't hold back," Dallin told him. "Go ahead and push."

A jolt of fear shot through Wil. "You said I could lose myself."

"But you won't."

Wil shook his head, eyeing the flame with wary distrust. "I'm... I can't. It'll—"

"The bleeding comes when you hold it back. Let it go. See what happens."

"It's too greedy." Pressure was building at the backs of Wil's eyes, sending a thumping pulse through his temples. "It wants... everything."

Dallin's hand tightened on Wil's shoulder. "It's only a candle. It can't do any damage. Holding back will damage *you*. Now *push*."

Dallin didn't understand. He couldn't see the patterns. Couldn't see the ravenous vacuum splayed out just beneath his vision. How could he not see it? It was so bright it was blinding Wil.

"I can't." Wil was warm—*hot*—the flame pulsing erratic, an echo of his own heart. And he couldn't pull it back this time—the fire might come with it and burn him from the inside out. "It's too big."

Its reality hung behind it, looming vast and bright as a sun, voracious. It crept into the crevices of Wil's Self and boiled his blood. Its heart *was* a sun, just as huge and blindly hungry, but trapped at the end of a wick, trying to stretch beyond its own form.

It saw the little piles of ammunition scattered around the room, a driving desire for the taste of gunpowder, and laughed its crackling laugh when it felt Wil knowing. Felt him wanting it too.

And it was starting to hurt.

"Listen to me." Dallin growled it, angry now. "Just trust me. I won't let anything happen. Push it, Wil. I know you can do this —*you* know you can do this. *Push it.*"

Wil latched onto the confidence in Dallin's voice, twitching his shoulder just so he could feel the weight of Dallin's hand shift against the skin beneath the linen of Wil's shirt.

Wil didn't push. It was too big for that. He clenched his teeth and *shoved.*

If he hadn't already been sitting down, the great *whoosh* and flash would've pitched him to his arse. As it was, Wil fell back against Dallin and sent him half reeling sideways with a startled grunt, but that hand never let go.

"Bloody *fuck.*" Dallin watched the fire reach out like a great hand through the doorway, fan over the wall of the passageway, and flare toward the ceiling, seeking fuel, then thin and choke itself on stone and mortar. A light scrim of smoke wafted as the flame weakened, snapping out its thwarted fury, then sputtered broodingly over the splash of wax and wick, all that was left of the ruined candle. One tiny blue flame floated in a liquid carcass of milky beeswax, and even that only lived a few seconds longer.

They sat silent, staring, watching the smoke fade to a thin haze at the ceiling. The hiss and final faint *pop* from the corpse of the candle had them blinking stupidly at each other and trying to rehinge their jaws.

The force had knocked them both back, Dallin's hip upending the pitcher when he'd landed. He sat now in a puddle of water, trousers dark and sopping. And he didn't even seem to notice.

"So." Dallin's voice was thin and strained. "That went well."

Wil couldn't help it—he barked out a laugh. He turned to Dallin, who peered back at him with eyes gone comically wide, and threw himself into Dallin's broad chest. Wil laughed again, louder this time, maybe a little bit wild, but with genuine humor and relief beneath it.

He hadn't burned the place down. It hadn't eaten him. He didn't hurt. And....

Wil reached up and swiped at his nose, fingers coming away with nothing more sinister coating the tips but a trace of gun oil. He held them up to Dallin and waggled them with a slightly hectic grin.

Dallin puffed an edgy little chuckle and scrubbed a hand through his hair. "Well." He squinted up at the sooted ceiling and then down to the pool of wax. He looked back at Wil with a waggle of sandy eyebrows. "It's probably a good thing we didn't start with the torches."

Not only the ceiling but the passageway wall and floor were black and singed as well by the time Dallin peered at Wil, judged him pale, and deemed they'd played at pyromania enough for today. They'd had to use four of the pitchers—and the blanket, when one of the lamps out in the hallway had exploded—and they hadn't even chanced anything bigger than the candles.

Most of Wil's efforts were spent on control, manipulation, and confinement. Making sure he didn't wander inside it all, misplace himself, or allow it to grow beyond what they could control was left to Dallin. Well, and putting out the various little blazes that cropped up in the periphery. There'd been a few of those. It was amazing neither of them had been singed, though that was likely because Dallin never let Wil forget to push *away*. After the first one, Dallin had ordered a pause so he could move the ammunition and everything else flammable he could find down to Wil's room. Not that it mattered—the flames would eat the dust in the air if they couldn't find anything else. Wil had to respect and admire the mindless craving for survival.

There was a touch of disappointment when Dallin called a halt, but relief too, and a great deal of satisfaction.

"You look like you're feeling well." Wil was sitting on the floor and watching Dallin shove the bed back to where it had been. He was moving very easily, as though he'd never been hurt at all. Wil was curious to have a look under that bandage.

"And you look like a cat with a mouse's tail hanging from its mouth."

Wil didn't even try to hide the grin. "I wish you could feel what it's like." He watched Dallin move around the small room, trying—likely fruitlessly—to put it back to at least a semblance of what it had been. Wil furrowed his brow. "I'll bet you could do, y'know."

Dallin looked over with a lift of an eyebrow, balling up the black-smudged, still partially sopping blanket. "Could do what?" He gave the blanket a dubious grimace, then gave it up and dropped it to the floor.

"Feel what it's like." Wil shrugged. "We share dreams, after all. And there's the calling and all. That would've been handy, if I'd known...." He shook his head. No beating himself up today. "But, I mean, there must be some kind of connection, right? Maybe you could... sort of follow me when I do it."

He watched with sharp interest as Dallin's face closed up and he looked away. In utter silence, Dallin retrieved the blanket again and paced slowly over to the doorway, kneeling to apply it to the scorch marks on the floor. He watched his own hands and nothing else as he tried to mop up the mess, leaving a faintly iridescent trail of moisture on the stone.

"Is that something you want to do?" There was a distinct edge of unease beneath the question.

Wil drew a knee up to rest his chin atop it. "Is it something you don't?"

"I didn't say that." Dallin kept himself busy with his makeshift mopping, peering across the passageway and at the marks climbing the wall there. Like he was avoiding Wil's gaze.

Interesting.

Wil narrowed his eyes. "Would you do it if I asked, even if you didn't want to?"

Dallin didn't have to answer—it was abruptly very obvious—but Wil was quite keen to see the reaction, the struggle to find the right words. He watched as Dallin dredged up answers in his mind, pitching them away one after one, until he settled on something he thought was the right thing to say. He dropped the blanket, and twisted to sit on the floor, back propped to the wall.

"I will do whatever it takes." Dallin's gaze was even, with a hardness behind it that nearly sent chills up Wil's backbone. Wil wasn't looking at Dallin anymore; this was Constable Brayden staring out from those intense eyes.

"What does that mean?" Wil asked quietly. "Whatever it takes to do what?"

"To right the wrongs. The things that happened, Wil... they offend me. I don't know how to say it any better. They offend me to my core. And now that...." Dallin waved a hand between them with a shrug. "The offense is keener. It would be wrong that it happened to anyone, and that's the way it started out. Now it's even more wrong because it happened to you. You asked me a while ago if I'd stop you from revenge. My answer is no. My answer is that you may have to work pretty hard to beat me to it.

So if you think we need to try whatever it is you have in mind, I'll do it."

Wil pushed away the selfish little bit of a glow blooming in his chest, concentrating instead on the somber discomfort he'd stirred in Dallin at the prospect of what had been proposed.

"You'll do it. But you don't want to."

Dallin shook his head. "It doesn't matter what I want."

"But it does." It really did. For the first time in Wil's life, it mattered at least as much what another wanted as what he wanted. And he wasn't even sure he really wanted it in the first place.

"It makes me...." Dallin's jaw tightened, muscles jumping and twitching. "It makes me uncomfortable. I don't like feeling like I'm invading the mind of another. I don't like the idea of another invading mine. The things in my head, they're... it's the most private place a person can own. They're for *me*."

Wil could certainly understand that. Except.

"You've been in my dreams for years. You've bidden me into yours. Is this so different?"

Dallin sighed uneasily. "I don't know. But that pushing thing you do... it...." His teeth clenched tight, and he shook his head. "This won't sound right, and please understand that I don't mean anything by it. But I saw that man in Dudley. I saw how he looked at you, how he looked at me when I touched you. And the boy at the stable—Calder said...." He trailed off and rolled his eyes to the ceiling. "How am I supposed to put this so it doesn't sound like I'm faulting you for something?"

The warmth Wil had felt a moment ago leached away. Something inside him had just gone chill.

"Well," he put in slowly, "you could say it plainly. Say that Calder told you what he saw, what it looked like. How he didn't quite believe I had no intention of dragging the lad into the nearest stall for a quick shag. How he was no doubt wondering if I'd used it to seduce my way through every man from Ríocht to here."

"He was... condescendingly sympathetic." Dallin shot a rueful glance at Wil and shrugged. "I, on the other hand, am thoroughly behind whatever you need to do to get what you need. I want you to understand that."

Wil had to make himself not clench his jaw or fist his hands. "How very... generous of you."

Dallin scrubbed at his hair, too obviously irritated. "See, I knew I wouldn't be able to say anything right. It isn't generous—it's a statement of simple fact. I want you to survive, Wil. And I want you to do whatever you have to do, whatever you can live with after, to do it. I want you to—"

"I've used it to defend myself." Wil's tone came out hard and maybe a little too cold. "And that by accident. I didn't even know I could do it, it happened by panicked chance, and I don't just go about...." He flailed, anger climbing, but the *hurt* beneath it was what made him keep going. "What d'you think Orman wanted that night outside Ramsford's? And what d'you think I was prepared to give him to make him think he got exactly what he wanted? If Palmer hadn't shown up, Orman would've gone away happily satisfied and blithely alive, and all it would've taken was a few moments of my time."

"Give them what they think they want," Dallin said softly.

Wil shrugged. "Women want to feed me. Men want to bed me. Well, some women want to bed me too, and some men only want to feed me. It's their own wants inside them that determine whether it'll be a pleasant experience or whether I'll end up running for my life. Some are more greedy than others." He sat back, keeping his gaze frank. "Some of it was very pleasant. I won't apologize for any of it." He raised his eyebrows. "Disappointed?"

Wil didn't know how it had happened, when it had happened,

but Dallin had somehow become the mean by which Wil judged himself. Likely because there was a decided lack of judgement, and it was easier on Wil's self-opinion that way—he liked himself a lot less than Dallin apparently did, and Wil had to admit he rather appreciated seeing himself reflected in those dark eyes. They showed him a much better image than any he'd ever even thought to look for before. Until perhaps now, anyway.

Dallin was going a bit red in the face. "And that's... see, it's not you or what you've done, and... fuck, Wil, *apology*, for the Mother's sake. *Disappointed*." He ground his teeth, hands fisted. "You can't hear it right, and I keep saying it wrong. It isn't you or anything you've done—do I really have to repeat, *yet again*, that every last bit of it... I don't think you *could* disappoint me. I'm afraid of disappointing *you*. Disappointing *myself*."

Dallin paused, mouth open, face going a lower flush of red, as though only now realizing what he'd said. He shrugged tiredly.

"When you first told me what happened at the Guild, that first day in Dudley, remember that? I walked out of that cell, and one of the first things that occurred to me was how easily a power like that could make even the best of men into the worst of men. And what you do, take that want and use it, that...." Dallin looked as if he wanted to tear his gaze away but willfully held Wil's with it instead. "I've already got the want, y'see. I'd be afraid I'd...." He didn't finish, just left it lying there, like a stone had just fallen out of his mouth.

That chill inside Wil thawed all at once. He really should have known better than to think... whatever he'd been thinking. That any intention Dallin had could be anything less than honorable. Dallin really was, very simply, a good man.

"That right there," Wil told him, quiet and hoarse, "that's what makes it possible to ask you. That's how I know. And I'm not quite as helpless as I was. You don't need to protect me from you. I can do that well enough on my own." He shook his head. "It isn't that people want *me*—surely you see that? They want what's *in* me, even if they don't know what it is. Some would open my chest and dig out my heart looking for it, and still not realize they didn't know what they were looking for. What you want...." A flush rose, hot and tight. "You *see* me. It's just...." There really was no good word for what it was, at least not in Wil's vocabulary. "It's just *different*."

He watched as Dallin sighed in defeat, and knew he'd won something for which he hadn't even meant to contend. Except now that the necessity had evolved out of the murky disarray at the bottom of Wil's consciousness, it made too much sense to put away again. Anyway, now that he was in it....

"Calder said your magic felt green, untapped. He said he shouldn't've been able to read you, which means you ought to be able to deny anyone you don't want mucking about in there. The Old Ones can all do it. You've more in you than any one of them. And you must've been doing *something* all this time—I looked for you. I looked hard."

Wil paused and thought carefully about what he truly wanted here. What he ought to want. What he ought to be saying to get it. And how he was going to do it without making an obviously touchy matter into something altogether untouchable.

It was hard work, this caring thing. And knowing you were cared for in return—probably more, and cleaner—made it all the harder. Made it... heavy.

"I don't want to be inside your head." Wil spoke it very clearly, putting all his sincerity behind it. "I don't want you inside mine. But I also don't want anyone finding me the way I found you in Lind." He swallowed as Dallin shot a narrow look at him but kept his voice calm and his expression open. "That second Watcher—he heard me. And I wasn't even calling for him. Or, at least, I didn't know I was. What if there comes a time when I need you to hear me? It's selfish, I know, and I'm sorry, but. Don't you think we need all the ammunition we can get?"

It wasn't fair. He was using Dallin's own sense of honor against him. But that didn't make the need any less needful. Perhaps Wil had only just thought of it, but now that he had and voiced the concern, there was no choice but to see it as imperative.

"Would you, um...." Wil shifted. "Should you maybe ask Calder if he could—"

"Not on your bloody life."

Wil sighed. "Then you're stuck with me, I guess."

Dallin's jaw tightened, gaze gone flat, almost angry. "Right." Irritably he picked up the drenched blanket, and threw it back down to the floor with a heavy *splat*. "I expect it's your turn as tutor. Let's get on, then."

After all Dallin's apprehension, all his heavy sighs and clenched teeth, it turned out to be incredibly easy. Wil had wondered, after he'd more or less tricked Dallin into it all, if it could even work. Wil had tried very hard to push Dallin that night in Dudley, after all.

There was no push to this, no patterns, no chaos. There was merely a reaching out, a concentrated call. A diffident rebuff that rocked Wil's mind only slightly. Some gentle cajoling, assurance, a request for trust. And then there was an answer. Hesitant. Not truly willing, but duty-bound.

Permission.

Connection.

Warp and weft.

I will do whatever it takes, Dallin had told Wil. There couldn't be more profound proof than this.

The denial was so much simpler. Almost nothing more than a mental *No*. For Wil, it was like butting his mind against a stone wall. He was fairly confident it would be the same for anyone else who might decide to give it a go. Dallin's belief was hard in coming —the knee-jerk *prove it* in him endlessly walking his mental watchtower, reason and logic its sentries—but once it came, it was unflinching.

They were both fairly exhausted by the time Dallin declared them through and himself tired and in need of the sleep he hadn't got last night. He still had that broodiness about him, his mood dark and discomfited, so Wil didn't argue. Anyway, it had to be going on midday by now, and Wil was starting to get hungry. They'd had a good morning's work, and though he was genuinely regretful that the exhilaration of taming fire—taming bloody *fire*— had been so thoroughly dampened by what followed, Wil couldn't regret the result.

"You'll need it." Wil made his voice soft and sympathetic as he and Dallin finished up assembling and loading the weapons. "We had to do it."

"I know." Dallin stretched his neck and loosed a heavy sigh. "Anyway, I'm glad it's done, and I'm glad you thought of it. It was... necessary."

Wil gave him a rueful smile. "Glad?"

"All right, resentful as hell with no right to be. Just.... It'll seem less appalling after I've slept, I've no doubt. I'm not angry with you. I'm not even angry, really. I'm just... out of sorts. Sorry."

"It's a lot to—"

Wil's response was cut short by the sound of booted feet tripping quickly down the cellar steps, almost running along the passageway. Urgency was behind the steps, hurried purpose.

Without even thinking about it, Wil's hand settled on the rifle and dragged it close, fingers resting over the trigger and the safety both. He only half noticed out the corner of his eye Dallin doing the same with one of the revolvers.

A contingent of the city's guard, perhaps? Had Wil's visits to Shaw's room been observed, reported? Had the Brethren managed to track their trail, following the wanted bills and the local gossip to the Temple's steps? A cold hand clenched around Wil's gut— Síofra?

Calder swung around the doorframe, a veritable explosion of wide shoulders and gray-blond hair thundering into the tension and ratcheting it higher yet. He didn't even pause at the state of the room, the smudges of soot, the shards of glass from the little eruption in the hall they had yet to clean up. He only stopped short in the doorway, peering intently at each of their wary faces in turn.

"They're here."

CHAPTER 6

W*ell, naturally*, Dallin thought. He'd been idiotic enough to forego sleep again last night, and then spent the morning trying to keep the Temple from burning down, and breaking down the very last barrier standing between him and the completely unbelievable—letting down the ramparts of his own *mind*, for pity's sake, and for someone who'd very frankly stated he'd use Dallin and then kill him if he had to. And all this after having jumped into bed with that very same man, who was, in point of fact, supposed to be Dallin's prisoner and who was convinced they were going to be the end of each other. Jumped into bed with him not once, but twice. Without, as had been bluntly pointed out to Dallin, even the smallest protest. Quite eagerly, in fact. One day after having woken up from a stab wound from which he'd apparently healed himself.

Oh yes, and there was also the small matter of promising the man for whom he was beginning to think he'd fallen quite hard—before he'd even begun to *like* him, for pity's sake, go figure that one—that Dallin would put a bullet through his head if it turned out Dallin couldn't protect him as he kept promising he would.

So of *course* they were here.

"Who's here?"

"A company of red and gold came through the gates about two hours ago." Calder shook his head. "There's a small contingent in blue and brown, as well, plus a few civilians with them. They're at the constabulary now."

The statement sank through a moment of strangled silence, twisting slowly from one possibility in a string of conjectures and into too-firm reality. Blue and brown. *Fuck.*

"All right." Dallin's hand went unconsciously to the weave of his shirt, which was not—and had not been for several weeks now —the blue and brown of his Putnam constabulary surcoat. A heavy twinge of loss hit him all at once, and he closed the hand into a fist. It was set, for better or worse. There would be no going back from whatever happened now.

Shaw arrived silently behind Calder, his mien edged with concern. "At least two of the civilians...." He slid a troubled glance at Wil and cleared his throat. "They're Dominionites. Traveling with Commonwealth soldiers. I'd never have believed it if I'd not seen it myself."

Dominionites. Surely Jagger wouldn't have allowed Síofra to ride along?

Dallin gave Wil a quick glance, saw attentive worry and not panic, and so turned back to Shaw. "You were there?"

"I didn't see them arrive. Brother Tranter was assisting one of the midwives last night and was on his way back to the Temple when the gates opened. When he reported what he'd seen, I went to the constabulary to see what I could find out."

Dallin winced. "You went to—"

"He knows better than what you're thinking," Calder put in.

"Oh yes, I should hope so," Shaw agreed. "I took some pots to the smithy's to be patched and recast. The shop happens to be only several doors down from the constabulary. I didn't speak to anyone, but I saw the soldiers idling in front of the building. They were giving the Dominion men a wide berth, but it was obvious they were together."

"What did they look like?" Wil's voice was far too soft. It was doubtful the others could tell, but Dallin marked the sharp reluctance beneath the question. Wil had asked because he had to, but he didn't really want to know.

Calder merely grimaced, his gaze fixed on Wil and all too knowing, keen and calculating.

Shaw took up the silence. "Dark-haired and fair." He shrugged. "Sorry, I was trying not to look like I was looking."

"Thin?" Wil pressed quietly. "Sort of... narrow-faced?"

Shaw seemed to twig to the disquiet this time. He frowned, softly sympathetic. "One of them, yes. He seemed to be the one in charge."

Shit. Dallin's gut curled as he watched Wil pull in on himself, watched Wil's eyes widen and his face blanch, watched paralyzing fear crowd out even the hungry intelligence in eyes gone dull and panicked. And there was nothing Dallin could do about it. An arm around the shoulders, a quiet reassurance—useless and perhaps not even wise. If ever there was a time for fear, right now was it.

Dallin stepped over to his pack where he'd draped his holsters and started strapping them on. So much for an afternoon kip.

"And what of those in the blue and brown?"

Shaw thought about it. "I didn't see any of those. I expect they were inside, and I didn't want to linger 'til they came out."

"It sounds like you did the right thing. I thank you." Dallin slipped on his sword belt, then shifted his glance between Shaw and Calder. "What happens if they come knocking?"

"We don't have to let them in. But if we didn't, they'd know why." Shaw shrugged apology. "I've nowhere to hide you but here.

I suppose you could stay ahead of them in the passageways for a while, but it isn't as though this place is a secret. They'd catch you up eventually."

That was... all too logical. Dallin blew out a long breath. "I don't suppose either of you knows of a safe place to exit the city unseen in broad daylight?"

Calder and Shaw exchanged an uneasy glance, some sort of dubious mental conversation going on between them via frowns and meaningful twists of eyebrows. "Not quite unseen," Shaw ventured, "but there is a place where you might perhaps be purposefully unremarked."

"Where?"

"It'll take some coin."

"It always does. Where?"

"Not far from where we first... met," Calder put in. "I can take you."

"That's... fine. Just. Yeah."

Dallin had known all along that when they left here, it would likely be with Calder as their guide, but he'd never really liked the idea. He'd much prefer Calder simply pointed a finger in the right direction and left them to their own plotting. As usual these days, Dallin's options were limited.

He turned to Wil. "Go get your kit together. Make sure that gun is loaded. I'll be down in a moment to collect the ammunition. We leave in five minutes."

For a moment Dallin thought Wil wouldn't move, perhaps couldn't, but Wil dipped a quick, jerky nod and silently quit the room.

Dallin turned back to Shaw. "Have you got anything he can take with him to eat? Food, it seems to—"

"Calm him, yes, I'd noticed." Shaw nodded. "Don't go 'til I get back." And then he too was gone.

Calder waited until Shaw's light steps faded up the stone stairs before he shot a sharp glance at Dallin. "It's him, isn't it? And you're not even surprised."

"Why should I be?" Dallin checked the tethers and ties, then stooped to slide his pack over his shoulder. "I've been Watching, haven't I, then?"

He didn't expand, just walked past Calder and down the passageway, fetching up at the doorway of Wil's room. Wil was already in his coat, crouched on the floor over his own pack, his back to the door. The tension around him was so tight Dallin thought he could reach out and twang it like the overwound string of a lute.

"I've lost my coat." Wil shook his head and stared into his open pack as though it might have mercy on him and swallow him whole. "It was here just a moment ago, I had your money in the pocket, your guns—*shit*, your guns, I'm sorry—but now I can't find it."

It made Dallin's heart clench, the lost despair in Wil's voice, the hunch of his shoulders. It was probably good that Calder wasn't hearing this.

"You're wearing your coat." Dallin kept his voice calm and low. "And I've already got my guns." He wanted to step over, lay a hand to Wil's shoulder, say something soothing, but again, it seemed like a lie, and Dallin sometimes had a hard time knowing if Wil would even welcome a comforting gesture.

Wil didn't say anything, merely looked down at his sleeve, blinking at the weave of the coat. He shook his head. His hand went to the coat's pocket, feeling at the bulk of Dallin's purse, before he darted a look at Dallin, wild eyes marking the guns safely in their holsters. Dallin had seen the look before, and not just in Wil's eyes.

I'm afraid, Captain. I want to go home. I'm only a farmer/tai-

lor/blacksmith/sixteen-year-old son of a poor man who had no other trade to turn to....

"Pick up your gun, Wil." *Man your gun, soldier.* Dallin watched as Wil's eyes drifted to the rifle lying beside his boot, hung there. "He knows we're here but not where. He wants your magic, but it's *yours*, and you've got it. We can get out of here before he finds us, and we can beat him if we can't, but I need you to pick up that rifle. *Now.*"

Wil nodded, kept nodding as his hand reached out, curled around the gun's stock, and gripped it tight. As if the cool of the metal itself had doused the feral terror, the bobbleish nodding stopped. Wil's shoulders unlocked, and he fetched a long breath into his chest.

"Right. Yeah. All *right.*" He laid a trembling hand to his pack, shouldered it, and stood with only a slight wobble. He turned to Dallin slowly, swallowing so hard it looked like he'd got one of those bloody potatoes caught in his throat. "Remember your promise."

"I remember all my promises. Including the one where I don't let it come to that." Dallin paced over, took up the ammunition, and distributed it between their pockets and the packs. When he was through, he looked at Wil calmly and cinched his pack shut. "We can do this. *You* can do it. Now let's go."

They left the same way they'd come. Dallin didn't remember much of their arrival, just a vague image of dead leaves and dried-up pricker bushes, but the set of the sun was nearly the same, and the weather hadn't changed—still cold and sunny, just edging on true winter but not quite there yet. He missed his coat, but at least he had the cloak. Even the wind was sighing past the tops of the walls as it had the day they'd first arrived. Dallin fervently hoped this day, as alike as it seemed, would turn out markedly different. He made sure both he and Wil had their hats in place, hunched in as small as he could, and took rear guard while Calder took point. Wil walked between them, munching nervously and without much enthusiasm on a biscuit.

The backstreets were even quieter than they'd been that day they'd rambled through them and tried to outwit the witless, who still had somehow managed to catch them out. Dallin quickly put away the self-chastisement—it would do no good, here and now— and concentrated instead on scanning their surroundings. Watching. It wasn't only about avoiding suspicion anymore—now it was about avoiding being seen altogether.

Wil's quiet panic remained, but he was thinking through it now, doing his best not to let it interfere with what they had to do, that furious, ground-in survival instinct taking over where fear would've had him paralyzed. He was watching too, his gaze snapping to all points, never resting in one spot for more than a second or two, assessing and dismissing, the badger watchful and wary. Good. Dallin could use those teeth about now.

Wil's glance lingered only once, when they flitted past the alleyway where Dallin had failed so badly and allowed others to drive their course.

Wil turned to Calder. "What happened to her?"

Dallin was surprised. He'd nearly forgotten about the haggard woman who'd spouted prophecy through her drug haze.

"She's gone to the Mother." Calder looked... smug. "She was only waiting for you."

Dallin narrowed his eyes but didn't pursue the cryptic remark, and he hoped Wil wouldn't either. One crisis at a time, and getting out of here was a lot more important right now. To Dallin's relief, Wil fell silent, wary glance slanting again to all points, gun gripped tight in both hands, index finger of his left hand twitching constantly over the safety. Dallin smiled grimly in hearty approval.

They walked silently for quite a while, pace quick but careful, ducking behind sheds and privies and even crouching on the ground behind a refuse cart once when no other cover could be found. The passersby were few but the risk of being spotted far too high. They were in one of the less prosperous parts of the city, shabby tenements and rundown little lean-tos the predominant architecture, and seemed to be moving steadily deeper.

It made sense, Dallin supposed. In his experience, the poor and determined had little choice but to find their way around the law, and he wasn't at all surprised that if there was a way to get in and out of Chester undetected, it would be in this part of the city. There was definitely something to be said for the resourcefulness of the desperate. Just look at Wil.

As if he'd heard the thought, Wil stopped abruptly and cocked his head. If Dallin hadn't been paying attention, he would've barreled right over him. As it was, he stopped too, frowning at Wil, who turned to him slowly, jaw set.

"We need the horses." Flat and sober, as if he'd just said *People need water to live.*

Dallin's frown deepened. "We can't—"

"We have to." Wil shot his glance to Calder, who was just now pacing quickly back toward them, having walked ahead before he'd noticed he was no longer followed. "We have to go get the horses."

Calder's eyes didn't roll, but Dallin could tell they wanted to. Calder pressed his lips together grimly with a disapproving glance for Dallin, then a stern one for Wil.

"It's safer to leave them, and we've already passed the turn to the city's stables."

Wil didn't even acknowledge him, just looked back at Dallin, steady. "We *have to*."

Dallin really didn't want to. Not only would it be too risky, but it would take time they might not have and make their trail easier to follow. But the look in Wil's eyes....

"Are you sure?"

Wil nodded. "And another for Calder."

This wasn't that dance of grudging, not-so-secret affection that had so amused Dallin since he'd bought the horses. Wil didn't want the horses right now because he liked them. In fact, Dallin was fairly certain Wil wouldn't think twice about leaving them behind or killing them himself if it meant a clean escape.

And what if I gave you a prophecy? Would you believe it?

Dallin slumped. This was close enough to one, he supposed. And yes, he definitely believed it.

"There'll be a staff there. Sneaking won't be an option."

Wil looked down for a quick second. By the set of his face, Dallin figured Wil had already known as much.

"I'll take care of it."

Dallin had no doubt. That was what worried him, even more than being recognized.

"Trust me." Wil met Dallin's eyes squarely, as close to calm as Dallin had seen him since Calder flung himself into the basement earlier.

Dallin sighed. "You'd damn well better know what you're doing." He shifted his gaze to Calder, hardened it. "The man says we need the horses. Take us to them."

Surprisingly, Calder didn't argue, but he didn't look happy about it. His mouth pinched tight, and he glared between the two of them before wheeling about and leading on without another word. Dallin gave Wil a dour smile, shrugged, and gestured him ahead.

Instead Wil leaned up and dropped a quick, chaste kiss to Dallin's mouth. "Thank you."

Dallin thought perhaps Wil should have saved it until they could make sure Dallin hadn't just gotten them all caught or killed. But he took it anyway.

Backtracking at first, then twists and turns into streets and alleys Dallin hadn't seen before. It was only a few minutes before he caught a whiff of the very distinct mingled scents of horse and hay, sweat and manure.

Calder halted at the mouth of a lane that opened out onto what looked like a moderately busy thoroughfare.

"We're in the southwest corner of the city. The gates are that way"—he pointed north—"and our exit is that way"—to the west this time. "If we get separated, head down the way we came and keep on until you hit the wall. Follow it west until you see a great wooden building, used to be a milliner's. There's a thick growth of trees behind it, and a midden heap. Behind that, there's an opening. A man named Rylan fancies himself the gatekeeper, and he'll want at least ten gilders, but don't give him more than four—tell him you were sent by the Exile." Calder shook his head. "I don't know if you'll fit the horses through."

"If we get that far," Dallin told him, "we'll worry about it then."

"I'll take him in." Calder nodded toward Wil, his eyes still on Dallin. "You stay here. No sense in risking both of you."

Wil frowned at Dallin through a tiny flare of panic, but Dallin narrowed his eyes. Why did everything Calder said have a vaguely sinister ring to it?

So if he dies, you already have your Guardian ready to go find your new Aisling for you? I don't think so.

Dallin didn't bother trying to keep the suspicion from his tone. "No. You keep watch, I'm going with him." He ignored the protests, just turned to Wil and nodded across the street. "Come on. Head down."

No one marked them as they crossed, just went about their business, whatever it was, and only slipped uninterested glances toward them then moved along. Weapons had been forbidden on the day they'd arrived here, so Dallin hadn't realized that almost everyone seemed to go armed as a matter of daily course. He cautiously approved. The city's guards and the constabulary might have a somewhat lackadaisical attitude toward defense, from the little Dallin had been able to observe, but apparently the citizens didn't. On the other hand, perhaps they were simply a particularly vicious, cutthroat lot. Dallin hoped he wouldn't have to find out.

Wil took the lead as they crossed the dusty yard, heading without hesitation toward the double doors of the massive building that housed the city's stables. It was a fairly busy place, workers coming and going, leading horses in from the paddock or out to be exercised. Several young girls were at work currying by the fence that separated the stables from the yard, sharing buckets and brushes between them, laughing and chattering as they worked, and calling out teasing advice to another as she trotted a horse past the paddock's fence. The girl merely smirked and flipped them a vulgar salute as she crouched in the saddle, the others shrieking good-naturedly before once again minding their own work.

Dallin tapped Wil's shoulder to get his attention. "D'you know where our horses are?"

Wil was smiling, watching the girls. He turned to Dallin. "I do, but we can't just go and get them. They have the tack locked up. We'll have to get someone to get it for us." His gaze shifted from right to left, looking for a likely mark, Dallin suspected. Wil smiled again when his eye settled on a towheaded lad leaning against an empty stall, staring at the girls and absently sharing bits of his apple with a docile little roan.

"Is that—"

"Miri." Wil was nearly grinning now. "She must've just had a bath. I told the lad to take care of them, told him they were pretty keen on apples." He looked back at Dallin, delighted. "I think he listened."

I don't think he had much of a choice, Dallin didn't say. He only jerked his chin toward the lad. "What d'you have to do?"

But Wil was apparently already doing it. "Shh" was all he said as he fixed his eyes on the lad. "Come on, then."

As though he'd heard, the boy's head came up, eyes gone vacant but with a bit of that hunger beneath his gaze Dallin had seen in the man in Dudley. Muted somehow, not nearly so feral, but still unsettling. The boy stared at Wil, mouth quirking up in a smile that was both thrilled and famished. Slowly, as if there was fishing line strung between them, the boy led the horse over to Wil and stopped in front of him, eyes for Wil and Wil alone.

Miri puffed out a happy snort and dove her nose straight at Wil's neck. Wil mostly ignored her, only shrugging at her, but he kept his gaze locked with the boy's. The boy stepped in closer, like he wanted to throw his arms around Wil, but he merely tipped in, almost but not quite touching. He closed his eyes and slipped a quiet sigh into Wil's cheek.

"I thought I dreamed you."

A tiny bit of a shudder moved through Wil, but he kept his smile as he laid a hand to the boy's arm. "Good lad." He pried the reins from out the boy's sweaty grip. "I need the other horse now. You remember?" The boy nodded, still smiling, standing there with his eyes closed like he was breathing Wil in. "Good. I need them saddled, all right? Will you help us?"

Dallin hadn't noticed until now that the place had gone eerily quiet. The girls had stopped their chatter, working silently now, eyes every now and then angling toward them, then scudding right over them as though they weren't there. The bustle of the place hadn't wound down, but it had... *quieted*. The shouts from the men tossing bales had receded to occasional grunts of effort and monosyllabic instructions. Even those working the horses had slowed them to lazy trots. It was like.... Dallin didn't know what it was like. It was like nothing he'd ever seen. Not like the inn at Dudley, but not terribly *un*like either.

He looked back at Wil. His breath caught.

The boy was still standing there, eyes closed, swaying with each word Wil murmured into his ear. Strange enough, all things considered, with the calm communion between the two uncanny and almost carnal in its mockery of some dark benediction... but Wil's *face* was what made all Dallin's instincts come up short and stagger back a pace.

Wil's eyes were half-lidded and pulsing out something that nearly hummed with calm purpose—glowing, they were fucking *glowing*, almost giving off their own eldritch light, unbelievable and yet right bloody *there*, undeniable, as much as Dallin would have liked to deny it. Like in the dreams, but stronger. Like in Dudley, but Dallin could actually *see* the power this time. It wasn't real, he knew; there was nothing physical about what he saw—it was simply as close as his mind could come to explaining what his eyes were telling him. Dallin had the oddest surety that if he asked Payton what he'd seen that night in the interrogation room, Payton would have said Wil's eyes were perfectly normal.

Only this time there was no fear behind Wil's serene gaze, no disquiet. Only a cool intent that made itself all too plain when Wil leaned in, brushed his lips over the lad's, and patted his arm.

"Go on, then."

The boy turned, looking right through Dallin. Dallin had to take a step back so he wouldn't get trampled when the boy led Miri down toward the stalls. Dallin gave his head a sharp shake.

"What are you doing?" It was as quiet and calm as Dallin could make it.

Wil's eyes were closed now, his head tilted to the side. "Pushing."

"Well, yes, but...." Dallin laid his hand on Wil's arm, almost shook him, but didn't know if that would queer it all, break Wil's concentration, make him start gushing blood, or make the stable's staff all turn on each other with teeth bared. "*All* of them?"

"Mostly the boy. But yes, all of them." Wil's eyebrows drew down, and he shook his head. "Don't talk. I have to focus."

Dallin let go of Wil's arm and couldn't help but step away just a little. Just looking at them all, going about their business as though their minds were elsewhere, it gave Dallin an uneasy chill, and a queasy little pit opened up in his stomach. In Dudley it had been as though someone had taken a cudgel to the minds of those people at the inn. With this it was a sharp, precise scalpel. So very different from the blunt force assault in that cell, where Wil had stumbled away from it bleeding, nearly hadn't stumbled away from it at all, and the other man had come away from it... well, for all Dallin knew, he was still catatonic. This was so much more... sophisticated. And in only what amounted to—he counted back—ten days, maybe?

Mother save them all—what would Wil be able to do with it when he *really* knew what he was doing?

I can turn myself invisible, Wil had joked once, tweaking at Dallin's reticence because he knew he could, and it had been mildly amusing at the time. Now Dallin thought it might not be too far off the mark. Perhaps Wil couldn't really make himself disappear, but he might be able to make others think he had.

Dallin wanted to look away, nail his gaze to the floor and not lift it until this unsettling business was done. Instead he kept his eyes on the lad as he unlocked what was apparently a storage cabi-

253

net, dragged out first Wil's saddle and then Dallin's, then went back for a third. Dallin should stay close, should be right where he was, in case Wil needed him—for what, Dallin was afraid to guess —but if nothing else, standing here and watching that lad saddle three horses was a waste of time they didn't have.

Dallin approached the boy warily, grabbing for his own tack, but he kept his hands away from Wil's things. That man back in Dudley had lunged at Dallin just for laying a hand to Wil's shoulder. Dallin didn't know if this was the same or not, if the imagined proprietorship reached to Wil's possessions, or if the lad even knew which were Wil's possessions in the first place, but Dallin thought it safest to let the lad take care of Wil's horse. By the way the boy was muttering to himself in a quiet little singsong, Dallin thought it best to just try to stay out of his line of sight.

He saddled his own horse quickly, cinched it all tight, the lad moving slower than was likely his usual wont, so Dallin saddled the one that had apparently been confiscated for Calder as well. Another roan, a little on the elderly side but with big hoofs and a big arse, barrel and flanks well-muscled, so he would do well enough for Calder. If Calder could even ride, which they'd neglected to address.

Another thing they'd neglected to address—Dallin was right now in the process of stealing a horse. Brilliant. He was already wanted—for desertion certainly, treason likely, possibly murder for that fiasco in the alley, and now probably for horse thieving as well. Of them all, horse thieving hurt the least.

Growling lightly, Dallin finished and straightened his back. Wil was still right where Dallin had left him, straight and tall. His eyes were open now, tracking everything, doing that oddly beautiful thing they did, eldritch and unfettered. As before in the alley, Dallin was struck by the wild allure of him. Dallin hadn't been exaggerating when he'd said Wil was like a minor god—when Wil looked like this, Dallin would swear he breathed in air and exhaled strength, winding it around himself in tensile threads of invincibility.

"The heart of the world," the lad murmured in that unnerving little harmonic buzz he'd been doing since he'd left Wil's side. "Blood to blood." His hands were opening and closing spasmodically around the reins of Wil's horse.

"They want what's in me, even if they don't know what it is. Some would open my chest and dig out my heart looking for it and still not realize they didn't know what they were looking for."

For the first time, looking at the blankly hungry look in the eyes of this otherwise handsome and most likely honest young man, Dallin thought he had some idea what Wil might have meant. The worship on the boy's face was almost predatory, as if he loved Wil enough to rip him apart.

And, all right, Dallin had had just about enough. Too much, in fact. He took up the reins of his horse and Calder's and tugged them over toward Wil, dismayed to see Wil was sweating now, somewhat pale, and a light tremor ran through his body. No nosebleed, but Dallin didn't like the way Wil's brow was twisting and his jaw kept clenching and unclenching in a too-obvious effort at maintaining control.

"We've got what we need." Dallin kept his voice low and smooth so as not to startle Wil out of whatever focus he was applying. "C'mon, let's get out of here."

Wil nodded slowly, waving the lad back over, then sliding his fingers up to his temple. "One more thing." He rubbed. "The crossbow," he said to the lad. "Get it, please."

"No."

Dallin made the protest even as the boy allowed Wil to take the reins from his hand and turned back toward the tack cabinet. Some part of Dallin was absently amused when the mare lipped at

Wil's hair—the greater part of him wanted to kick Wil's arse. *Hard.*
In fact, he'd forgotten all about the crossbow; it had been strapped
to the saddle when Dallin had left the horses at the post by the
gates when they'd arrived, and he hadn't even thought about
it since.

Dallin tilted Wil's chin up until that throbbing green gaze slid
into his. "I don't need it. It's done nothing but get in the way. Just
put a stop to this now—we have to go, and you don't look well."

Wil smiled at him, loose and too far away. "All the ammuni-
tion we can get." He reached out and latched on to Dallin's cloak.
"There's so much of it." His face twisted in vague bewilderment.
"I could wander forever."

Dallin didn't really understand what Wil was talking about,
but that last statement woke him to it like a hammer to the thumb.
He gripped Wil's hand.

"What are you doing? Pushing?"

"Tending." Wil sighed and closed his eyes. He swayed.
"Dreaming awake. It's... really quite lovely." A small laugh, and he
shook his head. "It doesn't hurt."

"Doesn't hurt, that's good, Wil." Dallin made himself squelch
rising panic. "I need you to stop it, all right?" The boy was coming
back with the crossbow, quickening his steps when he saw how
close Dallin had got to Wil, face darkening with possessive rage.
Dallin leaned down to growl into Wil's ear. "*Wil*, the lad is coming
back, and now he's armed. I'm going to get shot with my own bow
if you don't stop this."

"Amazing. So much to see...."

Without even pulling away or opening his eyes, Wil held up a
hand, flicked it. The lad stopped so quickly the mop of bright flax
on his head flew back from his brow and then into his eyes as
though he'd hit an invisible brick wall.

Dallin clenched his teeth, eyes flicking back and forth between the thwarted devotion of the boy and the beatific abstraction of Wil.

"All right, very nice, but stop it now. We have to go."

Finally Wil opened his eyes. Dallin almost wished he hadn't.

Dazzling muted sage flecked and eddied with churning malachite and twisted into Dallin's chest with a sadness and regret that was near physical, sliding from Wil's heart and into Dallin's. Deep and old, years of pain and betrayal, sorrow and abandonment, and all of it winding over them like a rime of misted rain.

"It doesn't hurt in here," Wil whispered.

All that pain, all that anger, burbling up from a well the depth of which Dallin didn't want to fathom—and there, inside wherever Wil was wandering now, it was gone. Inside with his patterns and his threads and his pushing, Wil was, probably for the first time in his life, free.

Dallin almost pulled away, but he didn't.

This was a connection he'd never wanted. If he'd known this was coming, back in that sooty, smoke-bitter cellar room, he would have backed away, shut himself down before it could cut him with the knowing. *It's all full of knives....* Dallin could feel them. And what was he supposed to do? Pluck one of them up? Plunge it into Wil's heart?

Three chirps of the lark scattered through the stillness, the faint snicker of a squirrel.

Dallin blinked. His heart lumped up tight in his chest.

Circumstances long forgotten or put away down deep in his consciousness where he wouldn't have to look at them, but the signal itself blared in Dallin's head like a claxon. It took too long for it to wend into his awareness, took too long for his memory to kick in and chitter the meaning to his instincts.

A young boy, gold hair long and swaying over shoulders already widening, loping through the fields of his country with a careless smile, pushing and shoving at his mates and laughing—

Three chirps of the lark, the faint snicker of a squirrel.

Danger—take cover.

Calder was still outside keeping watch, chirping the code Dallin only remembered through a strange, vague twist of fright and nostalgia. And then the warning stopped, cut off between one trill and the next—a sharp cry, then the sound of bootheels clocking hard on the dry, packed dirt of the yard.

Dallin threw his glance to the open doors, hands clutching spasmodically on Wil, squeezing so hard Wil gasped. Dallin barely heard it, his heart thudding the hammer to the anvil in his head as the blue-clad figure pulled up abruptly in the doorway. Dallin loosened his grip.

"Corliss?"

"Brayden." Corliss shook her auburn head and closed her eyes. "Oh *shit.*"

Limned in thin sunlight, her solid figure wavered just the smallest bit. Dallin didn't know if she actually swayed or if his own senses had hiccupped. Her blue and brown, always worn so proudly, was muddy and rumpled, and her hair, almost always in a tight knot at the back of her head, fell in long, wavy wisps around her face. She looked exhausted, face pale, dark circles beneath her tired eyes.

"You've been riding hard," Dallin said quietly.

Corliss took in the saddled horses, the workers, the boy, the silence....

"I've been praying they'd got it wrong." She looked like she was trying not to believe her own eyes. Her sidearm was still holstered, but the tethers were loose and her hand hovered just above the burled butt. She shifted her glance to Wil, skimmed it over the rifle in his hand, Dallin's grip on his arm. "Please tell me you've just arrested this man and were on your way to the Chester constabulary to turn him in."

Wil looked up at Dallin slowly, more alert now, like he was taking in the things around him as well as inside him again. The look was rueful, anxious—*caught and caged*—but hope took up the corners, waiting for Dallin to negate reality. "*I think perhaps you're the only one in the world I do trust.*" Dallin wished with his whole self that the next few moments wouldn't belie that tender, too-breakable faith.

"Brayden." The warning in Corliss's tone was all too clear. "Say it and I'll believe it. Don't make me arrest you."

Perhaps it would be wiser. Allow them to be arrested and then figure out a way to get them out of it. Or say what Corliss wanted to hear and then figure out how to get Wil away again. No danger of having to fire on Corliss and whomever the two others from Putnam might be. No danger of having to fire on soldiers beside whom Dallin would have been fighting ten years ago. No danger of either one of them getting shot while trying to escape.

Dallin shook his head and leaned in toward Wil. "Whatever happens, you get on that horse and you go, understand?"

"Brayden!" The horror in Corliss's voice was enough to make Dallin flinch.

He turned his gaze on her, hardened it. "You don't know what's going on here."

"I can bloody guess!"

Ever the mum, Corliss. Dallin pushed Wil back but kept his grip on Wil's arm. "It isn't what you're thinking. At least, that's not all of it."

"So you *are*—"

"It's bigger than that, Corliss, you've no idea what.... Didn't Jagger tell you anything?"

"Chief Jagger was arrested when word came back from Dudley that you'd absconded with the prisoner."

Dallin fell silent, stunned. *Arrested.* He shook his head slowly. "For what?"

Corliss's mouth thinned. "For conspiracy." Anger and betrayal flashed bright in her hazel eyes. "He wouldn't speak against you, wouldn't believe what they were saying, so they assumed he was in on it." Her glare flashed at Wil. "He's been in solitary confinement for weeks now—*I'm* not even allowed to see him." She looked back at Dallin, gaze going softer, pleading. "Tell me it isn't true. Tell me it isn't true, and we'll arrest this man and walk out of here together." Her hand still hovered at her holster, but the other went behind her back—reaching, Dallin knew, for the shackles at her belt. "You can still get out of this, Brayden. Everyone slips up. It's not too late to fix it."

Perhaps if she'd said "Dallin" rather than "Brayden."

Perhaps if Wil hadn't tensed and caught his breath when Corliss's hand came out from behind her back, cool metal clinking between her fingers.

Dallin pushed Wil farther behind him, keeping his eyes steady on Corliss. "I'm sorry."

"So am I." Corliss's gaze turned sad and regretful. Her hand finally settled on her gun, drew it from its holster, and aimed it at Dallin's chest. "Constable Dallin Brayden. By the authority of the Province of Putnam, Constabulary of the Commonwealth of Cynewísan—"

"*Stop.*" Wil very nearly hissed it as he raised his hand.

Dallin caught it. "No. Not her."

He didn't think he could stand to see Corliss with that blank look on her face.

"—you are under arrest on the charges of treason—"

Even though he'd known it was coming, it still hurt. *Treason.* Dallin couldn't help the sharp wince and near flinch.

"Then what do you propose?" Wil growled.

"—aiding and abetting a—"

"Get yourself to Lind," Dallin told him. "You know the way. You've got the money. Get out and keep running. Don't stop 'til you—"

"*Dallin!*" Wil grabbed hold of Dallin's arm with clutching fingers. "You can't let—"

"*Chosen!*"

A booming shout from out in the yard.

Wil froze, fingers digging into Dallin's arm so hard Dallin vaguely wondered if they'd meet in the middle. Even the mare, happily teasing at Wil's coat with her big yellow teeth, jerked up her head and snorted, dancing at the end of her rein.

A small gasp from Wil, a watery moan, then a broken whisper, breathless and terribly shaky.

"No... *no.*"

And with that one small puff of breath, whatever spell had held the stable workers in sway broke abruptly. Gazes sharpened, heads turned, confusion ran slow tremors over dozens of faces. Alertness honed their glances even as Wil staggered against Dallin, hand still clutching, holding himself up.

Dallin watched Corliss watching it all, watched her jaw set firm, watched her turn her eyes to Dallin and harden them. "I need help in here," she called over her shoulder. "Woodrow, haul arse!"

Woodrow? She'd brought *Woodrow*?

"Mister Síofra," she said with quite a lot more tact, "I'll ask you to stay where you are until the situation is more tenable."

"Wil." Dallin pried Wil's fingers loose, dismayed to his core to see the steady stream of bright scarlet dripping from Wil's nose. Wil didn't even seem to notice.

Damn it, he'd gone and pulled it back again. Didn't he know that would kill him?

Dallin took hold of Wil and *shook*. "You have to go."

"Chosen, dearest lost lad! Come to me now and all will be forgiven."

The tone turned Dallin's stomach. Paternal, just the right mix of command and kindness, condescending compassion. Dallin didn't know why he was so surprised Síofra nearly pulled it off—he'd had fifty years to practice it, after all.

"Constable Brayden." Corliss's voice was coming closer. "You will surrender your firearms—"

"Wil, get up on your horse."

Wil's dazed eyes turned slowly to Dallin, that looming panic from earlier now fully bloomed and flowering steadily. "I—"

"You can." Dallin snarled it. "You can and you will. Get up on that bloody horse, Wil." He closed his fist over the reins in Wil's hand. "Right now."

"Brayden." Right behind him now. A rolling click, the feel of a small circle of cold metal at his nape. "Don't make me." There was real pleading in Corliss's shaky voice.

Dallin's whole attention was on the fear flaring out of Wil's pores, on the sadness and desolation Dallin had touched before, when Wil had been wandering inside himself.

"Wil. *Will* Get up on your fucking horse."

Wil was still shaking his head slowly, tears crowding his eyes and dripping slow and thick down his blanched cheeks. "Don't... don't go away."

It almost made the tears come for Dallin too—fast and hard. He swallowed them and gritted his teeth.

"It's my bullet." Dallin tried to smile and failed. "See that? You didn't even have to throw me in front of it. So much for prophe-cies." Wil opened his mouth—to protest, to scream, Dallin didn't know—but Dallin cut him off. "I'm choosing you." He firmed his jaw and made his voice as hard and fierce as he could. "Now get up on that fucking horse. *Move it, soldier!*"

He didn't give Wil any more time for paralysis. He shoved Wil away, turned on Corliss, grabbed for the gun, and prayed with everything in him that Wil was lurching into the saddle as he did it.

Corliss's shock and disbelief that Dallin would actually attack her helped. Dallin was able to close his hand over Corliss's and prevent her from firing. He spun her and clamped his hand over her mouth. Corliss was fast and skilled in hand-to-hand, but there was no denying that Dallin was simply bigger and stronger. He used it to full advantage even as some part buried at the back of his heart mourned for the years-long friendship he was in the process of severing for good.

Dallin craned a look over his shoulder, relieved to see Wil already mounted. He wasn't leaving, though, only swiping his sleeve distractedly at the blood pouring from his nose and staring at Dallin with eyes gone impossibly wide. Dallin wished he had a hand free to give the horse's rump a sharp slap and get Wil moving.

Corliss was writhing in Dallin's grip, shackles clattering to the floor as her arm flailed back and whacked him in the head, digging the heels of her boots into Dallin's toes first, then kicking back at his shins. She was growling and probably cursing against Dallin's hand the whole while. Dallin ignored it all.

"Through the paddock." Dallin jerked his head at Wil's horse. "If she can't jump the fence, push her. You know you can."

"Lad."

From the doorway this time, softly satisfied. Dallin didn't even look, kept his eyes on Wil. He would have said Wil couldn't look more terrified than he had just ten seconds ago, but the dread notched up as Wil juddered in the saddle. He started to turn his head—

"Don't look at him, look at me," Dallin snapped.

"Come to me, Aisling," Síofra crooned. "He can't protect you. You know what he is—you know his destiny. Come to me now, and I'll take you home. All is forgiven."

"Wil, *look* at me, damn it." When Wil did, slowly, Dallin set his jaw and curled his lip on a derisive sneer. "Caught and caged, *Aisling*. Is that what you want?" He raised Corliss's hand— Dallin's around hers, hers around the gun—and pointed the barrel just over Wil's head. "It's either that or I keep my promise. Now move your arse, damn you. *Go!*"

The paralysis broke. Wil kicked his heels into the horse's barrel, tugged the reins, and crouched over her neck as she wheeled to the side. They took off with a low grunt and a clatter of hoofs. Dallin didn't know whether to laugh or cry when Wil shot his hand out on his way by the lad who'd saddled his horse, grabbed the crossbow from him, and just kept going, scattering beast and rider alike before him as he went.

A cacophony of voices burst from the yard, red and gold flicking past the open doors and through Dallin's peripheral vision, shouts and orders he didn't hear. He watched for a moment until Wil cleared the fence, then let out a long, tight breath and closed his eyes.

"I'm so sorry." Dallin let Corliss go abruptly and raised his hands. He rested them atop his head, took a step back, and lowered himself to one knee. "Two revolvers," he said as she spun, gun raised and aimed right between his eyes, "right thigh and left hip, a sword on my left, and a knife in my right boot."

Corliss was breathing heavily, disbelief still twisting through the betrayal in her shocked gaze. "D'you know what you've just *done?*"

Dallin nodded slowly, looked her in the eye. "I chose him."

He'd never been shackled before. Dallin stayed still, staring straight ahead, while Corliss guided his hands to the small of his back and snapped the iron about his wrists. He refused to allow his cheeks to darken, refused to allow his chin to dip. Dallin was proud of what he'd done, from the moment he'd made the decision to help Wil and not arrest him, and no humiliating procedure would dim that. Down on one knee, disarmed, searched, the ghost-weight of the badge they'd taken from his pocket uncannily heavy—all of it seared into Dallin's chest, but the burn for what he'd come to see over the past few weeks as his real duty flared hotter.

The eyes of every worker in the stables were on him. Commonwealth soldiers looked on from the door. Woodrow and Creighton stared at their boots. And still Dallin kept his head up. Even beneath Corliss's sad, disappointed gaze, Dallin didn't wither.

"It breaks my heart." Corliss whispered it as the clasps snapped home.

"And yet you're doing it."

She stood, stepped in front of him, anger flashing. "It's my *job.*"

"I began by using that excuse myself." Dallin met her gaze steadily. "Some jobs are bigger than others."

"You'd do the same in my place. You're First Constable of Putnam, Brayden—*First Constable.* Don't you even remember what that means?"

He shrugged. "That title no longer belongs to me. I have another now."

Corliss went nearly white with rage. "What could be so bloody important that you'd just throw all that away?" Her hands clenched into fists. "I could weep for you, but you're too damned stupid to weep for yourself!"

Dallin merely looked at her calmly for a moment, accepting the rebuke, the hurt, the disappointment. "In your place," he told her slowly, "I would have done you the honor of asking you that question before I'd done you the *dis*honor of shackling you and taking another's word against you." He paused, watching her gaze flinch and mist. "I weep only for the trust you owed me. Save your tears. I've no need of them."

Corliss lifted her chin, jaw tight. "As you will."

She left him kneeling in the center of the floor while the rest of the party watered their horses and milled about, awaiting instructions.

He loved Corliss like a sister, but Dallin couldn't regret her anger, her betrayal at his supposed treachery, the loss of her regard —any of it. His entire life was lying dead in this stable so far from what he'd called home, shattered around him, and he could concentrate on nothing but whether or not Wil had got away clean, whether he was safe, what kind of welcome he'd receive in Lind....

"You realize, of course," Síofra told Dallin quietly, pacing slowly across the floor to stand in front of him, black boots shining as they clicked and clocked across the wooden boards, "that I *will* find him and bring him home." He crouched down in front of Dallin, smiled, all charm and understanding. "You can't be blamed entirely. He's a very convincing liar." He chuckled sadly. "I can only imagine what he's told you."

I'll just bet you can. Dallin kept his teeth clamped tight and stared straight ahead. Síofra really was a smarmy-looking man. Narrow and pale, he might have been considered decent-looking at one time, but arrogance and calculation had turned fair looks tight and pinched. Dark hair worn longish in the custom of Ríocht, combed straight and tucked behind his ears; thin lips over straight white teeth that flashed brilliant with a practiced smile that could almost pass for charismatic; too-sharp blue eyes that could either look right through you or look right past you, but Dallin would wager they never in truth *saw* anyone.

I see you, though. And far too well. Too bad we didn't meet when we were both back in Putnam. Wil wouldn't have even had to tell me why he was running from you. And it wouldn't have taken me so damned long to decide to help him.

Síofra looked far too young for what Dallin assumed to be his years. He had to be at least two decades older than Wil, and yet he looked as though he hadn't yet seen his fortieth birthday.

Right, and I bet I know how you managed that, you soul-sucking weasel.

"He can't help himself," Síofra went on. "You mustn't blame him. The poor lad can't tell fantasy from reality most of the time."

That'll happen when you're force-fed mæting all your life, but you didn't manage to kill or steal his mind, did you? I'll bet the brilliance of it was like a shining gem just out of your reach, and that's just eating you up, isn't it? He fought you, and for more than fifty years you couldn't beat him.

Despite himself, Dallin smirked. It made Síofra's smile slip a bit, made the rage and hatred behind his eyes flash out just for a second, before he schooled his expression back to one of charm and concern. He leaned in close to dip his mouth to Dallin's ear.

"I know what you are." The whisper was a thin, silky drawl. "I know where you've sent him." He pulled back just a little, softening his smile, almost intimate. "I wonder if he'll think you've betrayed him when he finds what's waiting for him? Ah, but then, he won't make it, you know, so I don't expect we'll ever get an answer to that question. Pity." He sighed. "It's all been for nothing. He'll never even get out of the city, and you?" The smile twisted. "I believe the punishment for treason is at least one thing upon which Cynewísan and Ríocht agree." Síofra waved his long, pale hand. "Gibbets are the same everywhere, I expect."

None of it was surprising; none of it would get the rise out of Dallin that Síofra was obviously looking for. Instead Dallin leaned in himself and let his smirk curl wide and cocky. "He knows what you've done," he whispered back. "He knows what I am—he knows what *he* is. He knows *everything*." He mimicked Síofra's own little performance, pulling back, returning the smile, and letting it twist smug. "He knows you're coming. And he's ready for you this time."

Dallin was a much better bluffer than Síofra. Síofra's face darkened, rage suppressed beneath charm boiled up, and flowed over into the glitter of his eyes, the clench of his teeth. He stood, mouth tight, and glared at Dallin for a long moment before dragging his gaze away.

He turned to Corliss, who was waiting over by the storage cabinet, watching. "I'm done here, Constable." Clipped and thin. "I'll want to continue with this one at the constabulary. Bring him along with your men—I don't expect he can cause much trouble anymore. Let the local law deal with the other Linder. And after they've completed the search of the city and found the Chosen, see that these brave soldiers are housed appropriately in one of Chester's better establishments. On Ríocht's coin, of course."

With one last narrow look at Dallin, Síofra left the stable. Dallin watched him go, just barely keeping a snort under control. That man actually thought he was going to interrogate Dallin?

Fine. Let him ask his questions. They'd just see who got more information than whom.

Corliss made her way back over, and Dallin had no problem turning on her with a derisive sneer. "Taking orders from Dominion scum now?"

She colored only slightly. "You're hardly one to talk about what another does for or with 'Dominion scum.'" Her mouth tightened, and she shook her head. "You don't know what's happened, Brayden." She tugged at Dallin's elbow. Dallin got to his feet with only a slight grimace—his knee was bloody *killing* him. "Both sides are massing at the borders again. The talks have fallen apart, and according to the elders at the Guild, the only thing keeping them from blowing their war horns is the fact that General Wheeler has personally promised that the Commonwealth will find and return their Chosen. Those aren't just soldiers out there—they're infantry sharpshooters, handpicked by Wheeler himself. You're damned lucky none of them had to shoot at you—these lads don't miss."

"That doesn't answer my question."

Corliss *shook* him. "Síofra's *word* now determines whether or not war is declared. Síofra's *word* is all that's keeping the Guild from foaming at the mouth. Síofra's *word* will hopefully calm the Guild when he tells them Cynewísan did everything in its power to find their Chosen and return him to them safely, and then—" She stopped, face screwing up and eyes once again misting over.

"And then see that the Chosen's 'kidnapper' is properly hanged, I imagine." Dallin shook his head. "How long have we known each other, Corliss?"

She looked away, didn't answer.

"Since we were fifteen." Dallin barely managed to tamp down the growl beneath it. "I've sat at your table. I watched you bind your hand to Olin's. Your children have used me for a tree, all six of them, at one time or another." He leaned in, teeth clenching with an anger he hadn't even been aware was rising, but now that he was thinking about it—what right did *she* have to feel betrayed? "You should've known me better than this. You should've known that whatever it might look like, I did what I did because I had to, because the need was greater than the job."

"And how would I have—?"

"You should've found a way to ask!"

The bustle in their periphery paused for a moment, the stable workers and Commonwealth troops who'd been trying very hard not to look like they were watching suddenly sweeping keen glances their way. Woodrow met Dallin's eyes squarely for the first time; Dallin was surprised to note there was no judgment there, no anger, no nervous blushing. Dallin noted it, but Corliss distracted him when she set her jaw, took his arm again, and began to lead him from the stable. Woodrow and Creighton fell in behind.

The soldiers stared. Two of them spat in the dirt as he passed. Dallin ignored it.

They walked in silence until they were out of the yard, making the turn for the street that led to Chester's constabulary. Corliss was tense, brooding, but she leaned in. "What d'you want from me?" Her voice was whisper-thin, and her lips barely even moved.

Dallin breathed a small, silent sigh. "He means to question me. I want you to listen. To *all* of it."

She shook her head. "He's a close one, and he doesn't trust women. I doubt he'll let me."

"I didn't say you should *ask him*." Dallin couldn't help the way it snapped out of him. He reined in his temper as much as he could. "There's a book in my pack. Find it and read everything you can find on the legend of the Aisling, then get your arse to wherever they're taking me and listen." He lowered his voice. "I've never given you a reason not to trust me, Corliss, and I've never asked you for a damned thing. I've been a good superior to you while you've been at the constabulary, and for most of our lives, I've been a good friend. You do what I ask now, and whatever happens after, you owe me nothing."

Corliss gusted a heavy sigh and looked down at her dusty boots.

"As you will."

The Chester constabulary was newer than Putnam's and brighter, with its great wide windows and gleaming wooden floors rather than the bulky stone and stale surroundings Dallin had always associated with the law. He'd expected glares and derisive gestures when he was brought in—lawmen didn't generally take kindly to one of their ranks switching sides, and there was the mess with the gate guard, after all—but he was largely ignored, except for the few whose services were required to get him through the door and into an interrogation room.

Dallin wasn't taken to a desk to be processed by a bored minion, and he wasn't formally apprised of the charges against him. He was led straight down into the gaslit basement of the place, the same stone as the city's walls, and into a small dank room with no windows, merely a plain table bolted to the floor and two wooden chairs. Stark and dim and dusty.

He'd thought Síofra would keep him waiting, try to get him anxious and sweating, but he arrived with no fanfare a mere several minutes after Dallin was deposited by a bored bailiff. He sat across from Dallin, no charming smile this time.

Good. Perhaps they were to speak plainly, then.

Except Síofra didn't speak—just stared at Dallin, a pale glimmer in his eyes that was reminiscent of Wil but small and ugly, where Wil's was... pure? Dynamic? Just solely and simply *Wil?*—all burning intensity and cool cunning.

Dallin didn't know and didn't bother defining it. He merely rolled his eyes. "Right, that doesn't work on me. Save your tricks for your own minions." He tilted his head. "Orman ever recover?"

Síofra's calm façade slipped the tiniest bit before he caught himself. He shrugged. "I regret that our meeting has occurred under such circumstances."

Trying to be "friends," talk man to man. Too bloody predictable. Dallin just hoped to hell Corliss was out there listening to this. Because Dallin meant for her to get a bloody earful.

He raised an eyebrow. "I've no doubt." He smiled. "Then again, I've no doubt you regret we've met at all. You did try rather hard to prevent the possibility, after all."

"Ah, delightful, we're to be blunt, then." Síofra smiled too and sat back in his chair. "So the lad's been telling tales, has he?" He shook his head. "Perhaps I put too much trust in the boy."

"Trust. An interesting choice of words." Dallin raised both eyebrows this time. "D'you know what it means?"

Síofra chuckled. "As you will, then. Perhaps I should have been more... precise in my aim."

"Perhaps you should have been more precise with your questions afterward." Dallin shrugged. "When you drug a man and trick him into being terrified of the one meant to protect him, then trick him again into making him believe he was responsible for wiping out half a village, you really can't be surprised when he keeps a secret or two." He shifted, affecting a thoughtful frown. "What I don't understand is, why did you even think it necessary? I mean, let's face it—you already had him. He was already petrified of me, and you were going to stage your raid on Lind whether he knew about it or not. Why was it so important that he believe he did it?"

"Ah, that's right. You are—oh, I'm so sorry, you *were* a constable. I imagine you're used to asking the questions."

The condescending sympathy in the tone almost made Dallin laugh. Síofra really did think he knew what he was doing.

Except he wasn't so good without his drugs and his stolen magic. And he didn't seem to know it.

"My mistake," Dallin returned just as sincerely.

Anyway, he didn't really need an answer. Síofra had done it to make sure Wil stayed far away from Lind. Why Síofra had thought he needed to do it, seeing as Wil had been a prisoner all his life and there had been no real hope of escape, Dallin would certainly like to know, but he doubted Síofra would be terribly forthcoming on the issue. Dallin had asked the question mostly for Corliss's benefit, so he didn't pursue an answer he wouldn't get.

Instead he frowned and tilted his head. "What *was* the question, anyway?"

"I'm not quite certain I've asked one yet. But since you've brought it up—I'm very curious to know what you think the lad is about." Síofra waved a hand. "It doesn't really matter, you understand—he's mad and needs his drafts just to control his violent temper, and nothing he says can be trusted."

Dallin's jaw twitched some with that snide little "needs his drafts," but he managed to control the snarl. He kept his face blank.

Síofra leaned into the table, clasping his hands atop it. "*However.* Perhaps, if I knew more about the story he's given you, I might be moved to appeal for leniency once we reach Penley." His eyes widened, mock-apology. "Oh, I don't think I mentioned— you're to be tried in your capital before your elders. I've become quite... familiar with the High Seat, Channing."

Dallin would just bet he had.

He wished his hands were free. He would have liked to drape himself back over his chair for a more cavalier effect. He settled for stretching out his legs and slouching a bit.

"You assume it was necessary for him to give me a story at all." He quirked his lips. "You assume very many things. I thought you knew what I am."

Síofra's mouth pinched. "I don't *care* what you are." It came out through his straight white teeth. "You're no threat to me anymore."

"Perhaps not." Dallin shrugged. "But he knows what *he* is now. He knows what he can do." He cocked his head. "What frightened you the most, d'you think? You knew about the elements when you stole him away, so it must not've been that."

Síofra's narrow features froze. "It was him that called the storm outside Dudley, then."

Dallin almost jumped up and did a little jig. One little bit of confession, and from the man's own mouth.

Corliss had damn well better have her ear plastered to that door. Because Dallin hoped this was just the beginning.

"What else can he do?" Síofra demanded, all pretense at indifference abandoned.

This morning I watched him call fire and tame it to his hand. Bet that would send your stones up to your throat.

Dallin widened his eyes, all innocence. "P'raps when you see him again, you can get him sotted on mæting and make him tell you. That *was* how it worked, wasn't it? Steal an infant and then try to steal his power?" He let his face go hard. "But you didn't know what else he had in him, did you? You knew he was the Aisling, but you didn't know about the dreams, right? And when you found out, you kept him drugged for fifty years so you could twist them yourself."

Dallin just wished he could see Síofra's face when he found out the hard way about the pushing. He leaned in.

"I wonder what your dear, *familiar* Channing would think if he learned you'd been using a man's dreams to gain advantage against his country? Magicking without a license in Cynewísan is rather frowned upon, and I'd say magicking with criminal intent toward the Mother's own Gift wouldn't go over very well at all. How old *are* you, anyway? Ah!" Dallin sat back again. "But then, I suppose you reckon the elders won't find out, yes? Because the only one besides you who knows about it will never make it to Penley for trial, am I right?"

Síofra's complexion had gone rather gray—a mixture of rage and fright, Dallin guessed. His hands were gripping at each other so hard his fingers had turned wax-white.

"I rather thought 'shot while trying to escape' had a nice ring to it."

Dallin chuckled. "From the sound of it, I don't suppose there are many left in Putnam who will dare to object. Nice trick, that. How did you get them to arrest Jagger so quickly?"

"*I'm* to be asking the questions!"

If Dallin had a hand free, he would have held it up, placating. "Ah, right, sorry, I forgot." He dipped his head. "As you will."

Síofra sputtered for a moment, off balance. It was only with an obvious effort that he reined in his fury and too-evident unease. "*What—can—he—do?*"

Dallin allowed a snort this time. "You don't really think I'm going to tell you *that*, do you? Honestly, man, do give me at least *some* credit."

"Oh, I give you all sorts of credit, young man. But you've obviously heard as much about me as I have about you." Síofra leaned in, more confident now. "You know I can find out."

Dallin shrugged, unconcerned. "You can try."

Almost immediately the air thickened, grew heavy, and a light buzz fizzed at the back of Dallin's brain. Dallin set his teeth. It was getting more difficult to maintain the smirk, but he kept it, hardened it.

"*You've been doing it all your life.*" Wil's calm voice, guiding Dallin resolutely through the locks and chains of his own mind. "*Just find it and make it stronger.*"

The drone rose an octave, skittering over Dallin like tiny little insects crawling over his skin, slithering up his backbone. It was... familiar. Good thing for the shackles, else Dallin would've smacked himself in the head. Instead he barked a laugh.

"It was you!" He snorted. "I felt you coming. Shit, wish I'd known what it was before. Would've saved me an awful lot of wittering." He shook his head, still chuckling. "I kept thinking something terrible was coming, and all along, it was only you."

The buzzing stopped abruptly. Síofra sprang from his chair, and lunged across the table. Dallin consciously controlled his instinctive flinch and kept the smile. Síofra's long fingers curled around the edge of the table, clenched.

"Laugh it up, *Guardian*. Laugh all the way to the noose, for all I care. But then, as you say, you won't make it that far. Just know, as you hear that bullet coming for you, that it's all for nothing—I'll find him, and I'll have him. He's *mine*, and you've failed, as the two before you did."

Dallin let the smile drop, let his expression turn cold. "I wonder what Æledfýres thinks about that?"

He watched carefully as Síofra's expression went from livid to blankly stunned. It wasn't just surprise that Dallin knew how Síofra had found Wil—there was fear there.

Dallin took advantage. "What did you promise him in return for telling you where to find the Aisling? Or should I say, on what promise did you renege?"

Oh, this was just too rich. Síofra had lost so much color he was almost transparent.

Dallin pushed it harder. "I have to hand it to you. Biting the hand of a god. Pretty nervy. I should warn you, though—the Mother and the Father are sorely displeased with you. You might want to watch your back."

Presumptuous, but likely pretty accurate. Dallin had just more or less spoken for gods, but he thought They might be somewhat forgiving under the circumstances. Now if only one of Them would see fit to give him a bit of a hand here—pop loose the shackles or something, make Síofra choke to death on his own rage. Really. Anything. Dallin wasn't picky.

"I've nothing to fear from either of *Them*."

"Oh, I wouldn't count on that. They're quite cross that you've used Their Gift so badly." Dallin's teeth clenched, and he set his face hard. "And Their Gift is no longer addicted to leaf and help-less to fight you. So, you see, regardless of whether or not your bullet finds its target, *or* your noose, I've not failed. The Guardian has fulfilled his purpose."

Síofra's chin trembled. "You expect me to believe you've seen Them?"

"I don't really give a shit what you believe. I don't really give a shit about you at all." Dallin sighed. "It's so very strange. I've been expecting someone powerful, someone to fear, someone... someone with a bloody *spine*, at least." He shook his head. "You're so much smaller than I'd thought. It seems you're only scary when you're drugging little boys and stealing their power from them. It's... well, it's a little... disappointing, if I'm being honest."

And he was.

Síofra just stood there for a moment, seething. Dallin wondered if Síofra realized just how much information he'd given up during this supposed interrogation. Realized he truly didn't care. He didn't know exactly what he'd be able to do with his new insight, considering his current circumstance and his apparently rather limited lifespan, but it was something. A victory. Somewhat.

Please, Corliss, be out there and listening. And if anything happens to me, find him and help him.

"When next I see him," Síofra said, low and thick, "I'll be sure to give him your regards."

"Do that," Dallin said with a bored sigh.

"And perhaps I'll tell him you're the one who whispered his true name into my ear." Síofra's mouth curled up in a vile, humorless smile. "I'll tell him you were the one who gave me the key to his soul. I've no doubt he'll be...." The smile curled into a grin that turned Dallin's stomach. "Utterly shattered, I should think." Síofra dipped his head in an ironic half bow. "But you take solace in that purpose of yours, Guardian. Perhaps it will make your grave less dark and cold."

Dallin kept his face completely blank as Síofra turned slowly, walked to the door, and let himself out. A moment ago, Dallin had been almost exhilarated with the heady kick of knowing he'd gotten the best of Síofra, that Síofra was truly, in fact, as small as Dallin had said he was.

And then Síofra had parted with that last shot and left Dallin's ears ringing with it.

Have I a true name?

The question had been so quietly earnest, hope edged with trepidation. There had been real pain behind the anger when Wil had first told Dallin he had no name. And now it seemed there was one. Not only a name, but a key. A key to....

Dallin shook his head. Fucking hell, he'd just got done bulling his way through a thousand mysteries and secrets, and now here was another. And this one—

I'll tell him you were the one who gave me the key to his soul.

What the fuck did *that* mean?

Dallin shut his eyes, startled. There was a gentle little brush at the back of his mind—not the harsh, insectile buzz of Síofra trying and failing to force himself through the cracks of consciousness, but a light, grazing warmth. A request. No voice, no words, just knowledge, instant and clear:

"Get ready. I'm coming."

Dallin jolted and sat up straight, eyes wide and teeth clenched.

"Oh no, you're bloody not!"

The badger, snapping its teeth without looking first to see if he was latching onto a garden snake or the tail of a dragon. The crow, flying too fast to see the glass ahead.

The fear on Wil's face when just the sound of Síofra's voice had stopped him so cold it was like he'd died on his feet and forgotten to fall down.

Síofra was small without Wil's power to suck dry, but he knew how to get it. Considering him a small threat when Wil was safely away was one thing, but Wil ramming half-arsed into some stupidly brave mission to rescue his Guardian would surely get him caught again. If things went the way they looked to be going, Dallin's time might well be limited. Who would be there to help Wil this time? Who would care? Síofra had done enough damage already—what if he got hold of Wil, found out how to take and use the rest of all that vast power? Síofra up there, perhaps waiting, and Dallin down here, shackled and useless. And Wil was going to walk right back into it.

Dallin didn't even have any money to give bribing a go.

Bloody typical.

"Don't you dare, don't you fucking dare, Wil! I swear, if you show up here, I'll shoot you down!"

No answer, no sense of propinquity, not even so much as a

characteristic snarl or the snapping of ghost-teeth. Only silence, and into it the too-loud turn of the latch on the door.

Corliss stood framed by Woodrow and the bored bailiff from earlier. Corliss's eyes were avid, Woodrow's close to terrified.

Oh, thank the Mother.

"We'll take him from here, Tripp," Corliss told the bailiff. "He's our disgrace. No need for you to dirty your hands on him."

Dallin forgave her immediately. He stood as the bailiff looked him over with a disgusted grunt and waved his hand. Dallin made his way around the table, walked to the door with head bowed, and allowed Corliss to take one arm and Woodrow the other.

"I don't know how we're going to get you out of here without starting a war," Corliss muttered under her breath as they climbed the stairs, the bailiff lumbering his slow way up before them.

"I still say we just kill the bugger," Woodrow put in.

"And you want to take out a company of the Commonwealth's finest while you're at it?" Corliss pressed her lips tight. "The orders were clear. We're to serve and protect our 'guest,' and those boys are duty bound. We take one shot at the man, and they'll open all twenty guns on us."

Woodrow flung her a sour glance. "Well, I wasn't suggesting we do it *right in front* of them."

Dallin paused, waiting for the bailiff to reach the top of the steps and turn into the heart of the building. He frowned at Woodrow.

"Not that I don't appreciate the sentiment, and certainly not that I'm complaining, Woodrow, but... why are you here?"

Woodrow grinned—actually *grinned*. "Chief told me I had to get myself into the party. On account of how I told him I didn't believe what they were saying about you, and it all looked pretty dodgy to me."

Dallin raised his eyebrows. "You were gossiping. With Chief Jagger."

Predictably, Woodrow blushed.

Dallin shook his head with a wondering smile. "Forget what I told you before. You keep right on and gossip 'til the Mother takes you."

The grin came back. "Chief said I should've been an Aldrich man." Woodrow's broad shoulders squared beneath the remembered praise. "Said if we found you and you had orders for me, I should follow them like always."

"How *is* Jagger?"

Woodrow's smile fell, and he shook his head. "He looks bad. At least, he did when we left. I think that Síofra...." He shot a quick glance up the stairs and lowered his voice. "He's got magic, I know he does, and they kept letting him talk to the Chief all alone, and I think—"

"Who kept letting him?"

Woodrow's eyes widened. "Didn't Corliss tell you?" He frowned and shuttled a puzzled look between them. "They called Wheeler in from Penley to take command of the constabulary. He's the law of the Commonwealth now, and far too close with that Síofra fellow, if you ask me. First thing he did when he got to Putnam was cut loose anyone who wouldn't speak against you or Jagger. Then he up and had Ramsford arrested too. He had Manning in several times for questioning, but last I heard he hadn't been arrested yet."

Dallin almost staggered. "*What?*"

"They figured I was new and not loyal to anyone yet, so I was the one mainly to see to Jagger." Woodrow nodded gravely. "He told me to tell Corliss and Litton and Edda and—"

"Creighton," Corliss put in.

"Right, Creighton, he came along with us too—"

"I saw him." Dallin shook his head. "And don't give me any more names. It might be best if I don't know." Though he could certainly guess, if put to it—anyone who'd been brought in by either Jagger or Dallin himself, and who had the sense of honor Jagger sought in his officers.

Woodrow shifted uncomfortably. "He gave me a list of names and told me to have them say whatever those men wanted to hear, whatever would get them to let them stay on at the constabulary. Said if we were lucky, there would be a...." He glanced at Corliss.

"Countercoup," she supplied dismally.

Dallin's mind was still trying to stumble through all the startling information. Wheeler? *Wheeler?* What the hell was a career general doing taking over the law of the entire country?

"Is it true?" Woodrow's eyes were wide and somewhat frightened. "That lad—Creighton says he's a sorcerer, and the people in the stables...." His mouth pinched down. "Creighton says maybe he magicked you and that's why you—"

"Creighton wouldn't know a sorcerer if one walked right up to him and turned his nose into a potato," Corliss put in with a growl.

Dallin frowned at Woodrow. "Weren't you listening?"

"Corliss listened. I kept watch."

"I've not told him what I heard yet," Corliss told Dallin. "I thought it best."

Dallin looked back at Woodrow. "And yet here you are."

"Chief told me to." Woodrow shrugged.

Dallin didn't have a whole lot to say to that except "Thank you."

"If you two are through...?" Corliss gave them each a sharp look, then jerked her chin up the stairs. "We need to figure out what we're going to do, how we're going to get you out of here."

As though on cue, a roll of thunder rumbled its way through the building, vibrating the stone of the stairs, and shimmied right up Dallin's boots. He didn't even try to talk himself into thinking it a coincidence. His teeth clenched and every muscle in his body tensed.

"Wil? I'm going to kill you."

Dallin shut his eyes and tried not to growl out loud. "I don't think you'll have to worry about it." He turned a bit to the side. "Unlock the shackles but don't take them off, then get me outside. I think I'll be needing my hands." He waited semipatiently while Woodrow fumbled out a key and did as he was bidden. Free, or at least mostly, Dallin started up the stairs again. "Find Calder if you can, but I doubt I'll be able to wait for him. Where are my guns?"

"Creighton's got them." Corliss scowled. "And how am I supposed to find Calder? *You* sent him off."

Dallin had to think about that one before the sense of it clicked. "No, that wasn't Calder. He was only using the name when—it's too complicated, but his name is Wil."

"Then who the hell is Calder?"

"The man who was keeping watch at the stables."

"Ah." Corliss rolled her eyes as they reached the top of the stairs, then turned in the same direction the bailiff had gone. "I'll try, but I don't know where—"

Another blast of thunder shook the earth, like a bomb had just exploded over the roof of the place.

"Shit!" Corliss hunched in instinctively, narrowed gaze going to the ceiling.

Dallin sighed. "I've a feeling it's only going to get worse." He really was going to kick Wil's arse.

The Chester constabulary, when they reached the main corridor, had turned to bemused chaos. Officers had left desks and tasks to wander to the big windows, peering out at a sky gone dark and threatening in the space of only a few minutes. Citizens who'd been perhaps brought in for questioning or to file a complaint, even two men in shackles—all of them were gravitating toward the windows to stare at the brewing storm.

Dallin catalogued them without even thinking about it. That young man had likely been reported for prostitution, and they'd brought him in to give him a good scare. That woman had probably been caught trying to cast spells that hadn't worked anyway, and would be fined for magicking without a license. That other woman was trying to press charges against her neighbor, who'd dug himself a small tributary from the stream their properties shared and was siphoning most of the shared water rights.

Unthinking habit, and for the first time ever—standing here pretending to be under arrest in this foreign constabulary, in the process of widening the chasm between himself and the life he'd thought he loved—Dallin wondered how he knew these things.

"You've the gifts of a shaman—the gift of the Shaman...."

All right, then. Perhaps it was time to accept it, learn to use it, and keep moving.

The air had gone heavy, thick and charged. Dallin could feel a light tingle that was all too familiar, a quick shift in pressure that weighed against his skin, making it prickle.

He leaned in to Corliss. "Get me outside. Quick."

And then to Woodrow. "Get them all away from those windows. Stay in the center of the room and be ready to—"

That was as far as he got before the pressure flashed and popped his ears. He only just had time to pull his hands from the loosened shackles, grab Corliss and Woodrow, and drag them both down. Corliss bleated a surprised little *yawp* as her knees hit the floor, instantly drowned out when every window in the place exploded outward in high-speed showers of lethal shards. Two women in bailiff's uniforms were sucked out onto the street with the force, so fast they didn't have time to so much as yelp. Lightning flashed outside, thick ropes of yellow-white that dazzled the eyes and crackled far too close, sizzling the air and leaving it thick with the bitter-burned stench of ozone.

The entire room erupted into shouts and debris, people diving for cover, papers flying about in small whirlwinds. Pens and desk ornaments suddenly turned into airborne projectiles. It was all a dim distraction beneath the howl and roar of the wind.

Dallin didn't wait for Corliss or Woodrow, didn't even glance at all the constabulary officers with guns on their hips. He half stood, keeping as low as he could, and took a straight line to the doors. They were swinging on their hinges, slamming into the wall and then careening back as the air pulsated past him and sucked them closed to thud and hammer into the jamb again in a heavy staccato. Muted shouts and frantic orders were being called out behind him.

He waited for the air to shift again, expand around him, like being inside a living lung, and when it did, Dallin slid his fingers through the gap. He yanked the door back and threw himself through it.

The street was even more chaotic than the constabulary had been. Clumps of sod and sheets of tin from various roofs flew around clouds of dust swirling up from the ground in tiny cyclones. Hailstones pelted man and beast, tearing at timber and stone. Bolts of lightning shivered spasmodically over the tops of buildings, grazing dazzling fingers just close enough to tease an arc, then scudding over.

And in the center of it all, Wil stood in a pocket of calm, face set hard, brilliant eyes narrowed in concentration but still sweeping in every direction, seeking. Black hair whiffled gently around his face in the mild breeze enwrapping him. He brushed it absently from his eyes, tossed it from his brow, before clutching again at the rifle that now looked to Dallin like it was a permanent extension of those long-fingered hands. And Wil didn't even need it anymore. He stood alone, straight and tall, people staring at him in fear from beneath whatever cover they'd managed. Every element was at Wil's beck and call, and he held them each, danced their patterns, and wove their threads.

He was intensity. He was strength. He was driving will and stubborn determination. He was reckless passion and guarded distrust.

He was fucking *beautiful*.

"Mother help me." Dallin's breath sucked harsh in his chest, air pressure and stunned desire both. He was completely lost, cut from every anchor he'd ever known. And Wil was the only beacon he wanted to see. "How did I let this happen?"

As if Wil had heard him, he turned, nearly blowing Dallin's mind when Wil's shoulders sagged in relief and he grinned —*grinned*—as though pandemonium weren't swirling around them in wide destructive waves.

Wil waved his hand at the sky and *laughed*. "Air!" He broadened the grin, slanting it sly, and dipped a dramatic bow.

Dallin couldn't help it—he grinned back, then blundered down the constabulary's stone steps and into the street. He saw Wil's look of delight shift at the same time he heard Corliss's call from behind him, saw Wil's jaw clamp tight and anger flood the gleaming gaze as Wil's hand twitched at his side, fingers moving.

"No!" Dallin made a run for him, barked "Corliss, stay back!" over his shoulder, and closed the distance between him and Wil in four extended strides. "Wil, don't!"

Wil shot him a wary glance, flicked it like a knife back over Dallin's shoulder. "She's with *him*. They're all with *him*."

"Not in the way you think. Trust me, all right, don't—"

"*Aisling!*"

Dallin didn't know how Síofra managed to boom that thin voice the way he did, but it rang between them and drove a flinch from Wil. They both turned, Dallin reaching instinctively for Wil's arm—support, comfort, reassurance... whatever Wil wanted to take from it. Wil didn't shudder the way he had before, didn't shrink in on himself, but he tensed measurably, the same fear spiking his gaze. Just how much had it taken for him to walk back into all of this, knowing Síofra was here and likely waiting?

The air shifted so abruptly Dallin's chest tightened with the pressure. The hail turned to rain, a driving downpour, and the small pocket of silence in which they stood collapsed, rain soaking Dallin to the bone in mere seconds even beneath the cover of the waxed cloak. Small spheres of crackling electricity buzzed and bobbed around them, dipping to the ground, then rising and wavering. Waiting.

Wil half turned to Dallin, terrified. "He can... he can—"

"Not without the leaf," Dallin reminded him. "You're stronger than him. He can't make you do a damned thing." He jerked his chin. "Look at him, Wil. He's nothing without that leaf, and he can't take anything from you that you don't give him."

Síofra walked toward them slowly, smiling, the rain pelting him, drenching him, but he paid it no mind. Bold, he walked between balls of lightning as if he knew they couldn't touch him, proved it when he turned his hand and they pushed apart to let him through. Giving the lie to every assurance Dallin had just offered. Already drawing away power, twisting it and molding what Wil had done to his own purpose. Síofra's greedy eyes were solely on Wil, disregarding everything else, that same bottomless, cannibalistic hunger Dallin had seen in the boy in the stable—

It hit him all at once, made his gut clench and his mouth go dry.

He knew how this had to go.

Dallin looked at Wil, saw the fear, saw the years of control and trickery, the betrayal and the pain. Saw the strength and steadily growing confidence beneath it, saw the potential, and saw the terror that thwarted it. Saw what Wil needed to do, how this had to end, and the ripples it would send out through the rest of Dallin's country if it did.

"What if you figure it out and it turns out that it's either me or Cynewisan?"

Now here Dallin was, living the question. And what had he said back then, arrogant, reasonable Constable Brayden?

"Then I shall have to figure something else out."

Only there was nothing else to figure out. There were several ways this could end but only one way Wil could walk away from it.

Wil hadn't come back for Dallin. He'd come back because he knew what he had to do, and he was expecting Dallin to help him do it, even if Wil didn't know it. Dallin had bullied and pushed and swaggered, and now Wil needed it, needed his Guardian to stand at his back and tell him he could kill the monster.

Except killing this monster meant war. And not killing it meant Wil's future ended right here.

Dallin was just a *peon*, damn it. This shouldn't be his choice!

Choice. That was... laughable. There was no choice here. And if there was, Dallin had made it that first day in Dudley when he'd sat in a cell and listened to the shaky, broken tale of what had passed for Wil's life. And had kept making it, over and over again, ever since.

Jagger sitting in one of his own cells, caught up in the greater cogs of war's machinery, the fulcrum of which turned right in front of Dallin's eyes. Ramsford arrested, Manning questioned, countless faceless strangers dead already, and who among those Dallin had left behind might be next?

And why wasn't his heart bleeding as it should be doing?

Dallin swallowed thickly and cut the very last tie between himself and his life.

"You're going to have to kill him," he told Wil. "He won't stop 'til he's got what he wants or he's dead, and now he's got two countries at his back."

And they had none.

The Commonwealth troops had gathered behind Síofra, watching, looking to their captain for instruction, who in turn looked to Síofra. Síofra gestured them back, said, "The Chosen is mine," and kept coming.

A small whimper broke loose from Wil's chest, barely audible over the roar of the wind and rain, but the rifle came up, barrel leveled at Síofra, finger twitching at the trigger. Wil's dark hair was plastered to his head, thick sopping hanks dripping over his brow, into his eyes, but he kept his gaze steady, though his jaw twitched and his hands shook.

Síofra just kept coming, walking steadily toward Wil, still smiling, until his chest met the barrel of the rifle. "Chosen." He lifted his arms at his sides, welcoming.

"Don't call me that," Wil whispered through his teeth, shaky and small.

"And what should I call you, then?" Síofra's fake sincerity oozed through the words. "Aisling? Gift?" He lifted an eyebrow. "Wil?" His smile dipped sad, and he shook his head. "None of these are your name, my lad."

"*I'm not your lad!*" High-pitched and near to hysterical.

Wil's grip tightened around the gun. Dallin only watched carefully, a bit of warmth seeping into the chill in his bones as the metal in Wil's grip calmed him, steadied him.

Wil took a long breath. "I don't belong to you—you didn't choose me, you stole me—and I have no name because *you didn't give me one*. I was never anything to you, and I'm nothing to you now but a well you want to suck dry. You're doing it right now. I can *feel* you."

Dallin could feel it too, a small shift in the pressure around him, a tug and gutter of that tensile presence that leaked from Wil's pores. Thunder boomed directly above them, loud and violent enough to make Dallin nearly flinch, but Wil and Síofra stood perfectly still, eyes locked.

Light steps pattered behind Dallin, steady and familiar, and then the simple relief of the accustomed grip of his revolver was pressed into his hand. He glanced over at Corliss, a tangle of sopping auburn swathed like a cap to her head, sticking to her face, her eyes terrified, scudding between the three of them and settling on Dallin, asking. Dallin gave her a slight nod and a twitch of a smile he didn't believe any more than she did, then turned back.

Wil and Síofra hadn't even noticed. It was like only the two of them existed. Dallin gripped the gun in his right hand and laid the other on Wil's shoulder, just to remind him.

"We are one, you and I." Síofra closed his eyes and lifted his face to the rain. "Bound in heart and spirit. I feel you every time you open your soul."

Dallin didn't need the stray lightning to reach out and tap him on the shoulder for that one to click into place. "It's how he found you so quickly," he told Wil. "He can feel it every time you use your magic. He can follow you even when you're not dreaming. He will *always* be able to follow you."

He couldn't tell if Wil even heard him. No movement, not even a blink, just that steady hum beneath Wil's skin, that power leaking from him, thick and charged. Dallin could almost see Síofra growing more substantial, more present somehow, as he pulled it into himself.

"He's doing it now." Dallin's heart was racing, his gut curling and lurching, the revolver growing steadily heavier in his grip.

"Alive inside a cage, Wil. Don't make me do this." His fingers tightened around the burled grip. "Kill him," Dallin growled, low and frantic. "Kill him now."

Síofra opened his eyes. "I kept you safe." He jerked his chin at Dallin but didn't take his eyes from Wil. "I kept you safe from all of them. You know his destiny. And you'll stand here and listen to him trick you into betrayal?" He reached out his hand, palm up. "We're one, my lad, my Chosen. Come to me, and we'll sing your true name to the stars."

Wil's face had been set in stone; with that last cajoling whisper, it twitched, melting to confusion and pain. The air around them changed again—slipped. A staggering of control, and a shift Dallin could actually feel. The earth trembled, a shimmy of energy that spangled up from beneath Dallin's boots to tremor up his spine.

"Oh shit." Dallin's index finger, all by itself, slipped around the trigger of his gun. He flicked the safety.

"What?" Corliss touched her hand to the small of Dallin's back and leaned in. "What's happening?"

Dallin sucked in a shaky breath. "He's winning."

"I've a name?" Wil asked, lost and small as a little boy.

Síofra slid his glance to Dallin... grinned. "Ask your Guardian."

Wil turned to Dallin, the rifle sagging in his grip. His eyes were full of confusion, complete emotional upheaval, but no real accusation yet.

"He whispered it to me." Síofra pushed the barrel of the gun away and stepped in closer to Wil.

Dallin held Wil's wounded gaze as steadily as he could. "He's done nothing but lie to you your whole life."

Síofra edged closer. "He is the Mother's creature." His voice curled distressed, sympathetic. "Oh, my poor lad—you didn't honestly believe his lies, did you?"

His hand came up, reaching. Without thinking, Dallin let go of Wil's shoulder and knocked Síofra's hand away. He stepped around, shouldering Síofra aside, and pulled at the rifle's barrel until it rested against his own breastbone. Corliss gasped, but Dallin didn't hesitate. He lifted his own gun and pointed it at Síofra's head, marking out the corner of his eye as every soldier behind Síofra shouldered his rifle and aimed it at Dallin.

"Do what you have to do," Dallin told Wil, as calmly as he could manage. "Believe what you must, but don't let him touch you. He's taking it now—can't you feel it?" He pulled the hammer back on the revolver. "If you can't do it, say it and *I* will. We'll end it here."

Corliss gasped, dismayed. "They'll kill you. Brayden, you do it and the war starts right here and now."

Wil's eyes narrowed at her, flashed. Dallin was glad she was behind him—Wil already held a grudge against her, and he wasn't the forgiving sort. Of course, if he believed Síofra, Dallin wasn't going to be much of a barrier for long.

"Wil?"

Wil's chin trembled. "D'you know my name?"

"No." Dallin shook his head. "I didn't know you had one. Wil's always been enough for me."

"It's never been enough for me." A strained whisper, so very quiet beneath the steady wail of wind and rain. Wil jerked his chin at Síofra, but he kept his eyes on Dallin. "*He* knows it."

"So he says."

"If I kill him—"

"Then we find it another way. He said it was the key to your soul. D'you really want him walking about with that in his pocket?" Dallin firmed his tone. "This is yours. Of all the things you've taken on, *this* is truly yours. Say the word and I'll take it from you."

Wil stared at Dallin long and hard, skimming his glance over the soldiers, pausing on each and every one before peering over at Síofra, measuring.

"Lies." Síofra was smug. "He knows nothing else. He'll use you and take from you and empty you at the feet of his whore-goddess." Síofra's hand came up again, beckoning. "Come to me, lad. Come out of the rain. We'll warm your cold hands by the fire, just like when you were a boy, remember? You'd sit on my knee, listen to the old tales, and—"

"And drink...." Wil met Síofra's eyes, brow twisted tight. "And drink my draft." His eyes had gone dull with memory and... something else Dallin couldn't define.

"*Yes.*" Síofra's smile curled triumphant. "You've missed it, haven't you? The peace, the sweetness of the dreaming."

Wil nodded, slow and heavy. "I have."

Dallin's stomach dropped into his boots.

"He's an addict. He still wants it. I saw him wanting it."

Dallin could see him wanting it now. Could see the bone-deep wish for the simple serenity of standing beside a river and listening to it sing.

"...knives everywhere, and they'll never let me live it."

Could feel the remembered pain and the grief that had washed from Wil's heart and into Dallin's as they'd stood and watched stars reflected in a river's night-rippled surface.

I can't fight that. I've nothing to offer him but more of the same.

Dallin adjusted his grip on the gun. "Wil?"

Síofra stepped in again, hand still outstretched, stopping just short when the barrel of Dallin's gun came to rest against his temple, but he kept his eyes on Wil, avid. "You loved me once. You were as my own, and I took care of you, protected you. I was as a father to you, starless boy."

Wil just kept staring, standing there in the driving rain, brow twisted tight and eyes burning, flashing incandescent with the crackle of lightning. Dallin couldn't tell with the rain dripping over his cheeks, but he thought Wil might be weeping.

Slowly Wil turned to Dallin, face made of marble. He lowered the rifle, stepped in, and placed his hand over Dallin's. He pushed the revolver down.

"Wil, don't—"

"Do I look like I don't know what I'm doing?" Wil slipped the rifle's strap over his shoulder. "Trust me." With a small, sad smile, he leaned up and placed a warm kiss to Dallin's mouth. "Remember your promise."

He pulled back and turned to Síofra. Slowly the corner of Wil's mouth curled up, and he glanced sideways, looked at Dallin, sly and halfway wicked, then... *smirked.*

He took Síofra's hand.

CHAPTER 7

He'd known how this had to go, had known it for... he couldn't remember, didn't know where the knowledge came from, but it was no less real for its ephemeral origin—you either killed the monster or the monster ate you.

Dreams, he supposed. Too damned many dreams. Too damned many times walking through someone else's nightmares not knowing if you were the monster or the sacrifice, just knowing your feet wouldn't move fast enough and you couldn't scream.

Dallin was watching, too obviously afraid, but he didn't move away, didn't back down. "It's yours, it's in your hands, but.... Wil, it's only a name. Is it worth the risk?"

Only a name. Only everything.

Dallin didn't understand. How could he? He had one—*pride's people, from the valley, brave*—made of the hearts of mountains, and he never had to wonder.

Wil snarled. "It's *mine*."

He stopped there, choking on it, because it was far too big for mere words, and there was far too much of his Self tied up inside them. How did you say there was a blank, you-shaped space wandering around the universe, and it wasn't named *Wil*, and it wasn't named *Aisling*, and it wasn't named *Chosen*—not even *vicious little shit who never bloody quits*—and none of those names even began to define what you needed it to be? How did you say you were searching for a definition of yourself—your *Self*—and you could only find it in a word someone else had handed you, handed it to you because they loved you, thought you worthy of it? That all your life you'd thought you didn't deserve one, thought you were nothing, and then you find out it was there, *you* were there, and someone had kept it all from you, stolen everything about you when they'd stolen you, right down to that one little word attached to your Self?

"He has it, and it's *mine*."

Dallin said nothing to that, though Wil could tell he wanted to. Probably wanted to drag Wil away from here and just *go*, or maybe shoot Síofra and end this now, clean and quick. But Dallin only nodded.

And *stayed*.

Wil dragged his eyes from the only gaze that had ever really cared enough to look, to see. He eyed the soldiers, the guns, the men and women cowering in the street and flooding from the constabulary. Calder was there, flanked by the two men in blue and brown who had shown up with the woman Dallin called Corliss. They stood back behind the line of red and gold, Commonwealth soldiers all in a neat row, potential firing squad. Shaw watched from the steps of the Temple with some of his initiates and apprentices, worrying his thin lips, brown hair stuck to his skull, anxious eyes burning across the city's ruined square.

Even the horses were quiet, standing almost at attention where Wil had left them tethered half-arsed to an ale cart by the fountain —the first stationary object he'd come to when he'd barreled his way down the street from the stables the second time. Not running *from* this time, but running *to*.

Everyone was watching, waiting.

Wil put them all aside and turned to face his monster.

It was strange. Patterns danced all around him, wove themselves in and out of each other. Twining, then severing, tightening and slackening as time and synchronicity, synergy and stasis changed them, let themselves be changed, tangling down into continually shifting templates. A raindrop splashing against a stone, momentarily joining the weave of it, then changing it, rejoining the torrent, widening the pattern before slipping slowly to the ground, appending the shapes of soil and cobble. Everything had a pattern. All threads changed and rewove themselves, wed inextricably to water and earth, air and fire.

Wil couldn't see Síofra's patterns. No threads, no weave. Just a man-shaped blank spot sucking fibers of Wil's patterns into itself, forcing them into empty crevices, glutting itself.

He can't take from you anything you don't give him.

Taking the statement purely on faith, Wil staunched the flow, dwindled it to a trickle, just enough to maintain a tether. Almost shocked that he could even as he was doing it.

I couldn't find you. I looked for you, and I couldn't find you. You hid your thread from me, and now you're trying to hide behind mine. How are you doing this, and how am I supposed to fight it?

There was a push there. Wil couldn't see it, but he could feel it. Grinding at his senses, digging inside his head, whining and chittering, angry that it couldn't gain purchase. Harsh and brutal, willing to tear away layers of Self to find what it wanted.

Wil had felt it before, felt it the second before he'd heard Síofra's voice back in the stable, had kept feeling it since. Felt it in Old Bridge, in Dudley. Síofra was... one of them. Alike, somehow, somewhere at the core. He came from them. Or maybe they came from Síofra.

Too familiar. Wil tested its limits, felt for its boundaries.

Found them.

Wil smothered a smile and looked down at the ground to hide whatever light might be dancing behind his eyes.

I learned it from you. Isn't that ironic? Funny? Fucking hilarious? You took from me, but I took from you too. And I didn't even know it. But the funniest part? You didn't know it either.

He glanced again at Dallin, saw jagged worry, brilliant faith.

It's yours. You can do this. And if you can't, we'll make it ours. Just don't get lost inside it.

Wil didn't need any kind of connection to understand it—it was there, all over that hard-set face. When had big, scary, unreadable Constable Brayden become calm, reassuring Dallin with his heart in his eyes?

Wil took a long breath and leveled his gaze at Síofra. "As a father to me."

Síofra smiled and squeezed Wil's hand. "Blood to blood."

The touch, cool and too familiar, brought back comfort and revulsion both, horrible intimacy and deeply entrenched body-memory that made Wil shudder. "Blood to blood." Wil made his mouth quirk up in a return smile. "You know my name."

"Oh, my lad."

Síofra's face twisted into a mask of concern, a mimic of love that nearly scored Wil's heart with his pathetic wish for the reality. Wil made himself not flinch when Síofra reached up and brushed cold fingers over Wil's wet cheek.

"I know everything about you. I know things your *Guardian*"—Síofra spat the word—"can only guess, things that would turn him from you, things that would twist that honor of which he's so proud to righteous murder." He leaned in, and—slowly, gently—

laid a kiss to Wil's temple. "I know. I see. I only ever wanted to protect you, keep you safe."

The push ramped up to a whining buzz, seeking fingers crawling over Wil's mind, searching for a crack.

"Keep me safe." Wil let his cheek turn into the cold caress. "Keep me safe, keep me dreaming."

"*Yes.*" Síofra's eyes had a glint Wil used to think of as cajoling in his once-naïveté. Now he knew it for predatory. "You understand. It was too big for you, too much—it hurt your mind, so I took you to a place it wouldn't hurt, to keep you safe and happy."

"Happy." Wil had to pause and choke back bile. "And took it for yourself."

Síofra pulled back, grasping Wil by the arms. "I had to. You aren't well, my lad. You never were. It dragged at your mind, at your spirit. You weren't strong enough. You still aren't strong enough."

"*I think you are many things, but weak has never been one of them.*"

Wil tilted his head, genuinely curious. "Am I mad?"

Síofra's smile slid sympathetic. "Ah, my lad, my Chosen." He pushed sopping hair out of Wil's eyes. "'Mad' is such a harsh word. Unbalanced. Confused."

"*I think you're different. I think that what I might once have seen as madness is more just a way of coping and carrying on that I never would have thought of.*"

"I took the pain away." Síofra crooned it in that too-familiar tone that skittered down Wil's spine, sliding oily tendrils into his gut and twisting it into a cold, hard knot. "I took it all away for you. For *you*, Chosen. Always for you."

"And is that what you want to do now?" Wil peered into those blue eyes that had been so many things to him—intimacy and perdition, love and hate, want and revulsion. "You want to take it away? For me?"

The *push* was more a *shove* now. It yammered at Wil, demanding. Strong and unrelenting. Wil dug a mental hand into the weave of it and... tested its grip.

Pain spiked as he let it all slip just a little, just enough for Síofra to wriggle blade-splined awareness in through Wil's defenses. It *hurt*, bit into Wil's mind with razor teeth, and the push that seared in with it burned like venom.

The light in Síofra's eyes had gone fervent, elated. "Yes," he said, a bare hint of triumph behind the hard blue. "For you."

"All of it?" Wil twisted his brow and dipped his voice. "It's so very big. It frightens me." He shot a wounded look at Dallin. "He doesn't understand. He can't see it all like I can."

"Of course not. It's what I keep telling you, my lad. It's why I had to keep you hidden. He doesn't know you as I do, he can't understand."

"You forget that I see you."

Wil nodded slowly. "And you'll take it all?"

"Oh, my boy." Síofra pulled in a long, deep breath and unfurled a smile that was soft and loving, but Wil could see the oil beneath it. "For you."

The push was feverish now—behind Wil's eyes, lancing up his spine and drilling into his ears. Hungry, greedy, mindless, and exultant.

giveitgiveitgiveit

"For me." Wil pulled back, keeping his hold on Síofra's hand. "Blood to blood." He let his lip curl, teeth bared and grip tight, then—

"Open wide, then—*Father*."

—pushed back.

Resistance at first, saw-toothed and excruciating as the push washed over him, tangling into him, way down deep. Familiar, with a perverted sense of nostalgia, because oh, Wil had been here before, he knew this pain, except then he hadn't *known*. A bruise to the mind, a rending of the soul, and *fuck*, it *hurt*, but Wil knew now what it was, knew it was *his*, something of his own Self turned against him.

Sharp edges, like trying to take hold of the blades of a thousand knives, and all of it drilling into his mind, his Self. Tendrils of Síofra's pattern wound into Wil's as if they were hot wires under his skin, burning like acid and sliding into everything he was. Wil made himself not pull away, made himself take the pain, made himself *see* it, define its pattern. Almost cried out when he found it, but he didn't have the breath.

He pushed into the weave and drove in. His mind came loose, flailed out, reaching, grasping hold of the pain itself—*tether*—and latching on to the knots of agony wound around him. He did scream then, using the pain as a lanyard, a connection to Síofra's own Self, pulling himself in with it and prying his way into the pattern.

And then he was through. Just like that. Taking it over, and forcing it into the shapes he willed.

That's it? All my bloody life, and that was all I had to do?

Reeling, Wil paused, bracing himself, not quite able to believe he'd done what he'd just done. He took the threads in his hands and just looked, amazed by what he held.

And then he... *plucked*. Unraveled—

"Mutinous *wretch*! What...? Don't—"

—one, then two, and Wil dimly heard Síofra grunt, then throttle a scream, but Wil was already lost in sick fascination, the subtle brutality of the unweaving.

It was too easy. A lifetime of torture, and *freedom-revenge-ruination* was suddenly in his hands. All this time, all that pain, all the years of imprisonment—retribution shouldn't be so effortless. He should have to work for it, make it sweeter with the trying.

Color exploded before Wil's eyes, thinning and stretching out forever, burrowing into threads. Wil pushed at the emptiness with it, shoved and twisted, then opened himself wide and… swallowed it. Enraged—*easy, so bloody easy!*—he dug through it all, tore heedless with frantic fingers until the weave behind it lay exposed to him. He could feel Síofra's mind reeling, overwhelmed, and he followed it down.

Saw his own birth, heard the screams, paused and stumbled for a moment—*Mother*—when his own infant cries drowned out the harsh gurgle of murder in childbed. He tore himself away, flinging consciousness through a spiderwork of memory and forgotten memory, and ignored the screams of a mind rent and warped.

"Where is it?" He plunged mental fingers through a frantic wall of resistance and *tore*. Clawed through a Self so rotted and twisted, the man beneath it was barely there, shriveled and furiously betrayed. "*Betrayed?*" Wil seethed. "You *dare* to feel *betrayed?*" He tightened his grip, pushed harder. "Give me my name!"

"*Witch.*" Síofra's distant gaze was stunned, afraid but angry too. *Betrayed.* As though he had the *right.* He tried to drag his hand away, but Wil wouldn't let go. Panicked, Síofra pushed at Wil's mind, struck out with poisoned fangs that sank into Wil's soul and *burned*, but Wil dug his grip in with mental grappling hooks and hung on. "Filthy, ungrateful, mutinous—"

"Blood to blood," Wil said through his teeth. "Like a *father* to me. I'm only giving you what you wanted."

With a wave of his hand, Wil pulled the storm harder. He refused to even flinch against the greedy talons trying to shred their way into his Self, just struck back and brought the hail and the lightning. Built a wall about them with it and shut the world out. Shut Dallin out, because Dallin already saw too much, and Wil couldn't stand for him to see *this*.

Wil reached out, took Síofra's other hand, and yanked him in close. Wide, dazed blue eyes stared back at him, appalled and furious. Wil couldn't even feel disgusted with himself that he liked the look, fed on it. He curled the threads of horror and shock into his fist and rammed them into the weave.

"For me, all for *me*. Let me show you what you've done for *me*."

He spun the threads of his own weave through his fingers and hurled them.

Dragged from his bed screaming, small fingers clinging to the sheets billowing over the floor behind him as he's carried, terrified and weeping, to the chamber.

Held immobile in strong arms, choking as bitter tea is poured down his throat, the soft, flowery taste of the leaf fountaining in his mouth, his nose, strangling him.

Longing, a pathetic wish for arms around him, a shoulder on which to lay his head, long fingers brushing through his hair, a lap to curl into, the pleasant rumble of a voice in his ear—"They'll try to come for you, but I'll protect you, beautiful boy."

Dazed and stupid, stumbling around inside the only four walls he's allowed to wander, stone and mortar, latches and locks. Vague awareness that his mind won't work properly, unable to care, staring blankly at a fissure in stone, weeping for what he doesn't know he can be, laughing hysterically at nothing through the tears.

Driven into dreams that don't belong to him, facing monsters of someone else's making, writhing through someone else's lust, behind someone else's eyes, dream-kisses scattered along his throat, and knowing all the while it's not for him, never for him. Get their secrets, use their fears, push them along a pattern they won't want to go, but they will because there's an itch inside their mind, and he put it there when he stole their kisses and wore the faces of their monsters.

The simple word no *and the cataclysm of pain that follows it, digging into his mind and twisting inside it like a corkscrew, drilling sanity from him until he weeps, arches his back, and screams, "Yes, all right, just stop, please make it stop!"*

Harsh reality and the agony that comes with it, vomiting 'til his head nearly explodes, shaking and cramping and begging to be sent back into dreams.

Turning to Father, but Father turns away because he's been bad, he can't behave, he's changed the patterns and he's not allowed, and it hurt, and he couldn't help it, he had to—"I didn't want to, he made me, I couldn't help it, please"—but Father sleeps and doesn't save him, and he understands because he's been bad, but oh, it hurts, and he wantswantswants, but he can't have, can't ever have.

Tears burned Wil's cheeks. He could feel them scalding through the chill of the rain, and it pissed him off. Because why should he be weeping *now*, damn it? Anger and sorrow for a life taken away from him. Hatred and vengeance for the one who took it. It growled inside the thunder and exploded in a blast above his head. Betrayal beat a throbbing pulse in the air, shook the ground. And *still*, it wasn't *enough*.

"All for me, *like a father*." Wil gripped Síofra's hands 'til his own fingers felt as though they'd shatter. Snarling, Wil pushed and drove Síofra down to his knees in the mud, then pushed and drove Síofra's mind down inside Wil's own rage. Wil felt the crack, the fissure at the very edge of Síofra's mind, and crammed a thread of his own Self through it. "D'you still want what I have? You see now what you've taken from me. Shall I give you back what I've taken from you?"

Síofra's eyes had gone blank with dread, teetering on the edge of sanity. "Ungrateful wretch." He dry-heaved until he coughed up a thin spray of blood.

Wil pushed again. If it were anyone else, the meager resistance would have been laughable.

Easy, easy, so bloody easy. Why aren't you stronger?

And then he *shoved*.

Wil opened himself wide, showed Síofra *everything*. Pushed it into the emptiness, swallowed it and filled up the crevices. Threw pure power into the weave and watched as it stretched the threads, strained them.

"Blood to blood," he snarled. "Only your heart's too small and cold to take it all."

"Don't." Rain fell into Síofra's open, staring eyes. "Please. Don't."

Wil glared down at him, tried to laugh and... couldn't. Faltering, cold rain falling on the blaze of his fury and guttering it. He clenched his teeth, looked away. He'd been wild with it a moment ago, enthralled, reaching for revenge with every bit of rage inside him, flinging it out from himself, exhilarated. *I'm strong enough. I'm stronger than you. You can't hurt me anymore. You can't ever hurt me again.* Now he nearly stumbled beneath the weight of it, a mind balanced in his palm, that narrow face twisted in near madness.

"*Tell me my name!*" Wil let go of Síofra's hands and took hold of his coat instead—shook. "Say it, damn it. You took everything else away from me, I'll have my fucking *name!*"

Warm, broad hands settled on Wil's shoulders—*No, don't see this, I shut you out, I don't want you to see, how are you here, and how can your hands be warm when it's so bloody cold? How are you even here, don't you see how weak he is, how easy it was for him to take from me?*—and with the touch came immediate stillness.

"You're in too deep, Wil. Don't hold it back."

"I don't think I can."

No response to that one, just the weight of Dallin's hands firm on Wil's shoulders. Not holding him up, not holding him back, not *pushing*. Just there.

Wil took the comfort they offered—*Why do you keep caring? Why do you keep letting me take? Don't you see what's happening here?*—and dropped down to his knees, face-to-face with the monster who'd turned out to be nothing more than a greedy little man with greedy little power, who'd taken a small boy and convinced him he was weak and helpless, used him because... because....

"So... so *weak*." Hot tears squeezed from out the corners of Wil's eyes. "Weak and small, and I only wanted—" He shut his eyes tight.

"We all do," Dallin told him. "It doesn't make you weak. It makes you normal." He hesitated, then asked, soft and steady, "What do you want here, Wil?"

Wil faltered. What did he *want*? "I want him to—"

I want him to be stronger. I want him to be sorry. I want him to see. I want him to....

He swallowed a sob. "I want him to *bleed*."

Dallin tightened his grip and laid a firm kiss to the top of Wil's head. "Then make him bleed. End this."

He kept holding on. *Stayed.*

Wil almost wished those broad hands had pulled him back, almost wished that encouraging voice had dipped toward dismay and demanded he come away. Was cruelly glad they'd done neither.

He sucked in a long breath and drove himself deep.

All the time in the world, it was forever inside, and Wil touched each thread, following it to its end, then casting it aside before he took up another. Memories and inclinations, wants and

306

needs. All those things that built a person, and all twined together, pulsing in his fingers.

"He was a boy once," Wil murmured, surprised that he was so surprised when the bright-misted memories of childhood throbbed in his hand, all innocence and tactile need. "He had *parents*." A small, spare woman with a kind laugh and warm eyes. A tall, balding man, long nose and a cheerful gaze the color of morning.

Not fair, not fair, not fair—

The desire-driven consciousness of adolescence—the first kiss, the first thrill of intimacy, the first broken heart—branching and flowering into adulthood, seeding a life. Lust drove it all sideways; it always did. Síofra had believed once, he'd believed deeply, was devout in his beliefs, and he'd read, researched. Knew the legends by heart, dug through archives, outpaced the scholars and priests with his vast knowledge, and came to believe just as devoutly that he knew better. Proved it when he'd bribed his way into the ambassador's office, crossed the border for the first time. Invited into Temples as though he belonged there, permitted to read and study archives that would have got him hanged in his own country. Finally obtained something close to reverence in a secret brotherhood and watched possibility unfurl before his eyes.

Found the key.

A strand of memory, winding down into a morass of desperate resistance. "It's here." Wil could feel the edges of it. Down and down and down.... "It's down here." A shudder and a shaky breath. "Don't go away."

"I'm right here."

Wil latched on to the thread and followed it.

Deep and dark and cold. Like sinking into a pit of frozen tar. Scudding across forever, sliding into time and being spat back out again. A wide, bitter void beneath his feet, drawing him in.

He let it, tethered to himself only by the threads of pain acid-webbed around him. He tightened his grip and ramped up the agony so he wouldn't get lost. His own pain in one hand, a safety line back to his Self, and Síofra's strand of memory in the other, Wil pulled them together and plaited them. Joined them.

We are one, you and I.

Wil almost laughed. *Yeah, and I bet you wish you'd picked a different metaphor.*

Rushing through consciousness that wasn't his, striving through an alien vista with no markers to tell him which way to go. Only that thread, that fiber of remembrance inside a deep-dark pit of resistance. He clawed at its patterns, scrabbling-tearing-rending, ignoring the resonant throb of pain—his and Síofra's both, doubled and then trebled—until there was a give, the slightest break in resistance. Wil seized it, *push-push-pushed* at it with everything in him, shocked nearly stupid when the counterpressure abruptly broke and the weave frayed in his hands. Stunned, almost euphoric, Wil firmed his grip and slammed himself through, sailing reckless into the black, then....

Freefall. Unraveling.

Too fast, too uncontrolled.

Anchorless, Wil plunged headlong into the patternless murk, felt it closing over him, cold and black as well water.

"*Shit!* Wil, you're in too deep. You have to push it away. Do you hear me? *Wil—*"

Too deep.

Too right.

It was like being nowhere at all, pitching down into the unplumbed depths of a Self, skirting consciousness and setting his teeth against the deadly cold emptiness resisting-denying-thwarting him. It drew itself in against him, hiding from him what was *his*.

Wil growled and stretched for the boundaries, reach spanning eternity.

"Almost there. I can *see* it."

Could see the very end of the man who dared to call himself *Father*. Could see the shadow of his own Self caught down there in the darkness, biding in its little cage. A mantle of deception of its own design, weaving blindly, tangled inside a shroud of secrets and lies and betrayals.

Say my name, say my name, say my name....

A snarl and a gathering of strength. Pushing, tending, dreaming awake, all of them together. Wil twined it all in his hand, weaving it into raw energy. Elation nearly took him—*Dallin, you were right, I think can do this, I think I can do anything!*—as Wil shoved himself into the tight-woven strands of nothingness, grip fumbling but almost there, *almost there.* He reached, stretched—

"Wil, *no!*"

—and thumped with a jaw-jarring shock into... something. A presence. Alien and yet familiar.

Swarmed by awareness, overwhelmed by intent not his own. And he'd thought it had hurt *before.* Cold-sharp agony swamped him, shoving itself down his throat, choking him and snagging at his mind.

Far too big to be Síofra. Far too old to be sane. Far too cunning to be anything but vile.

Wil snapped his reach, started to pull back, but it was too big—

"Oh, shit. Wil? *Wil,* damn it, what are you doing?"

Sentience, crawling all over him, a more horrifying invasion than any tormentor he'd met before. Like something was peeling open his skull and peering into his head, cracking open his chest and measuring his heart, his soul. So strong, so aware—the master of greed, the god of lust, the demon of hunger—driving, chittering *hunger.*

This wanted more than souls. This was hungry enough to swallow worlds.

Blood to blood, it chuckled.

"*Wil,* damn it, *answer* me!"

This was more than just a memory.

I think I've just stepped into some very serious shit.

"Dallin?" Too faraway, too small. "Help."

"Don't pull back, understand? *Don't pull back.* Push it *away,* Wil, as hard as you can."

Too late. It reached again, and Wil panicked, jerked back, a whining little whimper knocking loose from his throat.

It knew him. It *knew* him, knew what he had in him. And it *wanted.*

Dearg-dur. Daeva.

Æledfýres.

"Oh fuck.... This isn't Síofra. This is the *real* monster."

Too slow, he was too slow—it smiled at him, laughed at him... *wrenched.*

Wil lurched, took what was in his hands, and closed his fists, snapped himself away—

"*Nonono, Wil, don't!*"

—hurtled, screaming, into forever.

Vast.

Dark.

Terrifying.

Alone inside time.

Not a dream. Not life. A dreaming half life, perhaps.

No. No, that wasn't right. A not-life.

Nothing.

"*I think there's so much more that if you're not very careful in how you use it, you could lose yourself.*"

He was lost, that was it. In a place with no color, no patterns, no path—

"*She fears for you, for your path has only just begun, and you refuse Her gift.*"

Path.... gift... he saw neither, and he didn't know who "She" was, but the thought made him want to weep, so he pushed it away. She should be here, damn it, should be... should be—

"*She is not my mother, and I want nothing from her.*"

It was so full of anger and betrayal, hurt and grief. It made his throat clog up, made his heart thud heavily, and he turned his face away. Sent his gaze out into eternal night.

Blank-black and oh, so dark. If he put out his eyes, he might see more. He hadn't known this kind of darkness existed. Pitch-poison and deadly comfort. Sink inside the cold, freeze away the pain, because oh, it *hurt*....

"Wil? Wil, are you in there?"

Quietly frantic—this hurt too, but not in his ears. He thought he knew the voice, but he couldn't remember how or who.

"Wil, damn it, wake up. We don't have time!"

Wil. It was... familiar.

"*Peaceful River. It's nice, isn't it? I want to live by one someday.*"

Water, river, peace, and a strong arm around him....

"*That's a very good wish.*"

...stars and confessions, songs and loss and contentment and grief.... A kiss.

"Calder! Shaw! Someone get over here. I need help!"

Calder.

River of stones.

"*...there's a river runs through Cildtrog....*"

"The Flównysse. I'm not sure how precise it is. It's been years, but this is how I remember it."

The flow of the river, the songs of the stars, the cool kiss of a gentle breeze against his cheek.

"How did you do this?"

"It's a dream, innit?"

A dream. A living dream, a dreaming life, a cold, dark, bottomless not-life where the stars had all gone silent and he was blind to the patterns, deaf, mute, senseless, and soulless.

"Mother save us, he's all-over blood! Is he shot?"

Mother.

"...there's a river runs through Cildtrog...."

Flównysse. Mother's Blood.

Blood to blood.

"No, not shot, he's just... he's bleeding."

Bleeding. Blood to blood.

"Help me get him up. Get to the horses—quick, before they realize what's happening. Corliss! You tell everyone what you saw and heard here today, understand? *Everyone.*"

"She can't—"

"What are you going to do? Shoot her to keep your damned secret? Look around you, Calder—*this* is what secrets bring. Look at *him.* I can barely even see his face through all the—" A hoarse snarl. "*Fuck* you and your secrets, now *move!*"

"What about Síofra?"

"Dead." Incensed. Satisfied. "Leave him."

Dead.

Síofra.

It should have meant something, but it only brought pain and shame and rage.

"I was a father to you, starless boy."

Starless. Soulless. Lost inside forever.

Holding a soul in his hand and closing his fingers. Finding a thread and ripping it out.

You're not Father. You're not anything, you never were.

"You accept a cage like you belong in one, beautiful Gift. And yet the keys to your prison are right within your grasp."

Father, help me. I don't want to be in a cage. I don't want to be lost.

"No, he'll ride with me. Through the gates."

"The guards—"

"I don't care if you have to mow every damned one of them into the mud. Get on that horse, point him at the gate, and keep moving. Don't stop 'til you get to the river."

Weightless and far away. Warmth through wet chill. Thunder and rain and a river of blood behind his eyes. A heart beating far too fast—*ka-thump ka-thump ka-thump* against his cheek—and a deep voice in his ear:

"Don't you do this."

Whispered and snarled at the same time. *Ka-thump ka-thump ka-thump*—the beat of a heart, the beat of hoofs on ground, the beat of his own mind against the bars of its cage.

"Don't do this, Wil, d'you hear me? Listen to my voice and follow it back."

Back....

Back where?

Back to where the pain was. Back to where it was all-over knives and sharp biting teeth and monsters waiting for you inside dreams that didn't belong to you, where the strong were weak and the weak were hungry, and you killed when you cared and if you cared you stopped moving and if you stopped moving you died and *Father* meant *Traitor* and *Mother* meant *Pain-Loss-Grief* and you were caged alive when you lost and you bled when you won, like a bloody river flowing from out your eyes—

"Is there anyone, d'you suppose, who doesn't want to kill me?"

"I don't want to kill you."

"The river, Wil. Find the river and go there. Wait for me there, all right?"

The river. Water, river, peace, a strong arm around him, stars and confessions, songs and loss and contentment and grief, a kiss.

Gunfire and shouts and "Out of the way, move it!" and jolting thuds that rattled his teeth, a broad chest against his cheek, ka-thump ka-thump ka-thump, and more gunfire, and "Calder! On your flank!"

I know that voice. I know this touch.

"The river. Find the river, Wil. I'll be there as soon as I can. I'll find you."

The river. Water, river, peace, a strong arm around him, stars and confessions, songs and loss and contentment and grief, a kiss.

"How did you do this?"

"It's a dream, innit?"

A slow smile, and dark eyes, and Why d'you do this to yourself? and comfort where there was pain, and confidence where there was fear, and no monsters hidden behind the blunt honesty, no judgment lurking behind the frank reassurance, only stars and water and songs and deep-dark eyes—

"It's beautiful."

Beautiful. He remembered it was beautiful.

It was... not quite enough.

He lost the thread and slid deep.

Wil stretched and loosed a groan, groping blind for the pillow and dragging it over his head. Burrowed deeper into the sheets. He felt... good. Rested. Content.

It had been slower the second time, more attention spent on exploration and the insistence on feeling every sensation, but no less intense. More of a sharing than a taking. A little more fear inside the pleasure. A tiny smile twitched at the corner of Wil's mouth. A little bit scary was all right. A little bit scary was... rather nice, actually. Reminded him to keep feeling.

"Bloody hell." He smacked himself through the pillow. "Go to bed a man, and wake...."

"Wil, damn it, wake up. We don't have time!"

Wil opened his eyes and frowned up at the drab gray of the ceiling. He stretched again. Strange dreams, too alive, too.... Had he been following? Had someone been following him?

He shook his head. No. No, they were safe here, holed up in the Temple with its damp stone and guttering lamps and pungent torches, and even if someone came and tried to take him away, Shaw wouldn't let them in and Dallin wouldn't let them have him. Safe. Here in this tiny bed they'd shared, broad, callused hands all over him, Dallin dragging reactions from him, bringing Wil back inside the moment with a well-timed kiss or turn of the wrist, making sure Wil's cries were ones of pleasure.

A considerate man, Dallin.

Dallin. He hadn't realized before just how much he liked the name, liked the way it rolled on his tongue.

"Wil, it's only a name."

Only a name.

"You don't understand. You have one—pride's people, from the valley, brave—*made of the hearts of mountains, and you never have to wonder*—"

"Stop it." He squeezed his eyes tight. What the hell was wrong with him? Ghost-voices in his head, awake and aware when they should be dead and buried, because they weren't real, they were someone else's dream, and he wasn't, he was *real*, damn it, real flesh, real blood—

Blood to blood.

"Mother save us, he's all-over blood!"

He dug his knuckles into his eyes. "Go away. Get out of my *head!*"

He'd never had this much trouble putting dreams behind him before. Never even had to think about it, never had to try. Wake up, blink away sleep, and forget anything that had happened while his eyes had been closed. It was easy. It was instinct. This disjointed overlap of dream-to-life-to-dream was... unnerving.

"Are you alive down there?"

"Dead. Leave him."

Wil shook his head, shut his eyes tight before blinking back up at the ceiling with a frown.

"Sort of?"

"Well, get your arse up and moving, yeah? We've got work to do."

Work to do....

"It's only a candle. It can't do any damage."

"I can't. It's too big."

Wil clenched his teeth and rubbed at his temples. Things were... off. Out of balance. He couldn't think straight. Had they been drinking last night? No. No, there was the river, then the kiss, then... more kisses, and....

A blank spot. A blank spot with dreams he didn't want to see inside it, so he pushed them away, cleared his mind, turned his head slowly, and just as slowly opened his eyes. He sighed relief. Tea and ham rolls. Breakfast in bed.

All right, then. This was good. Guttering lamps, uncertain light, damp stone, and Shaw's ham rolls going cold on the little cupboard just out of reach.

Safe. Not stumbling in blackness. Not alone.

Wil sat and knuckled at his eyes. Just a muddy mind this morning, that was all. His head would clear after a cup of tea.

He snatched up pants and trousers from the floor, slid into both, and slouched across to his breakfast. It was bloody *freezing* in here this morning, cold and wet—

No. Cold but not wet, no rain, just the chill of the stone floor against his bare feet, the damp of the air against his bare chest. He grabbed for his shirt, slid an arm into a sleeve... turned slowly to the door.

"Sleep well?" Dallin asked. His eyes were sad, his face stretched with tension.

Wil frowned. This wasn't... *right*. It wasn't how it was supposed to go. Dallin was supposed to be smiling. He was supposed to be looking at Wil like he wanted to shove him back into bed and not let him up again. *You are bloody evil.* He wasn't supposed to have worry in his gaze, he wasn't supposed to be dripping wet, he wasn't supposed to have that angry, welted burn flaring across his cheek, the ends of his hair on the left side of his head singed and slightly blackened.

"I feel... very strange." Wil shook his head, groping for sense, for words.

Put it all back to where it's supposed to be. Pluck the broken threads, reweave them into the right pattern. Warp and weft. Break-fast, shirt, Dallin at the door, then....

"Get rid of Calder?"

Calder. River of stones.

Dallin was still looking at Wil with that all-wrong sadness in his gaze. He sighed tiredly.

"Calder thinks you can't control it. He thinks you're weak."

"*No.*" Wil shook his head, angry now, edging on panic. "Don't say that."

"I didn't say it." Dallin shrugged. "He did."

"No, I mean—" Wil's heart was pounding. His eyes were burning. "That isn't what—you weren't supposed to say—" Bile crowded the back of his throat.

"Wasn't supposed to say what?" Dallin's dark eyes bored into him, seeing right down to blood and bone. "Wasn't supposed to say you're hiding? Wandering? Lost and trying not to be found?"

"No." A whisper, shaky and small. Wil backed up a pace and almost gagged when water closed around his ankles, grabbing him in an icy fist. "Why is there water?"

"Because it's still raining." Dallin's tone was sympathetic, but not enough to stop saying things he *wasn't supposed to be saying*, things he *hadn't* said, things that didn't belong here. "It's just as well. Hopefully it'll put out the fires in Chester. Though I think the constabulary is probably lost."

"The...."

Rain. Fire.

Hail and lightning and wind and thunder and mud soaking his knees, seeping over the tops of his boots—

"*Open wide, then—Father.*"

—and blood, so much blood, and not all of it his, gripping a mind tight in his fist and wrenching, the ground shaking beneath him like his own mental fist pounding against it in rage, weaving himself inside someone else's memories, following them down and down and down—

He gave his head a sharp shake. No. No, that wasn't how it was supposed to go. No more talking about Important Things, no tears, no running. Safety, a wide hand on his shoulder, thick stone walls around him to hide him from everything he wanted to hide from, reassuring words in his ear, someone at his back.

Breakfast, shirt, Dallin at the door, then—

"The *guns*. We're supposed to clean the guns."

There. The guns. Clean the guns and everything would be all right.

"We did that already." Dallin's eyes were kind. "Yesterday morning. And then we played with fire, and then Calder came, and—"

"*Shut up!*"

The tears were coming, burning hot against Wil's cold cheeks, and why was it so bloody *cold?* Cold and wet and rain and darkness so pitch he could almost touch it, taste it, wrap it around himself until he smothered inside it and forgot to care that he was freezing to death.

The lamps were all lit, so why was it so fucking *dark?* Safe inside his stone cocoon, so why did it feel like at any moment he might totter into some endless black abyss? Why was he shivering so hard his teeth were chattering? Cold and wet and—

No.

No.

He needed to get warm, put it all out of his head, a moment of silence, stillness, heat, a calm voice in his ear, he wanted, *needed—*

giveitgiveitgiveit

He stalked across the room, gripped Dallin by the collar of his shirt, and dragged him down—kissed him.

Agreeable. Compliant. Happy to oblige, as he always was. Dallin kissed Wil back, wrapping tree-trunk arms around him, and hauled him in tight. Deep and long—desperate and messy, and Wil didn't care—whiting his mind, calming the chaos, making everything seem right again.

Help me, I think I'm going insane, and I'm so bloody cold *I don't think I'll ever be warm again, and it's so dark in here.*

Tiny nips along his jawbone, broad hands on his back, and a heavy whisper in his ear: "I'm not here, Wil. This isn't real."

Wil clenched his teeth to hold back a whine. He shook his head against Dallin's shirt.

"Don't. Please."

"It isn't me." Soft and soothing. "I'm still looking for you. You're hiding from me."

"Just trust me, I won't let anything happen. Push it, Wil."

Wil burrowed in deeper, hands fisted tight in Dallin's shirt. "I can't. It's too big."

"Nonono, Wil, don't!"

"I think I'm lost." Raspy and thick, choked with tears and fear. "It's so cold, and I'm all alone. I didn't know anyone could *be* this alone. Please—I don't know what to do."

Losing control, losing the threads, losing his Self, losing everything.

The grip around Wil tightened. "My father told me that as long as I never forgot my name, I'd always know my way home."

"I don't know my name!"

"...you took everything else away from me, I'll have my fucking name!"

"You do. You always have done." So calm. So comforting. Dallin pushed Wil back gently, laid his hands over Wil's fists, balled tight in the weave of the shirt. "I know it too. I found it while you've been wandering."

Strong fingers threading through wet hair, lifting his head to rest against Dallin's, brow to brow—

"C'mon, Wil, I know you're in there, don't hide from me."

—that raw burst of healing intimacy sliding from Dallin's fingers and into Wil's skull, a slow-rolling wash of warmth radiating through him, rough fingertips settling over eight small scars carved into his scalp beneath his hair—

"Oh, fuck me." Breathless with shock. "Wil, you're not going to bloody believe this."

"Don't ask me for it, not yet," not-Dallin said.

Wil snarled through the tears. "It's *mine!*"

"And I'll give it, if you ask me, you know I will. All you'll ever have to do is ask. But think about this, Wil—what if he finds you? Do you think you can keep him from getting it?"

Weak. *Weak*, damn it, and too bloody vulnerable.

"You're not. But you're smarter than this. I know you are. You know it has to be this way."

No choice but to see the sense in it. No choice but to acknowledge that the only thing Wil could ever remember truly *wanting* was now in the safest hands possible. No choice but to weep angry, scalding tears that those hands were not his own.

His *name*. He actually *felt* his heart bleeding in slow trickles behind his breastbone.

"The river, Wil. I'm waiting for you there, but you have to come to me."

Wil shut his eyes and laid his head to Dallin's shoulder, hot tears squeezing from out the corners, wetting the shirt, winding into the weave. "But I'm lost." He blinked and squinted, staring at the threads of the shirt that were blurring beneath the spreading pink stain of his own bloody tears. "I don't know how."

"I'm wide open," Dallin told him softly. "I'm looking for you, waiting for you, and I've opened myself so wide I'm scared to death. You won't let me in, so it's up to you—*you* have to do this. Look for me and you'll find me."

"I don't want to go back." So small, Wil wasn't even sure he'd said it out loud. "I want to stay *here.*"

Here in this morning when he'd woken safe and content. Or perhaps in the night before, when he'd discovered it was all right to *want* safe and content. Not all of it, not the first time—he'd been too selfish then, hadn't given himself permission yet to believe— and not all of that harsh revelation that came after the first time.

But that second time, and this morning... yes, he could stay here with this not-Dallin, this dream-Dallin who somehow still didn't say everything Wil wanted to hear, stay here and relive those moments until everything just went away, until Wil dissolved into the black, and then it wouldn't matter because he wouldn't know anymore.

"It hurts, I know. Everything hurts, and you've endured it for so long."

"So *long*."

"I know." Not-Dallin set a gentle kiss to the top of Wil's head. "And I'm sorry, but you're not done yet."

Wil shut his eyes. "*Please—*"

"The Father needs you. You've seen what He fights. You've seen who."

Æledfȳres.

"Yes," Dallin replied, though Wil was *sure* he hadn't spoken that time. "He's been holding it all since you were born, Wil, keeping it all back, but how much longer d'you think He can keep doing it? He's dying."

"*I don't care!*" Terrified. Near rabid in the denial.

"You do. I know you don't want to, but you do. And I know you're scared, but you know I won't let you do it alone." Not-Dallin gently pushed Wil back. "He needs you. And as much as you think you want to, you won't let yourself stand away." He squeezed Wil's arms. "Find me, Wil. You know how."

A widening stain flowered over the weave of Dallin's shirt where Wil had wept blooded tears on his shoulder. Wil stared at the pattern, marking how the threads knit and plaited themselves —the kink of a fiber here, the jag of a strand there....

"Do *you* need me?" Wil kept staring at the stain, following the loops and lines.

Because I've only just this second understood that I need you, and it hurts to know it. It's bloody terrifying. Except knowing you cared stopped hurting when I found out I cared back. I think it might be all right that I need you if you need me back.

"I'm not real," Dallin answered. "I can't answer that. Find me at the river and ask me again."

It would do no good to weep, to scream, to beat at that wide chest and whimper that Wil was too terrified to move, too broken and lost to muster the strength. He did it anyway, let strong arms stay twined around him, hold him tight, rested his head against Dallin's breastbone, listened to the steady *ka-thump ka-thump ka-thump*, and closed his eyes. Wept until he couldn't breathe, that stain beneath his cheek widening, defining itself with each tear.

I'm wide open. Look for me and you'll find me.

Wil touched the stain with shaking fingers. Found a strand where warp met weft.

Followed it.

It isn't chill and frosted over this time. It's warm; the sun is shining bright on the water, glaring into his eyes. The grass is cool against his bare feet, green and soft with just a touch of dew from the mist of the river. The trees are full and flowering, fragrant apple blossom and heady dogwood, soughing whispers shivering through branch and leaf on the soft breeze. The chuckle of water over stone sings with the voices of the stars, though the sun eclipses their faces.

A wide, gold-limned figure bides on the strand, shoulders hunched, hands stuffed into trouser pockets, hair like chaff wafting and glinting red-gold-flax with every slight shift of the gentle wind. Those dark eyes are shut tight, brow twisted in concentration, jaw set hard.

Dallin's patterns are brilliant, altering and rethreading even now, a constant remaking. Gold to red to blue to jade—striating out from him in every direction in shards of burnished radiance, scintillating out into thin air, reaching, stretching.

Searching.

Seeking.

"I'm wide open. I've opened myself so wide I'm scared to death."

Open... doesn't quite cover it. Open is too small a word.

Bared, exposed, raw, and defenseless. Wil doesn't think he's ever seen anything so terrifyingly beautiful in all his life. Honor and fear, love and rage, pride and worry, virtue and sin—all of it scorching into Wil's eyes, a resplendent aura of lambent passion.

"You see me," *Wil had once said to Dallin. Wil doesn't think it's possible he'd looked half as astonishing.*

One tentative step forward from Wil, and Dallin spins, blinks. He only stares for a moment, as though he's not sure he's truly seeing what he's seeing. Then everything collapses, a chaos of color disintegrating, folding back into a fixed template with the relieved droop of Dallin's shoulders, the quick-fire release of tension from whatever was holding him strung together.

"Oh, thank fuck," *he breathes, shaky and thick, and he stalks over to Wil in five swift strides, jaw set, eyes ablaze. For a moment Wil thinks maybe Dallin's going to hit him, but then Wil's being snatched up nearly off his feet, hauled in, and crushed to Dallin's chest so tight it knocks the breath from him.* "When I tell you to run, you bloody run, and you bloody keep running, understand?"

There was a question Wil had wanted to ask; it had seemed so important, but now it's gone, and he thinks he doesn't really need it, doesn't need to ask, because he knows. That look, this embrace— whatever the question was, this is the answer. A tearful laugh wants to wend up from Wil's chest, but it's cut off by the strength of the hold.

"Keep telling me not to leave you alone, and there you went—" Dallin chokes it off. "And I've got Calder giving me I-told-you-sos and Shaw nattering at me to ignore Calder, and you wouldn't... wouldn't hear me, I couldn't find you, and damn you, don't you ever do that to me again!"

"Sorry, I...." No good. Wil pushes gently. "I can't breathe."

Dallin lets go so abruptly that Wil almost totters backward, would've done if not for the fact that Dallin is now gripping Wil's arms like he's afraid to let go. "Sorry." Dallin seems as close to losing control as Wil has ever seen him. "Sorry, I just...." His face screws up, and he shrugs helplessly, tightening his grip until Wil's sure it'll leave bruises. "Don't do that again, all right?" It's shaky, taken from a demand to a request from one word to the next.

Wil's ashamed no steady reassurance will rise to his tongue. Instead he reaches up and slides gentle fingers over the red-blistered burn, shiny and gruesome-looking, on Dallin's left cheek. "How—?"

Dallin's hand is over Wil's, gently pushing it away, curling around it. "Things got a little crazy in Chester. It's how we managed to get out relatively easily."

Wil frowns. "Fire?"

"Um." Dallin looks uncomfortable now. "The rain put most of it out before it could get out of control."

Ah. Wil thinks he sees now. He thinks he was seeing all along.

"Though the constabulary is probably lost," Wil murmurs, distant.

Dallin's eyes narrow. "How did you know that?"

Wil just jerks his chin at the burn. "Did I do that?"

"You weren't yourself."

Wil puffs a bitter snort. "Ya think?" He shakes his head. "How long?"

"...It's been almost two days now."

Wil scowls this time, unaccountably filled with sudden sharp *wrath.* "So why isn't it healed yet? Fuck's sake, Dallin, you need a nursemaid to bully you into healing yourself every time you get hurt? How did you ever manage to live this long without someone behind you all the time, nagging you to make yourself better?"

Dallin puffs a stunned almost-laugh, but it dies before it can make itself. "I've been...." *Dallin doesn't finish, just takes a long, deep breath, closes his eyes, and leans into Wil.*

"I've been using up everything I had on you" *is what he didn't say.*

Wil sags and leans in too, wrapping his arms, tentative, around Dallin's torso, soothed when a gentler embrace is wound around him this time.

"I know. I'm sorry. I can't... I don't know if I can do this." *Wil pulls back, pulls away, and walks slowly over to the strand to look down into the water. He could be blind and deaf, and still he'd know that Dallin was behind him the whole way.* "The things I saw...." *He shudders and clenches his jaw.* "The things I felt—feel—it's all just so... big. I don't know how to put it all in order in my mind. Everything keeps blurring together, slipping away, then slamming back into me, and I—" *The tears are rising again. Wil blinks them back.* "Calder worried what might happen if my mind broke." *Wil turns slowly to peer at Dallin over his shoulder.* "I think it might have done. And if that means I won't have to do what I know I have to do...." *He shrugs heavily and turns back to the water.* "Maybe it's not such a bad thing."

"And what...." *Dallin hesitates before he sets his warm, broad hand to Wil's shoulder.* "What do you think you have to do?"

Wil blows out a heavy breath and stares at the banks of rolling green on the other side of the river. "Æledfýres." *Like a lead weight dropping from his mouth, thudding at his feet.* "He gave me to Síofra. He's been trying to give me to the Brethren. He needs something from me, and he needs one of them to get it for him. And once

he has it, he can... I'm not sure. Finish the job with Father, I think."
He turns his gaze slowly back to Dallin's. "You know my name."

Dallin's head jerks back, and he stares at Wil, brow drawing down. "How...?"

"Because you just would—if anyone would figure it out, you would." Wil slides his fingers under his hair, over the lumpy scars on his scalp. "You were trying to heal me, to find me. I think I felt you, and you found my name instead." He drops his hand. "I've held the key to my cage all along. Fucking irony." Dallin opens his mouth, but Wil shakes his head reluctantly. "Don't tell me." The words are almost a physical pain in his chest. His name, his Self—he's wanted it for so long, it twists his heart to have it so close. "Seal it up tight, keep it safe for me. If I know it, he might find it, and then I'm really fucked." His hand goes back to his head, fingertips toying lightly at the raised symbols. "Can't read," he mutters, resentful. "No danger of me finding out by accident."

Dallin takes Wil's hand away, grabs up the other, and holds them both tight. "As long as you remember that it's yours, that you can have it for the asking."

A sad smile twitches at Wil's mouth, and he nods. "I wouldn't be doing it, else." He leans up and lays a kiss to Dallin's mouth—not the frantic, desperate one from when he'd been lost and trying not to know it, but soft and sweet, just a brief brush of intimacy, connection. Wil draws back and lays his head on Dallin's shoulder. "I want to sleep now. Real sleep. And then I'll... and then I'll come back. All right?"

Dallin sighs, then sags just a little—relief. "I'll be Watching."

Wil came awake by slow degrees. A vague awareness of his own existence first, broadening back into himself, getting to know the shapes of his mind again, then reaching out, stretching into his body. The aches came next, stiff pain striating out through his limbs and pooling in his back, making him heavy and reluctant to move. The scent of wood burning, then the heat radiating from it, warm and comforting. The steady in-and-out of breath, the incremental rise and fall of his own body in its rhythm, except it wasn't... it wasn't him breathing. *Ka-thump ka-thump ka-thump* against his cheek, and Wil smiled, slow and drowsy. He knew that sound. He knew that cadence.

Wil opened his eyes, blinking in the darkness, the undulating flicker of the fire scudding over his own hand lying relaxed in front of his face, splayed over the familiar weave of Dallin's shirt, the familiar curve of Dallin's chest. Squinting, Wil stretched his gaze farther, pulling the rumple of a bedroll into focus, an empty bowl on the floor, a waterskin. Then unbroken curved stone.

A cave.

The sound of rushing water came to him all at once, babbling and chuckling not far away. Wil could smell it—fish and loam, river reed and silt.

The Flównysse. Had to be. He'd finally get to see a real river after all.

Sighing, Wil tried to stretch without moving too much, but the aches flared and twinged, so he settled back in. He twisted his neck so he could get a look around.

He was, apparently, lying quite literally in Dallin's lap, Dallin propped awkwardly against what looked like Wil's pack and blankets, long body stretched out with Wil sprawled half along his torso and half on the cave's floor between his legs. A thick-furred bedroll had been pulled almost over Wil's head. Dallin's arms were locked protectively around Wil's shoulders.

"All right?" Dallin was awake, of course, his eyes half-slitted, peering at Wil with concern and trying to hide his relief.

Wil smiled. "I didn't know I'd be so sore. Some shaman you are."

Dallin's lip curled up on one side, sardonic. "You've been lazing about for four days now, going on five. And your brain nearly exploded out your ears before that. A little soreness you can live with."

"*Four* days?"

Dallin's hand tightened on Wil's shoulder, then ran gently up and down his arm. "You had a rough go of it."

Wil didn't argue. He still wasn't sure he'd made the right decision, or at least the right one for him. He had no idea, after all, if he was even sane.

"And how long have you been lazing about with me?"

Dallin closed his eyes and stretched. "A Watcher's job is never done."

Wil stretched too, a wide, satisfying yawn curling all the way up from his toes. "I see that burn looks better."

It did. Deep and almost gory before, blistered and raw. Now it was healed over with new pink skin, smooth and slightly tight, with only a faint telltale glisten of burned flesh.

"Someone came over all auntie at me and insulted my shiny-new healing skills. What else could I do?"

Wil stared at the burn, noting how close it had been to Dallin's eye. "How did it happen?"

"You've just woken. Don't you want—?"

"*How* did it *happen?*"

Dallin sighed and rested his head back. He stared at the curve of the cave's ceiling.

"At the gate." He scrubbed a hand over his face, careful of the burn, then let it fall and looked back at Wil. "You were out cold. I could barely feel your heartbeat. I'd never seen so much blood coming from one person. And then the sky just... opened up. And then the fires started, but the rain took care of most of them pretty quickly." Dallin puffed out a heavy breath, Wil's body lifting along with it as Dallin's chest rose and fell. "It was bloody pandemonium, Wil, you should've seen—" He cut himself off. "The ground started to sort of... roll, and everyone broke for cover. I thought that would be a good time to get ourselves out of there, so we made for the horses." He paused with a crooked smirk. "Well done, you, by the way."

Wil returned the smirk weakly. "Told you we'd need 'em." Trying for smug and not quite making it.

Dallin snorted. "Right, well...." He pulled the bedroll up over Wil's shoulders, then slid his hand beneath it, thumb dawdling absently along Wil's backbone. "We were trying to barrel our way through the gate, and they were giving us a pretty good fight, more than I'd expected, considering. I thought Calder was a goner for a few minutes there. But then these—" He rolled his hand, looking for words. "—just... *fire*, it came out of nowhere, great gobs of it, like a ghost was throwing balls of it, and the guards decided we weren't worth the trouble." He shrugged as though it was nothing. "One of them caught me, is all."

"It... 'm sorry."

"Ha." Dallin shook his head. "I'm not. Might not've got out of there, else. Anyway, at least the fire didn't follow us. The rain did, though. Great torrents of it, for bloody *days*. The planting should be damned prosperous in the spring, with all that ground water storing up. It finally let up two days ago."

Two days ago. When Wil had finally found his way to the river and at least a semblance of sanity. And then fell into a sleep so deep that for the first time in his life, he didn't think he'd dreamed at all. Or at least if he had, he didn't remember it.

He wondered briefly what would happen if no one was tending the threads, wondered if Father had been doing it and if it had drained Him even further in the doing, then put it out of his mind. Apparently the world hadn't stopped or blown up, so he'd worry about it later.

Wil turned slowly, trying not to grunt or groan. He folded his hands over Dallin's breastbone and rested his chin atop them. "Maybe Calder was right."

"I doubt it, but what about?"

Wil shrugged, staring cross-eyed at his fingers. "Maybe it's all too big for me." He chewed his lip. "Maybe I'm not strong enough for all this. I don't know what any previous Aisling had to deal with before, but I'm pretty sure none of them were fed leaf for years, and... other things." He kept his eyes on his fingers. "Maybe it really did drive me mad, and... I don't know... maybe it would be better if...."

He fell silent, brooding. He could feel Dallin's eyes on him, just looking at him, and Wil lifted his own to meet the stare. Found the dark gaze tilted, Dallin's mouth curved wry and just edging on humor.

Amused? Wil had just confessed doubts about the soundness of his mind, and the great pillock was *amused?*

Wil twitched. "*What?*"

"Nothing." Dallin shook his head and gave a soft pat to Wil's shoulder, almost condescending but not quite. "I'm just waiting for the badger to chew its way out and negate everything you just said."

A light flush flared at Wil's cheeks, and he looked away. "Shut up." He tried to growl it and couldn't.

Dallin had the decency not to snort out loud, but Wil could feel it rumbling anyway. Dallin's hand settled on the back of Wil's head, stayed there. "It's the middle of the night." There was a reassuring smile in Dallin's voice. "Save it all for daylight, yeah? We'll have plenty of things to worry about in the morning."

Wil's eyes closed again, all on their own. Lethargy had never left his bones, but now it sank in deeper, curling down as if it meant to stay. He frowned, then reached up and flicked at Dallin's hand.

"Are you putting me to sleep, Shaman?"

"Neat trick, innit?" Not a smile in Dallin's voice this time, but a grin. "I promise not to use it on you just to get you to shut up when you're in a particularly bothersome mood."

Wil dragged open his eyes. Huh. Maybe that was why he'd been sleeping so deeply for so long. It occurred to him that perhaps he should be vaguely pissed, Dallin making free with it like that, but it didn't feel like making free—Dallin had paused, waiting to see if Wil would object, waiting for permission.

Wil only scowled and burrowed under the fur, not being particularly careful with his elbows just for spite. "Bothersome," he muttered and let his eyes drift shut again.

This... was not at all the sight to which he'd expected to wake.

Wil blinked and rubbed at his eyes. Nope, still there.

He'd been alone when he'd woken mere moments ago, well rested and surprisingly serene, all things considered. No slow coming back to himself this time, just an instant of going from sleep to waking, an unconcerned understanding that he was alone —no big, broad, not-so-soft Dallin for a pillow this time—and then a sharp awareness of gnawing hunger.

Out for four days, going on five, and exactly how had he been getting fed? He wasn't *hungry*-hungry, certainly not starving, just really damned hungry, so something had obviously been managed. And now that the heaviness of a morning visit to a privy-loo-bush-whatever was knocking at his groin, Wil had to wonder—how had he been...?

Never mind. He didn't want to know.

He'd been dressed in a soft, sage suede tunic—far too roomy, but very warm—and drawers when he woke. It took only a few seconds to blink around the little stone hovel and locate some trousers. His, from his pack, he was pleased to see. And his own drawers too, while he was at it—*thank you, Dallin*—though all the food Wil had stashed in the pack was now gone. Gone over rotten and binned, he supposed. His shirts were all gone too, though there was a pair of trousers and three pairs of stockings—remnants of Miss Afton's generosity on behalf of her departed Esmond back in Dudley, and Sheriff Locke's foresight. Upon less casual inspection of his surroundings, Wil noted the rifle was missing, though the knife had been set neatly atop his pack. The absence of the rifle bothered him somewhat. He hoped he hadn't lost it in all the... whatever had happened while he'd been... swooning.

Swooning. *Swooning.* Like a... like a... swooning... thing.

Weak.

He'd growled, dressed, and ambled a bit stiffly to the mouth of the small cave, squinting into bright daylight—

And found himself peering out onto a camp of at least twenty brawny blond giants. Massive shoulders bloody everywhere. At least a third of them were women, and even they were at least half-wider than Wil.

Hair long and pulled back at the temples in beaded braids, the way Calder wore his, or queued in long tails down their backs. More than a few of them even had feathers twined at the ends of the plaits. All of them wore varying shades of the earth—browns and greens, russets and grays—all of them in leathers and suedes and flaxes, all of them in short, heavy animal-skin coats, lined in fur or wool, and all of them armed. Bows and quivers, guns and holsters, swords and scabbards.

They milled around a central fire pit bigger than the smattering of individual blazes that radiated outward from it. Kettles or pots of water hung over them from makeshift tripods. Ownership seemed to be defined by saddles and cooking supplies set up around each fire. Another several behemoths stalked the perimeter, keeping watch.

Wil didn't choke on fear when he saw them; he choked on astonishment. The fear came after. Not really fear, exactly—more an overfaced disquiet.

He'd gotten used to Dallin, certainly, but this was... different. Wil didn't feel so puny around Dallin. It was a good thing Wil had never stumbled into this place before he'd come to know Dallin and learned to see his own small education as lies, else Wil might have fallen down dead from terror at his first look.

Too bad they kept themselves so secluded and didn't breed outside their borders. A country full of men and women like this, and Ríocht would never dare fire another shot. For the first time, Wil wondered just how many from the Dominion had been lost—wasted—on that vile raid all those years ago. People like this didn't just let someone walk in and take from them, after all.

They looked very much a part of this place, their beiges and greens blending with the terrain they trod. Hunchbacked foothills sprouted almost at their feet, rolled upward and outward, plumped with tree cover like the backs of great green sheep, unbroken but for a brown strip of road that wound up the spine of the anchoring highlands.

Lind.

And with the steady mutter of the river behind—*just* behind, on the other side of the rock formations in which this little beehive of caves nestled—Wil guessed he was now standing in Cildtrog, birthplace of Dallin Brayden: *pride's people; from the valley; brave.*

On the whole, Wil would say his introduction to the place, after all the drama of deciding to come and then trying to get here, was rather anticlimactic. Just as well.

With a nervous glance outward, Wil found Dallin, picking him out easily by his short hair, though it seemed he'd managed to appropriate a proper coat from one of the Linders. He was standing just at the edge of the campsite in intense conference with Calder—naturally—and Shaw and another three giants. Wil couldn't hear anything from here, but for all the body language, they might as well have been screaming. Dallin was shaking his head a lot, jaw set hard, eyes narrowed, riding right over Calder and anyone else who dared speak, with what appeared to be a rather scathing opinion of something. Calder's tanned face had gone red, eyes just this side of wild, and if he didn't stop pointing that finger at Dallin's chest pretty soon, Wil mused, he was likely to lose it. Shaw just looked worried, while the others stood a little apart, watching calmly. Every now and then, one of them would interject with something, Dallin or Calder would listen and respond, and then it would all begin again.

A debate over the worth of Wil's life again? A reliving of the mess he'd apparently made in Chester? In Dudley? All the way back to Old Bridge? Ríocht and Cynewísan? Everywhere in between?

Wil sighed, eyeing the little enclave, then eyeing the fire pit. The smell of cooking meat was wafting toward him now, tapping at his empty belly, which in turn started shrieking at his brain. He wanted to know what was going on with Dallin and Calder, but he wanted food more. Well, all right, he wanted food first. But before that, he'd have to wade through a sea of giants.

He ventured slowly from the darkness at the cave's mouth and into sunlight, placing his boots carefully in the spongy, winter-pale grass. He was still stiff and sore—a lot more than four days of sleeping could account for —and somewhat dizzy, eyes dazzled in the bright light of day, and a headache he hadn't noticed while he was lying down was sending a dull pulse through his temples.

"...*your brain nearly exploded out your ears....*"

Wil supposed a lingering headache was a small thing, by comparison.

Horses were penned in what looked like a rough-fenced pasture on the outskirts, smaller paddocks scattered around it, and Wil reconsidered his assumption that this was a temporary camp. He was pleased to see Sunny and Miri—and the one he'd more or less stolen and hadn't had time to name yet—milling around with the rest, and made a note to greet them after he'd begged something to eat from whomever was cooking whatever that meat was that was making his mouth water.

He shoved his hands in his pockets and hunched in against the breeze, regretting almost instantly that he hadn't thought to hunt around for his coat. It had been so warm in that little cave, and the sun had been so bright outside it—it hadn't occurred to him that he might need to keep warm until he was enough steps away from it that the want of breakfast outweighed the want of the coat.

Watching his steps on the slippery ground, Wil paused by one of the small fires—this one sporting a good cast iron kettle almost at the boil—dragged his hands from his pockets, and crouched over it for a quick warm-up. The heat beckoned, welcoming, and Wil stretched his hands under the kettle and over the flames.

"...*great gobs of it, like a ghost was throwing balls of it....*"

Curious, Wil shot a quick glance to all points to see if anyone had marked him yet. It didn't seem so. He turned back to the fire, flattened his hand, and watched as the flames skutted down, compressing over the edges of the small pit like the petals of a fiery flower, tongues of it licking at damp earth, spitting and sizzling.

He shook out his hand and blinked it away.

Only the tiniest of pushes, but the headache stretched and tendriled behind his eyes now, and he rubbed at them. He probably shouldn't have been messing around with it so soon, but it made him feel better to know it was still there.

Furtively Wil swiped at his nose, relieved when his fingers came away clean and dry. Dallin would kick Wil's arse for him if he did anything stupid so soon after Dallin had more or less sucked himself dry to heal him. Now that Wil thought about it, it seemed ungrateful.

He shot a guilty glance over his shoulder. Dallin was still in heated consultation and looked like he was nowhere near finishing up yet. Good. Wil just wouldn't mention his little test when they were finally done with their pissing contest.

He snorted and turned back to the fire—

Almost fell backward on his arse.

A pair of tall fringed buckskin boots rose up from the ground, long, thick kid-covered legs sprouting from the tops and climbing up—and up and up and up.... Wil followed the line of the wide body past the buff and sheepskin coat, finally craning his neck, gaze coming to rest on candid indigo eyes set in a grave young face, an uncertain smile crooking over wind-chapped lips and crinkling the small semicircle of cobalt tattoos inked over a sun-browned cheekbone. Wil only controlled the anxious little start that shuddered through him because they were markedly different from the others he'd seen.

The young man stared for a moment, seemingly unaffected when Wil just stared warily back. Wil was just starting to squirm uncomfortably beneath the regard when the young man finally quirked his brow ever so slightly, then dipped a small bow.

"Hunter Calder."

Wil couldn't help the twist of his mouth, the quick drawing away of his gaze. Bloody hell, was he going to be stumbling over Calders for the rest of his—admittedly probably short—life? His throat was suddenly dry, the aches and twinges in his bones tightening as tension took hold of him in a tight fist. None of which was helping the headache.

"Um. Wil." He kept his head down, eyes to the ground.

The young man—Hunter—cleared his throat and scuffed the heel of his boot in the spongy sod, digging a small channel in the soft grass in its wake. "You are a sorcerer, then?"

Wil shot him a sideways frown and raised an eyebrow. Sorcerer. Ha.

Hunter gestured at the fire. "I saw a woman command fire once. When I was very young." Wil thought Hunter looked very young now. He couldn't remember when he'd seen such ingenuousness in the eyes of anyone but a child. "Made it burn every color of the rainbow, but it didn't dance to her will. We young ones thought it quite clever, even so. She called herself a sorceress, but the Old Ones called her a trickster and sent her away."

Wil chanced another glance up, sorry already he'd been so stupid as to do what he'd just done out in the open like that. Dallin would kick Wil's arse twice over. And now that Wil had done it, opened up, he couldn't stop seeing the patterns.

Hunter didn't look like he was about to run for a noose or anything, but one never knew.

Wil turned his gaze back to the fire, and shut his eyes when he couldn't make the shapes of the threads recede, couldn't make it all stop pulsing behind his eyes. Anyway, what was he supposed to say?

Hullo, I'm the person who pointed the way to the raid that took out every young male between ten and twenty before you were born

—good thing you weren't *born yet, though, amiright?—and I've been told it wasn't my fault, and I've been told I was tricked, but that doesn't quite take away the fact that I did it, does it?*

"No, I'm not a sorcerer." Wil looked away. "I'm just...." He thought about it but couldn't come up with anything with which to even vaguely define himself. "I'm just nobody."

Hunter hunkered down on the other side of the fire, head atilt, quizzical. "The Old Ones do not call upon the *Weardas* to guard Just Nobody. The Old Ones do not command the *Weardas* to cross the Bounds to defend a Domin—" He cut himself off and waved a hand. "—to defend an outlander Just Nobody and escort him into the very heart of our country."

Wil had nothing to say to that, and even if he did, he thought it best to keep his mouth shut until he knew just what these people had been told. "*Weardas?*"

"Ah." Hunter squinted thoughtfully at the sky for a moment, then looked again at Wil. "'Guard' suits best, I expect. Perhaps 'sentry.'" He shrugged. "Some of the First Words encompass many meanings."

Wil thought of all of those meanings for *Wæpenbora* Dallin had rattled off in that little inn outside Dudley, and nodded. "Is that what your marks say?"

Hunter lifted a big chapped hand unconsciously to his cheekbone. "So I'm told. At any rate, it's what they mean."

A distinction Wil could certainly understand. "You don't cut them into your skin, then. Like the Old Ones."

Hunter's open expression took on a subtle weight. "You have been to Lind?"

"No." Wil wondered if he'd said too much already. He waved over his shoulder toward Dallin. "My...." He trailed off, confused. Just exactly what *was* Dallin to him now? And would whatever they were to each other be acceptable here? "My friend—" He caught the word as it came out his mouth. He'd never called anyone by that descriptive before.

"Ah, I wasn't thinking." Hunter grinned. "You are the companion of Dallin Brayden." He placed a hand over his heart and dipped his head, as though the name itself held some sort of reverence for him. "You would be aware of some of our customs, then."

Wil looked down, curling his fingers over the flames, and tried to ignore the things inside them, the things inside everything around him. He shivered. "Some, I guess." He really should have gone back for his coat. The chill was working right through him, despite the fire. He kneaded at the headache. "You knew of him before?"

Hunter's blue eyes widened in surprise. "Of course. All in Lind know of the Lost Shaman. We have been waiting for him." He didn't seem to notice Wil's discomfiture. "Tell me...." Hunter paused, somberly probing. "*Did* he truly destroy Chester with his spells to rescue you?" He leaned back at Wil's bit of a flinch, seeming to twig to his own lack of discretion, and dipped his head. "Forgive me, but... he has been spoken about since I was a boy. He's become somewhat of a legend. Many spoke as though he was lost forever. I don't think I expected to set my own eyes on him, and now...." A light flush crept to his tanned cheeks. "We didn't arrive in time to see what happened in Chester—we joined your party just outside it. But I saw him fight against your countrymen, you see. I thought perhaps, now he's home, he might... teach."

It took a moment for the sense of it to get through the growing pain behind Wil's eyes. Hunter was just too bloody *bright* with his gyrating reds and golds. It was distracting and even painful to look at, drilling into Wil's eyes with too much... *hereness.*

"Fight...." Wil squeezed his eyes shut, then popped them back open. He squinted. "*My* countrymen?"

"Ah yes, I expect you wouldn't remember."

Soft sympathy, a tiny bit of condescension toward the weak little Dominionite who'd apparently had to be rescued by the big, strong Lost Shaman in Chester and then defended in some skirmish Wil hadn't even guessed had happened. Just as well, he supposed, or he might have been throwing random fireballs into the middle of the chaos and setting them all ablaze, regardless of who was who.

"Ten of them." Hunter paused for a quick sneer. "They skulked outside the Bounds and tried to prevent us from entering our own country." He lowered his voice, eyes sparking with anger as he leaned in. "They wore marks they did not own."

"Oh." Wil closed his eyes again, rubbing at his brow this time. The Brethren. Of course. He'd almost forgotten about them. "They are no countrymen of mine."

If Hunter heard it, he didn't acknowledge it. "Dallin Brayden led the defense when they attacked, took command from our own *Weardgeréfan*, and turned it to a thorough rout. They say he was a captain—in the *cavalry*."

Wil opened his eyes at the awe in Hunter's voice, peering into an indigo gaze gone bright with something both light and dark at the same time. Lust, but not the sort Wil was used to seeing in the eyes of a young man. A warrior trained for battle, too obviously in his prime, and with no war on which to exert that hunger.

Hunter's gaze went softly avid. "What's he like?"

Wil stared. He tried kneading at the base of his skull this time.

Oh, for pity's sake. The boy was in love with Dallin. Listening to stories about him since he was a child, romanticizing it all, and now he'd seen his Lost Shaman, and he'd gone and lost his head.

And how was Wil supposed to answer a question like that?

Well, let's see—he's strong enough to break me in half if he wants to, and yet I don't think I've ever felt a gentler touch. He

341

could easily strut around and take anything he wants, but he never takes from another without permission. He's denied his magic his whole life, and then in the space of less than a week he learned to heal himself of a stab wound and then heal me of... something I don't want to think about. He had a life he loved, a job he was very good at—I know, I saw him do it up close—and he walked away from all of it because he thought it was the right thing to do. He's intensely passionate, but you have to pay attention—you have to look beyond the self-possession to see the coals burning behind his eyes. But you'd better be careful, because he'll look back and see you too.

"What's he like?" can't be answered with words. You have to be there beside him and live it with him to even begin to understand who and what he is. And even then, he'll likely surprise you.

Wil frowned.

Oh hell. Does that mean I've lost my head over him too?

A flush warmed his cheeks, and he shook his head, but he stopped when the pain flared out and wrapped around his skull like an iron band tightening. He sucked in a thin breath and stood —a little slowly and awkwardly, as though he'd aged fifty years while he'd slept.

He'd got up too soon, that was all this was. He should've stayed in the dark little cave and waited for Dallin to come and coddle him some more.

Weak little Dominionite in the middle of all these great big Linders, needs to be rescued and defended, coddled and cosseted, then condescended to by someone who wasn't even alive when I'd already done my worst....

He had to get out of here.

He wasn't even hungry anymore.

"I'm sorry," he told Hunter. "This must be your own campfire, and I didn't mean to impose. I was only—"

"I'm pleased to share it. And I'd be pleased to fetch you some breakfast and guide you around the camp, if you like."

Wil blinked, eyes narrowing before he'd even registered the vague bit of suspicion creeping into his awareness. "You want to fetch me breakfast?"

"Or tea." Hunter gestured to the fire. "The kettle's almost at the boil."

Oh, for the love of.... This boy didn't think Wil was going to put in a good word for him with the Lost Shaman, did he?

A prickly little jag of *mineminemine!* jabbed Wil in the gut, and he clenched his teeth, throttled it down, closing his eyes and rubbing at his temples. The headache was chewing right into his brain now, edged and pointy behind his eyes, and he couldn't stop the threads from winding in front of them, spiking into them like shards of glass reflecting too-bright sunlight.

Too much. Too big.

Weak.

"Are you well?" Hunter's tone was filled with concern, his hand taking firm hold of Wil's elbow.

"Fine." Wil's voice was faint and shaky, not quite supporting the lie, but he pulled his arm away nonetheless. "I'm fine, I just—"

Except he apparently wasn't fine, because he was talking one second—*blackblackblack everything too dark too big too black*—and the next he was sitting on his arse in the damp grass, the heavy throb swarming up his backbone telling him the descent had not been a graceful or gentle one. His head was going to split—it was going to split right open and dump his brain out onto the ground.

"*Fuck.*" Wil drew his knees up, planted his elbows atop them, and held up his thumping head with his hands. Pressure was building up behind his eyes as if he were pushing, except he wasn't. He wasn't doing *anything*, just bloody *sitting here.*

.... Sitting here in the middle of Lind, a place he'd been warned not to go. Not everything Síofra had said was a lie. In fact, almost everything he'd ever told Wil had at least a seed of truth in it.

Maybe it wasn't just a headache. Maybe it was whatever Calder had done to Dallin that first day in Chester. Hunter was a Calder. Maybe he knew how to do it too. Maybe he wanted Wil —*weak little Dominionite companion*—out of the way so he could get close to the Shaman. Maybe he knew about Wilfred Calder—a *Seeker*—maybe he was a brother, a cousin, and decided to take out his frustrated thirst for enemy blood on the weak, helpless Dominionite. Maybe *all* Linders knew how to seek, and here Wil was, trapped right in the middle of them, all those eyes on him, all those minds trying to pry into his, all those patterns trying to wend into his own, subsume it, obliterate it, push him out of it, send him out into the darkness—

There were hands on him, wide and strong, but they weren't the *right* hands, so Wil shrugged them off sharply. He growled. Voices fuzzed in his head, splotches of light spangled behind his eyes, and the ground kept wanting to roll out from beneath him.

Too vast. Too deep. Too alone.

Standing on the edge of a black abyss, patterns all around him— too bright, too painful, and none of them his.

Weak. Letting Síofra take from him, hiding in the darkness, letting others fight his battles while he was busy swooning, and now unable to keep anything at all at bay, wide open, and everything crushing inward, pressure and weight, pressing him down and down.

Great ripping *pain*, crowding in, crowding out. He gripped his head in his hands, dug his fingers into his scalp to try to keep it from exploding all over the grass. Everything was too loud, too bright, too altogether *there*, overwhelming, and hands kept coming at him, so he kept snarling and shaking them off, until—

"Wil?"

The right voice, the right hands. "Not...." Wil squeezed his eyes shut tighter, dug harder into his scalp. "Not *weak*."

"Weak?" Genuine confusion, then genuine conviction. "No, never."

"Don't need rescue."

Idiot. Stupid. Denying the need when it was so obviously wishful thinking.

"No, Wil." Dallin's voice was somewhere between wry amusement and raw anxiety. "You're usually too busy rescuing me to take the time for your own."

Wil hadn't really been looking for a "right" answer, but that was it. He reached blind. "*Help.*"

CHAPTER 8

Dallin turned on Calder, jaw set. "*This* is why you should've told me."

He shouldered away the young man crouching beside Wil, not pausing for pleasantries, and dragged Wil upright. The young man didn't go away, merely moved to Wil's other side and hovered, honest concern on his open face. Dallin measured, then dismissed him, shifting his glance to Shaw as he arrived behind Calder, huffing and blowing with the exertion of his sprint, then to the three who came behind him. Dallin shot a heated glare at every one of them.

"You don't *fuck* with people like this."

He tightened his grip and took a slow step forward. He dipped his head to Wil's ear. "I'm sorry. I didn't think you'd be up yet, and I got... distracted."

"What...?" Wil turned his face into Dallin's coat, gripping at it with clutching fingers, breath thin and fast through clenched teeth as he stumbled and lurched, clinging but trying to keep his feet. "What *is* this?"

Confused and in pain. Not quite frantic yet, but getting there.

Dallin didn't blame Wil. Dallin could feel the weight as though it was on his own shoulders, invasive and unrelenting. He reached for it, found it, and set himself to sorting the balance.

"It is your destiny, lad," Calder answered.

Dallin's teeth set tight. "You say one more—"

"You must heed the Old Ones, Brayden."

"If you don't get the hell away from me, I'm going to heed my more violent inclinations and shoot you in the face."

"Now, Brayden," Shaw chastised mildly, "you're allowing your temper to rule your reason."

"I do that sometimes."

"Destiny?" This from the young man, still lingering and looking as if he intended to follow where he clearly wasn't wanted. His eyes had gone bright with interest. "Is that why you saved Wil, then?"

Wil growled and pushed into Dallin harder. Dallin stopped short to turn a narrow stare on the boy. "Who the hell are you?"

The lad gulped but lifted his chin. "Hunter Calder."

"Of course you are." Another bloody Calder. Brilliant. Damned prolific family, the Calders. "You assume too much, like everyone else around here." Dallin dismissed Hunter once more, adjusted his grip on Wil, and started walking again.

"The heart of the world." Wil's voice was slurred and dazed, and he sagged against Dallin. "Too much, too big."

Dallin had to stop short and tighten his grip to keep Wil from slithering to the ground. Yelps went up all around as every fire in sight flared up, spat, then burst from their pits like fists unfurling, as though someone had just thrown oil on them, before settling back into their confines. Dallin shot a quick glance around the camp. No one had been hurt, but every eye, sprung wide in surprise, stared at the various fires, then shifted wary glances first to the Old Ones and then to Wil. Reflexively, Dallin shot a sharp look at the sky—nothing brewing yet—then laid his hand to the crown of Wil's head. He closed his eyes and tried to shut everything else out.

There was too much—both crowding in and crowding out—and Wil was growing too frantic to let him help.

"Settle now." Dallin kept his voice low and soothing. "You have to let me in, all right? Like in Chester, remember?"

"Heart of the world." Garbled and breathless. Wil sagged in Dallin's grip, clutching his head. "Fuckfuckfuck, it *hurts*, make it *stop*."

"I'm trying, Wil. Just try to calm down and let me."

It wasn't pushing, not anything like what Wil did, or at least what Dallin understood about what Wil did. More like opening up, letting his intuition reach out, decoding what he found, deciding what the problem was, and then trusting it. Finding a lack and filling it. Finding excess and taking it away. Asking.

It didn't even feel like magic, really. It felt more like common sense. Earthbound and almost rational, once Dallin had allowed it out of its cage. No whispers in his mind, no mental pictures. Just a deep-down, indefinable *knowing*. A conscious, willful act of *letting* himself know, of not demanding a definition or explanation. Knowing, then doing. Stepping out of his quickmud. With both feet this time.

The heart of the world, Wil had said—so had that boy back in the stable—and now Dallin knew all too well what it meant. It had stayed at bay while Wil slept, that deep, mindless, dreamless sleep Shaw had shown Dallin that first night, but now that Wil was awake, it seemed to gather at him as if he was some sort of lodestone. Which, now that Dallin thought about it, wasn't too far off the mark.

"It's this place. I'm sorry. I couldn't keep my promise, and now you're paying for it."

"Promise?" Wil sighed, some of the coiled tension running out of the set of his shoulders. He wasn't clawing at his head anymore as he'd been, just holding on to Dallin's coat now. Equilibrium was coming slow, but it was coming. "You always keep your promises. I should've pushed, you were right, I should've pushed, I shouldn't've pulled away, I'm sorry, I didn't—"

"Wil, it's all right. You don't have to—"

"—didn't mean to burn you, too deep, too *weak*, I can't make it go away, I can't stop *seeing*—" He staggered and shifted a muzzy gaze up at Dallin. He blinked, then shut his eyes again tight. "I have to sit down."

"You have to go to Fæðme," Calder put in, reaching out and setting a hand to Wil's arm.

Wil swung blind and smacked Calder's hand away with a mumbled "G'the fuck off me."

He didn't wait for Dallin to guide him down to the ground. He more or less started to fold his legs and slide down Dallin's side, trying to plant his arse where his feet had been. Dallin just sort of teetered sideways and followed Wil down, helping as much as he could with the awkward maneuver and the resulting awkward position.

"Too damned many threads," Wil breathed, strained and thin. "It *hurts*, it fucking *hurts*, and I can't stop seeing them."

"Here, let me help." The boy—Hunter—had somehow got hold of Wil's elbow and was trying to help hold him up. Wil didn't growl, just kept babbling, so Dallin didn't order Hunter off, else they might all three end up in a heap.

"Wil," Calder persisted, "you must talk sense with your—" He glanced at the small crowd they'd drawn, mouth pinched. "—with Brayden. There is no reason for you to be in this pain."

Calder turned back to Dallin, eyes hard, worried. One thing for which Dallin had to give grudging credit—Calder really did care about Wil. If only Calder wasn't so bloody *sure* he knew better.

"You must take him to Fæðme. Only there—"

"I will take him to Fæðme when he has been told what it means for him, and *if* he then agrees to go—not before." All of it shoved out from between Dallin's teeth. "If you'd bloody *told* me about all this before we reached the Bounds, I would never have—"

"But Fæðme is forbidden," Hunter put in, one hand still resting on Wil's arm, the other hovering behind him as though he was afraid Wil was going to topple backward. "It's sacred ground. Outlanders are not permitted." He frowned up at Calder then the three Old Ones still silently looking on behind him, then back again at Dallin. "Is he not from Ríocht?"

Dallin bristled. "And if he was and needed healing to save his life, would you deny him?"

Hunter pulled back, surprised by the vehemence with which Dallin had asked the question. He blinked. "It would not be my place." He shot a bewildered glance up at the silent elders. "I expect I would do as the Old Ones instructed. And...." He flushed, suddenly distressed. "And the Shaman." His head dipped low. "Forgive me, I forgot to whom I was speaking. I should not have presumed."

"Right." Dallin scowled. "My point."

Hunter only shook his head, looking at Dallin attentively as though he was waiting for Dallin to pull wisdom from out his arse and hand it over. Dallin couldn't help the jag of anger. Hunter was only a boy, only knew what he'd been taught. It wasn't his fault. Still, that blank belief made Dallin's jaw go tight and his fists curl.

"I didn't mean to offend. I only mean to help." Hunter jerked his chin down at Wil. "He is in much pain. You can heal him, surely."

Wil had stopped the steady stream of apologetic jabber, but he still hadn't opened his eyes. Now he drew up his knees and covered his face with his hand. He was still holding on to Dallin's trouser leg. Despite the tight grip, Dallin managed to plant one knee in the grass to kneel over Wil.

"Too many eyes." Wil was muttering in a steady stream, but it wasn't exactly *babble*, so Dallin didn't panic. "It's too much. I can't stop seeing it all. Make them go away."

"Easier said than done." Dallin had been trying to make them go away for bloody days. He shot his glance upward, ratcheting it into a glare at the crowd of gawkers. "All right, everyone move along."

He was satisfied but still discomfited that they backed off immediately. Since they'd run headlong into this little war party—mere miles from Chester and still fleeing breakneck when they'd more or less collided—and word had spread of Dallin's identity, the unaccountable near-reverence had almost done the job of unnerving him where all the violence of the escape had failed. And it continued to make him edgy every time he found himself on the receiving end of it.

He turned back to Wil as everyone but the five he most wanted to go away did so. All right, four—Dallin supposed Shaw could stay. Wil liked him, and Shaw had been damned helpful the past couple of days.

"It's this place, Wil. It's nothing to be afraid of. It's a lot, but there's nothing inside it. Do you understand what I mean?"

That had been Dallin's biggest worry—terror, really—at least while Wil had been so lost, so unreachable. That what Dallin had felt inside the chaos when Wil stood in front of Síofra—that presence, that overwhelming greed and intent—had somehow followed Wil down into the dark. It wasn't until Wil finally found his way back that Dallin could breathe easier, could sleep and pay attention to things other than constant meditating and searching.

Wil nodded, very carefully, but kept his head bowed and his body curled in.

"Good." Dallin rubbed at Wil's back. "We're going to figure out how to keep it back. I'm taking some of it, but you're stronger than I am. You're going to have to push it at me so I can take more."

That got Wil to open his eyes. Worry. Instant knee-jerk refusal. "No, I'll—"

"You won't. It won't hurt me. It's what I'm here for." Dallin glared up at Calder, at the others. "So I'm told."

Thorne—the eldest, and up until this point, seemingly the most reasonable, in Dallin's opinion—finally spoke. "That is *not* what you've been told." He stepped forward, crouching down on creaky knees beside Dallin to peer at Wil with a gentle smile. He reached toward Wil, but stopped short when Wil reflexively pulled back. "May I?"

Wil squinted at Dallin with a frown, questioning. All Dallin could do was shrug tiredly. The pain in Wil's eyes, in the tight set of his white face, the confusion—if Thorne could take that away, Dallin wasn't going to begrudge it.

"He won't hurt you." Dallin said it with a warning flash of his glance to Thorne. "But it's up to you."

"I am Denton Thorne." Thorne dipped his head low. "I am pleased to welcome you to Lind, and I am overjoyed to make your acquaintance." His smile pinched. "Wil, yes?"

Wil nodded slowly, still wary, still pale, and obviously still very much in pain. Dallin wasn't sure how much sense was getting through it, but Wil seemed to be following the conversation, at least.

The little Dallin had been able to help so far hadn't been

much. He didn't want to do what needed done out here, but he would if he had to. If Thorne didn't hurry it up, Dallin was going to knock him out of the way, fragile old bones or no, and do it right here under the eye of every man, woman, and beast in the camp.

Permission granted, Thorne laid his fingertips to Wil's brow, pulled in a long breath, and closed his eyes. "You have been lost for a very long time, my boy." Thorne frowned and adjusted his fingers. "You do not know the joy that moved through Lind when Calder sent us word from Chester that you had been found." He smiled. "Doubly glad, for 'twas your Guardian who found you."

No smartarse comment from Wil as to the exact circumstances under which Dallin had found him and what had resulted immediately after. Wil must really be hurting.

"So you really were looking for me?"

The soft yearning in Wil's voice nearly pierced Dallin's heart.

Thorne kept the fingers of one hand on Wil's brow and ran those of the other through Wil's hair, tucking a hank of satiny blue-black gently behind Wil's ear. Dallin was both surprised and relieved to see Wil's posture slouch just a fraction more, a further release of pain and the tension it wound around him like a coiled spring.

"We looked, my lad. Believe it." Thorne shot a conciliatory glance over at Dallin. "Though our methods were...." He lifted an eyebrow, wryly expectant.

"Antiquated," Dallin supplied.

"Antiquated," Thorne agreed.

"Amateurish."

"Hm, right, and...." Thorne's mouth twisted, sardonic. "What was the other?"

"Incompetent and negligent, I believe were my exact words." If Thorne was expecting Dallin to flush and take a single one of them back, he was going to be sorely disappointed.

Thorne merely nodded and turned back to Wil. "All of those things and more, brave lad. We would prostrate ourselves at your feet, but young Brayden tells us you might be moved to...." Again he looked at Dallin, expectant.

This time Dallin did flush. "I believe I suggested that he might kick your arses."

"And that you might hold us down for him, yes?"

Dallin was saved from answering that one by Wil, who looked worried, but Dallin was extraordinarily relieved to see a bit of defiance creep into Wil's pained gaze. "Calder said you would be expecting *me* to prostrate myself. That I'd sinned against—"

"The only sin here is our own." Thorne's tone was soothing. "We have waited for our Lost Shaman so that he may guide us, as he always has done. Now that he is home, he has wasted no time in pointing out our sins and mistakes to us rather plainly."

Wil looked from Thorne to Dallin. For the first time, a faint smirk touched Wil's lips.

"And has he spent the last few days 'guiding' you, then?"

Thorne returned the smirk. "In a manner of speaking."

"You have my sympathies." Wil smiled up at Dallin, somewhat weak and thin, but it took the sting out of the tease. "He's 'guided' me a bit too."

Thorne grinned and pulled his hand away. "The pain has lessened?"

Wil nodded. "Thank you, it has." He rubbed his fingers over his brow where Thorne's had been. "Calder said Fæðme—"

"Not here, lad." Thorne patted Wil's cheek. "Let your young Brayden get you settled and fed. The pain will return shortly if we don't let him tend to you. You and he have more work to do." He waved at the others behind him. "We will come to you afterward." He sent another meaningful look at Dallin. "All will be disclosed,

354

and then we will hear your decision." He turned back to Wil. "Is that acceptable?"

"My...?" Wil's brow twisted in confusion, but he merely looked up at Dallin. When Dallin shifted an encouraging nod, Wil turned his gaze back to Thorne. "It's acceptable. Thank you."

Courteously, Dallin helped Thorne to his feet. Not so courteously, he set his gaze on Shaw alone. "We could probably use your help, if you don't mind."

Shaw gusted a weary sigh. Dallin didn't really blame him. Dallin had been putting Shaw in the middle since he'd joined them, using Shaw as a sort of buffer between Dallin and Calder. It was either that or they'd end up knocking each other out, so Dallin maintained the tacit parameters and pretended at decorum. Since the bone over which Dallin and Calder were snarling was Wil, however, Shaw had been remarkably cooperative. He nodded his agreement while the Old Ones, one by one, sidled past Wil, dipping full bows to him, and left them to themselves, thankfully chivvying Calder along with them. Wil just sort of blinked after them, then up at Shaw, then Dallin, then... he frowned and lifted a questioning look at Hunter, who, like his apparent kin, didn't seem to take a hint that his presence was not welcome.

"I can help," Hunter said, somewhere between a demand and a plea. He shifted his glance from Wil, to Dallin, to Wil again, then spread his hands and dipped as close to bowing as he could get in his half crouch. "Wil from Ríocht, please forgive me for any affront and allow me to make amends." He lifted his head and flipped an anxious glance at Dallin. "I can fetch whatever you need, if you'll just tell me. Food, medicines—"

"Tea." Wil rested his head in his hand again, eyes closed. "You said you'd fetch me tea."

Hunter grinned and nodded enthusiastically, eyes bright. "I did."

"Please do, and...." Wil squinted up at Dallin, blinking him into focus. "What was that stuff Mistress Slade gave me?"

"Mistress...." Dallin had to card through several days of chaos to place the name. "Oh." The healer in Dudley. "Meadowsweet and skullcap."

"D'you still have it?"

Dallin shook his head, rueful. "I lost my pack in Chester."

Wil turned back to Hunter. "Can you find some of that?"

"I don't know meadowsweet." Hunter looked crestfallen. "But mæting would surely—"

"Did I *ask* for mæting?"

It was sharp-edged and through Wil's teeth. Dallin wasn't surprised, but Hunter certainly was—he reared back and blinked.

"I'm sorry," Wil said, voice low now and with none of the strength of mere seconds ago. "I didn't mean to... just... I don't want mæting."

"Poppy?" Shaw put in.

"Actually, wood betony will be better for this," Dallin said. "It grows like a weed around here, and most use it for amulets and charms. Shouldn't have any trouble at all finding a good supply."

Not with all these *Weardas*. Dallin had found over the years that almost everyone who carried a weapon also carried a good luck charm in some form. Those who were regularly shot at tended to be a superstitious lot, and Linders were the most superstitious by far.

Dallin shifted his gaze to Wil. "It will help you relax. It won't put you to sleep, and it won't... do anything else."

He left it there. It didn't matter if Shaw or Hunter understood what Dallin didn't say, only that Wil did.

"Fine." Wil closed his eyes again, kneading at his temples as though he was trying to dig right into his skull. "Whatever, just... *something*. Quick."

"All right, then." Dallin nodded at Hunter. "You heard the man. Tea and wood betony. Drop the dried petals right into the tea —a good palmful of them—and make sure you don't get any leaves or anything else in there, only the petals, mind. Once they've sunk to the bottom of the cup, bring it along." He waved Hunter off. "Get on, then."

Obviously pleased, Hunter sprang to his feet and hurried away. Dallin just shook his head. Another bloody Calder. What was he supposed to do with *another* bloody Calder who wouldn't fuck off?

"Right, then." Shaw clapped his thin hands together and quick-stepped over to Wil. He crouched down and took hold of Wil's arm to wrangle it over his shoulder. "C'mon, lad, up you get."

Dallin helped haul Wil to his feet, keeping firm hold while Wil staggered. Wil wouldn't open his eyes, and his brow was drawn in tight again.

"Shall I carry you?"

Dallin hadn't meant anything by it but necessary help, but Wil snarled, snapped, "*No*, you shall bloody *not*," and tried to pull his arms away.

Dallin caught Wil as he wobbled, suffering some more snarling with some added growling.

"Hey. *Hey.*"

This as Wil jerked away from both Dallin and Shaw, obviously too sharply, because he gasped, clutching at his head with both hands before he bent at the waist and gagged up nothing. Dallin didn't wait for Wil to settle down—he took hold of Wil again, keeping him from keeling face-first into the grass. Wil didn't fight Dallin this time, only stood there, bent over and breathing hard.

"Wil, I'm not trying to... whatever you think I'm trying to do, just—" Dallin shook his head. "You asked for my help. Now let me help you."

"I *will*. I only.... Not *here*. They already think I'm fragile and halfway mad, and now you want to bloody *carry* me."

Pointing out that Dallin had pretty much lugged Wil from Chester to here would probably be a very bad idea right now.

"I don't *want* to bloody carry you, I asked you if I *should*. All you had to do was say no." Dallin frowned. "And *who* thinks you're fragile and halfway mad?"

Wil let Dallin straighten him up some, then let himself be slipped back beneath Dallin's arm. He took a shaky step.

"They all do. I could feel it. I can *still* feel it. All of them." Wil slid a squinted gaze up at Dallin. "I can't stop seeing it all. It's everywhere, even when I close my eyes, and it hurts."

"Let us get you settled back in." Shaw reached up to guide Wil's head to Dallin's shoulder. Dallin was fairly impressed that Wil let himself be guided, that he closed his eyes again and seemed willing to at least try to let Dallin lead him. "Brayden knows what to do, all right? We'll get you tucked back in and let him do his work."

Wil lifted his head and blinked up at Dallin. "Yes. Please."

Dallin sighed, nodded, and led the way back to the caves.

Relief shouldn't be coming this hard. In fact, Wil shouldn't have even woken yet. He should have stayed under the sway of that heavy sleep until Dallin lifted it away, but it was as though Wil was becoming immune to those small things Dallin could offer by way of respite. Or, perhaps, this place was just too much—*too much, too big*, Wil had said—and anything Dallin could do would always come up just short of enough. Guardian or no, chosen or not, this sort of thing was just not what Dallin was good at. Give him a gun, a sword, a bow, or even just his fists, and he'd stand against anything and take his chances, but this....

It was enough to make him doubt his own snarled assertions to the Old Ones just an hour ago. Well, would have been, if he wasn't so unwaveringly *sure* this was how it had to go.

"Wil, you have to listen to me, all right? I can't do it if you won't let me."

"I *am* letting you. I just... I can't... you're making it worse."

"Because you won't let me make it better!"

"Brayden," Shaw chided softly.

Just that, just his name, but it had the desired effect. Dallin drew in a deep, calming breath and let it flow slowly from his chest.

"I'm sorry, Wil. I don't mean to be impatient." Dallin adjusted his position, knelt in front of Wil, and slipped his fingers into Wil's hair. He began a gentle massage. Wil was stiff and tense, but he didn't jerk away. "It's going to get worse before it gets better, and I'm sorry, but it can't be helped." Wil still wouldn't open his eyes, squinched tight in pain, so Dallin did with his voice what he couldn't with his expression, measuring his words carefully, setting his tone smooth and low. "You have to open up, just like you told me in Chester, all right? You do it quick, and then you push it right at me—in to you and out to me, as fast as you can."

Wil shook his head against Dallin's hands. "You don't understand."

Down to a strained whisper now. If Wil didn't start cooperating soon, Dallin was going to have to put him out again. Except then Wil would simply wake sooner than he should, and the whole thing would start all over again.

"Then explain it to me." Dallin kept his voice as soothing as he could, what with all the anxiety ramming through him.

"You were *there.*" Wil's hands came up and pressed over Dallin's—not for any kind of intimacy, Dallin was sure, but an animal instinct pressure-to-pain. "Síofra couldn't.... I pushed, I pushed it *all,* and he couldn't—"

"Síofra was not your Guardian. You told me once I was as chosen as you, and this is one of the reasons why."

Dallin had argued long and loud with both Calder and Shaw about this, and they were halfway right. Dallin didn't have the spells and prayers he was supposed to have spent the past twenty years learning, and he certainly hadn't trained for it or practiced it, not even once. And perhaps it was cockiness made necessary by the immediacy of Wil's need, but Dallin *knew* what he was doing in this, the same way he knew a person was guilty or innocent just by looking at them.

Shaw, after coming around somewhat to Dallin's point of view, had speculated that perhaps, down deep where even Dallin never looked, he'd been training himself without even knowing. Dallin didn't necessarily believe that entirely, but it had convinced the Old Ones enough to leave him to it. They'd even chastised Calder —albeit mildly—for his vehemence in his protestations. For now. Because if Dallin couldn't keep Wil under control, or help him find a way to keep himself under control, there was no doubt the next armed standoff in which Dallin found himself was going to consist of him against twelve magic old men.

The problem, as Dallin saw it, was that even those twelve old men, as versed in magic as they were, had no real idea what they were dealing with in Wil. Power over elements they understood, and on those things Dallin would happily take their advice. But the dreams, the pushing—they were as ignorant about it all as Dallin was about tatting lace. They hadn't touched the edges of Wil's power as Dallin had. They hadn't stood inside it and felt Wil wield it. They hadn't looked at it with inward eyes and seen, understood—*known*. Dallin had. Dallin did. He wouldn't be taking this kind of chance, else.

Of course, that surety hadn't prevented him from dousing the fire in the cave down to coals. He'd taken all the guns and ammunition out and stored them in Shaw's the first night they'd got here. Dallin might be sure, but he wasn't going to take stupid chances.

He closed his eyes, laid his brow to Wil's, and took a long, deep breath before pulling back again.

"Wil, look at me."

He waited for a moment, but Wil only kept sitting there, eyes squeezed tight, breath thin and fast. Dallin slid his hands down to Wil's shoulders, shook just a little, and firmed his tone.

"Open your eyes and *look* at me, Wil."

With obvious unwillingness, Wil slitted his eyes and squinted at Dallin against the dim light. Dallin waited until Wil's gaze was semisteady and locked with his—liquid and shifting, overbright with that eerie light, and pulsing at Dallin, *painpainpainpain*— and Dallin firmed his grip on Wil's shoulders.

"Do you trust me?"

Because if Wil didn't, it was all pretty pointless. And not just this, but everything.

Wil shut his eyes again, thin tears squeezing out the corners. He slumped and leaned in to rest his head to Dallin's chest. "Yeah. *Yes*, you arse."

Dallin hadn't known how incredibly tense he'd been, waiting the perhaps three seconds for that answer, but he blew out a sigh before he could help himself. "Then do as I say, all right? Let it in, then push it out—at *me*, only at me. Not everything, just the pain. It won't hurt me, I promise."

"And what happens if it does?"

"Then I expect you to choose yourself, like you've been alleging you would." Dallin dropped a brief, soft kiss to Wil's head, gave his shoulders a squeeze, and pushed him back to sit somewhat upright. "What'll it be, Wil? Are you a man of your word, or was it all talk?"

Wil's face twisted into a snarling scowl. "You're crap at manipulation." He pressed harder at his head. It took a while, but he eventually gave a small, conciliatory nod.

Crap or not, it had apparently worked.

"All right. Good." Dallin grinned, cheered and relieved beyond sense, despite the fact that he'd just talked Wil into turning what Dallin knew to be almost boundless and pretty damned potent power directly at him.

It didn't matter. This was right, Dallin *knew* it was right, and he'd stopped caring quite a while ago just how he knew anything. If he had anything that could be called magic in him, it was this.

"Do it now. Let it in and then send it out, but do it quick. It's going to hurt like a bugger until you push it at me, so don't hesitate, all right? Just the pain, not the rest."

"Just the pain." Wil dared to wrench open his eyes and level his riotous gaze at Dallin. "You're *sure*?"

Dallin lifted an eyebrow. "Do I look like I don't know what I'm doing?"

Amazingly, Wil smiled back—small and weak and fleeting, but there. "I don't think Guardians are supposed to be so cocky."

Prideful, Calder had called Dallin, and arrogant and possessive too, while he'd been at it. Dallin half admitted the potential truth to it, though not to Calder. Dallin might have even allowed the arguments to sway him, if he weren't so deep-down *sure*.

"It'll work, Wil. Trust me, all right?" Dallin kept his grip on Wil's shoulders and braced himself. "Do it now."

All he could do was watch as Wil closed his eyes again, tensing even more in Dallin's hands. Dallin could feel the reluctance, the fear... the shift as Wil tentatively unlocked whatever it was inside him that was trying and failing to keep everything at bay and extended a shaky reach—

Wil screamed, anguished and wrenching, as it all flooded at him, excruciating and overwhelming. He balled in on himself, flung his arms over his head, and screamed again.

Bloody *damn*, this place was powerful—it fair reeked with it —and all of it pounding in on Wil. Dallin could feel it, like invisible iron filings scattering at a magnet, sharding right into Wil's mind and his soul, splitting and rending beneath its almighty weight.

"Don't hold on to it, Wil. Push it away."

Dallin could feel the flow of it all, could feel the thrum and shudder, but not the pain, just Wil's anguish beneath it. Could feel Wil frantically trying to weed through the threads of it, sort them and shove them away from himself. He was sliding down into a state that was near senseless—a wounded animal mindlessly trying to lash out and curl in at the same time, screaming to make its throat bleed.

"Damn it, Wil, you didn't listen to me before and you ended up lost. Now don't—"

"*Fuck off!*" A snarling shriek, hoarse and *this close* to hysterical.

The smoldering bones of the fire flared once again to life, spat and roared, then whooshed out and up. Shaw yelped and reached out a hand.

"Don't touch him!" Dallin ordered.

That was all he needed—Wil's mind was ready to snap, the pain was that great, and in this basic, wounded-animal state, he might take out whoever got near him. Dallin didn't want to think about the sorrow and guilt Wil would have to deal with afterward if he somehow managed to kill Shaw.

"*Wil!*" Dallin shook him, harder than before. "Wil, listen to

363

me. Don't hold onto it, don't try to sort it—just push it right at me. I won't let anything happen, I promise, just send the pain—"

He jerked abruptly back and away as if a great hand had just reached out and shoved him in the chest. It knocked the wind out of him—he couldn't even let loose a small yip—as he was thrown backward with a force that hurled him across the small cave, slammed his back to curved rock, drove him into it, compressed him between immovable granite and mind-numbing power.

Oh fuck. This wasn't just big—it was bloody huge!

Dallin took it all, pulling down every barrier and letting it flow over them, letting it drive into his body and his mind, seep into the cracks, and fill them up. His body instinctively tried to double over with the pain, but he was pinned like a bug to a cork.

Mother help me—is this what he's been feeling all this time? How could he stand it?

Breath was just a memory. Dallin's chest was caving beneath the force of it all.

Out the corner of his eye, Dallin saw the fire climbing up the wall of the cave. He heard the rumble of thunder, then he was deaf and blind, unable to move, to claw air into burning lungs. Still he let it wash into him, took it all, and invited more.

He could feel Wil inside it, distant and still confused, but sanity was returning, relief was slowly taking the place of agony. Dallin reached, setting himself like a baldachin beneath the onslaught. He showed Wil the channels, showed him how to use them, and then was swamped by the bald grace of Wil's reprieve when the stanchions held.

Part of Dallin smiled, smug and satisfied—*Ha! Fuck you, Calder, told you I knew what I was doing*—the rest of him saw the dark void of oblivion beckoning.

He let it come.

He was propped on his hands and knees when the black receded, head hanging, lungs wrenching and gasping, and vaguely glad he hadn't ended up in a helpless heap. There were far too many hands plucking at him, far too many voices nattering concern.

One set of hands was rougher than the others, clutching and almost shoving, where the others were just shaking lightly, almost petting. One voice was angrier than the others, frantically growling and demanding, where the others were low and worried.

"Dallin!" A sharp shake and a near snarl. "*Dallin Brayden!*" A smack this time, right to Dallin's ribs. It smarted good, but if Dallin had even an ounce of air in his lungs, he would've snorted. "You son of a bitch, you promised, you *swore*, I trusted you, you said—"

"I *said* not to hold it back and to—" Dallin had to pause to catch his breath. "—and to do it *quick*."

Wil went loose against him. "*Oh* thank *fuck*." He leaned down and dipped his head beside Dallin's, careful not to lean too hard lest he knock Dallin over, but leaning in just the same. His hand tightened on Dallin's shoulder, and he blew out a long, shaky sigh. "You scared the shit out of me."

Dallin finally managed to lift his head, squinting up into Wil's worried face and marking the lack of even the smallest drop of blood, the color to Wil's cheeks. He sagged, letting the hands help him lean back and plant himself semisteadily on his arse on the floor of the cave.

"Now you know... how *I* feel." He was still wheezing.

Dallin's gaze went first to the fire—blazing again but banked lower than an inferno, thank the Mother. He checked what little sky he could see through the cave's mouth next—still blue and cloudless, with no threatening rumbles muttering in the distance. Though, when his eye drifted groundward, Dallin noted a few too many loiterers standing around mere paces away, both worried and excited whispers flitting among them, and gazes all pointed into the little cave. Dallin trusted they weren't getting much of a view and dismissed them. He blinked, trying to clear his vision, and saw Shaw right beside Wil—one hand still on Dallin and one resting lightly between Wil's shoulder blades, support and comfort.

Dallin gripped Wil's arm. There was still some bit of worry in Wil's gaze, and he was still pale and drawn, but color was creeping steadily back into his cheeks, and his eyes were no longer wild and filled with pain and feral power—just green.

"All right?"

Wil gave Dallin an incredulous glare. "*Yes*, I'm all right. Are *you*?"

Dallin had to think about it for a moment. "A bit of a headache, but yeah." He narrowed his eyes. "You're sure? It's all...." He waved his hand. "It's holding?"

He didn't really have to ask—he could feel it, almost a low hum thrumming somewhere at the bottom of his spine—but it made him feel better when Wil nodded and smiled.

"I don't know quite what it is, but yes, it's holding. C'mon, let's get you over there where it's more comfortable."

Dallin let Wil and Shaw help him up, though he didn't feel at all wobbly—just that bit of a headache—but his back was going to hurt like hell later. He was already on his feet, trying to stretch his shoulders beneath all the hands, when he noticed for the second time there were a few too many of those hands. He turned, frowning, and found that... that boy, that... Calder's kin... what the hell was his name?

"Hunter. What the hell are you doing here?"

Hunter blinked, wide-eyed. "I...." He turned and waved

confusedly at the mouth of the cave, where a pewter cup lay in a pool of what was likely the tea he was supposed to bring Wil.

How long had Hunter been standing there? How much had he seen, and how much of it did he plan to report to the others? And how much did Dallin really care about what Hunter did or who he told?

"If Calder put you on us to spy, you needn't bother. You'll find I'm not quite as secretive as he would apparently like. All you have to do is ask."

"Spy?" Hunter looked genuinely confused, genuinely... hurt. He shook his head, adamant. "I would... no, I never—"

"Leave him alone." Wil was still shaky but apparently gaining back his equilibrium along with his snark. "He's not his uncle. He means well." He leaned in close and dipped his voice. "He bloody worships you, y'know. Have a care."

Dallin frowned at Wil, then turned the look on Hunter with barely suppressed suspicion. *Worships.* Dallin didn't quite know how to take that one, and had absolutely nothing to say to it, so he didn't even try. Instead he looked back at Wil.

"Uncle?"

"Well." Wil looked away. "I just assumed. Here, let's get you over there and sit you down."

It was the avoidance of the gaze that made Dallin narrow his eyes.

No, you didn't. You know. And he didn't tell you, did he?

"I could feel it. I can still feel it. All of them."

Dallin wondered just exactly what Wil had seen, and how much. Wondered what all that knowing might do to a person's head.

"You assumed correctly." Hunter dipped his head with an uncertain tilt of a smile, following along as Dallin shrugged off his helpers and sat down on the rumpled bedroll. "I am the son of Garrick Calder, brother to Barret Calder."

Dallin refrained from asking if Garrick was still alive, and if there were any more Calders running around the place waiting to pop up and not go away.

"And are you close?" Wil's question was quiet. He didn't look at Hunter as he sat down beside Dallin.

Dallin saw Shaw frown when he caught the tone. But Shaw kept silent, merely leaning against the stone of the cave's wall, folding his arms across his chest, and watching. It had been necessary to fill Shaw in on quite a lot of Wil's history after Shaw had more or less commandeered Wil's horse and joined them in their escape from Chester, but Dallin didn't remember telling Shaw about Wil's nonencounter with Wilfred Calder. Perhaps Shaw was in the process of twigging to the coincidence of the names now, or perhaps Calder himself had filled him in.

Hunter shifted an uncomfortable shrug. "Our families shared *inhíredes.*" He paused, brow creased in thought, expression brightening when he settled on the right word. "Household," he translated for Wil.

"So...." Wil looked down, tugging at his fingers as though they were too close to his hands. "You would have grown up with his son, then."

Dallin was very careful to keep himself from sighing and rolling his eyes. This insistence on seeking rebuke and snatching at guilt that didn't belong to him was getting wearisome.

Hunter's eyes had gone round, cautiously eager. "You have seen Wilfred?"

"I—" Wil stuttered into silence, shut his eyes, and rubbed at his brow.

Hunter wouldn't have been told why Wilfred crossed the Bounds. He wouldn't have been told why Barret had cut his Marks and followed later. And he obviously hadn't yet been told that Barret had found, in a sense, what Wilfred had left looking for. Without even knowing exactly what he was looking for.

It *still* set Dallin's teeth on edge.

Keeping his tone even, he made himself say, "No, we haven't seen Wilfred." Dallin watched with a small pang as Hunter sagged and his earnest gaze dimmed. Dallin shot a quelling glance at Wil —*There, are you happy now? You're not the only one you hurt when you insist on punishing yourself*—and looked back at Hunter with a bit of a frown. He was so young, so full of illusions, as all young men were. His disappointment showed all too clearly, and Dallin was at a loss as to what to say to it.

Shaw saved him. "Here then, lad, did you manage to find some of that wood betony?" He pointedly didn't look at the former contents of the cup still lying spilled across the stone floor. Dallin didn't even want to guess at which part of the previous half hour or so Hunter had walked in on that had startled him enough to drop it.

"Oh!" Hunter jumped to his feet. "My apologies, Wil from Ríocht." He dipped a small, diffident bow. "I...." He looked over at the cup with obvious chagrin. "It.... When I...." He shook his head with a light flush. "I'll fetch another." And then he was gone, snatching up the cup smoothly as he went, scattering the crowd that had gathered outside with a few sharp, imperious words and animated shooing gestures.

Dallin watched him go. He turned to Wil with a grimace.

Wil still had his head down, fingers working at his brow—more to hide his face now than a reaction to any lingering pain. "I know, I know. I'm sorry."

"Brayden will perhaps forgive me for speaking for him," Shaw ventured softly, "but I believe the point is rather that you've nothing for which to be sorry."

Well, then. Not only did it put Dallin's thoughts into concise words, but it rather answered the question as to how much Shaw knew.

"I know." Wil said it with a heavy sigh this time, finally lifting his head. "I know it with my head." He turned his gaze on Dallin, apparently marking the skepticism there. "I *do*. I just." He shook his head. "It feels... unfair that I should be here, in Wilfred Calder's country, among his people who loved and miss him, and using his name."

Dallin was immediately sorry for any cross thoughts he'd had a moment ago. He propped his arm behind Wil and leaned back—hopefully just enough light contact for comfort.

"His own father said he would have willingly shared it. And you've only kept a part of it."

Lame, lame, lame—but then, there was no good argument. Dallin would have felt the same in Wil's place. Then again, how would he know? His name had never been in question.

"Perhaps," Shaw said slowly, thoughtfully, "perhaps 'using his name' is not the proper way to think about it." He peered sharply at Wil. "Perhaps *honoring it* would sit better."

Wil's brow drew in, pensive, and he looked down again, fingers twitching at each other but not yanking and twisting as before. Thinking about it but seemingly not howling inside.

Dallin had had plenty of cause over the last several days to be thankful Shaw had followed his impulse toward adventure that day in Chester. Here was another. And the now-shaman's former vocation—to which, granted, Dallin hadn't twigged 'til he'd seen how Shaw sat a horse—might prove extraordinarily handy, if Shaw would ever open his mouth and own it.

"I've brought the kettle this time!" Hunter ducked through the cave's opening, kettle in one hand and cup in the other. He didn't wait for instruction but crouched down in front of them and poured steaming tea into the cup, offering it to Wil before putting the kettle to the side.

Wil accepted the tea with a flimsy smile but leaned in to mutter quietly to Dallin, "I don't want to hurt his feelings, since he's gone to all the trouble—twice—but I really don't need it anymore."

"You will. We're not quite through yet."

Wil still didn't move to take a sip. Instead he stared down into the cup for a long moment, then lifted a tense, half-embarrassed look up at Dallin. "It's... it smells...." He looked down again and shook his head. "It's flowery, and I—"

Dallin didn't need for Wil to finish, which was good, because it was all too clear that Wil couldn't. Dallin blamed Hunter for even mentioning bloody mæting in the first place.

As casually as he could, Dallin folded his hand over Wil's, guided the cup to his own lips, and took a sip himself. Slightly bitter beneath the lavender and honey, but not bad. And definitely not laced with anything more sinister than wood betony and some spice. Dallin pushed the cup back at Wil.

"It's fine, no worries." No fuss and no accusation. "I'll have a cup when you're through." Dallin twitched his shoulders and shot Wil a small smirk, deliberately dropping the subject of the tea. "Don't know your own strength, you."

Wil returned a rueful smile. "That'll teach you to reprimand me when I'm being pummeled by—" The smile slanted into new uncertainty. "What *was* all that?"

"That was—*is*—the Aisling's legacy."

Wil and Shaw both cut their gazes toward Hunter, frowning. Dallin merely turned to Hunter with a challenging lift of his eyebrows.

"One of the things over which your uncle and I vehemently

disagree is secrets. I don't like them. He thinks they're a necessary part of life. What do you think, Hunter?"

Hunter's own eyebrows went up, but in surprise and near chagrin to be so pinned to the spot. "I think... um." He looked to Wil for help but found only bemusement to match his own. He answered the challenge, rather than the question. "Was that why you quarreled with the Old Ones?"

"Part of it."

"No one has ever quarreled with the Old Ones." Hunter's expression tottered between intrigue and rebuke.

"Then this is new for them. If I have my way—and by tradition, I should—it's the first of several new things." Dallin sat forward, draping an arm over his upthrust knee. "Haven't you ever wondered what they do up there in that great Temple? Hasn't it ever angered you that you're kept so far removed from your own religion?"

Hunter looked down and studied the floor. "It is the way of things." He lifted his head. By the new light in Hunter's blue eyes, Dallin could tell he'd hit a nerve. "It has always been the way of things."

"That doesn't make it right." Dallin waved his hand. "Sit down." He waited for Hunter to comply before he went on, "You know of Ríocht's Chosen." Hunter's glance went immediately to Wil, narrowing. He nodded. "Do you know the legend of the Aisling?"

Again, Hunter nodded, the vague suspicion in his gaze dulling somewhat to... Dallin wasn't sure, but he thought it might be disappointment.

Hunter shrugged. "The Beloved who sings the songs of rain and sun to the Mother in the People's voices. Some still burn offerings to him in times of drought or flood, but most have forgotten."

Dallin hadn't known what answer he'd expected, but this one

piqued his interest. He'd never heard of the Aisling until Manning had hit him with it the first day he'd met Wil, and Dallin had lived here until he'd been twelve.

He tilted his head. "How d'you know of it, then?"

"Calders have walked Lind since the Mother birthed it." Hunter seemed ingenuously proud. "My name's song is quite long."

Ah. Dallin couldn't help but wonder if the concept of the Aisling would have blindsided him as it had done, had his father lived but another two years. He pushed it away and caught Wil looking at him with something soft and sympathetic. Dallin offered a reassuring smile, then turned back to Hunter and gestured at Wil.

"Hunter Calder, I'd like you to meet Ríocht's Chosen, the Father's Gift to the Mother, and my friend—the Aisling. No bowing necessary." He ignored Shaw's bit of a gasp and turned to Wil with a small smirk. "You don't want them all bowing to you, right?"

"I...." Wil's mouth was hanging open, and he stared at Dallin, wide-eyed, but he managed a dazed shake of his head. "Um. No?"

Dallin couldn't help an answering grin. "You're not drinking your tea." He waited for Wil to take an obligatory sip, still frowning in surprise, then turned back to Hunter, keen to analyze his reactions. If Dallin had his way, Hunter would be the first to know all the deadly deep secrets, but by no means the last.

Hunter was looking rather blankly at Wil. "*Dúil.*" He said it softly, slowly, then slid his gaze over to the fire and out the cave's mouth to the sky. A frown gathered at his brow as he turned back to Wil. His expression had gone awed, almost overwhelmed, but there was instant belief—helped, no doubt, by the dancing fires and threat of thunder in the clear blue sky only a little while ago, but not nearly so much *Prove It* as Dallin had waded through. The immediate trust was somewhat disturbing but still exactly what Dallin had been hoping for.

"Brayden." Shaw was softly cautious. "Do you really think this is wise?"

Dallin turned to Shaw, all smartarse smirks and cheeky retorts gone. "I think it's not only wise but necessary. We have Commonwealth soldiers pawing the ground and tugging at their reins at the Bounds. Roaming the countryside somewhere out there is a band of who knows how many nutters who want to steal Wil and push him out of his own mind. And in case you'd forgotten, *all* of them know exactly where we are. That's not even counting what the Guild's reaction will be when they get word their emissary is dead and their Chosen once again missing—*kidnapped* by me, no less, and with too many witnesses for even the Brethren to silence this time.

"Lind is a tiny piece of land, relatively speaking, caught right between Ríocht on one side and the rest of Cynewísan on the other, and Cynewísan wants us just as badly as Ríocht does. The very *last* thing any of us needs right now is more bloody *secrets*." Dallin paused, throttling down the anger welling at the back of his throat, and took a calming breath. "Considering all that," he told Shaw more evenly, "I think it's the smartest damned thing I've ever done."

He turned to Wil. "I'm sorry, I should've asked you first, but—"

"No, it's...." Wil was frowning, but not angrily. "It's smart, you're right. I just...." He shook his head. "There are soldiers at the Bounds?"

"Ah. Shit. Yes, sorry." Dallin shrugged. "I forgot you'd need some catching up." Not forgotten, really—there'd hardly been a moment, after all. "They didn't exactly chase us here, but they might as well have done. The result's the same, after all. The company that escorted Síofra to Chester is there, no doubt with reinforcements by now, and if not yet, then soon enough. Nine of the Old Ones have been out there with a good number of *Weardas* since we arrived, keeping them from crossing over and trying to avoid making it necessary for countrymen to start shooting at each other. The Brethren are lurking out there somewhere, but if past observation means anything, I don't think they'll have the brass to try anything on that side of the border." He grimaced. "Though there's nothing stopping them from going around and trying from their own side. Besides lack of intelligence, of course."

"I'd heard you had some goodly trouble from the Brethren."

"Did you, then?"

"Hunter told me you'd run into them." Wil shrugged. "That you took command from their...." He peered at Hunter, expectant.

"*Weardgeréfan*," Hunter supplied absently.

"I didn't *take* it," Dallin argued. "I just sort of—"

"Just sort of started giving orders and didn't remind the commander he was in charge when everyone followed them."

Dallin scowled. It was rather on the mark, so he couldn't really argue.

Anyway, Wil didn't give him much of a chance. "So the rest of the Old Ones are a few miles away at the Bounds playing diplomat, then. Where does that leave us?"

"Quite thoroughly pinned. The only thing we can do is get Lind ready for a standoff and possible battle to give us time to do what we came here to do. I think the best way to go about that is to fill our defenders in on exactly what they're defending, so they at least know what they're fighting for." Dallin gave Shaw a look. "I've found that men who know their cause tend to put a bit more heart behind their aim. We might be asking these people to fight their own countrymen—just because Lind likes to pretend it's not a part of the Commonwealth doesn't mean its soldiers will jump to take up arms when we say so. I think they deserve to at least know why we're saying so."

"Yes, you would." Wil reached out and flicked Dallin's more and more unruly fringe from his eyes. A throwaway gesture, but the intimacy behind it touched Dallin's heart and pleased him absurdly.

Dallin jerked his chin at the cup. "Drink your tea."

Hunter had been rather quiet. Now he peered up at Wil, measuring and still awestruck, then turned his gaze sharply to Dallin.

"You are the Guardian, then." He shook his head. "Has the Shaman always been the Guardian?"

"That's sort of the point, yes."

"But...." Hunter's face screwed up in bewilderment and budding ire. "Why should.... I don't understand. Always, when the young ones are taught religion, we are taught of the past Shamans. We are taught that only the Shaman may welcome outlanders, only the Shaman may leave the Bounds and still *be* the Shaman. My uncle had to cut his *Marks* from his face!" He was getting agitated now. "*Never* were we told the Aisling and the Guardian were real. *Never* were we taught that those outlanders the Shamans before had welcomed were the Aisling come to live among us." He shook his head, hands stretched out toward Dallin. "I just... I don't understand."

That was betrayal lurking behind Hunter's eyes. Dallin filed that reaction away too. A whole lot of resentment toward the Old Ones was healthy, in his opinion, and more than deserved, but if it wasn't doused very quickly, Dallin would end up with a rebellion he didn't want and chaos they could all do without.

"Don't think too harshly of them. Lind's laws have kept you all barricaded against the rest of the world, and they had their reasons when those laws were made. But it didn't stop the world from changing outside the Bounds. The Old Ones are wise and kind, but they are also men—very *old* men. I'm told Thorne lost count of his age after he passed his hundred-and-fiftieth year, and no one even remembers how long ago that was." Dallin softened his tone. "Men are fallible, and you can't blame them for being so." Though it would certainly make Dallin feel better if he could. He sighed. "Who knows? Had I grown up here, had I not been taken away and lived in the world for all those years, I may have thought the same way as they do."

He actually doubted that one, in his heart, but he wasn't sure if that was merely wishful thinking, so he didn't say it aloud.

"The Mother's will." Shaw raised an eyebrow when Dallin shot him a sardonic glance. He shrugged. "You would argue the course of your path, Dallin Brayden? You, who has seen both the Mother and the Father?"

Dallin narrowed his eyes. "How did you know that?"

"Um." Wil raised a hand and gave Dallin an apologetic grimace. "Sorry." He dipped his head at Dallin's scowl, cheeks coloring slightly. "I didn't say it was you, I didn't say it was anyone, really, I just sort of asked if it was normal, and I didn't say what you'd been told—"

"No, no." Shaw's smile was wry. "He was almost as close with information as you are."

"And." Wil squirmed. "Well. He made me skillet cakes."

It was slightly accusatory. Which, considering what Dallin knew of Wil's appetite, was a pretty believable explanation. Dallin wondered what else the two had discussed in Shaw's rooms in the Temple while Dallin had been preoccupied with recovering. Wil wasn't about to tell him. He was too busy pretending to drink the tea.

"You have seen Them?" This from Hunter, whose voice had gone down to a hoarse whisper as he turned a look of such awe and adoration on Dallin that Dallin almost wanted to smack it off his face.

Dallin sighed. "Yes, I've seen Them."

"Does it bother you so?" Shaw asked with interest. "For a man who has seen and spoken to his gods, you seem rather uneasy with the Divine. The words and messages from the Mother and the Father should not be kept so close to one's own chest." It had the tone of light rebuke. "Part of a shaman's calling is to impart the wisdom he is gifted by Them to all."

"A cleric I am not," Dallin replied tersely, slightly stung. "And I intend to impart whatever I must to effect the changes I think necessary, so save your reprimands, if you please."

For the first time, Shaw pulled away from the rock wall. He frowned and stepped slowly over to stand behind Hunter. "Why do you hate them so?"

Dallin's brows snapped down. "I don't hate anyone. What are you talking about?"

Shaw shrugged. "All right, then. You dislike Calder intensely. You tolerate me because of Wil. I suspect only a proper upbringing and your life in service has kept you from being out-and-out rude to the Old Ones, though you've bordered on disrespect more times than not." He laid a hand on Hunter's shoulder. "And only your kind heart kept you from trying to shatter a boy's faith to suit your own ends." He paused and pierced Dallin with a finely honed gaze. "You disdain belief, and you scorn believers. And yet you've seen the Mother and the Father both."

Dallin's teeth had gone tight. His cheek twitched and ticced without his consent, but he kept his temper.

"I neither disdain nor scorn. I merely cannot respect *blind* belief. People are weak, and the weaker they are, the more they rely on what they've been told is stronger than themselves, even beyond all sense and reason. I've seen too many—" Dallin clamped his jaw, snatched up the cup from Wil's hand, and downed the rest of the bolstered tea, wishing it was something a hell of a lot stronger.

"Hm," Shaw hummed into the resulting silence. "I imagine you have."

Dallin couldn't help glaring. *And you would know, wouldn't you—shaman?*

Shaw patted Hunter's shoulder. "Come, lad. Wil's not had his breakfast yet, and the Old Ones are waiting." He peered over at Wil while Hunter got to his feet. "We'll likely be a little while."

Dallin rolled his eyes but didn't say anything, merely watched Shaw chivvy Hunter ahead of him as they made their way across the green to the communal fire. Aggravated, Dallin got up, went to the kettle, and poured another cup of the tea.

"Why *do* you hate them?"

Dallin gusted an irritated sigh as he turned to Wil. "I don't *hate* them, I just—" He pointed to where Shaw and Hunter had just been. "It's people like those, people like Calder, who made it possible for Síofra to do what he did to you. D'you think no one at the Guild ever had a question as to what was going on? D'you think not a single one of them ever thought what was happening to you was wrong? But they *believed*, they put faith in something they'd never even bothered to question, and watched horrors happen because they *believed* that Síofra was doing the will of the Father. Without ever *once* having heard the Father's will from His own mouth. It—" He ran a hand through his hair. "How can you *not* hate them?"

Wil was staring at him, thoughtful. "Faith didn't put me in my position—one man's choice did."

"And the *blind* faith of dozens of others kept you there because they *chose* not to see the wrongness of it. And shall we talk about the Brethren and their *faith* while we're at it?" Dallin puffed a derisive snort. "I've seen the look in their eyes, I've seen it in the eyes of too many others before them, and I've seen the same damned look in Calder's eyes too. That isn't faith—that's mania."

"Where have you seen it before?" Wil peered at Dallin with a very keen interest and a soft depth to his eyes that reflected an odd sort of accepting compassion Dallin had never seen there before. Wil tilted his head, voice low and gentle. "Is this why you won't talk about your time in the military?"

Dallin twitched, his lip curling before he could help himself. He took a gulp from the cup, wishing again for something stronger.

"It isn't that I *won't* talk about it." He shrugged, inexplicable discomfort, and walked over to the cave's opening. He leaned into its curve. "There's nothing to say. I served, I lived, I went home. A great many others have bigger stories to tell."

It turned quiet for a long moment, then Wil was suddenly there behind Dallin, slipping his hand lightly to the small of Dallin's back, propping his chin on Dallin's shoulder. Dallin took inordinate comfort from it despite the unfathomable disquiet roiling in his gut.

"It was children." Wil said it quietly into Dallin's coat and tightened his hand just a fraction when a small shudder flittered up Dallin's backbone. "Wasn't it?"

No denial would come to Dallin, though he wanted one desperately. "Why would you think that?"

Wil sighed. "It's why the children in Kenley haunt you so. You went and turned them into your own private ghosts. I'd thought it was what happened here all those years ago, but... I expect that would only make what you saw in the army worse." Dallin twitched and firmed his jaw, but Wil didn't back off. "It's always worse when it's children."

And just like that, it was all *there* behind Dallin's eyes, all of it, *in front* of his eyes, inescapable. Things pushed down and throttled, smothered mercilessly and buried just as deeply as that day more than twenty years ago when he'd left these Bounds locked beneath the bench of a tinker's cart. No tears came, no wrenching sorrow. Just that fiery rage burning in his chest, in his head, acid boiling in his stomach and searing up his backbone.

He lifted the cup slowly, drained it, and then just as slowly lowered it. He gripped it in both hands. The sun was high above the tree line over the hills, sharding into his eyes, but it took the shadows away, so he kept looking.

"Dozens of them." Dallin nearly didn't recognize his own voice, the way it came out almost low enough to be tentative. He stared unseeing out onto the green, not watching the morning activity, not hearing the good-natured shouting or the blow and chatter of the horses. "Cut down by the hands of their own mothers." He shook his head, leaned it on the rock, and closed his eyes. "We'd plowed through Carrick and on into Maghera." A hard clench of his teeth, and he looked at Wil over his shoulder. "A league and a half from the Guild."

Wil didn't say anything, just met Dallin's stare with calm expectation. Dallin turned away again, shifting his gaze up to the tree-covered hills, the Temple resting atop them and hidden behind constant evergreen.

"They knew we were coming. I can't even imagine the stories they'd heard." Dallin turned his back on the world outside their little cave and looked again to Wil. "You have to know this—the Commonwealth *never* wiped out noncombatant villages. We *never* turned our guns where guns weren't turned on us. Even when.... I mean, the women of Ríocht, they're not allowed to touch weapons, so they'd use anything they could get their hands on— shards of glass, broken farm tools—but even then we only deflected if we could, disabled if we had to. And never, *ever* a child."

Wil nodded somberly. "I believe you."

Dallin hadn't really known how important that was to him, that belief, but it seemed to quiet a tiny bit of the acid in his gut. He looked down.

"I don't know what they'd been told, but they obviously thought it better their children died at their own hands instead of ours. *Mothers*, who—" His teeth clenched again, eyes burning, and he pushed it away in one long, heavy breath. "They'd piled the bodies outside the gates and burnt them. Dozens and dozens of...." He pounded his fist to the rock beside him and flashed a wrathful glare at Wil. "And it wasn't only the once.

"They had *that same look*, every damned one of them—that righteous piety, that burning madness behind their eyes, worse than any bloodlust I've ever seen in even the most vicious soldier. They were told we were monsters by people they trusted, and they believed it blindly, believed it enough to murder their own children. They thought they were sending them to the Father. What kind of—who could believe in and worship *any* god who would demand such a thing?" Dallin dropped the cup, heedless, and held out his hands, palms up, vaguely shamed by the near-pleading, the remembered grief and revulsion that must surely be showing in his face. "Now, you tell me why I *shouldn't* hate them. Tell me why I shouldn't hate *anyone* who shows me that same sick, mindless conviction behind their eyes."

Wil only kept looking at him—not judgment, not pity—just looking, that same soft compassion he'd started out with, unchanged. His hand was resting on Dallin's chest now, a warm, consoling patch of damp where palm met skin through Dallin's shirt, fanning out in thin stripes beneath Wil's fingers.

"I can't. I would tell you instead to do what you intended to do, and don't let anyone sway you." Wil pulled Dallin down, kissed his cheek, then pulled back. "I would tell you to teach."

"I'm not a teacher. I won't presume to—"

"No?" Wil tilted his head. "I can shoot now."

"Extraordinarily well."

"I can ride."

"You can stay upright on a horse. There's a difference."

Wil ignored the contrary obduracy. "I know how to start a fire in the rain." This time Dallin stayed silent, just raised an eyebrow. Wil grimaced and smacked Dallin's chest. "Yes, all right, but you get the point." He paused with a frown, eyeing Dallin with soft interest. "You're being deliberately difficult."

"Yes."

"This makes you uncomfortable."

"Yes."

Wil nodded. "All right, we'll stop talking about it. Except that... well, they've been waiting for you." He said it as though it should make such obvious sense, when it just *didn't*. "And anyway, in case you hadn't noticed, you've been talking about telling your people all about their religion, shaking out the secrets, and handing out truths. What is that, if not teaching?"

Your people.

His people.

It was... strange. And Dallin didn't want to talk about it anymore.

He brushed his fingers through Wil's hair. "You're feeling better, then?"

Wil sighed with a small, saddened twist of his mouth but allowed the distraction. He dredged up a clouded smile and patted at Dallin's arm, then ambled back into the cave and sat down.

"Much. A bit of a headache, but it hardly compares." He tried to hide a shudder. "What did you do?" And then he frowned. "You're still doing it. Or... am I doing it?"

Dallin shrugged. "Little bit of both, I expect. I don't know if I could explain it properly. I just sort of... balanced things."

"Warp and weft." Wil smiled. "And you said you didn't have magic."

"Mm." Dallin turned and set his gaze back out onto the green, kicking lightly at the cup with the toe of his boot. "Apparently I've more than one calling." He jerked his chin toward the camp. "They're back with your breakfast. Let's get you washed up and fed, yeah? We've a long morning ahead."

He hadn't been sleeping very well the past few nights, dreams repeating and driving him awake so often he might as well not even try anymore. So when he watched the three shamans file in, each of them dipping low bows to both him and Wil, each of them smiling serenely, Dallin felt weariness creep in, muted but insistent.

This little conference was to be the result of two days of almost continual arguing, defending, assuring, and Dallin quite resented the fact that they hadn't allowed time for him to talk to Wil about it privately first. Dallin could insist on it—they put up a good fight on some things, but they always acquiesced when their "Shaman" put his foot down, as it were, and though it was convenient, it still made Dallin want to hit someone. Who was he, after all? And who were they to let him stroll in and take control, simply by virtue of legend and ancient law? And all right, so it wasn't truly legend—Dallin had accepted the reality of what he was, what Wil was, as he'd sat stunned in that inn their first night out of Dudley—but how could these men just... just *hand* him Lind? Expect him to guide its fate and everyone's in it?

Dallin turned to Wil, noted the shuttered gaze, the wary attention, and silently approved. As much as the simple acceptance annoyed him, Dallin still wasn't entirely sure there wasn't some kind of trap lurking beneath it all. Calder, after all, had been one of these men before he'd cut away his Marks. How many of them thought as Calder did? How much of all this was simply information gathering until all twelve could convene and vote on Wil's fate—with or without their Shaman's consent? How much of that control they seemed so eager to hand Dallin was, in truth, control, and how much of it was stalling?

He kept silent as they seated themselves on the stone floor, moving a bit slowly and cautiously, all of them, but surprisingly less rickety than Dallin would have expected from men of such advanced ages. Then again, doing what they did, immersing themselves daily in the power of this place, good health and longevity were rather low on the shock scale.

Dallin shook his head. How was it he could be remembering things he'd had no idea he'd even once known? And how could he have forgotten so profoundly that he hadn't even known there was anything he *had* forgotten?

"Forgive our eagerness, young Wil," Thorne began, "but we have waited so very long." He gestured to his right, to a broad-faced man with a full beard of silver-gray and a shaggy mass of the same on his head. He was thick and swart, round-cheeked, a man who appeared to thoroughly enjoy his food. "May I present Æweweard Marden," Thorne said, then indicated the man to his left. "Æweweard Siddell." A scarecrow made of sticks, hair only just beginning to go iron beneath the gold, thin cheeks clean-shaven though cragged with obvious age; Thorne's junior by a few years, but age sat heavier on him than any of the Old Ones Dallin had met thus far.

Both men once again dipped their heads, hands laid over their breastbones in a gesture of deep respect. Marden reached into his tunic and withdrew a thin, fine-wrought silver chain. A small dagger-shaped drop of crystal quartz dangled from its end, clear and flawless, catching the light from the cave's mouth and spattering prisms over the walls and his cragged face.

"A small gift." Marden extended it to Wil on the tips of his thick fingers. "You are full of questions. Used properly, this may help you find answers."

Taken aback, Wil started to reach out but stopped before his fingers touched the stone. "And what is the proper way to use it?"

Marden smiled as though the question itself satisfied his own curiosity. "Why, whatever way you choose to use it, of course."

Back to those same cryptic answers Dallin had been getting for two days now. He almost growled.

"It is also known to offer protection," Thorne put in, "and to aid one in...." He paused, searching. "Forging links," he finally continued. "Making difficult unions less difficult." He nodded, encouraging. "Go on, then, lad. It's all right."

Wil shot a glance over at Dallin. When Dallin only shrugged, Wil leaned forward and allowed Marden to drop the chain over his head. Wil sat back, frowning, but his fingers closed over the stone with a strange delicacy before cupping it lightly against his breastbone. It took a moment for Dallin to twig to the odd emotional jumble twisting in Wil's expression.

No one's ever given him a gift before. And he's scunnered.

Wil tried to speak—couldn't. He cleared his throat. "I don't know what that means." He watched his finger through the clear stone as it stroked slowly along the smooth line of it. Swallowing heavily, Wil looked up at Marden, a soft shimmer to his eyes, and nodded. "Thank you. It was very kind of you."

Siddell was next, extending his bony hand, thin eyebrows raised encouragingly as Wil slowly held out his own, palm up. "Sun and Moon," Siddell said as he dropped a small smooth charm into Wil's hand.

Primitive-looking, though somehow more beautiful for it. The shapes were vaguely male and female—the woman made of fiery gold sunstone; the man cool and opalescent moonstone. The Mother and the Father, Sun and Moon, fused together into one. Their arms were outstretched, one eternally reaching for the other, a forever-dance of intertwined love and faith.

"Balance and harmony." Siddell closed his fingers over the charm and folded his own gnarled, blue-veined hand over Wil's. He smiled. "You feel it already."

Wil nodded slowly. "It feels... extraordinarily old. It's been...." He closed his eyes and held the charm to his chest over the crystal at his breastbone. "Its dreams are so very deep and... and *long*." He peered at Siddell, once again taken aback, almost to the point of anxiety. Wil held the charm back out in an open hand. "I can't accept this—it must be thousands of years old. Time before time. I can feel it."

"Then it seems to me that you can indeed accept it, for it seems it belongs in the hand of one who knows it."

Wil shook his head, his expression too close to distressed. "You don't understand. I *can't*. It's been touched by Her own hand." He held it out to Dallin, near panic. "Here. You should have it. It isn't for me. They've made a mistake. It should be in the hand of one who... who—"

"Who deserves it?" Dallin cut in softly. Wil only stared at him for a moment, then shunted his glance away, dipping his head and pointing it stubbornly at the floor. Dallin folded the charm into Wil's hand as Siddell had done. He squeezed his hand tight around Wil's fist. "These men know all about you, Wil. They *know*, just as She does. If you think you need some sort of absolution, they'll happily give it to you, so will She, but you're the only one who thinks hiding from Her deserves retribution."

"I've not been *hiding*."

"No?" Dallin set his arm over Wil's shoulders. "I know a little bit about hiding. I know it's possible to hide things so well you forget you'd ever buried them in the first place. You of all people know I've likely got you beat when it comes to denial. If I'd not hidden away so much of myself, I really might've hacked my way into the Guild when I had the chance all those years ago. I'll always owe you a debt for that. I'll always be sorry."

He gave Wil's hand a light squeeze around the charm. "You hated Her and you loved Her at the same time, and both combined to keep Her from you. That's all this is. Not failure, not disloyalty, not weakness. You built up walls to survive, and you've forgotten how to let Her through them. That's all right. She's never stopped loving you because of it. She's never stopped trying to help you, reach you. That's why I'm here, remember?"

"For Her," Wil whispered.

Dallin sighed. "You're such a stroppy idiot sometimes." He tugged at Wil's hair to soften the sting of the rebuke. "For *you*, y'daft dolt. And not because I owe you, so don't even start. I'm here because of you. You said you trusted me."

"I *do*, I... it has nothing to do with—"

"Then trust my word."

Wil shook his head, frustrated. "It doesn't have anything to do with trusting *you*."

"It will have." Dallin pushed Wil away and nodded toward the three shamans silently watching them, gazes keen and observant but benevolent. "They're here to tell you what's expected of the Aisling. I'm here to remind you that it's all up to you. But you also need to know that...." No. Not yet. "We'll get to that. Right now, trust me in this." Again Dallin squeezed Wil's hand around the charm. "You should have it. Accept it graciously, and let's get this done."

He withdrew his hand and sat back. Making his opinion clear, he hoped, but leaving it up to Wil.

Wil only sat there for a moment, slightly hunched, staring at his fisted hand. Slowly, like the petals of a reluctant flower unfurling, his fingers loosened, opened, the little charm lying in his palm glowing iridescent in the combined light of the fire and daylight creeping in from outside—coral-gold and irised-pearl, tatted in a perpetual stone embrace.

Shoulders drooping, Wil peered up at Siddell through his fringe, then closed his hand over the charm again. "Thank you. I'm sorry. I didn't mean to sound ungrateful. It's beautiful, it's more than—" He bit his lip. "Thank you."

Siddell bowed his head with a smile, then turned a hard gaze on Dallin. Measuring. Strangely, all of them were staring, and more at Dallin than at Wil. Perhaps Dallin had stepped outside their expectations for their Guardian again, as it seemed he was entirely too wont to do. He didn't care now any more than he'd cared the other fifty times he'd done it.

"Well, then." Dallin returned their stares evenly, with perhaps a slight touch of defiance bubbling beneath it. "Shall we get on?"

ABOUT THE AUTHOR

Carole lives with her husband and family in Pennsylvania, USA, where she spends her time trying to find time to write. The recipient of various amateur and professional writing awards, several of her short stories have been translated into Spanish, German, Chinese and Polish. Free shorts, sneak peeks at WIPs, and other miscellany can be found on her website.

Website: www.carolecummings.com

Join the Rocky Ridge Books newsletter to find out when the Aisling trilogy and more of Carole's work will be available.

ALSO BY CAROLE CUMMINGS

The Aisling Trilogy

Guardian

Dream

Beloved Son

The Wolf's Own Series

Ghost

Weregild

Koan

Incendiary

The Queen's Librarian

Blue and Black

Don't Fear the (Not Really) Grim Reaper

ALSO FROM ROCKY RIDGE BOOKS

The Diversion Series from Eden Winters

Diversion

Collusion

Corruption

Manipulation

Redemption

Reunion

Suspicion

Decision

The Mountains from P.D. Singer

Fire on the Mountain

Snow on the Mountain

Fall Down the Mountain

Blood on the Mountain

Return to the Mountain

The Wrestling Series from D.H. Starr

Wrestling With Desire

Wrestling with Love

Wrestling With Passion

Wrestling with Hope

www.ingramcontent.com/pod-product-compliance
Lightning Source LLC
Chambersburg PA
CBHW030914050726
47498CB00003BA/737